THE MONSOON DRIFTER

Armin Boko

authorHOUSE®

AuthorHouse™ UK Ltd.
500 Avebury Boulevard
Central Milton Keynes, MK9 2BE
www.authorhouse.co.uk
Phone: 08001974150

First published by AuthorHouse   10/29/2010

ISBN: 978-1-4520-9589-9 (sc)
ISBN: 978-1-4520-9588-2 (e)

This book is printed on acid-free paper.

THE MONSOON DRIFTER

Divorced from the turmoil of recent history, some dislodged victims of it and protago-nists of this novel remain work of fiction.

Armin Boko

Dedicated to those returning from wars as 'damaged goods'.

Contents

CHAPTER ONE

MAN REBORN

On sunrise the inmates road gang left the prison gates behind them never to return. Max alone was kept back in the cell until close to lunch time, when the guard arrived and dumped a bundle of clothes on the floor.

"Here, the warden sent you this, and you've got ten minutes to pack. So don't stuff around!" The guard departed, keys and all, and left the steel door open.

That implied early release. Without a parole regime or other benefactors to help his cause, it cought Max by surprise. Ten minutes to pack was no problem. He could have done with less. Other then a roll of manuscripts, some miniature wood carvings done with a 40W soldering iron and a tooth brush, his earthly belongings included only a swag of tatty clothes now left behind. By contrast, the bundle of clothes the guard brought in were a real eye opener. New, fitting and quality wares including leather shoes. He finished dressing up hurriedly, and left the cell for the exit corridor with shirt buttons still to be done.

Prison authorities here worked with precision, not to island nor Swahili time. The deal was for him to be released at midday. As the church bell chimed in noon, his senses began to take in changes around his confined universe.

From a dark sound proof corridor he was entering an open square under blinding tropical sun and a cacophony of noises that come with the traffic and crowds. The sun on equatorial zenith blinded him at first. It made him slow down on the lonely walk to what promised to be freedom.

At last that final step. The the borderline between it and slavery, and he was out in the open. To his left stood a gendarme guard under arms at shoulder height failing to take notice of him. Max Horvat felt his heart beat racing, and the walking pace wanting to follow. He remained to be convinced this wasn't some kind of a prank by the warden or worse. As he was to find out these apprehensions had no justification.

How the times have changed. Even here in the most remote of places. The coral brick colonial penetentiary on Mahe'Island in the Seychellois Republique, one that over the centuries remained the resting place of notorious pirates and cutthroats was to see out its last remainig inmate. And if he was a free man again that would have completed the circle. From a round the world solo sailer to a convict, to a free man again. Albeit one whose very existence was under cloud. To begin with he was destitute. His yacht sunk, discharged without documents, and worst of all without friends. For all that mattered he was a fortyeight years old new born orphan. But free, at least for now he was.

1

Wether he would manage to pick up the broken pieces once more in his tormented life, littered with upheavals, that remained to be seen.

A few paces into the open square he threw a backward glance, only to find the squeeky iron gates remained open.

They were in fact never to close again. He also became aware of being under surveillance. A few years inside did volumes for one's power of sensual perception. A thought flashed through his mind. Perhaps they were not through with him after all this theater. Indeed little if anything of what transpired today so far could be rationaly explained. Eventually it would all fall into place, bit by bit. He was apart from all else on a discovery tour. Right now all he could do was keep his wits together, and refrain from jumping to conclusions. Scanning the square a large poster next to a bus stop attracted his attention. So that was it. This prison was to officially cease existance. Instead, priceless realestate that it covered was to be put to better use. After all, a jailhouse can be buildt on a garbage dump. In its place according to the poster was to come a forty stories condominium of luxury suites. Each priced at over $2 million and sold off right from the design board to mostly the nouveaux rich of South Africa(SA), whose ranks lately included many Xhosa professionals. Those breathtaking views over the turqois channel and offshore inlets were alone estimated to be worth the asking price.

Pleased with himself at to having worked this one out, he soon decided it was no good kidding himself. This was the easy part. But why would they let him go? Never mind the SA investors. To them, the banks and the builders he ment nothing. As it turned out, he served less than a half of an eight years stretch on dual charge of illegal entry and homicide with diminished responsibility. Sure he was a model prisoner. For this he was well treated in return. Sure he did all sorts of useful tasks on work release, but why the sudden clemency? Why would they spare him and the cost-free labour? He figured there just had to have been a third hand in this. It didn't help that to all of his questions so far he'd received no answers.

To begin with, who for heaven's sake knew he was still alive, having been left for dead on that faithful morning in the waters of Farquhar Lagoon? Only to be rescued by a miracle called Dr Marcus Botha and his spouse Jean.

And he had not the vaguest idea of their whereabouts. Then of course, back to the authorities here. But to them he couldn't be more than a pain. Furthermore if anyone at all had interest in him, how come nobody ever dropped in to visit him? For close to four years he'd seen visitors aplenty. Not as much as a single sod came to see him. Despite all of this, driven by intuition alone, he remained convinced. There was a third hand involved and it would have been costly.

Whoever was implicated in his release to freedom, had to have been familiar with the local politics. It had to have been someone who not only knew and cared for him, but also knew how to move these fickle islanders where they weren't keen on going. And just as importantly, knew how and whom to bribe.

Suddenly, he first felt then saw a dark blue Citroen pull up alongside of him. So close his right hand actually slid over the front mudguard. The driver's door opened ajar, and a husky male voice called out to him to take a seat. For an instant Max by instinct almost made a run for it. Only to quickly decide against it. It would have been worse than futile to run in his condition. To run would have equaly been a valid excuse for the gendarmes to finish him off. Notwithstanding the fact if they wanted to dispose of him, surely they would have done it by now. There were so many ways available to them. Or was it just another game of cat and mouse? He had no way of knowing. Max finaly took a seat opposite an overweight middle aged driver in Sheraton's livery. They were alone and Max could spot no guns at hand. This relaxed him to a degree. He felt confident of being more than a match for the driver should the need arise.

As silently as the car pulled up, it took off gliding in low gears over what used to be potholed and dusty streets of the Victoria's waterfront. Milling along the way among the usual layabout deadbeat suspects. The goodtime girls in their flimsy colourful frocks, the currency smugglers, spies and touts. Often one and the same.

Once on the open road the driver silently reached for a manila folder and passed it over to Max, with a curt comment.

"A one way ticket to Jo'burg, and you'd better be on it."

Max examined the folder. It was just as the driver had said. A one way ticket to Johannesburg, on the Air Seychelles Shorts 360. These ancient flying coffins had the looks as well as a reputation to go with it . But just then the twenty six year old turbo was his only chance. Or he was as the driver put it a gonner. Just like in the wild West movies. A gonner. Back to another prison no doubt to serve out the remainder of the sentence. Perhaps a lot worse.

Attached to the air ticket was his Australian passport with a month left before expiry date. One hundred rupees, the marine registration papers of Sounion, the yacht he lost and its log book. Missing was all of the the $ US cash he had on him when taken into custody, and it was a considerable amount.

Gradually the driver became friendlier, ignoring any mention of money matters.

"Soon you'll be at OT", he said.

Max didn't get it.

"Oh sorry, you would remember the place as The Johannesburg International Airport. Now they renamed it after Oliver Thambo. The new political master of South Africa. And they renamed most of the rest, without adding another brick to it. You'll need a new street directory as well once you set your foot there."

Obviously the driver was well informed on his past. That much became clear to Max. They arrived at the airport with time to spare. Over a cup of cappuccino the chauffeur opened up. Yes, he didn't drink, not on duty anyway. Yes, he was a married man, with two daughters, both studying medicine and very smart. His name was Jacques, but Jack was OK. But when it came to throw some light as to who was behind all this , he'd just slip conveniently into French Creole. Spoken at speed incomprehensible to Max. Jack was under orders performing odd jobs outside doorman's hours at Sheraton Hotel. Sending doughters to uni cost heaps. They parted company quasy amicably and shook hands, for the want of anything more appropriate. Within minutes he had new company.

Next thing he noticed, there was a very long legged middle aged groomed state official, Max was certain he'd never seen before seated in Jaque's chair. He spoke in faultless English and seemed to have an air of military bearing about him..

"My name is Gaston and you'll follow me. Keep your passport in the pocket."

Max did as told. Then moved towards the Passport Control check with fear and some trepidation. He needn't have this time. Even so, he just couldn't control that fear in his bones. It was at this Passport Control desk check four years ago that he came to grief on the previous attempt to leave the island. A passport without an entry mark and blank on further computer checks spelled trouble. Soon the senior staff got to deal with him.

"Nothing to explain", tried Max with bravado. Just another bum tourist, why should you care at all?" But care they did. A number of political agitators, gun smugglers from the mainland and foreign mercenaries spotted in recent times caused the Immigration to double check on all foreigners.

What followed next was an interrogation. A torrent of questions. "Who was his boss? Who was he working for? Where did he stay? When did he enter the country?" On and on it went. He fudged the best he could. Gave answers which turned out to be false upon most ordinary of cross checks. With sole purpose in mind to avoid Dr Botha and his wife to be pulled in as accomplices. Some two hours later, after Departures board indicated the SAA Boeing 737 was airbone with the couple on board, he duly confessed. All this was four long years ago. No wonder he felt twitchy. But on this occasion it all went smoothly. Thanks to tall handsome authority figure of Garson. Obviously a highly ranked security official. A big predator .

At last the boarding time green light came on. Here relieved of immediate problems, the nagging question as to who was behind all this wouldn't give him any peace. Who payed for all this? Who donated the clothes he was wearing? They were quality clothes and a surprisingly good fit. Who for heaven's sake went through all of this trouble? Who knew about him at all? World outside had practically ceased to exist for Max. His clock had stopped running years ago. He didn't have a clue.

Eventualy the ancient Shorts 360 taxied for take-off. In deafening noise it began to climb, wings shaking perceptivly. Soon the sparkling scenery of the Morne Blanc granite bold peak came into view. Then Ile Therese and the fringing coral reefs surrounding it. From his window seat he was privileged to view some of the most stunningly beautiful scenery on Earth. Next in order to catch a better peripheral view, he crouched lower down on the seat to the point where his hands touched on the the trousers cuffs. But wait! What was it he just felt? There was something hand stiched inside the left cuff. Upon inspection it turned out to be Barklys' Visa card. Still shiny in wrappers. Max found his hands shaking out of control once he read the name on the card.

Adam Malek.Dr Adam Malek to be precise.

He continued to stare at the card in utter disbelief. The shock that cought him was such, he slumped back into the seat with force. It startled the male passenger next to him.
And then the memories of the hell underground he and Adam went through eleven years ago began to flood back in a tide of uncontrolable emotions.

* * *

Eleven years on, he could still clearly remember the disaster that struck in that gold mine at Dreifontein. The date was engraved and stuck in his mind. Second of June 1991. One-and-a-half kilometers under ground in the bowels of the earth on that faithful nightshift he stood next to Adam Malek operating a pneumatic drill when it happened.
Without warning a faulty compressed air hose coupling snapped and let a loose heavy steel reinforced hose fly whipping through the air. Hissing like a reptilian beast the air hose cought Adam Malek under the safety helmet, and smashed in his lower jaw. Then with somewhat diminished force continued on and fractured Max's nose. Still on the rampage it went on to sweep the floor of all the dust that had been there since the Silurian period.
Soon the dim lightning of the miners headlamps could barely penetrate through the chocking dust. Two Sotho miners nearby heard the commotion and bravely raced in to offer help. Max in pain and bleeding profusely ordered them more by sign language than the **Fanagalo** miner's parlance to shut off the compressed air valve and to unpack the stretcher. Adam lay unconscious on the dusty ground. Max turned him onto the injured side and jammed his thermos bottle stopper into Adam's

mouth to stop him chocking on his own blood. They lifted Adam into the nearest half full pan and alarmed the shift foreman. Within an hour on the first available **kibble** he was winched up to surface and medivaced to expert medical care.

It was later reported that rapid intervention probably saved Adam's life. No big deal though. Accidents, injuries and death are a part and parcel of underground mining. So much so, those in charge take a pride when the statistics fall below the average. Every bit of ore, coal or gold that has come from underground mines had been payed for by miners' blood and sweat. Not to mention disabilities, silicosis, lonely neglected miners' wives and greaving families. This case somehow aroused more interest.

A few days later, Mine's manager dropped in to see Adam in the recovery ward. Adam's speech was restored and the pair spoke at lenghth about Adam's prospects.

The manager soon found out Adam not only had the degree in Geology, he had ideas which if correct would simplify the exploration, and if useful would also make it a lot faster and more economical. Exploration costs were escalating and of major concern.

While by no means convinced, manager's recommendation to the owners was to give the young Pole a try. In any case a man like this was wasted on a production drill rig. That was a modest beginning. In a way that accident might have been the best thing that happened to Adam for a while. Years later, his ideas proved correct. Gold exploration would never be the same again. Within those years, Dr Malek became one of the top gold explorers in all of Africa. A position that carried him all over the continent. With it came big salary, bonus increases, prestige and a lot of clout. The other side of the coin of course was that his life was in constant danger supervising exploration crews in the most God forsaken wilderness. Just managing to survive the lowless streches of the Congo for one was an achievement in itself. Here the natural instincts were essential.

Adam would negotiate and cooperate with some of the most feared characters on the continent. His one advice to all was, let them be in no doubt you are more valuable to them alive. If only for a day longer. But then again, there was always a chance of running into a a real cretin. There was no shortage of despicable scum for whom the Law ment nothing. Many of them in their early teens.

A heavier penalty still were frequent periods away from Loland, whom he married two years ago. Adam missed her company as much as her gregarious nature. She was the twin sister of Jean Botha. They would meet regulary, including **ousis,** the elder sister Vivian. Still single in her mid-thirties and acting as Science Master at a nearby Catholic gymnasium. A round of bridge, or just plain debate over anything under the sun made certain there was never a dull minute.

It was a joy to be there, and be a part of that circle. Adam could sleep on hard ground, eat millie millies, smoked grasshoppers, bush meat and not complain. But he'd be found missing the three sisters. Discussions and polemics he had with Viv alone were a never ending topic of conversation. Viv gave one an idea she was a frontline woman's libertarian. Enough to caution your average male not rush in, she was also compassionate to a fault. Like a soft boiled egg. Hard on the outside, soft on the inside. That's how Adam summed her up once. Her choice of clothes didn't help either. In order to cover a birth mark, summer or winter, she would wear a turtle neck. Blouse or pullover, but a turtle neck. And her choice of make-up was stark. None.

"I want to be made up inside my head. Not be dolled up." She'd comment when pressed. In all, enough for your average male to pay respect. and the guard well up.

As often as not Dr Marcus Botha would be absent from the bridge rounds. His skills were too much in demand. Saving lives from road and mine accidents, where every second was precious, led him to improvise a portable mini op-room, including the local anesthetics. All of this gear including blood serum supplies he'd have packed in a case the size of an average suitcase, and have it stored in a refrigerator ready for the next emergency call. At times Jean who was a theater sister would join to assist. Most often Marc would preffer to go alone. Even when he could have delegated and sent out junior staff.

Needles to say, his name was all over the media, as was the ongoing warfare with the Minister for Health given the nickname 'Beetroot'. Any person less in public eye she would have fired without hesitation. With Mark she chose war of attrition. One morning an intern called on Marc and showed him the vacancy for the position of Chief Surgeon Emergency Ward advertised in the Johannesburg Star. It was in fact Mark's present position.

He called on the Minister over the phone and let her have it with both barrels. Of course he played into her hand. His position become untenable. Suddenly the Docent's position at UCLA Los Angeles USA offered to him only recently looked heaps more attractive.

He put the proposition to Jean and she less than agreed. He in turn pointed out the advantages. His breakthroughs in application of cryogenics and new serum formulations to the severely wounded were finding acceptance. Before long the US Army got interested. Dr Marcus Botha had bright carrier prospects ahead of him. But not in his native land. Here the Minister not only refused to fund the research, she demanded to censor, and co-author all of his future publications.

"Typical of the vindicative incompetent upstart. Just look at her. The whole system is in shambles and she wants me out." That's how Marc put it to Jean.

"We'll have to move. There is no choice. Like it or not Jean."

"Think of your friends here Marc. Think of our family. It is not just you and me." She would resist. And then, it would remain to settle the SA financial affairs. They soon found out the only sensible thing to do with Rand savings was to spend it. Rand was well dawn. Then the foreign currency limits on top of it. A thousand dollar a head limit ment they would have to start from scratch in what used to be a very over priced realestate of California.

There was also the security problem. Los Angeles when it came to crime, as Marc was to find out on his visit to the place was barely an improvement on Jo'burg. Around *iGoli* they killed for a meal ticket. Around LA more often just for kicks. And one look at the World and Oceans map of the world prompted Jean to make a comment.

"We might as well join the chicken run and emigrate to Perth. It is a lot closer. We've got friends there."

Marc pretended not to hear this, and suggested they invest in a solid ocean going yacht. One could live aboard as well. That would have temporarily at least solved the accommodation problem. Jean never easily beaten had reservations.

"First you've got to get there sailer. Ever heard of Cape Horn?

She remanded him that yachts can and do sink.

"Yes." Marc admitted. "You are not wrong there. It reminds me of Max, that Croat in Seychelles."

All this was taking place with the three sisters and Adam present during the Easter break. Adam who was a sharp listener took all of this in. Finaly, something clicked loud.

"What did you say Croat's name was?" Adam couldn't wait to hear the answer.

"Max …something, I'm not the best on names."

"Well, can you tell me what did he look like." Adam continued quizzing.

"Why? Solidly put together. About six foot tall. Deep scar on the left cheek, ginger beard. Blue eyes. The name went like... Orvat, could that be right? But wait. Why do you ask?"

"I am not sure of course. There cannot be too many blue eyed Croats by the name Max. Apart from sailing aspects in your story. Otherwise the description is pretty close to that of a man who once probably saved my life. And the name is Horvat, the 'h' is not silent. H as in Loch."

"Yes, you are right." Jean chipped in. "Horvat is right. I remember now. I ended up donating over a litre of blood to him. Why didn't you ever mention this?"

"I didn't, you are right Jean.", Adam replied. "Why? Perhaps I've been too busy. I don't know. But that has just got to be him, damn it. Tell me all about what happened there." He turned to Marc visibly aggitated.

A tragic story of what unraveled on the waters of Farquhar Lagoon came out, followed by description of Max's slow recovery and jailing. At least the story how the Bothas found out and saw it. And then, still remembered what happened four years ago. Memories can be fickle.

At this point Adam joined in the conversation, telling them what happened last time he saw Max after the mine accident, and hospital recovery treatment.

Adam was still in the recovery ward when Max dropped in to visit him. For once he got back at Adam in the Polish version of *howyergoingmate?*

"Yak se chujesh bratko?" To which he got back:

"Nje tak dobze." Meaning not so hot. Max slipped a bottle of Chivas Regal under Adam's pillow.

"Maybe this will make you feel better and warm you up. I came to bid you farewell my old mate. I'm off to war". Max added.

"You what?" Adam half got out of bed.

"Yes, you heard it. You know what happened when the old USSR fell apart, next Chechoslovakia, then the rest of the Eastern communist block. You were in Poland to see it unravel. You saw the 35% unemployement. You saw the coalmines in Silesia close one after another. That's why you like thousands of others came here, looking for work. Somehow it all fell into place. Without wars" Adam chose not to interupt.

"But not so in Balkans. They all managed to part peacefully, except for Yugoslavia. When it came to Yugoslavia's turn Serbs got the tails up…Serbia is where Serbs live. That's how indoctrinated they got. Majority actually bought that Nazi propaganda. Crowds in Belgrade lined up to see off their armour off to invade Croatia adorned with garlands and jubilation." Yet another chapter of Balkan madness and European incompotency was to unravel.

Hystorical records show Milosevic in 1991could do no wrong. To put it in context he had the necessary backing of US, Brittain and France. That is until the savagery and genocide the Serbs were up to, exposed by brave reporters on the ground, night after night became an embarrassment to great powers. In early sommer of 1991 his homeland Croatia stood to fall to Serbian conquest. The ultimate disaster. They, the Croats had to fight. If with bare hands. According to Max there was no choice.

Adam just stared at him. Lost for words.

"And that was the last I saw him. Years ago." Adam continued.

"Months later I got a postcard from Pech in Hungary. Max wrote to me he'd been one of very few who managed to escape from the hell that Vukovar was. And then nothing. Up to Jean telling me about your misadventures in the Seychelles.

7

"For Christ' sake!" Vivian commented." That is some CV for you. The poor devil hasn't had the best of times. Still some character. No matter how you looked at him."

"Wait now until you hear his side of the story." Marc went on to explain how they nearly ended up in strife themselves for complicity.

Even so, there was a lot more to the story they never got to know. It was the story of the Monsoon Drifter that remained to be told much later.

Just then, the landline phone rang for what was a sequence of news and messages. Mostly bad.

First, the Police Commander from Nylstroom wanted to talk to Dr Marcus Botha. Jean picked the phone and fobbed the policeman saying Marc was out attending a road accident. If she could pass on the message. Sure, the message went, his grandfather's funeral was on at 10 in the morning tomorrow at Nylstroom, and sincere commiserations to the family. Stop.

That was the first she knew about Marc's beloved **oupa's** death. The first anyone here knew. Not long thereafter a call from a certain Gaston at Mahe'wanted Adam to know the parcel was on the way. Stop.

By now Jean was almost mortified to lift the receiver. Positioned right next to her chair she let the next one go.

Adam picked it up on a bad mobile line. It was from the Lord's Resistance Army in Northern Congo bordering Uganda. So they have kidnapped his crew yet again and the ransom quoted was astronomical accompanied with usual tirade to follow.

"Whitey, **worungu** plunderers of Africa, your crew is going to end up impaled as bush meat." On and on. In return Adam called them every unprintable name that came to him. That he knew only called for more respect. Most Europeans don't know a first thing as to how to approach the outlaws. Still the LRA held all the trumps.

"Wait until I can arrange finance. But first you must promise not to hurt my men. Yes, you have my word." Adam knew he had to negotiate.

The sum they eventually agreed upon was less than a tenth demanded. That he knew he had to pay. So did the management. You live here or die by your own word. One thing was clear though. He would pull out of the Congo after this, if it was up to him to decide. It was not. How to accommodate General Mzkwe's ransom demands was for the CEO of the **Shellberight Mines Ltd** to decide. He told the one-eyed General as he liked to present himself as much. Now remained to find the CEO. He could have been just about anywhere with school vacations in full swing. Try as hard as he may he got nowhere. That is when Adam decided to drive to CEO's Parkhill adress himself. Perhaps the house servants could help .

This left Marc back on the phone trying to extract more information about his grandfather's demise. Also without success. Marc was deeply hurt by the news and wanted to drive off to Nylstrooom before daybreak. Only to hear Jean come against it. Still it didn't matter how you looked at it. They had to be there by ten in the morning. That ment some night-time driving, dangerous or not.

"Why don't you try for some armed escort?" Jean suggested.

"Why not! What an excellent idea. I have just the right team in mind. A couple of demobbed SAS heavies. I met them once while game fishing off Port Elisabeth in Natal."

Du Plessis brothers were guns for hire. Wasting no time, Marc, Loland and Jean got busy packing the station wagon. Not forgetting the weapons and ammunition.

Vivian left to herself, summised the situation.

I see that leaves me to meet Max at the airport." Without anyone objecting, she also got down to work.

All this was happening at Bothas' villa, during the customary family Friday's get together. With one difference. Since the latest break into her flat Vivian decided to update the security system. Tradesmen were still busy testing it. That's why she moved in temporarily to stay with Bothas.

Here she found there was a problem. Clothes she brought with her were mostly tracksuits and tennis gear. What was she to wear? And did it matter? She decided that it did. With Bothas gone she took the liberty and started trying out Jean's outfits.

One by one, until there was a pile of discarded clothes on the bed. She hadn't spent so much time in front of the mirror since the teens. Emboldened by the experience she took hold of a lipstick. One more look in the mirror and she was happy with what she saw. In the last act of break with the past, she liberally applied Jean's favorite French perfume. Jean will understand. If not lough at all this.

"Life is too short old girl." She told herself. "It is high time to get switched on!" She returned to the pile of clothes on the bed, pulled It on the floor, got more agitated in the process and kicked into the pile for a good measure.

"No more VV this VV that. I'm through with time wasting dills. And stuff you Gino! A reference to her ditched boyfriend!"

She wrote out in lipstick a poster with Max' name on it, and drove herself to the airport. Arrival was right on schedule and unusually efficient Customs controls saw her arrive just in time still catching breath. Max was in the crowd waving his left arm in the air trying to attract attention. As he spotted the red poster and Vivian, he began to move forcefuly through the crowd.

"Hallo, are you Adam's wife?" He asked as he approached closer. "I am Max Horvat. Pleased to meet you."

"No, no". She corrected. "I'm Vivian de Villiers. Adam's sister in-law. Adam would be here, except he's got some urgent matters to attend to. He sends you his regards. We'll drop in to see him tomorrow. Right now it is too late to drive to Botha's place. We'll call in at The Emerald Guest House. Ten minutes drive from here. Boy, you must be tired. Tired and hungry. Let me take your luggage." She sportingly offered.

"Luggage?" He just loughed and pointed out the plastic carry bag holding a manila folder, a tooth brush, ship's log, some manuscripts and little else of value.

"That ought to do it for luggage."

If the first impressions ment anything, she had a real buzz. Here at last was a man. A real life figure. Most men these days seemed to Vivian as conformists and HMV. Only too eager to please the master. Heads bent down over their computer screens cowed in funk lest the master detected defiance.

"Not so? Well, how else does the vacuous political correctness get accepted? Men have ceased being men. Just look at yourselves! Bejuweled like Gypsies. With sperm counts of a pidgeon. I mean, reduced to vent off your pent up frustration in ethanol driven mob frenzy as fans in a football match. And I'm sick of footy. Oh, yeah, job insecurity, house mortages kids and the like. I accept. But wait, did it all happen overnight? Like hell. Real Men like Selous or Pretorious must be turning in their graves. Even the once fiery Eugene Terrablance looks a lost cause."

All this and more was flashing through her mind as they had a close searching look at each other. For his part, not knowning any better, he felt envious of the lucky man whose pride and joy she would have to be. By the time the Ford Fiesta driven by Vivian pulled into Emerald Guest House drive in it was past midnight. They called at night shift porter's desk and the room she booked ahead. She also brought in a takeaway Chinese from the airport and a bottle of so so OBiKWA Chardonney. Over the re-heated meal he couldn't but notice the disparity in the colour of her skin. Alabaster pale neckline and arms that were well sun tanned. She quickly spotted the object of his attention.

"Tennis." She explained. I used to play in the A grade in my younger days. Of late more of a social persuit. Mainly mixed doubles. That can be a lot of fun though."

Well, he thought, that at least explained some of it. The other observation that struck him as odd was the fact there was no jewelry. None at all on her to be seen, yet she was well made up.

"You don't miss much. Eyes of an eagle." She passed him a compliment.

"And you are a good mind reader." He countered.

"We have a lot to tell each other." She tried to keep the conversation alive.

"I agree. Just for start. Tell me if you don't mind. How exactly did Adam manage to find out about me? And how did he manage to have me bailed out of that hole?"

She told him what she knew from Jean and Marc. Also vaguely about Adam having some dealings with a high ranking Seychelloise public servant who insisted to be called Gaston.

"No idea what his real name was. Adam never saw him once. All of the dealings, and I am only going on what Adam told me, went via a Sikh middleman.

Adam had Gaston once on the phone. He swears the character comes from the ranks of the military. Active or retired? No idea. It cost Adam a fair bit in time and money, but boy, was he determined to get you out. I think , Adam also mentioned the deal was upon your release for the second payement to be made. With this all records of your sentence to be erased. That is all I know Max". She modestly concluded.

"Whoosh! You know more than I thought you would. I am much obligded."

She had another close look at Max and noticed he was barely making any impression on the contents of the wine glass. Very telling, she thought. He would fancy a cup of cappuccino after the meal if possible.

And so it went on. With each minute they were more and more into each other's private life. In normal encounters it would take days, weeks, and perhaps longer for two until now perfect strangers to get to know each other. Here it was numbered in hours. There was no time for finesse and infantile silly games.

"Mind you, I knew much about you before I met you. It gives me a start. But boy you must be exhausted! We'd better try and catch some sleep. Leave the coffee for now." They cleaned up the table. She'd sleep on the couch and he in the double bed. He refused to accept her proposal. To settle the issue Max tossed a coin. She called the couch.

"I told you so." She triumphed.

He showered and ducked into the bed. Within minutes he was sound asleep. It took her much longer. The noise of aircrafts landing near-by didn't help. There was no curfew at OT.

Finaly, she too dozed off. For how long she couldn't tell, when a loud cry call from Max in a foreign language she didn't understand woke her up. He was going through another nightmare, back in Bosnia's war charging a Serbian machine gun post. She alarmed hurried across the room then called out loud.

"Max, Max! It's me Vivian. You are here with friends. Wake up!"

As he woke up, shaking his head and her standing aside of his bead, she became aware of being naked. She often slept naked in summer. Exposed here it somehow didn't bother her in the least. What little light came through the large bedroom window facing the golf course arrived from the pale moonlight. Enough candle power for him to see her.

"Max, be easy on yourself! No more bloody wars. What you need is TLC, not bloody war. Snap out of it!"

He looked her up again and her trim body. Somehow he just couldn't believe what he was seeing. Gradualy relieved from his trauma fit, Max composed himself somewhat. "Come in TLC." He reached out a hand. She took it with some hesitation. He could feel her trembling.

"Come in TLC. You'll catch a cold."

"Least of my concerns. I promised Adam I'd look after you, but I don't know if this was a part of the bargain. It's also been a while since I have been with a man. You know what I mean. I could be a bit rusty."

"Then what should I say. All I have been having was dreams. Years of it. And here is another dream. It feels like one. Please tell me I am not dreaming Vivian."

He woke up next just in time for lunch. She left him a written note on the table. As he moved towards the table he saw his life size mirror image. What he saw called for closer inspection. There were lipstick marks in most unlikely places and his back had finger nail scratch marks as if an ocelot had jumped him.

The note instructed him to stay put. She wouldn't be long and signed, 'Good morning to my dear friend.'

Before long she was back burdened with a collection of shopping bags.

"Been shopping as you can see. I hope I wasn't away for too long". She added having a guilty glance at her wristwatch. "Did you find my message?"

"Find it, …yes of course. But tell me what are we going to do? We've overstayed the checkout time deadline.?"

"Well, since we have to pay for it, we may as well stay here for another day. It is my fault. I should have returned on time. Fancy a round of golf? Or tennis?"

He looked at her long and hard.

"Let me tell you something Vivian. You and Adam have so far done so much for me I'm at a loss trying to figure out how to pay you back. Here I am almost back to rejoin the human race. That after being a convict only 24 hours ago, as you well know." She protested loudly.

"Why are you so hard on yourself? From what I heard what you did was in self-defence. So why? Perhaps I'm not the best person to put that question since they accuse me of the same fault, but why torture yourself. Just try and take it in. I owe you as much as you owe me. Is this the way to build a relationship? Establishing who owes more to whom. Wasn't loving one supposed to be about giving?"

"Too right it is, but try and put yourself in my position. All take and no give."

Again she gave him that look of controlled displeasure, which comes with years of teaching.

"Why?" She protested? "You and me ought to start talking less about you and me and more about us instead. I don't know where this will lead us. I do know it would be a good start. So what do you say partner?"

"No". He objected, " I like the dear friend better. None has ever called me that before."

She turned closer towards him and let the shopping bags slide to the floor. In the same move she slung her arms around his shoulders.

"Max, listen to me. I've seen men before. Slept and even lived together with a few. Only to see it over time fall into a void of nothingness. Leaving me more lonely than before. I may be wrong. It wouldn't be the first time... I don't quite know how to put it. You certainly gave me more to think about. Heaven knows how long is this between us going to last. If it is for just one more day, I'll thank my Lord for the gift."

He was cought completely off guard. She was disarmingly open about most intimate of one's feelings. He'd never discussed love affairs. Most men have a mental block and cannot discuss this with best of intentions. Kids these days are different. They cannot stop

Traying to say something in reply, all he managed to do was an incoherent mumble. She spotted his state of confused discomfort and skillfully changed the subject.

"I just blew the budget", she said pointing out to the merchandise. And there was a present for him. Loads of underware and socks he was in need of, and a sports jacket. She was presenting him with gifts. Only to find him deeply embarrassed and hesitant to receive it.

"On one condition". He conceded." Give me the bill for all this, and I'll see you back one day, OK?"

"Fine, if this makes you feel better." She knew his self respect would demand nothing less. And so the afternoon went on, mainly in a lively conversation. He wanted to know more about her orphaned childhood, and she described that thirst for knowledge that every scientist worth his or her salt recognizes as the inner fire without which it all becomes pointless.

"And it may be so anyway in this upside down world." She added.

"Why upside down?"

"Why! For all numbers of reasons. Look, when I was a kid at school a clip behind the ear was what you got when noughty. We as kids feared the teacher. Here teachers live in fear of getting assaulted by the pupils. Similary, blacks used to live in fear of whites, and with a good reason. Now, the whites live in fear of the African. Just wait until you see. Then look at the mess this country is in. Only a handful of Africans have realy benefited from the changes. The elite, the BEE mob. You'll hear plenty from them. Believe me. And guess what? They employ servants just the same as the well off whites. Only more so. Given a choice whites are recognized as a more compassionate and honest employers. Man, we here have lost the plot. So many empty promises, so much spin and so much hot wind. Feet of clay, a Chinese desease? No man. None wants to payrole people if they can help it. Even the checkout girls know before long it will all be fully automated. Globalisation that's what they call it I hear. Impoverisation, more likely. And let's not mention the youth. Man, what's the point in busting your gut trying to teach the youngsters binomial theorem and trigonometry when there are no jobs for them?"

Max was a patient listener. He had to be. So he took it all in a without a comment.

"Well, what do you think? Am I right? How do you see it?"

"Look, I have been inside." He insisted. "Shielded no less from some of what you observe. Certainly in no position to comment on SA's present position. I must say the Rand currency has been devalued. But you do comes as a sharp observer. I'll grant you that."

"Sharp you say, or harsh?" She wasn't sure she understood.

"Sharp, you couldn't be harsh if you tried, I don't think."

She smiled back at him. "Little do you know my good friend! Oh, enough of this idle talk. I nearly fargot to tell you. Adam is dropping in to see you, about 4 pm. He wanted to know how you were getting on."

"You didn't tell him?" Max probed.

"Tell him? Of course I did. We in the family circle hold no secrets from each other. Of course he knows. I wanted him to know. I got the impression he was pleased to hear it. And then something else my dear friend." She paused for breath and went on uninterrupted.

"With Adam rest in the knowledge he is determined to get what he wants. It may not always be what you expect...No Max, we hold no secrets from each other. This gets to be very embarrassing at times, but it does bring us together. It started in Cape Province during my childhood, when mother fell ill to TB, and dad got lost at sea in a storm. It was me who changed nappies for my younger twin sisters and put bread on the table. No Max, once you are inside our Capees circle it is for life."

In the interim , after a lunch on the run, Max put Barklays' ATM to test using the 020791(Second of July)as a punt pin number. It was spot on. He withrew R300, and made a note of it. To him this was an advance that had to be payed back one day. As for Adam's methodical approach to life and things, it got Max thinking. He was beginning to feel there was more at play here apart from their camaraderie. Just how right , he was to find out the same day.

But first he had to get busy. ID papers, passport and driver's licence, all needed renewals. As a resident adress Vivian told him to to use hers, that flat at Parkhill where they were headed for anyway.

At close to four o'clock Adam rang the buzzer. He had news from Ian McLarty. Known to all as Boss and CEO of 'Shellberightmines Ltd' whom he'd managed to track down on the mobile inside the Kruger Park. Somewhere near Pretoriuskop. Boss was out with his grandson. Over a poor signal strength Adam wanted to hear what Boss intended to do about General Mzkwe's ransom demands.

"General, pig's arse!" Boss cursed. "Footslogger more likely. Tell you what Adam. Present those darkies with anything that comes to your mind to divert attention from yourself for long enough. Give them chocolate, biscuits, kudu biltong, football gear. Anything but grog and Play Boys. I want my men back. If it helps trade in the drill rig. It has payed itself I don't know how many times already. Trade in the concession if it has to be, but bring back my nephews and yourself included. Offer them nuggets, but strictly no cash! That is where we went wrong the first time. I feared they'd be coming back for more. As for calling the Ugandan army to help? Bloody hell, they are more trouble than worth. Amin or not. Forget it!" Boss was to conclude the instructions by ordering Adam to get cracking.

"Get the next plane to Entebbe. No time to loose. Bookings are heavy."

"Hold on Boss!" Max called out. "Before you hang up, there is one more thing. Do you remember that Croat who saved my life at Drifontein?"

"Yes I do. That was along time ago. What of him?"

"Well, he is back here and could do with a job."

"I see, of course you are short a security hand. It has to be one who knows the trade. What is his experience?"

"He's come through wars in the Balkans. One of a handful who managed to escape the Vukovar hell."

To Adam's surprise Boss knew about Vukovar, and commented to the effect he just hoped Max was better than Frans that Belgian drunken SOB Adam fired a month ago after the last debacle in the Congo.

"Vivian tells me he doesn't touch booze." Replied Adam. "By the way he is in top nick according to Vivian's hint. I've got myself a real man, she boasted openly, so what do you say Boss?"

"I say he is on, with one proviso. He is to sign to the effect that mine accident at Drifontein years ago was on no account to be subject of a future, nor present litigation. Did I make myself clear?"

"Phew." Adam let off the air." Now I see why you are a CEO. I wouldn't have ever thought of it. But then again, I am convinced Max is not the litigious type."

"People and times change." Boss pointed out patiently. "Have been around the traps long enough to know first hand."

"So if I have understood correctly over this bad line, he is to be offered a job as a security specialist. What money?"

"Offer him the going rate plus danger money bonus. That ought to do it. And bring my lads back. Oh, and promise to keep out of the media. Not a single ruddy word to anyone. Media pests and blasted reporters least of all! Is that clear?"

To Boss it didn't matter that Andrew, the older of the Mc Larty brothers was twenty, and John eighteen. To him they were still his boys. What Adam didn't know was that Boss himself many years ago came from the same Clyde school of hard knocks. He did very well for himself, but when he first disembarked in Durban from the P&O liner Orsova, all the money he still possessed was in coins. He had no underwear to change into, and nobody could understand him. His long rise to the top started from the bottom of the social and mining scale. A long way down. It took years, and made him into a legend.

Now Boss was obviously getting impatient. Plus the fact it was against his prudent ways to discuss shop over an open line. There was also the four year old tugging at his saffary shorts. Adam cought onto that and wished Boss and his grandson happy holidays.

"Copy. Over and out."

With a few minutes to go before 4pm the buzzer rang. Adam opened the door without waiting for invitation. He was in hurry. No time for niceties. Nor idle gossip. So much to do, and so little time. He spotted Max and Vivian at the table, then wished them a good afternoon. Without further ado he took a vacant chair opposite Vivian and decided it was time to get down to business.

He opened the briefcase, pulled out the Employement Contract, and handed it over to Max.

Max obligingly took the document. He proceeded to read it from cover to cover. Fine print included. All this to somewhat impatient Adam.

"Who drafted this contract?" Max asked quite composed.

"Why, I did." Replied Adam." That's how Boss wanted it."

"He doesn't miss much, now does he."

"No Sir, but what about you? If you accept, we are off tonight to Entebbe. I have to know."

"What!!" Vivian exploded. "We've only just got together and you can't wait to undo us. You are a monster Adam. A monster. I suspected your motives before, now I know, you a self-centred…cold fish."

She found Max showing his displeasure over the course of events.

"Just wait you two. Since this obviously has mostly do with my signing or not signing, let's settle this first. I will sign the employement contract. It offers me payed employement. I am actually going to get payed for what I do, as I did before the clock stopped running for me. You two don't know what I am talking about. Just trust me. It is a moral booster to one's sense of self-esteem as much as the cold cash that comes with it. And if we are to fly tonight to Entebbe, that is a part of the job. We cannot get in this life what we want. Only what the good fortune delivers. If our relationship cannot withstand a strain or two, then I don't know about our future Vivian. We should come out of this stronger. Not weaker."

He looked silently at Vivian, pleading for understanding. It took a long pause. Finally she approved. Where only days before she would have not positively responded. Perhaps the two were on the same wavelength after all. Acting out of her usual demeanour she finally relented. Max was right after all.

"Excuse me Max, and you Adam. I felt there cheated again. I just couldn't help my selfish self." Adam now turned his attention to his sister in-law. What a remarkable transformation. In years they have known each other, he'd never seen her like this. The calm, matter of fact Viv, quick to put anyone in their place at the first sign of weakness was here exposed as just another valnurable woman. And the looks. The released, freely flowing shoulder length jet black hair shone with opalescence under the incoming light in response to every movement. Add to that the silk blouse. Top buttons undone, and braless. No more turtlenecks. As he looked back at her again, he imagined one more button going undone.

"Enough to drive a fellow nuts!" He concluded to himself.

"Thanks for signing this." Adam told Max with a comment that could have been interpreted in more than one way.

"I take my hat off to you. Man, you melt icebergs. You have done what only a magician can do." Max let that go unanswered. He was already busy starting to collect the details of the mission to bail out the drilling rig crew from the General Mzkwe's rag tag army. This needed to be well planned and Max never needed a lesson in work ethics. They would check out Emerald Guest House first thing next morning.

* * *

CHAPTER 2

GRANDFATHER'S FUNERAL

There had been droughts in the Limpopo province before. Many droughts over the years. But the one in the *Anno Domini MMII,* the worst in living memory was a mass killer. It didn't stop at taking the infirm.

Around mid-morning the mercury was already over the 40 degress C in the shade and climbing. Into the second year with no rainfall there was no green to be seen anywhere. Limpopo, which meanders for much of the SA Northern borders had ceased to flow. Its tributaries and smaller streams including the Crocodile and the Olifants River had been dry for months. Around the shrinking pools of green slimy polluted water that remained there was now a strict pecking order. The big and strong would deny the weaker access to the drinking holes. Smaller game crazed with thirst were doomed. For vultures, hyenas and other scavengers it was a time of plenty. In places the vultures were too full to take off when persued by surviving crocodiles.

Here and there a troupe of baboons could be observed frantically digging in dry river bed low stretches. Any small pools of liquid that filtered up would be viciously fought over. Young ones didn't stand a chance. They would succumb from thirst or mauled, bleeding from the vicious bites inflicted by their own kind. All semblance of social order was gone. Even the male on guard for big cats would leave the post and join in the free for all.

All this was made infinitely worse by clouds of blow flies infesting the bloated corpses lying all over the place. And that sickening stench of cadavene. The all pervasive stench of death. One couldn't wash it out. It stayed on, adsorbed in the hair and adhered to the clothes fabric for days.

In the worst of that drought at Nylstroom, later to be re-named to Mamibulla, to the south of the Olifants River there was a funeral in progress.

The diminishing white tribe was to give parting forewell to the collected remains of Dannie Botha, who was until his violent death the last remaining white horticulturalist in the area. Two nights ago he'd been cut down by a burst of AK-47 fired from close range. All this in front of his family log house that stood on that *kopi*, in the middle of nowhere, surrounded by wilderness for five generations of Bothas. It was built to last and before there were any Zulu *impies* or ANC cadres nosing about scavenging for easy pickings.

Danny died ridlled with bullets before the night fall. What was left of him the postman found delivering mail. Now destined to depart forever from the only land Danny knew and loved. Around the scene stood a crowd of mostly *blankes*, middle class whites.Doctors, dentists, architects, engineers from Pretoria, Jo'burg and Vereeneging. Apart from the armed guards present, all family members..

They came to see off *oupa*, who stubbornly refused to leave and move into the relative security of the city with one of his kin.

He'd shared with Venda farm hands what there was to share. Ate at the same old timber table. He saw to their sick and helped their children. He spoke *tsiVenda*. He payed

respect to their pagan tribal custom, when it was against his religion's better judgment. He was almost one of them and God-father to a few. No, they wouldn't harm him. He was certain of it. Besides he could not stick it in the city. And he was correct. His workers did no harm to Dannie. They barely managed to escape themselves. It was the ANC cadres from down South. Men who came here with guns and a mission to kill another *whity*.

Once upon a time a man like Dannie was safe and respected in the bush, but the times had changed. The raw courage, the open mind and a pair of working hands was now no more than, like standing naked in the snow. One needed an army for protection. This was insane. A lone whiteman's life anywhere in Africa was getting more precarious by the day, and uninsurable here.

Hordes of Zimbabwe escapees were also roaming the wilderness looking for something to snatch. A country called Rhodesia used to be the granary of Southern Africa. The same country renamed to Zimbabwe under a looney butcher Mugabe couldn't feed itself.

Only days before, suspecting trouble was getting closer, Dannie asked his life time Bushman friend and night watchman Zweni what he thought of the security. To which the Bushman chose to remain silent. Not a click. They could just menage to keep wild life at bay as it was before this new menace.

Dannie knew the man too well to insist. The answer was there in the unflinching gaze that Dannie knew how to read. This, and countless wrinkles closing in told Dannie of fear.

From then on, neither man was off guard. Dannie wasn't going to move. A stocky powerful man in his mid seventies he was still more than a match for most. Besides Dannie never moved out of road for anybody in his life. Black or white. He would chew on his pipe, methodicaly re-adjust the ancient greasy felt hat, and if provoked spit on the ground from the corner of the mouth. It was almost a ritual.

One of the dying breed he refused to ask for help. When Zweni finaly spoke, he suggested asking for help from the scattered neibhourhood farms or even the *Boeremag* underground. They Danny said were just like the *ANC*. A crowd led like sheep. And he detested crowds and loud mouths. One went with the other. No! *Dankie!* Thank you.

The ANC hitmen knew all this and more. In a grudging respect to the silver-haired old *Bure* they went to a great deal of trouble planning the attack. Here an ex *FRELIMO* hand a part of the raiding party came up with a plan. A land mine was planted on the last dirt road hairpin descending towards the homestead with Dannie and Zweni returning from a shopping trip. The powerful explosion lifted Toyota *bakkie* clean off the ground, turned it over and rolled it down hill before it jammed against a mopani tree. It cought the bushman in between and killed him. Dannie had the left foot severed, still pinned in the upturned cabin. Moments before the explosion he caught a glimpse of men running through the bush. Bleeding badly and ready to meet the Maker he instinctively felt the end was near. But not without a fight to the finish.

Somehow, with all the strength he could muster, Dannie got hold of his Whinchester carbine and crawled out of the cabin determined to fight to the end. He feighned dead, with loaded carbine between the knees. Two Africans out with their *pungas* fell for it. Dannie was a deadly shot and finished another two fleeing through the woods. Now on his back he tore a shirt sleeve and apllied a clumsy tornique, but it was no good and the pain was excrutiating. He had no choice but to crawl towards the homestead and look for help. He didn't know there was none there left to help. Then just short of the steps leading to the homestead and out of ammunition, the ex Frelimo hitman and the only ANC raiding party surviver, spotted him and took no chances. He went on to empty the AK-47 magazine at Dannie's sprawling body almost at his feet. All that was yesterday.

Now the funeral was in progress.

The crowd arrived in their BMWs parked in full view of the cemetery. Surrounded by some hard men led by du Plessis brothers. Armed to the back teeth and nervously showing off weapons. Police was conspicuous in their absence. Nor was there an African face to be seen except for the undertaker. As it was planned, four Africans were to be buried later on in the afternoon. Not a single one from a local **kraal**. Those who would have gladly come, and there were many, cowed by the tribal witchcraft doctor, an ANC cadre chose to stay away. The **inyanga** threatened to put a spell on anyone attending, now under the spell of silence and grief. An air of defeatism was deeply felt by all. This wasn't just a loss of a beloved family member. The loss was more profound. It spelled the end of an era.

Here and there a puff of dry hot wind would kick up a swirling cloud of fine talcum powder. The silent crowd lined up to allow the Rev. Marius Muller of the Dutch Reformed Church to address them. A tall, very upright man he would have commanded respect in any crowd. As a young man, he'd flown Spitfires with Ian Smith of Rhodesia in the Battle of Brittain. Both decorated war heros. Now he addressed them, in Afrikaans at first. He spoke in cold anger, cursing those who killed Danny, and those behind it, wishing them hell for eternity as fitting punishment for killing his old school mate Dannie.

Then, because it was ment for a wider audience, or for some obscure reason, he continued his sermon in English. He looked agitated driven by anger as cold as steel.

"The savages!" His voice boomed and could be heard a long distance away without loudspeakers.

"The black savages!" He called out once more.

"Where is the world now? Where are all those bleeding hearts now? None is as blind as the one who doesn't want to see."

Where indeed? Danny Botha was only one more **nja nja** of the statistics that read 147 white farmers killed alone this year and counting. The world Father Muller was refering to was not interested. Not your WCC, UN, CNN and least of all those callous power brokers in their ivory towers, who draw straight lines over continents and then call them national borders. Those who make fat contracts for weapon sales to Mobutus and Amins, and then go on merrily *yacking* away of freedom and democracy, next allow butchers like Pol Pot a seat at UN or go to play golf with **bapak** Soeharto. Those two butchers alone have killed over three million innocent people. But who cares? So the corallory to all this was, ...well, the racialisam by blacks or Asians, many times more brutal than anything dished out by the whites, ...well, that is just fine. Father Muller was ready for another onslaught.

"What sort of devil's creation was this? This was not sporadic violence in a violent country. No! This had to have been given a nod right from the top."

Father Muller felt now suddenly grown old well above his years. He was past caring about personal safety. Past worrying of becoming the next ANC target which he must have known couldn't fail to eventuate. His congregation was no more. Moved overseas, into the cities or been moved underground. Monies for the church repairs ran out. The broken in doors and windows stayed broken to allow dust and wild life in. A pair of owls with chicks was nesting in the tower rafters. This grave yard was a disgrace. Life as Father Muller had known had ceased to exist. And he was getting more dispirited and physically weaker by the day.

"In a century from now", he was fond of saying: 'They'll need archeologists to prove the white tribe and civilization existed around here once. It is all going back to bush in my lifetime.'

He continued with eulogy and his clerical chores to a crowd by now in a very subdued mood. None more so than Dr Marcus Botha. A heart surgeon and by now the leader of the Bothas clan. He made a decision to visit the deserted property. Scene of his early pre-school childhood. This was also to be the last homage to his beloved *oupa*.

To young orphaned Marcus, the old man was everything. Marc's mother died unaided, alone in the bush delivery so he could live. His farther could never forgive himself for letting that happen. Never re-married, and drifted aimlessly through the wilderness for the rest of his life. Now if just the thought of having lost the old man was painful enough, worse was to come.

They drove in long convoy at speed. Guns at the ready and having reached the base of the homestead hill spread out military fashion securing the parimeter. The place was deserted of humans. Marcus, a natural leader carefully approached the building, weary of booby traps. He became intrigued by all that red he could spot from the distance. It couldn't have possibly been all blood. As they closed in, it was for all to read.

ONE SETTLER -ONE BULLET! Followed by the ANC colours and the spear and shield emblem. It wasn't at all factual, but the message was chillingly clear.

Marcus felt his blood pressure rise and the finger on the M16 trigger tightened another notch. As he approached closer he could see the windows and doors were missing. Nor was there any sign of the Toyota bakkie. It was all taken away. As was the machinery, and everything else portable of value. Including many hunting trophies and valuable big cat skins. Then came the greatest shock. Inside the fruit shed and coiled up on the floor was a large *donga*. A reticular python, gorged full on Tchumba, an eight months old Rhodesian ridgeback guard dog. With a bullet lodged in his hindquarters whilst guarding his masters body, he was unable to escape when the snake got him in the night. Clear collar belt stud indentations could be observed on the snake now sluggishly trying for escape.

Jean returned from the fruit orchid. A herd of starved elephants had raided it the first night it was left unguarded. To top it all, Barklays' assessor was to reposses the property next morning on a pretex of a loan repayment default that didn't yet eventuate.

Marcus called in other members of the Botha clan. There was a brief but animated discussion before a mutual agreement was arrived at.

This place, where their forefathers had existed through the hard times over generations was soiled beyond any hope of redemption. Farther Muller was right. Within two generations the old *Bure* had lost it. Air conditioned offices don't produce strong leaders. Those hardy souls who crossed the Drakensberg in ox-wagons and wouldn't bow to British empire at its peak only to be put down by brutality of concentration camps and scorched earth policy; those valiant God fearing men the enemies learned to fear; they were no more.

All this and more was going through Mark's thoughts. He knew he'd never see this place again. As a gesture of final defiance he took off his sunglases and trod on them. He wanted to see this place now for the last time and store it in his memory. The way it was. Not the way it appeared through coloured glasses.

"God **verdomme!**" Demnation ." He swore and spat on the dusty earth in front of him in utter disgust. Just as he'd seen his *oupa* do. Then put the 35mm Leica to work. The anger he felt wouldn't let go. He swore again.

"**Verdomnis!** We've lost our heritage, our roots."...

They departed in a cloud of fine dust that had only just settled. Left behind them was a homestead and fruit sheds on fire. Two large almost dry water tanks riddled with bullets and a python shot to bits.

Jean veiled and dressed in black stood silenly beside her man. She as a mixed blood, or what used to pass under apartheid as coloured might not have shared the admiration for the deceased. A man of few words. A hard man. A hard drinking man as well, but he was a part of this rugged world recognized and appreciated by all. No more.

She turned to face Marc.

"I know how you feel. The bastards who are behind this ought to be crucified." Marc stayed silent for the rest of the non stop drive back to Parkhill. Once at home, the first thing he did was to e-mail a stinging resignation letter to the Minister for Health. Also contemptuously called 'Beetroot', after her recommended cure for AIDS.

* * *

CHAPTER 14

THE GOLD FEVER

Men will go literally to the end of the world in persuit of the yellow metal. Platinum may be more precious, but it is gold bug alone that does it. From the freezing cold of Alaska to the waterless ovens of the Australian Tanami desert, men will be found defying heat, cold, hunger, malaria, civil war and just about anything else in relentless search for gold. The Big Yellow. Anything short of a mine field.

Only with this in mind could one begin to comprehend the complete disregard for common sense that brings one into Northern Congo. Oh, there is gold *thar in them hills..* There are natives digging up the alluvial stuff with garden tools and naked hands. Bone lazy characters who let their women do all the chores and carry the burden. They can be observed actually engaging in hard physical work and of their own volition. At least those not enslaved. Only gold fever can do this. And this is not to mention the big boys looking for the mather lode with their modern gear.

Big boys like Dr Adam Malek. He was convinced the eastern shores of what used to be called Lake Alfred held promise of a big find. This was all the more important to the company as their gold reserves in Gauteng looked as good as depleted. Company's plummeting share price reflected that.

His two men drilling crew had done a first class job. The Mc Larty brothers were new to the job, but picking up fast. Never a word of complaint from either of them. The exploration results were still to be announced to Jo'burg's bourse, the JSE, and a tighter drilling grid was required before that. That's what needed to be done. It would have been by then had that Mzkwe character not kidnapped the crew. This practically under the noses of the Blue Helmets.

A battalion of Pakistani engineers UN troops was stationed within shouting distance. Well, that's what the UN military wanted the world to believe. It was a half truth at best. The remainder had more to do with gold fever. As it appeared at a time, Mzkwe, general or corporal actually managed to pull it off. How? It remained to be explained. The fact was he, Adam Malek would have to see to it that his crew come back alive. He had one assistant to help him. And one only. Max Horvat. Not the best of odds by far. This mission promised to test both of them to the limit.

By the time Adam and Max arrived at Entebbe four days later, the trail had gone cold. They were kept back by the red tape burocratic whims and no matter how many phone calls and prompts, it was to no avail. What with the entry visas for DRC, the yellow fever and hep B shots. Just to mention the most pressing matters. What the pair didn't know, was that for once being late actually worked for, and not against them. Far from being negligent, the men from Lahore actually persued the outlaws for days, suffered casualties, but pushed on and surrounded the guerillas.

Somehow Mzkwe managed to slip through the tall grass. Most of his men did not. Nor did the soldiers take prisoners. Once the guns fell silent a foot patrol stumbled upon the drill crew, both men shackled and tied to a post. They were in a shocking state. Beaten, filthy and badly done over by mosquitous. It took days for them to be scrubbed clean in a lazarette.

Mzkwe was on the run and the drill crew under medical care made promising recovery. Thankful to the Pakistani soldiers for saving their lives, they in turn divulged all there was to know about the search for gold. To say the audience was mildly interested would have been a joke. After a demonstration, the old rig was running again and a Pakistani engineer was getting acquainted with controls and the mounted detectors.

Adam modified a standard Minelab 3500 detector so a thin probe could follow a withdrawn drill bit and test the hole, down to 200 meters. He completely changed the drilling mud composition as well. They did away with expensive core recovery and fire assays. Furthermore using activated montmarillonite clay-cement slurry they would after a week manage to re-drill for the core imbedded with the separated gold collected at the bottom of the hole. Weighing recovered gold and co-relating the impulse strength from the mine detector thin probe was sufficient information to rate the hole. It took some trials, fire assays, statistics and calibrations before Adam got reliable and reproduceable results .

Of course, what one did with the recovered gold was one's bonus for exposure to this merciless place. This did not escape the Pakistani soldiers. They were equally exposed. Away from home. They also lost men here. While the officers were on good pay, the same could not have been said for the ordinary soldiers. And that's how the yellow fever took hold. The officers happily joined in. They got the drill back to work, as well as their own backhoe. Day and night. There was at first no shortage of diesoline nor mechanical savvy.

There was a looming problem though. The drill crew had to be released. No question about that, and the media informed. As it was, a Congolese TV reporter addressed them in French, the official languages in CDR, only to be told in Urdu and English for a good measure to rake off. A discussion took place. It was obvious there would be attempts by the gold exploring company to rescue their men. Whoever was sent from SA up here had to pass through Entebbe. That was the only sensible way in at the time and remains so.

Major Tariq Laksam, units top ranked officer decided to hang around the Entebbe Airport in order to intercept Dr Adam Malek. Some sort of a negotiated offer was to be made quietly on the side. Major Laksam, a lawyer was also the right man for the negotiation.

He took with him an adjutant. A tubby red nosed Kashmiri for whom the army after Indo-Pakistani disastrous war defeats and Hindu retributions was the only family he had left in this world. Pinocchio as he was better known in the batallion, also held deepest of admiration for the Major. A better choice for a life guard the Major couldn't have made if he tried.

* * *

In the interim, as the delay to the Entebbe flight continued, Vivian with Max moved back into her flat. There was a list of maintenance jobs left to do.

The second night back an intruder tripped the alarm. Max expecting this sooner or later, quietly slipped through the garage entrance and took the intruder by surprise. A youth of 14 at the most Max thought. Skin and bone and frightened. Max disarmed him and frog marched him into the flat. He was told to take a seat. Soon he owned up, this was the second time here. Vivian was by then a ball of fury. Max let it go for a while, then put a number of questions to the boy.

It turned out, the Beretta pistol he had belonged to his uncle, and he was over eighteen. He had no parents, no schooling to speak of, no job and of course no money, and pleaded on his knees for Max not to call in the cops. They beat the living Jesus out of him the last time. Max then asked Vivian to offer the boy a meal. He had to repeat it.

"Is this the other cheek?" Vivian demanded to know as he began to eat.

"Not at all, but we may just give this urchin a word of kindness. A kind word, I don't think he's had in his life." Max replied. He emptied the Beretta magazine and gave back the boy busy gulping down the cheese sandwich the pistol.

Max took his name, the address, quietly slipped R20 note into youth's pocket and escorted him back into the night. His name was Mawindy and he slipped into the night like a ghost with the parting words:"***mNumzame, dankie** Baas* Max ."

"You never cease to surprise me Max." He heard Vivian comment and objected.

Would it be any different if I was starving in his shoes. I'll go one further. If all that money spent on security was instead spent on keeping orphans like Mawindy out of mischief would the rich be more secure, I wonder."

"If only it was that simple!" Objected Vivian still visibly fuming.

Any chance of a quiet night kip was gone. They watched TV, played rommie, and drank coffee. She'd ask him over and over again about his childhood and previous marriage. To Max this was like opening old wounds that never properly healed. She was doing him no favours. How could he explain that. It was only natural that she wanted to know. Finaly, just before dawn exhausted and fully dressed they fell asleep on the sofa in each others arms.

With first daylight the phone rang. Vivian got up, still drowsy and in a mood.

"Who could it be at this hour?" She had no idea.

"May I speak to **Baas** Max?" Mawindy called. By then Max was standing next to her and overheard the call.

"Max here, where are you Mawindy?"

"At Soweto catching the train to the city. Did **Mefrou** want her laptop back?"

Madam wanted the laptop back real bad. And all those CDs he took, don't forget." One could hear the noisy crowd and a train pulling into the station before the line went dead.

"What did you make of that?" Vivian was undecided, too afraid to raise hope.

"Wait and see. He must have broken off with his uncle. If so, that puts him out on the street. I'll tell you what. Get some **brekk**y going, and a good serving for three. I am hopeful Mawindy is going to turn up.

He did before she was about to take a drive to the school. Max saw him in and asked him to join the breakfast table. Smell of freshly done beacon and eggs was for Mawindy a new experience. Soon he was into it. Max let him eat in peace and Vivian let him handle it. She was testing the Toshiba laptop. A top of the line Satelite 20 machine, and still under warranty. For her modest salary quite an outlay of money. More irreplaceable still were numerous back-up discs. It was all there. The laptop battery was flat, but the computer fired as soon as the mains power got connected. For an instant she was elated. One more look at Mawindy changed all that. He had a black eye and face bruises clearly fresh.

"Your uncle?" She was guessing.

"Ja, ***Mefrou***, but I knocked him out cold. He won't beat Mawindy any more."

She went for the first aid kit, then cleaned up Mawindy, s face. Max watched her from the side. Words were superfluous. Her action spoke louder than words could. A man she could have chocked only hours ago had now care lavished upon him money couldn't buy.

"There you go Mawindy, does it feel better?"

He smiled awkwardly exposing a broken tooth and feeling proud as a man should.

"Oh, she added, and the name is Vivian. No more *mefrou*. You have done something that took a lot of courage Mawindy. Not many people have a lot of courage. It is a precious thing. By the way Mawindy. How did you get that name? It is not a Zulu name, is it?"

"My first and last year at school, we were sixty to a class. I'd fight them for the access to the window, calling out, 'my window'. Since then the name stuck. My Zulu name is **Lubungu**, but everybody calls me Mawindy. I've gotten used to it by now."

Max couldn't believe how she had changed. It was genuine. No theatrics. He looked around the other package Mawindy brought with him. Amongst the meager private things that all fitted into a shopping bag, a long handle painter's brush stuck out. That and a few used up stencils

"Are you a painter?" Max enquired..

"Ja, ***Baas*** Max. Painter and signwriter. And I can draw as well. Nobody's got money now to pay for a job. I do a job and they don't pay. Or pay so little it cost more for the paint. What can I do?"

Just you hold on there!" Vivian interrupted. She had been to the school only yesterday. The vandals completely messed up the façade. It must be re-painted soon.

"I won't make rush promises, let me first see the head. The school principal was on tightest of budgets, but maybe, just maybe we can do something. You two wait for my call. I have to speak to Frans first. Shortly thereafter she drove the clapped out Ford Fiesta out of the garage and off to work.

The two men now left behind to themselves got onto man talk. Discussing bruises on Mawindy's knuckles and tatty clothes not to mention cheap shoes falling to bits gave Max a start. He had an idea. Mawindy and Vivian notwithstanding other differences looked to him pretty close in statue and height. As it turned out also in shoe size. For a Zulu Mawindy had slender limbs. Max took a mental note of it.

Before long the phone rang. Vivian got a positive response from Fransois van der Waal, the school Principal. But! Wait for it.

"Could the two of them make it to the school?" Frans wanted to see what Mawindy could paint first.

It was Max's turn.

"Could she spare a pair of her tennis shoes? She had a crate full of them.

"Of course she could."

"And a training suit? "

"That as well."

"Great! That's it then."

They took a taxi, and Mawindy arrived. Freshly shaven proudly advancing in his newly acquired gear. The Head didn't let them wait too long. A tall bespecled academic who played it straight to the point.

"Here young Zulu man." He started addressing Mawindy and deliberately choosing to speak in English taking note of Max' presence.

"You have half an hour to show us what you can do. And you Vivian here are the keys for the tool shed. The paint and stuff. It's all there. Now I have to go. See me back after the bell."

Max watched all this and then it hit him. "Why!" He exclaimed.

"Why don't you Mawindy go and paint an African motive. Paint what comes to you naturaly. If you are as good as you say you are, I think the little devils are going to feel a part of it. And if so they may not vandalise it again."

Vivian agreed it was a good idea. Mawindy was given a selection of paints, brushes, a pair of white overalls, and left to himself alone undisturbed.

That half an hour was going to decide his future. Mawindy knew it. He got down to work. What he wanted to paint was imprinted in his head for keeps. He just never had a chance. He split the façade into three parts. The right hand one from the viewers point was to depict the scene of his farther's burial. He got killed in a mine accident. The distraught mother featured in the foreground holding little Mawindy and his younger brother by the hand.

The painting was done in bold strokes life size, and when Mawindy thought the time was up, he put down the tools and broke down sobbing. He wasn't the only one to be tested. Francois van der Waal was one of them. Quietly watching Mawindy from the background, he stepped forward and gently placed his hands on youth's shoulder.

"You are on Mawindy. You are on, and if I have to pay for this out of my own salary. But first I'll call on the Minister. Let's see what she thinks. We might have something here. Meanwhile, if you have nowhere to sleep, you can stay in the garden shed until we find better."

Frans and Vivian left for the lecture rooms. Mawindy recovering pose now looked at Max. What did he think?

"What do I think? Let me see the rest of it first. I'm no arts critic. Don't listen to me. Don't listen to anyone. Just go ahead and do your own thing. You get that?"

And he did. The remaining two parts of the mural were even more striking. The one on the left was a mine cave-in rescue scene. Everything in this scene was true to life. Max could tell.

To know this, Mawindy must have toiled and seen it first hand. Miners tormented faces. The sweat and dust. It was all there. The one in the middle had miners inside the **kibble** being winched to the surface. Just at the point where the first rays of deflected difuse daylight enter the shaft piercing through the darkness. Packed in amongst the living was a figure of a bloodied lifeless miner, still being supported upright by his mates.

Frans arrived after lectures anxious to see the progress. What he saw took his breath away. Without a word he got on the phone with a massage for the Minister. He had something of outmost interest to discuss with her.

Her assistant passed on the message without delay. What intrigued the Minister was the word outmost. Frans was a measured man. She knew that from previous budget cuts. Not prone to exagerations. So what got him so excited? She couldn't wait to find out. Instead postponed an appointment, and ordered the chauffeur to step on the black Mercedes 600. In next to no time speeding through the traffic she was at the school gates.

What she saw brought tears to her eyes. It was more than arts. For a city buildt on lives and sweat of the miners, what recognition was there from the city in return? Practically none. Perhaps this was a new beginning to set the records straight. She was soon followed in by the press entourage. That mural with paint still fresh was now a focus of attention bombarded by flash lights. And Minister insisted Mawindy take her portrait.

Life was never going to be the same for the young **umZulu**. He was destined for a meteoric rise. Singled out by destiny for fame. One out of millions.

Vivian returned from the school with Max. She was tired after a poor night's sleep and a stressful day. And she'd done some soul searching. It was a mood Max hadn't seen her in. He correctly sensed there was trouble ahead. It soon came in form of an unprovoked outburst of bad temper.

"Hell man I don't know what is happening to me any longer. And you for one, crowd me every which way. What is it about you? You seem to be always a step ahead of me, and yet you just got here. No matter what it is you have got the solutions before I've spelled out the problem. People take notice of you. Some had never seen you before. Look at Frans. He'd never spoken a word of English with me. You come along and bingo! Look at Mawindy. How right you were. But why didn't I think of it? After all I'm a pedagogue, not you….You go out into the night and bring in a mugger. You survive the war, and God knows what else….Your lovemaking as well. You send me to the Orion Nebula with speed of light, only to crush back on Earth. It's just too much. All I seem to be is your shadow. Blow it! You have got everything man."

"I'll tell you what I've got here Vivian. Nightmares and what is left of R300. That buys a pair of cheap shoes."

"No, not money. You've got things money cannot buy. If you hang around here you'll do very well. People take to you, believe me. Black and white. It's just that poor me is no more than your shadow I'm not used to being. For the first time Max tensed up. Don't take anyone or anything for granted, lest it turns on you. That's how he saw it but kept it to himself.

"Well, what do you have to say for yourself Max?"

"If I have given you offense, I apologise." He tried cought flatfooted.

"There you go again. I knew you'd say it. Oh, so correct. Why don't you for once loose your temper. Or call me a silly bitch. I could live with that. Or slap me once and tell me to shut up. I could, I think live with that. But no man. You are so perfect. So composed. No weakness in you boy. All the failings are in me."

"Vivian!" Max sharply raised his voice. Here was a man of short temper getting genuinely annoyed.

"If you keep this up, I'll have to spank your bottom."

It wasn't so much the threat. She knew he was never going to lay a hand on her. Strong men do not beat their women. More the raised voice. He was human after all. That brought her down from the clouds of despair. All the same, the damage was inflicted.

Max felt he was from now on with Vivian on shaky grounds. Before the year was over , he was to find out how just how tremor prone and how shaky.

* * *

The SAA DC-10 from Johanessburg landed in the late morning and late. Nothing unusual about that. They most often do land late here, and some leave early. That's Africa. To Major Laksam it made no difference. Early or late, a job was a job was a job. That's an axiom. All there was to it. Just another call of duty. No more no less. And once more for the fourth day running he was out there surveying the exiting passangers.

From the whites disembarking it was easy to exclude backpackers, spies, mercenaries and well off tourists. He was on the lookout for a middle-aged businessman by the name Dr Adam Malek. Finally he spotted the man who fitted the description. Two men in fact, engaged in lively conversation.

Major Laksam timed his approach and addressed the two men collectively with : "Dr Malek, may I introduce myself."

Of course he received Adam's attention.

"Major Tariq Laksam from the UN 106th brigade. Dr Malek I have news for you. Where can we talk?"

By then it was too late. Sharp reporters have been persuing UN about the clashes with LRA and the missing drill rig crew for days. Here they had the quarry cornered. Before he could budge, Major Laksam and Dr Malek had microphones literally shoved into the face. The media circuis was on for real. Adam kept quiet and for a good reason. Now all attention was focused upon the Major. And he was up to it. As dapper a soldier as you are likely to see, the Major accounted for the clashes with LRA Mzlewes men. Concise and brief as the military can be. Omitting nothing and giving away nothing.

"Any prisoners taken?" He was asked.

"None." He countered refusing to elaborate.

"Casualties?"

"Two dead, four lightly injured."

"Any sign of the missing drill rig crew?"

"Yes."

"Well…, what of it?" Major' tall upright figure seemed to be more intimidating now. "They are in our field hospital making a full recovery. That is all I am in position to report to you gentlemen. For more you have to talk to their company officers here." He pointed to Dr Malek who was anything but ready to accept the invitation having promised Boss to stay out of the media attention. But what could he do? Finally at pains, almost panicking, he decided to pass it on to Max. At least Boss would know whom to blame for the debacle.

"Here Mr Max Horvat, our liaison officer can fill you in."

In the next instant, the TV cameras turned to Max expecting him to throw a bit more light on the subject. Trouble was, Max knew no more than anyone else by now knew. He had to think fast of something, and very fast, lest they looked like fools.

"Major Laksam!" He was addressing the officer not the TV cameras.

"We are deeply indebted to your brave men and thank you for it. To the families of your fallen we extend deepest sympathy….Now can we move ahead, please!"

He ellbowed the reporter next to him with positive force, as if it was the most natural thing to do. The crowd gradually dispersed.

Far from disgracing himself, Max' TV interview, broadcast across Africa, as brief as it was had unforeseen consequences for some.

None more so than one John Ngezi now Assistant Police Commissioner in Dar es Salaam. To him this TV report on Tanzanyan evening news was a most unsettling blow.

For it was none other than Ngezi who pronounced Max Horvat as good as dead. Four years ago in shooting tragedy that took place on Farquhar Lagoon, Seychelles.

It was a child, whom Max had fathered and never seen Ngezi was watching play in front of him. Little Maxine became Ngezi's stepdaughter.

It was Max' wife Aisha, whom he Ngezi finaly won over after years of sweating on it to become his wife. With Max coming back from dead so to say, Ngezi felt it was all threatening to get undone.

He was at last happily married, and Aisha was in early pregnancy expecting his child. But how was she going to take the bombshell? Because that's how Ngezi felt the calamity of first order.

Right now Aisha was busy playing with Maxine. Sure he'll have to tell her, but not just now. Ngezi made a snap decision. He got onto Air Tanzanya's desk and guzzumped a seat on the first plane to Entebbe. There was a lot to do. There was also a financial side to the story that needed to be given careful consideration

* * *

Boss back in Jo'burg was elated. It was also the first time in his life he had a good word to say about the **Pakkies** and The UN. Boss was impressed by the cool nonchalance in which Max got the media pests on the back foot. He passed the praise onto Vivian, who'd do French translation work for him when needed…

Major Laksam was annoyed. His cover blown he reprimanded the adjutant for having dirty boots. On the move, the Major, Adam and Max escaped from the media reporters into a busy restaurant.

"I hope this place is not bugged." The Major was cautious.

"Not by us Sir. That's a fact." Replied Adam, having recovered his pose.

"Well then, let us get down to settle a few things here now. Shall we?" Adam agreed. "We came to pick up our crew and the equipment. We thank you for the rescue, and grieve for your losses."

"That is all very well, except…, you gentlemen must have come across what passes as gold fever. Believe it or not, my men are infected."

Major went on to describe the predicament in full detail to disbelieving pair sitting on the other side of the table.

"I thought about dressing this up a bit, but gave up in the end. Even the truth sounds fanciful, I know." The Major was fortright.

"What to do now? What do you two suggest? Is there a compromise. If so I am authorised to negotiate. Of course none of this ever happened. That is the key"

Max was the first to recover from the shock. He knew about gold fever.

"Deliver our men back. The rig we can, I think from what Dr Malek indicates be leased to you free of charge for, …I don't know? Perhaps six months. In any case how about we fly over in your chopper and see our boys first. Does this sound reasonable to you Adam?"

Under normal circumstances Adam would have objected to his junior usurping the authority. Here he was grateful to have someone as quick-witted as Max on his side.

"Man why do you think I went through all the trouble messing around with those shonks in Mahe'. Am I glad to see you back on my side!"

With this they sat down over a leasurly meal and exchanged more mutual niceties with the very engaging Major. All over soft drinks and tea.

Over two hours passed by, before the Major snapped and got busy making enquiries about the worsening weather situation. He soon got the answer back from the officer on duty at the Entebbe UN Compound. A rain depression was closing in. From experience the Major knew how bad it can get in these parts. Flying a helicopter in such deluge was nothing short of inviting a disaster. Now he had to decide. Fly without delay or stay put and see out the storm.

Just about to announce the decision when a PA message for Max 'orvat came through. There was an urgent message for him at the Information Desk. Vivian, he was almost certain, but now what? Wrong again! The message read:

"I couldn't reach you any sooner. I've got important information on your daughter Maxine.

Hopping to see you soon, and wishing you all the best. Late boarding, if you miss me leave a contact address behind."

Air Tanzanya, Dar es Salaam, Signed...........(John Ngezi), Tel 255-2221-18424.... Stop.

If he'd been kicked in solar plexus Max couldn't have possibly felt more back-winded and off sorts.

It took a while but eventually he put some of it together, then rang up the number given. It was from Dar's Airport. The desk clerk passed the incoming call to impatient Ngezi.

"Yes, Ngezi here."

"Well Ngezi. Where do we start? It is Max here at Entebbe returning call?"

"You do remember me Max, don't you?" It came back quick as flash.

"Inspector Ngezi. If I remember correctly. We met once I seem to recall with me in a bit of a spot. To put it mildly. How could I ever forget?"

"Right man. Almost right. They have kicked me up the ladder a bit higher since. For you, what matters is that we have to meet each other ASAP. There are matters to discuss of vital importance to both of us...." After a short pause he went on.

"And have no fear. You have no criminal record, and no charges pending. I give you my word on it. This is about family matters and some financial aspects. More than this I cannot tell now. Look I am arriving at Entebbe on Air Tanzanya in about five hours time. Wish I could be more precise. As it is I'm late boarding. See you soon. Meet me at the airport."

Max took it all in, missing nothing spoken, and that gut wrenching feeling only got worse. What the blazes was Ngezi on about? At least he'll be able to meet Ngezi on neutral groud.

He got back to the see the Major and Adam heading for the UN helipad and a take off.

"Wait". Max held them off." I have to stay on to meet someone." And he went on to explain."

"All right with me." The Major spoke. Adam just nodded in agreement.

"We'll stay in touch. Not so easy in these parts, but we'll try. It may also be smarter for one of us to stay on safe grounds."

They parted company. The pair made off towards a running UN Range Rover outside. Within minutes there was a Russian made cargo UN helicopter dronig away into distance heading 318 degrees T and about to cross The Lake Albert into North CDR.

Max left alone just shook his head. It was on overload. He couldn't keep up with the events unraveling all around him. He'd come a long way in a very short time. For start there was a Visa card in his name with a fat salary advance on it.

Then the mobile in his shirt pocket went off. Vivian this time. She asked him if he was well, as if to cheer him up. Nothing was said about the last outburst. And yes, Mawindy sends **Baas** Max thousand greetings. He'd done the portrait, and the Minister was lavish with prize and reward. Lots of love Max. She hung up before he could utter another word.

That woman had him raking his his brains. What does a man do now? He only wished he knew, and this was no time to romance. It was Ngezi he had to deal with first. He booked a double room at Blue Avocado Hotel in Kampala. Adam liked the atmosphere there, then hailed down a mini bus taxi already half full with passangers and paultry heading for the city

* * *

Before his departure to Entebbe life at Vivian's place began to assume some semblance to normalcy. Meals were set at regular times. One timed TV news, and the sleep came by easier. Max had his hep B and yellow fever shots, anti-malaria pills taken and best of all, some money to spend. He diligently studied all the land maps covering Uganda's border with Northern CDR. In particular the military maps showing every detail of importance, and for long enough to retain it in his memory. It took hours but to his way of thinking it was indenspensible.

He constructed a hot chilly spray can and practiced for hours karate and judo exercises, thus tried to engage in skills he thought naiivly would come handy to a would be security officer. He had to get ready, ... well, in his own amateurish way.

She was getting ready for the resumption of regular school hours. Any day now, that the enrolements were over. It was back to teaching time.

Still they managed to spend most of the free time together often engaged in verbal duels. Every once in a while she'd fire a real broadside stinker. Like:"You men are so complicated and yet so simple. Look, I admitt almost every damn gadget that was ever produced was invented by a man for the benefit of a woman. Granted. That's brilliant, only to let it all go into wars and weapons. Rockets and bullets and mass destruction. Where is the sense in this?" Bullseye! He had to fight back..

"Why blame men? What about QE I, The Iron Lady, the Amazons?"

"Yes, I suppose you have a point. But does it answer my question? No!"

"Look Vivian, we can blame each other, it somehow always ends up being the loosers fault. The wars I mean.

In fact when you examine history of the wars, it makes you think war and not peace is the nature's way. A lot worse now with modern weapons, for sure. In the middle ages the rulers used to be at the front in the thick of the blood and guts carnage. These days the rulers press computer buttons and give us spin. Then make sure none of their kin has to go and fight. The **homo modernicus** has got it made. Just press a button and a village goes up in flame. That's great. Just great!"

"So what are you saying?"

"It is not so much what I am saying. It is what I have seen. We are just no good. The sadists who commit unspeakable atrocities don't look like the Lucifer with horns and a long tail. No. They look just like you and me. Just your ordinary folks. Some do it only when blind drunk, others can do it cold sober. And some of the worst do it in the name of the religion. "

"My God, you must have gone through hell." She moved closer to him.

"Still promise you will tell me more." She insisted.

"I see, you don't take no for an answer. Tell you all there is I will Vivian, but it is a long story. Not just now. I have to be emotionaly ready.

The story of the Monsoon Drifter, so called because that is how he saw himself would have to wait.

* * *

CHAPTER FOUR.

MZKWE'S CAPTURE

Major Laksam's helicopter flew into a blinding downpour before reaching the western shores of Lake Alfred. Experience and skills of the pilot saved the craft as it was being tossed about on the downdrafts of cold mountain air. A few minutes longer, and they wouldn't have made it. The powerful engine began to misfire and splutter. Even so, the landing was much too hard. The landing gear required a mechanic, and almost certainly new shock absorbers.

For one who'd fought in the swamps of what used to be East Pakistan, Major Laksam couldn't remember ever having seen so much water and rain. Rapids were disecting the bivouc camp. The major tapped the pilot lightly on the shoulder, as to say, well done.

His second in command, Captain Imran ul Huq appeared to meet them and escort them into the assembled barrack office. There was nothing outstanding to report, apart from the Kampala's HQ ordnance and provisions bills. One item requireing some answers was the high fuel consumption. Please explain, general's note red. Next Major Laksam got onto the Kisangani HQ and was warmly greeted by his old comrade in arms Gen. Khan. They fought together in the first Indo-Pakistani confrontation in the lowlands of what is today Bangla Desh. Until the Pakistani front all around them collapsed, their armoured division was winning and taking Indian prisoners. Until surrounded on all sides, next it was their turn to go into a POW camp. The treatment dished out to them was humane and correct and to this day Gen. Khan tries to impress on his subordinates to uphold the discipline and the ethics.

"Our's is an honourable profession. Let nobody forget that. Given orders one shoots to kill. One does not kill when there is no call for it." The Major got onto the *sparky* in the com-room contacting the HQ.

The officers freely discussed over the scrambled frequency modern military radio the strategic situation. The General wanted to know what threat the LRA still posed around North DRC. Here it got tricky for Major Laksam. Mzkwe was still on the loose. How many men or boys more likely he still had the Major couldn't answer. He'd only just returned. Then there was a question of troop rotation. Khan could not be more specific, but there was talk in Rawalpindy's HQ of a posting closer to home, still with the UN. It spelled Afghan.

Would he be interested? Major could smell a rat. He tensed up. Army life had its pitfalls. One can get to the rank of Major in most armies based on seniority and modest ability. Hence there is real hope only for a few hand picked and chosen ones to advance. On family connections and wealth influence his chances were nil. That left merit. That ment every word had to be meassured, if he ever stood a chance of promotion.

"You know me General. I'm here to serve my country. It is for you to decide."

"I hear you Major. There will be a decision soon. I'll keep you posted. By the way, I have cought onto the extra fuel consumption. No harm done. The boys have earned it…Over and out."

How did the General cotton onto the gold mining fuel consumption, he had no idea, but a good guess. He'd served shorter than Captain ul Haq and had been promoted ahead of him. Naturally this creates tension. But there was a way to drive home a truth or two. He asked Captain to report without delay.

"Captain ul Haq can you report to me on the security situation. Where is the LRA hiding? What are they up to? And what weaponry still remain?'

"Major Laksam, we have lost contact since the last skirmish. As to how many men or boys are still with them, we are in no position to tell."

"And why not?

"Well, Major you have seen it for yourself. The weather."

"You mean to say there are no foot patrols outside of the parimeter?"

"No, ..I mean yes Sir, there are no patrols."

"And I take it there are no ambush teams out there either?"

"Trenches are full of water Sir."

"Then bail out the water Captain. Use your helmet to do it. Soldiers have been doing it for generations."

"Hardly likely LRA would try to sneak in in this weather."

"Wrong again Captain. Didn't you know, that's exactly how they got in the first time to kidnap the drill crew.

"With all due respect Major. You know, I wasn't here when it happened."

"True, still no damn excuse. You are an officer. It is your business to know and to lead. If you don't know, how can you bloody well lead? Tell me!"

"I see your point Sir. Foot patrols and ambush teams to set up. Did I get it right?"

"See that you get going Captain. The General is getting pissed off impatient, and that cannot be good for either of us. Unless you'd rather be posted to Afganistan…Now **diiismiiised!**"

Meanwhile Adam got to see Mc Larty brothers. They were still being tested for malaria, otherwise gaining back on lost condition, and dressed in army camouflage gear. What Adam wanted was a private conversation, with nobody else around within earshot. For this to happen they had to wait for a break in the weather. When it came it was late afternoon. The men trudged towards the claim in mud up to the ankles.

"I think we are finally alone. Now tell me where are the grid maps and drilling results. John was ready. He held it under his armpit and presented the file to Adam. Page by page, figure by figure Adam went over it. It seemed too good to be true.

"Let me ask you a question John. You two didn't do a fiddle here just to please the boss?"

"Never. *Gen* Boss, cross *me* heart! We did as you trained us. And every figure has been double checked. And the recovered gold re-weighed more than once."

"From the results here we are on a good prospect. It all ties in. Flaky alluvial gold here is only the false bottom. Even more rewarding could be that hillside over there about a kilometer from here. I am almost certain that is where the true ancient river bed was."

"Outside of our claim." Protested John.

"That's true for now. It belongs to Beersheba Syndicate. I've checked with Kinshasa. Have you boys seen anybody over that hillside?"

"Some *Twa*, pygmies from the distance once. Harmless. Otherwise, not a sole."

"Good for us. Now listen here. We have to lodge a claim in Kinshasa before others get wind of it. The BS hasn't done any exploratory work here. They consider it too unsafe, and I agree. Their rights to the claim expire in two months. Promise me not a word about this to anyone. You'll be richly rewarded. I'll make sure of this. Get it? Not a single word to anyone! Remember, this is your uncle Ian speaking."

At 18.00 hours, the field kitchen bell signaled dinner time. They gathered under the canvas. Staple military diet, corned beef, rice and beans curry. Followed by luke warm weak tea. To Adam all this was just fine. What mattered was the fact he got on well with the Major and Adam had a proposition to make. It was a task to be carried tomorrow and included mine detectors. As for the rest of the evening, it was spent on idle talk, until there was a commotion and shouting in Urdu, he could not understand. Then he saw a one eyed character followed by two more youths marched hands tied up behind their backs.

"Pinochio!" Someone shouted." Look what he's cought!"

Sure, the tubby red nosed soldier marching in the prisoners had some ressamblance to the cartoon character. But looks often deceive. So this time. There was nothing remotely funny about Major's adjutant. Once under the canopy with everybody present he got firmly hold of Mzkwe's untidy hair, shook him up and yelled at him.

"You filthy, murderous, stinking scum as much as fart here, I'll drop you!"

The Major was onto this in no time.

"What was this I heard soldier?"

"Sir, I was only kidding." He said that with a dead pan face. Then snapped heels to salute so hard the moustache shook. They were all laying about in fits. Except for the Major. He turned to Pinochio.

You have done well corporal. I'll have you in for promotion. Now get these savages and get them to sing, then report to Captain ul Haq. **Understood?**"

"Yes Sir!" And one more salute. None loughed this time. They led the prisoners for interrogation. Apart from Mzkwe these were killers with child faces and scores to settle

When Captain ul Haq reported to the Major next day, it was all in place. Anybody can srew up once. Ul Haq thought to himself. This time it better be good. Asked more or less the same questions, Captain had substantive answers for all of them. And a captured arms cache. The hope, false as it turned out later, was it spelled the end of LRA in their district and for good. It remained for the Major to pass the good news to Gen.Khan when Adam walked in.

"You promised to see me Major."

"I seem to recall you having mentioned a mine detectors job. Did I get that right?"

"Yes Sir."

"At ease Adam. You havn't signed on yet. I believe this is a sensitive matter."

It was. What Adam was proposing to the Major was what you may call extra curricular. But the Major owed him one. For a good measure Adam played his last trump. He pointed out to that hillside that promised to be the next Ashanti."

" Do you know who holds the rights to that? At least for the next two months."

"Why? No idea."

"You would have heard of the Beersheba Syndicate?"

Majors face took a strange twist. It was more than just location of the last Australian Light Horse cavalry charge well known to all military academy graduates

"I get it. No choice at all to a Moslem. So what do you propose?"

"Before I can say anything I would like to try your standard service mine detector." Fully charged?" Adam insisted.

"Yes. I've taken a note of your request. All modifications have been carried out. Compotently and as you requested"

"Spot on. That's terrific. Thank you Major!"

Modifications were absolutely necessary. Despite the fact that modern gold detectors owe their existance to early mine detectors, these were nowdays absolutely useless as gold detectors. Advances in discriminator circuitry are the major reason. A modern mine detector would discriminate, ie supress a signal, set against a motor car on the ground of size. Equaly costly, it would reject a nail on the ground of symmetry and shape. All this had to be circumvented and some printed boards removed.

It was time for testing to find out what the detector can pick post- modification.

As they climbed for hundreds of meters approaching the BS claim, it occurred to the Major to ask how it was possible for alluvial gold to be found on the hillside.

"I really don't know. It may sound a silly question to you."

"Not at all Major. A thousand million years ago there was another pile of dirt on top of all this. Kilometers high. Bit by bit it got eroded and washed away. We cannot tell with certainty how big the pile was. Nor what was a high and a low a thousend million years ago."

"Oh, I see." An admission of an intelligent officer to lack of knowledge outside of one's field of expertease. Fools and pretenders never own up to it.

* * *

CHAPTER FIVE

MAJOR'S DEAL

Major Laksam reached the heights of the BS claim first. He was long legged, fit and a mountain climber. Adam struggled behind him breathless, and he was carrying no gear.

They spotted the tin plate claim notice. More than a half rusted in. There was no sign of anyone having been around here for a long time. Apart from ample animal excretion mounds.

"Just here Major."

Adam thought as good a start as any for what he had in mind."

Now let us have a look at your mine detector. "

Adam tried the threshold and sensitivity adjustment, and found it similar to the earlier BSS base gold detector models. And just as efficient. A steel screw, piece of metal 5 grams in weight from a foot deep gave a clear signal. The smallest coin, the same.

It seemed to function. Apart from the extra long shaft he found a pain.

"Now let us start on what we came for."

Adam took a line on large trees surrounding the claim and began gridding close to it. He didn't go very far before the detector started whining. Adam pulled off the ear phones and passed them on to Major standing close by. The Major could hear the signal even before he placed the ear phones overhead.

"Music to my ears."Adam commented." That mellow meeowing sound of gold. It takes a good ear at first, but one gets better with practice."

"Is this why you brought me up here?" Major wanted to be certain.

"Part of the reason. This signal you just heard has to be gold. I had no idea how good your gear was. As it turns out, for this claim it is more than good enough. What that means is you people don't need us to find gold. It means you found this on your own. Good for the moral and good for us. And me and my men are no more than by-standers. It avoids a whole lot of complications. As for the claim, thresh it all you like in the limited time you have here. You'll be doing no more than scratching the surface.

"Well, well, I cannot remember anyone so generous. So what is it you would want in return?"

"First, a complete discretion."

"Goes without saying."

"Second, get me a safe passage escort to Kisangani and back, under, whatever pretex. Can you do it?"

"Gen.Khan is there and he wants to see me. So escort? Yes, no problem. Safe? Not at all. We get shot at. Mind you, we retaliate and hit back with all we've got. By now they may think twice, but safe? No, you have to take your chances.

"I accept Major. To guzzump BS I have to see the Minister for Resources myself. It cannot be done any other way. This'll be costly."

" That's your problem. OK. I'll get you up before dawn."

The Major returned to the spot where they picked up the signal. It took a while to dig through the sticky clay soil but soon a piece of shiny yellow metal emerged to see the sun. A pretty, still jugged nugget about 20 grams in weight. And there was more. Signal strength increased with depth. Adam expertease told him he was on a winner.

"Or, one more thing Major. Before you leave, fence the access path. It was the only way in or out. And for a good measure place mine field signs. In French, English and kiSwahili. Then have your men or machines return all the dug up soil whence it came from." The Major frowned. Adam was getting ahead of himself.

"For a civilian you are doing well here issuing orders."

"And you Major for a lawyer, if you should think about leaving the military, you'd do very well in SA. Boss spoke to me briefly and he offers you a salaried directorship with us. You can go a long way in SA. Not a bad start if you ask me."

"Thank you for the offer. The Mayor declined. Within himself he wasn't so sure. Posting to Afganistan border held no attraction to him. He feared the old comradeship in arms with Gen.Khan had outlived its user date. At this point Major Laksam in a dark mood decided to return to the unit. Gold didn't do it for him. He refused to take the nugget.

Trouble was by then he couldn't extricate himself from the mess the gold find got his unit into. Gold does get people into a bind.

The break of dawn saw them just over Djugu, and then westward on to the province capital of Kisangani. In little over two hours they over-flew the ground that took Stanly and his carriers months to cover. Flying low they encountered no hostility. Morever just the sound of the helicopter gun ship was enough to see what life there was scatter in all direction. This included the remnants of *Twa*, as well as wild life. The pilot couldn't help himself but to overfly the Stanly Falls on the on the Laulaba river. Better known as The Congo.

Two armoured PC carriers escorted the Major and Adam. The first stop was a call at Gen.Khan's HQ. The general knew all about their adventures and let them know. Of course with the latest agreement between The Major and Adam it was all above board. Well, almost. The news from Rawalpindi wasn't so good. New posting to Afganistan was official. Orders arrived in latest dispatches from home. Ten days to fly out and join the division. The Major took that as a demotion. Without a murmur to indicate his displeasure and hurt pride. A mark of a truly classy officer.

The second stop was the pre-arranged meeting with an official from the *Ministere de'l Mineral Reserche'*. Adam's rusty French was no problem. When it came to dollars these characters were cognizant of good English. A deal was struck. The new mining lease incorporating the BS lease all in one. Signed and registred. It didn't help BS's cause that no work whatsoever could be shown to have been done on the leases over four years. For now Adam was sitting pretty. But not for long. All this was to change soon.

With the main objective achieved, Adam made a phone call to Max at Entebbe, and that from a street vendor's mobile. Public phones here were non-existant. Hence there was little for either of them to hang around for. Kisangani was a shadow of former Stanlyville. The civil war devastation and African decay was only too evident all around. A white face far from welcome..

Without delay they re-fuelled and took off on the return flight, choosing a more southerly route. Via UN post at Goma, and finishing off on a northerly dog leg over Lake Albert. Again without encountering hostilities.

"It must be you Adam." Major was suggesting. This is the first time I have been over this ground flying for hours without a shot being fired. Upon arrival The Mayor passed orders to start packing. All to an audible sound of disappointment from the troops. As Captain ul Haq came to meet him, the Major just gave him a silent cold stare

* * *

As far as 'Shellberight Mines Ltd' was concerned, except for the rig, this was an all time exploration success. That rig was expensive and originally difficult to ship across the lake. All in pieces. Towed up into the mountain. What to do with it now created a real problem. Adam had no way of getting it back. Heavy rains made any thought of roughing it over the bush tracks a lost cause. To fly it back, he would have to go back to Kampala and try his luck. Off hand he knew of none able to tackle this. Equally he couldn't just leave it despite it having payed itself off, as Boss told him.

That's where the phone call to Max from the street hawker at Kisangani comes in. Adam needed help, and thought Max could always be reliant upon to come up with the goods and sound advice.

Max, about to see off Ngezi at the Entebbe Airport picked the call on his new Nokia toy. They brought each other up to date. Adam popped the question.

"You are a man of ideas Max. What do you suggest we do with the rig, before I get to ask Boss. I can't get it to the Lake Albert. It is all one swamp from end to end?"

"What about your army friend? Hasn't he got that Russsian chopper you flew from here?"

"Major Laksam is up to his neck in trouble. So much so the top brass want him off to Afganistan."

"I see. that doesn't leave much choice. Other than to extreme levels of violence. My old Lee-Einfield rifle mothballed fired after 50 years. So should your rig. Just give it all the machine oil and canvas you can find, then burry the thing. Once the dry season comes, it'll be there unless someone knicks it before. You don't have any choice remember."

"I'll think about that, Adam promised."

"And when do we go home?"

"I wish I could be more specific. As it is, I have to fall back on my own resources. The best shot now that LRA here is rooted, would be to walk down the mountain and pay the fishing folks to get me across the Lake Alfred back into Uganda. One plus the other, give it four days. Have seats reserved on the flight to Jo'burg."

"In four days, 4x4, understood, including myself of course. OK Adam. See you then, and regards to the Major."

Re-joining Major Laksam's camp came to Adam as a sobering experience. Men were busy packing the guns and equipment for an aerial lift to Goma, thence Afganistan. One more night here, and Adam's crew would have to sleep under open sky, without the military to protect them. Never too keen on this project in the past due to extreme levels of

violence, Adam felt even less enthusiastic now. It looked, the LRA locally was done for, but their leader Joseph Kony was busy negotiating with Kampala. There were inter-tribal conflicts that made mockery of national borders and would never end. Lendu vs Hemu, Tutsi vs Hutu, DRC against the lot, and hopelessly divided. Prospects of better times ahead were zero. As if this wasn't enough, *Ministere du Minere* revised the Ordinance No 81-013/1981, whereupon the Minister could revoke a prospecting and/or mining permit at his discretion. One after another foreign mining companies felt the pinch.

Anvil Pty(Aus), BarrickGold(Can), AngloGold (SA), they all got a bloody nose. Despite all the help, the state owned miner Kilo-Moto OKIMO could not make a profit. DRC was a hopeless case, and it will never amount to anything.

Anyone else other than CEO of Shellberight Mines Ltd would have capitulated. Boss worked on his instincts, and would never let an opportunity go begging..

'The last man standing will pick the fat booty.'

That's how he put it. And he was determined to have another crack at it. Never mind lack of infrastructure and horrendously expensive exploration. The stubborn Scott gaffer wasn't in the mood to capitulate. He was a born fighter.

And there was one more thing to consider. An oil geologist over a sundowner drinking session let Boss into some secretly kept seismological data on Lake Albert.

There was oil there, and big time. The oil man was certain. But then, the Biafra war came, the civil war and cheap oil. That was years ago. The oil was still there and the price was climbing ever higher. Before long Boss was certain the Big Oil would be there to get it. With all the back up required. What price a gold lease next door then? All this Boss kept to himself. And he had still another trump up his sleeve. Meanwhile encouraging his men to perservere.

'One more shot *me* lads. One more shot, then we'll decide.'

What that trump was would become clear when the game was up, and not a moment sooner. The rest was based on the need to know.

That's how Adam was supposed to find himself with du Plessis brothers in Kinshasa. In not too distant future, unexpectedly and against his better judgment. But his luck was to change for the better.

* * *

CHAPTER SIX

NGEZI MAGIC

Ngezi landed just after dark. Max picked him up at the Entebbe Airport and they drove off in a hired Renault to Kampala's Blue Mango Hotel. Ngezi had stayed there on previous occasions and told the receptionist to extend the booking for another night. The four times a week air service had no return flight for Dar es Salaam for the next day. He insisted all bills to go on his expense account. Max thought it foolish to argue against that. All the more so since Ngezi made it known to be under-using his expense account.

Once upstairs in the apartment, they took a shower and Ngezi asked Max if he felt like something to eat.

"No thanks, I've just eaten at the airport." Max replied.

"Anything to drink? No, sure?"

Not put off, Ngezi got the room service on notice. Before long there was a bottle of Californian Zinfandel on ice. Ngezi was very partial to a good drop of light rose.

"Anyway, you are more than welcome should you change your mind."

Max was still surveying Ngezi's generous midriff, which did not go un-noticed. In fact not much of anything would escape Max' power of observation. Despite this, Ngezi's deminour was friendly to a fault. He could not have been more social. Just like magic, Max thought. Ngezi magic. Max had met men with charisma in his time, but he thought Ngezi was a natural charmer cut above the rest. A real joy to be with.

"It's the diet." Ngezi suggested." My sweet tooth is the undoing. And what about yourself? How do you menage to stay so trim.?"

"Same as you Ngezi. It's the diet. The food so bloody tasteless it puts one right off."

Ngezi liked that at first. Then before long that smile began to fade. He reached for the small suitcase on his lap.

"I brought with me the family album. Let me show you."

One by one photographs of Aisha, Maxine and Ngezi rolled before Max' eyes. The kid had blue eyes. She was nicknamed after it. Aisha seemed a lot heavier particulary in the hips, and if he wasn't wrong pregnant as well. Wedding photographs taken in front of St Joseph's Cathedral followed and Ngezi still kept silent. Both of them were chocking on emotions. One more photograph of Maxine showing that capricious nose and challenging posture that was pure Aisha. Finaly Ngezi could take no more. His hands dropped.

Now they eyed each other. Not as adversaries. Ngezi was struggling to say what his family ment to him, but Max beat him to it. He knew how to read pain.

"Let us lick our wounds first. It still hurts but I feel for you and your family. We have to sort this thing out before you go."

"I could not agree more Max. Not only this. I want us to remain friends, and for you to be able to drop in and see your doughter. Any time. As soon as old enough, she is to be told about her real father. It will be done. Trust me. I hope you see it my way."

He paused before continuing, mental strain still written in his face.

"Of course you are entitled by Law to ask for our marriage annulment, and all the rest. We can remain as best of friends, or we can battle it out in courts where the wigs are the only winners. I just hope you see it my way."

Max took a while to digest the full implication of what he'd just been told. He was taken in by the sincerity of the man. It was genuine pain sharing , and there was no way he'd do anything other than absolutely agree.

"I promise to you Ngezi no harm will come to you family that is of my doing. I know, my doughter I've yet to see could not be in hands that are more loving. So here my friend, we'll have a drink to your magic, and I haven't had a real drop in four years.

You make friends where others make enemies. Here, let's toast to Ngezi magic."

"You flatter me Max. No. Let us drink to our friendship and little Maxine."

Max was once more impressed by Ngezi's ability to sum up a situation under severe emotional stress, and still arrive with the most sensible outcome.

"How do you do it?" Max wanted to know.

"Just a part of the training." Ngezi replied. Now that could have been a part of the answer, but it didn't matter. Just about everybody can vouch for more than a single case of retard in the Police Service. No different to any other institution, to be fair, and perhaps not quite that bad in the reformed Police Force of old. More respected and more efficient then. Most would agree. No matter how one looked at it, Ngezi stuck out. He was a true work horse. He would accomplish in one morning session what took others a week and forever to do.

"Just where do you get that drive and zest from?" Max wanted to know.

"The upbringing I suppose. My Lutheran background. Mind you with Aisha's Catholicisam, I come a poor second. By the way, did you know my grandfather on father's side was a Prussian officer Von Luderick or …something, I lost track."

"The name Ngezi doesn't sound Prussian to me. Perhaps von Ngezi? No."

"I leave it to your intelligence to work out why. My forefathers came from Mashonaland a century ago, to escape the raiding Ndebeles. Raiders with long shields. That's what I have been told as a child. So the name is Shona, and I cannot speak a word of it. Just great! Something to be proud of. Just another *bone-headed **Morungu***. Well, pardon me, not quiet. ***Morungu*** is Shona for a redneck. That much I do know. But little else."

"I am a bit of a crossbread myself."

It was Max' turn." From what my grand mother quietly whispered to me one Christmas, I've got Venitian corsair blood in me. Not that it makes me feel any different, and I detest Venice. To our people rule of St. Marks lion was the dark ages."

By then the second bottle of Zinfandel was starting to exact toll.

"Guess what?" Ngezi spoke." Whatever else, no one can accuse you nor me of inbreeding."

Max thought this was the funniest comment he'd heard in years. It was becoming more and more obvious the two were in more than one way, two of a kind.

A male bond was in the making. The common interests, the this and that and the other. It had all run its course. This was the genuine article. It happens, not at all often, but it is all the more precious when it does. More naturally under duress. In the war trenches or deep underground. On this occasion it was neither and it was spontaneous. They genuinely enjoyed each other's company and Ngezi insisted he be called by his first name.

They spent the rest of the eveninig and well into the night exchanging information. There was so much to tell each other, sleep was out consideration. Copious cups of strong cappuccino didn't help. Towards two AM Max thought of not imposing himself any longer and suggested they went to bed. Ngezi wouldn't have it. Still as sharp as ever. He wanted to know about Max' plans for the future.

"Look Max, you come to this part of the world as a round the world sailor. Right? I know, your yacht got smashed up and sunk. By now I think I have cought onto the rest of the story. But let us get back to your original idea."

"What's the use?" Max protested. "Sounion my old yacht is no more. All I can do is dream?"

" Yes. I hear you. But just for a moment. Let us assume you had your Sounion, or a similar ocean going yacht back. What would you want to do then? You are free now. I don't know of anyone in this world who is more free than you. So, which way would you jump my **fundu**?" Sorry my friend, I slip into **kiSvahili** so readily.

Max thought hard but could not figure out what Ngezi was driving at. Instead he sounded off disillusioned.

"I don't see what is the point labouring on this."

"Good, I understand you Max, but all the same. Would you stay or continue on? Don't get me wrong. I am not trying to talk you out of your plans. Never to see you again. On the contrary. The sooner you turn up at our place, the happier I'll be!

This is about **you** and **you** alone. What is it that you would want first and foremost. Life is short. We all know that, but carry on as if it would never end. If I can be of any help in whatever you decide you want to do, I'll do my best, rest assured."

"John." Max was calling Ngezi by his Christian name for the first time.

"Look, I've just returned to life so to say. In five days since, more has happened to me than in years before. I've been fortunate in meeting some people who have been on the whole kind to me. And I met a woman. Well, I don't know, we get on up to a point before I begin to feel lost. Now you ask me this."

"No!" Ngezi stood his ground.

"I did not suggest you go and tell the world to go and jump. Look I've got a yacht. No. To be more blunt, what I ment was simply this. How would you like a replacement for Sounion? What you do with it is entirely up to you. Can this proposition be misinterpreted?"

"Mate, believe me, I still don't have the foggiest idea what you are driving at. Maybe I am getting a bit drowsy, it is getting on after all. You know damn well I am practicaly broke and yachts cost oodles of dough."

"Snap out and listen." Ngezi shook him up by the forearm.

"You can have another yact. All you have to do is get your brains in the gear. If I am not mistaken, you have been born under a lucky star. Aldebaran or Deneb? Now just listen to this."

"On Easter Monday our Customs received a call from a fast ferry on route to island of Pemba. They reported a foreign yacht out of control drifting aimlessly in perfectly calm weather and a crew acting strangely. All less than five nautical miles offshore. Thus in our territorial waters. The junior officer on duty did the right thing, and took the patrol boat to investigate

What he found he had trouble accounting for. It made no sense. Of the five crew he could account for four. The Captain of the vessel was missing. Here it becomes strictly a Police matter. Stuff all to do with Customs. I received a phone call at home and we put out to sea again. We got there just in time to stop an Arab dhow crew from boarding. Needles to say they were dark about it. I had to pull out my service revolver to make the point, and see them on their way cheated of plunder. I soon found out what the Customs officer found strange. There was almost no diesoline left on board. Batteries were shot. Sails hanging every which way. Loose sheets overboard. One snagged and fouled the propeller. And the awful smell. There was feaces on decks and a pile of unwashed dishes growing molds. They'd been drifting for days.

We took them in tow. The foreighn yacht is in Customs pond under guard. Police investigation is still ongoing. It could turn into alledged murder of the Captain by the crew."

"And the dope?"

"The forensics Analysis Report came up with pure MDMA. That is *Methylenedioxymetamphetamine.* Ecstasy as sold on the street. The lilac wonder psychomimetic that makes people climb power poles and gives life time of hell for a short feeling of euphoria. Expert medicos tell me it stuffs up one's Serotonin levels for good. Suckers who use it end up demaged goods. In any case, the four crew are drying out under arrest and facing long sentences. One has already confessed. The Captain refused them access to the drugs they were smuggling. They fought on deck in the night and he fell overboard. Somewhere off Pemba Island. The Captain never stood a chance of being fished out. Now back to the yacht. That will be of more interest to you."

"NZ registred?" Max queried after a Polinesian name.

"Kai Vai, Sydney, Australian vessel. I'm certain of that. The Spray Eater.

"How big?"

"LOA(length over all) on the registration certificate reads 12 meters and 15 tonnes displacement. Is that big?"

"No, just about right. Fibreglass?"

"No, it said something like cold molded timber. Whatever that means. I know my power boats. This is out of my league."

"Think hard! Anything else? Like single mast or two master? Auxiliary engine, radar? You know that sort of gear you'd find often on a power boat as well. If I'm not mistaken?"

"Yep. A BMW twin diesel, Furuno 12 miles range radar, Flemming wind vane self stirrer, GPS, Engel 12 V 3-way fridge, and wait for it. A four man Zodiac life raft."

"Quite a bit of good ocean going gear. Compliments to your memory. So what happens now to the yacht that it is impounded?'

"Until the Police concludes the investigation nobody is allowed on board. Once the clearance is given, the yacht will be offered in an open auction for sale to the highest bidder. Considering the mess the boat is in and the bad publicity surrounding the case, I cannot see too many bidders pushing the price up."

"Think again John, I have a vague idea I have heard that name Kai Vai before. In Maori it does stand for spray eater. Is there anything odd you remember about the yacht that springs to your mind. It could be important. For instance. The genoa. Was it a sulf furler? Or just about anything at all unusual that you can recall?"

"Now that you come to it, yes. I found this odd. Once you got inside the cabin, the horrible mess notwithstanding, there was a lovely touch of varnish, and this strong odour of brandy. We checked it out. There was no liquour of any kind to be found. Those sailors got high on something else. Anyway we could not explain it."

"Brandy you mentioned. Now wait for this." Max took extra care to explain what that brandy odour ment.

"An Auckland boat builder, and one of the best by the name John Lidgard specialized in cold molding boat building technique. Apart from special free flowing grades of epoxy resin and hardener, one needed the best quality boat building timbers. Like huon pine. Cut and wasted long time ago. Except, you won't believe this. A brandy distillery in Auckland decided to replace the old huon pine vats with stainless steel ones. The discarded old timbers got picked up by guess who and for a song. Cut in the timber mill to 5 mm slats. Triple laid and glued they made immensely strong hull structure. With the boat's interior releasing over the years some of that lovely brandy scent. How do I know all this? I'll tell you. One afternoon on anchorage in the Whitsunday Islands I was fortunate to meet the man and we shared a cup of tea aboard a 41 footer cold molded yacht called Regardless. The cognac aroma was still there after years of construction."

"So what is your position on the subject so far?" Impatient Ngezi wanted to hear."

"It is like this John. If your namesake buildt it I'd want it. If only I could afford to buy it. It sound like a middle of eighties design. You don't get tossed about in one of those. A sea kind design. And the gear is very good. What you have told me about it is enough."

"That's what I wanted to hear from you. Just tell me what do you want to call the yacht. It may be advisable to change the name because of the bad publicity. I don't know. Some folks are superstitious and myself I don't hold any views on that one. In any case you leave all of that to Ngezi."

Exhausted, both finaly fell asleep fully dressed. Ngezi was the first to wake up. He walked up to Max snoring away in the resting chair.

"Wake up Sinbad! We've got work to do." Max began to stir then looked at the wrist watch.

"Is this AM or PM? I've lost track of time. I think I need a shave."

"Don't bother having a bleeding shave. You look more masculine unshaven." "Oh, thanks a lot." Max objected." If you are going to show photographs to Aisha, I insist on having a shave first."

"All right if you are so determined. Meanwhile I'll eat all of that breakfast coming up." Not an idle threat.

And so it went on. Just before noon they turned up at the UN Kampala compound. Ngezi produced his Interpol Accreditation Pass to the white helmeted UN Police Guard who in turn contacted the HQ. Soon they received a wave on signal. Not as much as a customary search for weapons to delay them. All curtesy, Brigadeer Singh was keen to find out what he owed to an Interpol visit.

"It is not your unit Sir." Ngezi was quick to reassure the much relieved host. It was the Pakistani 106th battalion in DRC they had to get in touch with. They needed access to Brigadeer's UN HF radio band. Any help would be warmly appreciated. How could the Brigadeer refuse after that. Contacting the old enemy was cordial. After all it was all under UN command.

"Come with me to the communications room gentlemen."

He ordered the sparky to contact the troops from Lahore. Major Laksam picked it up. Ngezi introduced himself and passed the michrophone to Max. Normaly, interstate telephone conversations around the Congo were most trying. If at all possible. And it was the security of men that was in question. Major understood. Within minutes he had Dr Adam Malek on the receiver. Ears all around, it had to be brief and not giving away anything sensitive. Adam was up to it.

"We are fine, thanks. Stop. Off tomorrow early Stop. Just got back from Kisangani. Stop. Book a flight home in four days. Stop. Four men, one is a native. Stop. Meet us at Butiaba when we get there. Stop. On our own, no assistance. Stop. Regards and Love to all, Adam. Over and out.

The HF line was loaded with bad weather induced static, but Max was satisfied he understood the message. And if that message sounded trivial it was anything but. None of what was ahead of the Adam's crew could have been described as plain sailing. The truth of the matter was the exact opposite. For start, it remained to be decided where and how to mothball the drill rig. It might have been old and written off in depreciation many times over, but it was Adam's baby, and for him held a special place in affection for machinery. It was this rig and the new ideas he introduced that made him. And the rig was in excellent working order. It had to be taken care of. And then another problem.

They had to depend completely on their own resources to make it back. Through the deluge, coastal mosquito and leeches infested swamps.

The Major promised to equip them with light weapons captured from the LRA cache and to donate the wet weather gear. But that was all he could do. Army escort to the shores of Lake Alfred was out of the question. It was by now a swamp from end to end. As far as the eye could see.

Adam pressed for time decided not to waste any and used one of long costeans dug up by soldier's backhoe to bury the mothballed drill rig. Gallons of used engine oil and all the cotton bed sheets the Major could spare came handy. Adam made sure he had the exact position before departure and used the GPS coordinates noted down as reference for the future.

One more greetings session with soldiers. Lots of hand shakes. A bear hug with Pinnochio. One final backward glance and they were on the way descending towards the Lake Alfred.

It took a hard slog and most of the daylight before the group reached village Laba. Men exhausted and absolutely filthy called in at a thatched hut.

The scene with uniformed men entering caused panic and set children screaming. Soon other villagers armed with cultural weapons turned up. Adam greeted them in kiSwahili. Gradualy the panic subsided. One elderly fisherman who spoke halting English looked them up. Their army tunics in particular. All from close quarters.

"*You no Pakistan*!" He pronounced. He was firm on that. There could be no doubt.

"Damn right." Adam confirmed." We speak English."

"*Oui, Angle, Angle.*" The fisherman was happy to be proven right.

"*Che voules-vous?*" He was a French speaker after all. And Adam could only string enough together to explain what it was they wanted. No *femme!* No women, no food. They wanted a motorized boat to take them across the Lake Albert back into Uganda a place called Butiaba. Some 70 Km in straight line across the lake with nothing in between.

"*Un canot a'moteur*.." Adam tried.

"*Que?*"

"*Un barque a'moteur ?*"

"*De quell cote ?*"

"Butiaba."

"*Ou?*"

"Uganda." They fell silent. The meagre light thrown about by a single kerosene lamp showed puzzled faces more than anyting. Uganda was a long way from here. Longer still for someone crossing in an open boat.

The weather was unpredictable to put it mildly, and there was nowhere to look for shelter in a blow. Add to this a problem of making it back against prevailing wind and current. There were no takers. Until the old fisherman who thought the TB he was carrying made a long life most unlikely anyway, decided to put in a bid. He badly needed money for medication and a new wife. He faced Adam and proposed.

"Tant l'argent Monsier !"

"Combien ?"

"Deux cent dollars pour un homme. OK?" A high price indeed. But a high price for a high risk job. The fisherman stood if he made it back to earn more in one day than he would in a full year fishing.

"OK." Adam accepted. But, half in advance, the remainder on delivery. They shook hands on the deal. At two hundred dollars a head Adam was still comfortably within budget, but taught by past mistakes it was always prudent to huggle.

After a brief weather check the fisherman returned and pronounced boat trip would have to wait for daylight. Lake spirits were too restless tonight. It was pitch black out there under cloudy night sky and there were bad spirits about nobody could deny that. At night up to their worst evil saurcery. Fishermen have gone out before never to return.

They set out in the morning instead. Having rested more than slept on hard ground in the court yard and taking turns at two hourly watch. To greet them, the grey sky above pregnant with heavy cumulus clouds ready to discharge the load at anytime. The long boat powered with 40 HP Honda got a final check. Fuel, oil, food, drinks and weapons were all loaded in followed by four men. They left the small village and within an hour it was pouring down in buckets. They used the hand portable GPS unit to navigate. Course due East. Rain continued for most of the way and kept them busy bailing. They reached Butiaba with an hour of daylight to spare. As if by a welcome home, the sky cleared.

Not that it got much easier at Butiaba. Still no modern facilities of any kind, and no telephone network. Again it was left to do the door knock.

Followed by one more night sprawled on hard ground inside a sweaty wet weather gear fully dressed. This gets to one. After days of this the skin begins to smell funny and an uncontrollable itch comes with a foul mood. The men experienced all of this. Fortunately Max calculated with a possibility of them arriving early and he turned up in a hired Renault van the next morning to pick them up.

A few days of R&R in a good hotel and long cold showers restored the men to their fighting trim. On the fourth day they boarded the SAA Boeing 737 and flew off to *iGoli*, also known as Jo'burg or Johanesburg. To home and the Sisterhood welcome.

The old fisherman begged them to keep quiet about him. He had so much money on him, the poor devil was sure to be a target. Adam understood and offered advice. They agreed to deposit second half of the cash in a Barklay's saving account.

CHAPTER SEVEN

KAI VAI AUCTION

Ngezi returned to Dar. Within days, the missing Captain investigation was closed. The accused made to face the charges. One more puzzle for the coroner. This allowed the Customs to publicly auction the impounded yacht 'Kai Vai'.

Marine survey report that came with the offer was only factual in as far as stating the obvious. The yacht was in a mess. No denying that. Neither was any effort made at any stage to rectify matters. She was to be sold in 'as is' state. As for the surveyer expertease, nobody wanted to know. This suited Ngezi just fine. He empowered a family friend to do his bidding. There was no reserve. The auctioneer started at $2000. A single hand rose and then in no haste.

Once, twice, …before another bidder got up bidding $4000. From there on it just escalated. On every occasion Ngezi's proxy bid up a thousand higher, the emacipated, bearded junkie face under dark sun glases at the back of the crowd would raise it. This continued. The latest bid at ten times the opening one leaving Ngezi's proxy desparate for instructions. But it wasn't the friend Ngezi rushed to consult. It was the auctioneer. Ngezi produced his Police badge and declared the auction invalid on technical grounds. All hell broke loose.

The Customs were put out of joint before Ngezi told them the second bidder was on a Wanted List of Interpol. He'd only just recognized the drug dealer from the posters. Besides, only with more drugs still left on board did it make sense to bid that kind of money for an supposedly:

Old timber yacht , with ceased engine and sails 90% shot'.

They looked for the wanted Lebanease dealer, but he'd vanished by then. It left Customs with a job on their hands. They got sniffer dogs on board. That should have been done in the first place. By the time they cut through the fiberglass skin of the false keel, 200 kg of pure Colombian cocaine came to surface.

When the next auction came a week later, the yacht was in a more disgraceful state than ever before. Only one hand rose at $2000 bid. Ngezi got the registration transfer papers to fill in before deciding to wait. He phoned Max, urging him to retain the name.

'Kai Vai', for spray eater in Maori? Too good a name to change, I say. And then paper work all over again? Ngezi was obviously too busy and tied up elsewhere.

"Yes. Leave it as is." Max agreed fully convinced just the same.

Ngezi pleased with himself, hired a shipright from the Yacht Club with the brief to get the yacht tip top. Otherwise still in perfectly sound hull condition, back to A1 state and ready for the ocean. And a week to do it in. A tall order.

Once the mess got cleaned up, the diesel air bled, the oil changed and a few more adjustments later, she started first up and ran quiter than a sawing machine. A new mainsail and selfurler, new batteries, antifoul, slipping costs and Ngezi had a 12 meter LOA ocean going yacht in sound shape for less than $12000. A gift. He couldn't wait to pass the good news to Max. A week later Ngezi was contacting Max.

"Sinbad, you old salt, when I you comming to pick up your ship? She'ready. A beautiful piece of craftsmanship, and it all works like a Swiss clock. This is my wedding present for you."

"Who is talking wedding?"

"I have my sources and from what I hear this girl Vivian is going to eat you, marry you or have you shot. Take your pick."

"Shot gun wedding, that's what they used to call it. That was a long time ago Ngezi,"

"I know my *fundu*. I was only testing you. Just in case if you need a JP to do a civil ceremeny, call on papa Ngezi."

"Thank you papa Ngezi. I'm still strugling over the last one."

"That would be the third time lucky. Do you believe in it? Like the old superstition all good numbers are three? Or changing a boat's name brings bad luck, you belive in that one, don't you?"

"You do know how to get your man Ngezi. Memory of an elephant."

"Part of the job. So what do you say?"

"Boss , he's on cloud nine. Doesn't want us near him for a week. Trouble is this is a long leg Dar to Durban. It can get pretty rough. Most often also chocker block full with shipping. Normaly it takes a crew of 3 and as many weeks. 3x3. I'll see if Adam or Vivian want to crew for me. I'll think about your offer, and thanks a heap for the present. Phui, some present! We'll see about wedding. So far she hasn't spoken. I might not be the right man for her anyway."

"And you havn't asked. You fool! It is for her to decide right or wrong."

"Sure. In any case if we are to wed you will be the first to know. It will be civil, and it will be you my friend to do it for us. Now I've got to go Ngezi. And regards to that lovely wife of yours. See you there any day now. Bye."

CHAPTER EIGHT

THE SISTERHOOD

With men out of town on various missions, the three sisters decided upon a council of war. There were four matters to be threshed out. Loland set the ball rolling.

"I feel we give in too easily. Whatever it is just look at us. I've been wanting kids for years. All my *hubby* has to say to my wishes is for me to wait another year. And then another. The right time never *come*. I refuse to take any more excuses. As of today I'm off the pill!"

"Can't remember when I've seen you so *bolshie*." Vivian was surprised.

"I'll second Loland." Jean pitched in." I mean, just look at them. Out there like boy scouts challenging the wilderness, dodging malaria and the bullets. As if it was the most natural thing in the world. So pre-occupied with their testosterone driven mucho caper, it never dawns on them that here back at home, one has sleeples nights worrying oneself sick about them coming home in one piece. I'll join you. As of today I am off the pill myself. And you Vivian, don't tell me …?"

"Bravo you two. As for me, I havn't been on it for a year or so. "

That settled the first point on the agenda. Of course the men were to be told about it. Just when? Well, eventually. One didn't keep secrets in the circle.

"Now we come to the second point." Again Loland held the agenda of the meeting.

I've checked out with my gynie man. He tells me I should conceive without problems. Jean got the same result. I don't know about you Viv but it seems there's going to be children in our circle before long. Perhaps we ought to plan ahead, just in case. You know what I mean. If worst *come* to worst what happens to the imps. I'm no Cassandra, but hey. Are we just going to let it be?"

"A bit academic at this stage. Don't you agree?" Vivian was non-plused.

Not deterred, Loland came back with more. Obviously she'd given this some thought.

"What if we didn't know who the father was and left it at that. Those kids would be our kids. As long as one of us is around they would not become orphans like us. Don't lough! Australian Aborigeenes practiced this for ages. No orphans *boyo*, until we came along to save them."

"Hang on Loland!" Vivian interjected wanting to know more.

"What are you suggesting? A free for all? I don't believe this is coming from you."

"Oh so clever **ousis** . Only you, Vivian can have ideas. This has nothing to do with promiscuity. It is us and them. And us and them only. Anyone steps out of line it is curtains. After all that is how our pagan fore-fathers survived. I may be an RC on my CV but the truth be told, pagan heart still beats in me." Loland persisted .

"We are the circle. One family, so why not bring the men in? And have a new family where nobody leads and all follow. Where nothing can be agreed upon unless we all agree. Like, ...well like the UN Security Council, where every member has a power of veto."

"Loland!" Vivian objected in dispair." UN is a shambles. For goodness sake, what did you have to drink before you came here? I hope the Bishop doesn't get to hear this blasphemy."

Jean watched all this in good humour, before commenting on Marc's likely reaction. "He is so prudish, I'm convinced he'd abscond rather then jump in bed with either of you."

"Hold on sister right there. Maybe not. Why don't you try him out. And you Viv. Haven't you noticed the way Adam looks at you since you've come out of the shelf. That Mr Wonderful! Hasn't he turned you around." Loland wasn't beaten yet, and she could punch.

"After all, one can always say it was only a joke."

"So that's the gratitude I get for bringing you to up." Vivian was mildly cross.

With widely differing opinions, that left the second point unresolved. The remaining matters to be trashed out were tied up with finances. For the fact that all of them were employed professionals, their finances were in poor shape. Unpayed mortgages and car loans for start. Money slipping through the fingers.

Vivian took over the debate.

"Let me tell you two. We used to share bread leftovers hard enough to break one's teeth on. Nothing was ever thrown out. Now loafs of bread are thrown out because they happen to be two days old. And then, look at yourselves. Compulsory shoppers, both of you. You want to save? Ha! Save or just talk about it. Budget my girls, budget and stick to it. The only way."

The twins, both blushing got to serious thinking after the impressive ear-bash.

At this point they got interrupted. There was a knock on the door. The Postman had two letters from the Ministry of Health. Both addressed :c/o *Senior Research Fellow, Dr Marcus Botha.*

"News to me", Jean commented. The title on the letters implied Marc's promotion to Level 4(out of 5) of the Public Service and this following a stoush with the Minister and Marc's angry letter of resignation.

"Maybe I should also resign." Loland was equally astounded. Not so Vivian, poor actress that she'd always been. Loland cought onto that.

"You Viv wouldn't by any chance have anything to do with this?"

"No use covering up. Yes, I did a bit to help matters, I admit."

As it was she moved hell and high water to convince the Minister it was in mutual interest to retain Mark in SA.

When Marc got to eventually read the letters, it turned out the second one was an invitation to the Symposium on Advances in Heart Surgery to be held in Laussane. Marc was to present his research papers. The Minister had booked ahead pending his acceptance. As if she doubted he'd accept. The Minister was all charm, and post scriptum sent regards to his sister in-law Vivian.

Tea and scons party continued somewhat subdued, until the other two men arrived. All on a high. They were over the moon. The success stories just kept rolling in. Boss for one, told Adam and Max to clear the blazes out of the office. He didn't want a sight of them for a week, only to press an envelope into the hands of each containing fat share bonus issues.

Marc was elated and no longer tempted with the prospects in the USA, having just spent some time there. He found LA no safer than *iGoli*. If anything more brutal. True, around Gauteng crime rate was on the increase. That didn't mean in LA one had to be less street wise to survive.

The jubilation is very infectious. Particulary when buildt on solid foundation as this one was. The men were soon crowded and made to feel heroes. Loland had champers on ice ready, and as usual took charge.

"A toast to our heros! You are not ordinary nine to five men."

That's how she called it. Max for one never felt a hero in his life, but was overjoyed just the same. He missed Vivian, and the cosy home warmth. It was all here in harmony, and he felt a part of it. Until Loland once more ventured headlong into unchartered waters.

"Our men are not only good providers, " Loland proclaimed, "but also good lovers. Whole of SA, not only us can take pride in their achievement. So let us sisters welcome them home and give them the key to our Sisterhood circle."

And she continued unabated.

"This evening every desire they have, and I mean every desire will be fullfiled. It is not for us sisters to negotiate. Not today. We play Swazi rules tonight. And may the best genes win!"

She all fired up raised the toast once more. Aroused and in full gusto.

Max looked at here with fascination. She belonged to the barricades getting tired men motivated off their lazy back sides. But then he felt something else. Not missing anything, Vivian spotted him with his hands busy. She looked him in the eye and called out to him to feel free. If it made him happy, she would be happier still. Now it wasn't the wine he drank, Max could take easily a lot more before it got to him. No. It was the spell of the sisterhood he was to be initiated into that sent his head spinning. Next he looked around and noticed Adam's arm over Vivian's shoulder. This left Marc and his spouse also turned on by the spectacle and feeling light hearted.

"Now feel free my heros, we'll show you what a real home comming is. And the last thing, I may have have an announcement to make. But this can wait."

Loland felt she'd done her bit, moving in on Max. The twins nodded in agreement.

It remained for the next morning to sort out who slept with whom. At the breakfast table Loland told men the sisters had had enough of the pill, and to put it simply the sisters loved them all. Now a part of the circle. To her surprise there was not a murmer, much less an objection.

"Men! Not so difficult to lead after all." Loland still by Max' side, commented to Vivian later on.

"Just how much of this is to your credit Loland?"

"Let us not get into a squabble over this *ousis*. Between us tell me what did you think of Adam?"

"Do you realy want to know?" Loland was in for a big suprise.

"All right then, listen to this. A finer, more considerate man I have never met. So the next time you come complaining to me over Adam this and that, I'll break an ashtry over your head, and I mean it."

Well, that was the long and the short of it. Thereafter, it was planned they pay off two mortages and move eventually altogether into Bothas' five bedroom villa, and with joint input pay off the reminder of outstanding loans.

"Screw the banks." Loland jubilantly called out. Before letting off more steam.

"Screw the pill and the Progestin. We want to be women again and we want kids."

The loudest of the three sisters, she was to be last one to conceive now holding the latest bank'statement on the saving account showing insulting 0.1% interest rate.

"Give me that free of encumbrance title! It can't happen too soon. Vivian is spot on!"

* * *

To Maximilian Horvat this should have been the harbour of peace. A true *Dar es Salam* he'd dreamed of. A place, where one can do so much of what realy counts in life. He wanted to join Vivian and teach Science and Maths, for which he was well qualified, and would hopefuly receive the necessary clearances. A lousy pay for sure, but to him money came a poor second. He was never going to be rich. For a good week he felt relaxed.

Then it happened. The time bomb went off. The only thing suprising was that it should happen here in the midst of harmony, where he was least expecting it. As usualy, it was just before dawn when those dreadful images of Vukovar came back to haunt him. His screams woke up Vivian laying next to him. Once more she got physically hold of Max and shook him with all the power she possessed.

"Wake up!" She screamed at him. As he woke up violently shaking and bathed in cold sweat, she begged him once more to tell her what it was that was tormenting him.

"Let go of me Vivian." He pleaded.

"You don't want to know it so dreadful." But she insisted.

"Tell me what do I have to do to make you see you are not alone. You are so full of life and zest to build...Then this."

"That is because I've witnessed so much death and destruction. Let go of me Vivian. I'm damaged goods. I have thought of putting an end to this more than once, but this takes more courage than I seem to have."

"You have been alone for far too long my dear friend. But you are not alone now. You have me, and my big mouth, I know, but there is a big heart that goes with it. You have the circle. We are all for you. And it is not as if you lacked courage to fight. You have fought and won. So why give up now?"

"How can you fight what you cannot see? This thing, they call it the black dog in the Aussie gets me in the night. Sometimes I can feel it coming. Do you know I shot my own brother. He begged me to finish him off."

"Max listen to me….", there she broke down and failed to finish the sentence. She embraced him and he could feel warm tears rolling over his face. It took a while before she could continue. More determined then ever.

"We'll fight this thing together. Call it what you like. Black dog or whatever. We'll fight the beast together and if it is the last thing I do. We'll also ask for help. In fact I already have. Marc spoke to a colleague of his, a psychiatrist. He wants more detailed information to be specific, but from what Marc tells me, the shrink wants you to offload your burden and share it. Share it with me, with the circle, with the world. You cannot go on feeling guilty for the war.

Slimy vermin that causes wars lives in palaces, high offices and stock exchanges. Offload! That was one word the shrink repeated over and over again. And then be done with it. He suggested you write it all down once, so there is no need to re-open the old wounds. How about it? I'll take a week off. Frans promised to stand in for me. I'll be your secretary for a week until we write it all down. We'll let the poisoned boil out until you are fit again to do your best. Wether you love me or leave me after that I'm old enough to cope and forgive. All that is up to you. But for now, we don't give up! And before I forget, another advice. When you present what you have experienced let it be described in the third person. In simple terms. Not me and I, but him and he." She paused out of breath, before continuing.

"How this is supposed to make a difference I don't know. Worth a try I suppose. So how about we take a week off. Drive to Kruger, or wherever you would like to go and start getting serious?"

By then, Max fully awake recovered most of his composure. He looked at her in bewilderment.

"You leave me speechless. A big heart all right. I just hope you do not live to regret it. Have warned you."

"You have and I heard you. And it makes no difference. So how about it? Kai Vai can wait."

Max could feel her intensity of emotion threaten to overwhelm his defences. So he tried another tack.

"Or maybe not. Was it Kruger Park you mentioned? How about Dar es Salaam, I can't wait to thank Ngezi." What he realy ment had more to do with the yacht and Maxine.

Of course there was more to it. Viv cought onto that, looked at him with an approving nod and a hint of a smile. She felt it was not all in vain after all.

"I thought you said, Dar to Durban leg needs at least three crew due to heavy shipping traffic, and three weeks to do it aboard a traditional cruising yacht. 3x3 as you like to put it. I cannot stay that long, and then that is only two of us. Don't forget I am a novice."

"I didn't say we would sail it back. I am not even sure Ngezi is not playing tricks on me. He is a fascinating character. I think you'll like him. Sharp as can be, but also forgiving of strugglers who don't come up to his standards. And a true workhorse."

"So what are you suggesting?"

"Well, let's have a look at Kai Vai. If it is as good as Ngezi makes out, we can get a professional crew to bring it down to Durban. I have a few adresses of yachtsmen experienced in offshore yacht deliveries. One is a Kiwi I used to do Astro navigation with. Meanwhile we can do what you wanted. I'll let you nanny me. Be my secretary, and promise to try my level best to get that black dog beast under control. Now, how is that?"

"LBW."

"Go away, I am serious." He objected.

"I think you are taking after Ngezi, and he seems to be a bag of tricks. I'm looking forward towards meeting the living legend."

"So two return tickets to Dar on SAA?"

"Sure Max, they insist on foreigners having return tickets. You have no choice. I hope you can afford it. I cannot."

Max foolishly cashed in his share bonus issue, and sold his part of the gold brought back by Adam."

"No problem Viv. I'll try and spoil you for a change."

Next morning they were airborne." He was getting used to a frequent flier life.

"Havn't flown at all for years. Now I can't stay away from the blasted tarmac."

They landed unannounced and booked at The New Africa Hotel. A bland but functional hotel, strategicaly well situated it the city. She unpacked and turned the Toshiba laptop on. No rest for the wicked.

"Do you know if I dictate, this machine will actually put it into writing?"

"No Viv. I'm way behind on these inventions. A lot of catching up to do."

"It is a program called Dictaphone."

"Would it do for me? I mean, would it recognize my voice?"

"Most probably not. It has to be trained. Like a dog."

"Vow vow, in that case , how is it going to put into print anything of mine?"

"You'll just have to train it yourself. That's how. It takes one long session." "And wouldn't my voice recognition erase yours, and un-train it for the want of a better expression ?"

"There is a way of getting around it. I'll show you."

The late afternoon session Max spent repeating the questions put to him by the Dictaphone software. There was more than one hick up with the pronounciation. He swore at the bloody machine a couple of times in number od languages. Did that help? It in the end it worked out up to a point. If he spoke deliberately slow and drawn out, the machine would accept some of his dictation.

"Max, I know, these software programs have their share of problems. Mind you, it's not easy. There is English, and there are variations on English barely compatible with each other. Just ask a fellow to pronounce the word **fast,** and listen to what you get back."

Exhausted after a trying session they were ready. Max suggested some R&R. Vivian obliged with a suggestion to drop in on the Yacht Club. Max agreed.

"I knew it. Just what took you so long?"

They took a taxi and signed on as temporary members. Max told the Commodore he knew Ngezi well and that was enough. They deposited some cash at the reception's desk. One ate and drank in the club on pre-payed credit only. No cash on premises. After a few drinks a waiter came to pick up the glases. Max asked him for the direction to the boat yard. He wanted to see a yacht. The waiter showed him the way towards the balcony overlooking the yard instead. They followed the lead and right below them Max could see a yacht fitting the description. At the overhead oblique angle given he couldn't read its name though.

"That could be it. If so, I don't know why it is still on hard stand. Ngezi spoke of it as ready to go. He was soon to find out why. It had nothing to do with the boat. A traditional cutter about mid-eighties design. A more sea kind boat of this size would be hard to find. No barn like cockpit, nor reverse sheer nonsense. Built for comfort not speed. These boats unlike their modern sisters don't buck as a yearling colt in the ocean swell.'

"Yeah, but you still don't know if this is your boat, do you?" And they weren't the only bystanders admireing the yacht.

Standing right next to them, judging from imposed overhearing of the loud conversation, was a pair of medicos returning home following a difficult task with *Medicene sans Frontire,* MSF in Sudan's Dafour hell.

It turned out, the Elliots surgeon couple only arrived this ***arvo***, and flush with ***dough*** wouldn't mind a ***tub*** like this. Shame it wasn't for sale. Bloody shame. No guessing where they came from originaly.

As for the yacht. Was it, or was it not Kai Vai?

"One way to find out." Max suggested.

They returned to the reception and phoned Ngezi at home midway through his dinner. Aisha picked the call. No voice recognition needed. Max found he was struggling for words, panicked and passed the receiver to Vivian, who asked in turn for Mr Ngezi, who in turn came close to choke on his knockies, unaccustomed to to have females on call at home. It ended with Vivian passing the phone like a hot potato back to Max.

"Hallo, Good Evening John. We're here at your Yacht Club."

"You what?...Here in Dar, our club...be blown, ...sure, we'll be there to meet you in, ...well give us an hour or so."

You noticed he spoke of 'we'. Aisha and possibly the doughter were on the way as well. From here on Max was on needles. Vivian had never seen him twitching so nervously before.

Neither was Ngezi faring better. He'd solved two Sudoku puzzles rated diabolical while memsahib was seriously busy rummaging through the wardrobe. At last Ngezi let off a little steam.

"Let us know when you'ready, dear."

That was the strongest term Ngezi was capable of when it came to confront his spouse. Finaly she emerged dressed to kill. Ngezi was stunned.

"Wow! Was all Ngezi managed. Not so Aisha.

"It is Saturday night. There is a ball at the club. Remember you promised?" Well, that was so long ago, Ngezi wasn't so sure he promised. Besides, his memory was never questioned before. But it didn't matter. To a ball they'll go. It ment he had to dress up as well. That only took minutes.

They arrived at the club quietly to find Vivian and Max, both casualy dressed on the balcony overlooking the boat yard. Ngezi sneaked up and tapped Max on the shoulder.

"Hallo you two. Nice to see you again Max, and your partner. May I introduce myself.."

He couldn't quite complete the sentence when Aisha puffed up from climbing the stairs and lagging behind spotted Max. At this point all protocol went by the wayside. She sort of shuffled up on high heels in top gear, charged and threw herself around Max' neck as only she could. No half measures for her.

"My saviour!" She exclaimed, then kissed him passionately on the lips."

"If it wasn't for you where would I be? Some old pervert's plaything at best. Look at me now! Hapilly married, a lovely doughter of yours and John's on the way." She turned around to Vivian and Ngezi somewhat taken aback with all the passion.

"You'll just have to excuse me. I promise, I'll be a good girl from now on." They burst out loughing. Then it was Ngezi's turn, trying to cool things down.

"What do you say Max?" Pointing towards the yacht on hard stand below the balcony.

"A classic, excellent sea boat."

"Wait until you see her inboard."

"John! Cannot this wait for daylight? "Aisha had other ideas.

"Sure dear."

Ngezies proceded towards the dancing floor. John had a reservation. As much as he could think of better things to do, Ngezi was a natural when it came to dancing. It was a joy to watch him waltzing on the air. Max found out on the same dancing floor he was out of his depth. Vivian foot sores were proof enough, but she valiantly endured. The contrast between the two males on the dancing performance could not have been more stark. Vivian decided to offer consoling advice.

"Don't let that get to you Max. He was attending dancing lessons when you fought wars."

"Tell me my guardian angel, what else have I to do, before you give me the flick?"

"Run off with another wench. Nothing short of that." And she thanked him for understanding and patience. That helped to soften the embarassment Max felt. Vivian went on .

"I know I can be a hand full, must have rubbed a lot of Romeos the wrong way. Until you came along to tame me. Now I can prance like a cub ready to roll over for a tummy tickle. I wonder what happened to my sef-esteem. But do I care? Disgusting, isn't? And you are the first man I came across who had enough faith in me to look behind the bravado and fireworks I front up. For this I will always remember you. No matter what. You liberated the woman in me and showed me the way. Not those silly periodicals.

"Eyh Vivian, who is talking rememberance? Look at me. I'm still here. Would you like me to always be at your side? If so, why don't you marry me?"

He had been planning and rehearsing to say it for days.

"I thought you'd never ask. Of course I would Max. Never in all my life can I remember anything I wanted more." It all came to a head now.

They embraced on the dancing floor and Aisha was quick to spot it.
"John!" She called out loud. Max found love again. You cannot guess how happy I am to see it."

"It makes two of us." Ngezi, quick as flash, instantly cought on and applauded with a huge sigh of relief.

* * *

Late Sunday morning after church service at St Joseph's they met again at the Yacht Club. On this occasion Maxine joined in Ngezi's arms. Max couldn't get his eyes off the child. The second time he'd lost a doughter. Except the circumstances were entirely different. If the first doughter was lost to Chetnik's bestiality in Bosnia, the little one here could not be in better hands. If the first loss was a cause to despair, the second one was a cause to regain faith in life. The child was not to be tempted with a bonbon offering and clung to Ngezi calling out Papa.

"She'll be told my friend. You have my word on that. All in good time."

"No need to apologise John."

They took a long walk into the boat yard. Reaching the hard stand holding Kai Vai, Ngezi passed Maxine into Aisha's waiting arms and climbed up the cradle holding the yacht penned up. He unlocked the entry, removed the wash boards, then slid down the companion way into the cabin. Max followed closely behind.

"*Struth,* can you smell that brandy? This was Lidgard buildt all right. Just like I said."

"You are right Max. It smells like a distillery. But smell or no smell, she is yours with all the documents that follow transfer of ownership. Wait for the official transfer of ownership to your name, and that is the end of paper chase. She is registred in Canberra of all places, and as yourself carries the Australian flag. But that can wait. There is nothing to stop you from sailing in the name of the previous owner. What got him to join with those loonies is still unclear. It smells of blackmail. The court case against the four is due in a fortnight. We'll see what pans out. Meanwhile here are the documents.

Max took the folder and red through the Australian Ship Registry form. Mind you some of those Aussie beaurocrats everything afloat was called a ship. Never heard of a boat, yacht, cruiser, but ship. Some ship at 12 tons displacement. The rest read as expected:

Kai Vai, buildt by John Lidgard, Auckland 1986, in cold molded timber WEST technique; Bowden design;cutter rig 36 feet LOA;2 cylinder BMW 20 HP diesel auxiliary. Registred in the name of one Jan van der Haag, and a Sydney address given. Anyway he left the transfer form unfilled, as if he'd red the future change in ownership.

Left alone Max continued excited to systematically examine the inventory. He wrote a checklist and went ahead.
Mainsail:Brand new 10 oz cloth…………..Tick…..Excellent
Selfurling genoa, new Hood cut…………..Tick….. "
Inner jib/cum storm sail………………..falling to bits, rust stained, a bit iffy?
Twin BMW 20 HP diesel………………..I'd walk on hot coals for 15 HP more

Fleming wind vane self stirrer................Bullseye
Seaphone VHF..................................very useful
Cat 2 safety gear............................. costly
12 miles range Furuno radar..................? Never used a Furuno before?
Indian Ocean charts, weather maps and , List of Beacons and Lighthouses and Pilot books. It was all there. Once in water, the 500 L water tanks and 200 L diesoline could be filled, curtesy flags and pennants hoisted and she was ready to sail again.

"It is very comprehensive I must say." Max was full of praise, anxious to hide his excitement. Ngezi watched his every move before he spoke again.

"I'm glad you like it. Myself, I only know what I have been told when it comes to yachts. I always had my doubts how can anyone go around the three oceans powered by an engine I can lift in one hand. Or, by the way, before I forget, there is a small double truncated dinghy, I think they call it a pram. It sits two seagulls in comfort. Padlocked on a chain. Just inside the gate. You'll see it has Kai Vai stenciled on it. Don't forget to lock everything up. This is the reason why I had to wait for you. To moore the yacht would only encourage the thieves. As it is the yard shares a night watchman with the club, for what it's worth…And now I conclude my Sunday sermon……Lordy Allelhuja….."

"Not much different to anywhere else in the Third World. And not just the Third World. My Sounion got broken into twice at Pitwatter." Max pitched in.

"That much is true. If the lazy menfolk got off their butts more often and spent less on dagga, khat and what not to help their cause, I'm certain there'd be less crime. As for Africa, it is the wretched women who do all the work….Anyway, I'm happy you like the boat."

"And how much do I owe for the repairs and new sails."

"Max, have you forgotten what I told you over the phone only days ago? Kai Vai is my wedding present to you and Vivian to do with it as you wish. And if I may pass one more unsolicited word of advice. If you don't marry that lady, my friend you have rocks in the head. And as for money matters? No, I am not avoiding the issue. Loss of your yacht and close shave with death comes in now. It is like this.

"When Ismail Hassan Aidid, alias Hamoud, plus dozen others got buried by Rene on Farquhar, after you shot him in self-defence, Interpol cracked his codes and got onto one Stayerishe, an Austrian bank. Hamoud had millions stashed there, and still has. We have been squizzing the bastards ever since to recompense Aisha for the suffering she endured. They payed first installment, a pittance, and ever since the lawyers have been having a picnic. I can now add the replacement cost for your yacht, sunk by him, but man, these people are unbelievable. Just when you think you have got them where they have to admit liability, they come with some other outlandish crap nobody ever heard of.

Hamoud , as far as I know had no will, and no next of kin to claim his estate. But then, his Somalia is Somalia. Arse end of Africa. Anything is possible. More about all this for later."

* * *

Back in the New Africa hotel after a Sunday dinner, Vivian took a seat and soon started adding sums thereby loking more distressed by the minute.

"Not my big mouth again!" She spoke in a tone which was only a note below anger." Why can't I keep my big trap shut?" She went on having a monologue admonishing herself.

"Why?" Max picked it up…What's bugging you?

"As if it wasn't enough to put you off by my tantrums, next I'll have my sisters baying for blood."

"Why, I still don't get it. What are you mumbling on about Vivian?" Max was once more scratching his head. "Much more of this and I'll end up bold."

"Oh, sure, I owe you an explanation. I foolishly gave my sisters a dressing down on their spend-thrift ways. Made a big deal about budgeting one's way. Now guess what. We're broke. And the marriage ceremony will only make it worse. You go from broke to broker. But then that's not right either."

"Let me see those figures."

Having gone through the arithmetic Max had to agree. Her savings and the $A 1800 he still held with the CBA, The Commonwealth Bank of Australia were not enough to meet the expenses for even a modest wedding. She continued.

"You know Max, the old saying, there is no fool like an old fool. Right on the money. Here we are carrying as if we owned the world. Two middle aged fools with heads in the clouds. That's what we are."

"I suppose we could borrow some from the bank. A few bits of gold I have left wouldn't go far. But you are right Vivian. Living on the credit card is for eighteen year olds. They have a future, or at least they ought to have a future. The fault is not yours, blame me. I brought us up here. Therefore I and not you am responsible for the budget fiasco. It is very prudent of you all the same, and very sobering, I must admit. So let us figure out how best to manage this. I am certain we'll find a way."

Half an hour later, Max was about to weigh the gold nuggets left, no closer to a solution. But help was on the way. There was a call from the reception that broke the doom and gloom. Mr Ngezi was in the foyer. As always, very descret, dropping a call card. Soon he joined the two, and came to the point without much ado. He had some papers for Max to sign. One of those delt with Max' divorce from Aisha. Here Ngezi went on to explain to confused Max.

"I try the best I can to avoid the Legalese mumbo jumbo. Put in simple terms, the Law gives Max a choice. Either spend anything up to five years and complex process of court procedures, and/or produce signed affidavits of **x** number of witnesses, who would have known him for **y** number of years, then wait for the outcome. All so, the Death Certificate would be annulled, and then go for divorce.

Or much simpler, sign the divorce papers on the ground of desertion. Here and now. Why? All this to avoid the bigamy charges. To Max none of this made a convincing argument. Instead, he was relaying on the judgment of his friend Ngezi. A JP after all.

He signed the forms for the divorce consent. According to Ngezi he was about to be free by Law to marry lovely Vivian de Villiers.

It still didn't do anything for the financial squeeze, but it helped to inspire a change in mood. With Ngezi around it was impossible to be in a somber mood. Vivian looked relaxed as well. Ngezi wanted to know about the wedding. Dar or Jo'burg, church or civic, big or small, when and where, and so on. Boss was hinting at Dar. Why? It was to became clear soon. Now Max laid the cards on the table for Ngezi to see. It was all empty talk.

"Mate, just as well we have you here. Guess what! We only just figured out, the wedding may have to wait."

"But why?" Ngezi was not at all pleased.

"Well, let's not go into it any deeper. Suffice it to say, we'll have to go back to work before we can afford a decent wedding."

Ngezi didn't like this at all. He red this as funk and turned on Max..

"Look at this my *fundu* One has to make choices in life. We all do. For you the choice is plain. Stay with this charming lady, or sail the seven seas. Which is it going to be?" Despite being of the same age group, Ngezi was more and more acting as if he was Max' custodian.

"I don't see what the heck you are getting at." Max protested loudly.

"OK. Now listen to this. You must have seen those two, the Australian surgeon couple. They are looking for an ocean going yacht. Pay cash on the spot. In $A, on Australian bank account. It is an Aussie yacht. A dead simple transanctiopn for all."

"How do you know all this? It is all news to me."

"Things come to my attention. Let's just leave it at that."

"But you presented us with the yacht as a wedding present?"

"Sure, and I also mentioned, feel free to do with it as you please. I care about you not the damn yacht. Did I not explain myself?"

Max felt his head spinning. Yet he knew Ngezi was right. So was Vivian. It was he who lived as if there was no tomorrow. Immature in his ways. Head in the clouds. He felt intense attention focused upon him by both, Ngezi and Vivian. Both individuals he found as pillars of strength. Unlike his own tendencies to drift, these two were unwavering. Yes, he was wobbly on finances. Destined never to be rich. Equally, he also had dreams of sailing the seven seas in a beautiful yacht Kai Vai. Clearly one had to make a choice. It could only be one or the other. It was one of those rare moments where a decision made will set a definite course for the rest of one's life.

He wasn't sure how long it took before the silence was broken. Time is a relative thing. Things can happen in a flash of a second. Only to see years go by of Lord's precious gift with nothing to show for, except wastage and grey hair..

Finaly he spoke in a firm voice. His mind was made up for all time.

"Go ahead John. Here is the ABC for today. Tell those medicoes the yacht is for sale, and take their holding deposit. This lovely lady of mine is the brains in the family. And I have just swollowed the anchor."

All Vivian managed to do after this was blush and choke on emotion.

* * *

In his Jo'burg office, Boss back from Easter holydays sliped into the work routine. The IN tray got a look first thing in the morning. Boss noticed a pile of telex messages. Obviously Easter didn't stop business nowdays. He emptied the tray and began to sort out the wheat from chaff. Usually he'd scan a page in matter of seconds before decision was made on what to do. This morning it took much longer. A lot of stuff was in French, moving Boss to comment: "Why don't the frogs learn a proper language!"

Off hand boss could not think of anyone who could do both, speak French and be trusted, apart from Vivian now in Dar. So he continued, and deeper into the tray found a fax from Gome UN Post with Adam, back in the Congo asking for directions. All in code. Plan Alice or Plan Beatrice? Adam was of the opinion it was too late to try and buy out BS. So goodby Alice. Pakistani soldiers cashing in their gold soon gave the game away. It didn't take long for spies to sus this out, and the BS men to start splashing money big time around Kinshasa.

Now Beatrice was of the Amazon kind. Fight to win. They all played dirty anyway. Boss could see this far ahead, and du Plessis brothers, back from lending security to *oupa* Botha's funeral were just the men for the job. No more amateurish stunts. The stakes were too high. Du Plessis were old mercenary hands with a formidable reputation and scores to settle. As well as a hidden arms cache left from the Biafra war. A tougher pair of white mercenary hands loaded with menace would be hard to find.

Without having read the contents of the other telex, sent from the Ministry of DCR Resources, Boss instinctively knew what it was all about. It was like a game of poker. One bluffed to see the other upping the stakes blink first.

He sent a return telex to Adam. Uncoded and signed. Lots of Love, Beatrice! Close to the bottom of the pile was one telex from BS, more or less insinuating Boss had to do with the minefield on their claim. What a load of tripe! Seriously! Boss knew nothing of it.

Then came the invitation to wedding. He was cordially invited to attend the marriage ceremony of Vivian de Villiers and Maximilian Horvat. In line with his plan, to be held at St Joseph's Cathedral Dar es Salaam next Wednesday, at 6pm. Boss liked both of them, and without delay reserved a seat on the flight to Dar Wednesday morning. That called for a strong jug of black coffee to sooth the nerves. What a bloody drama! The letter from the oncology ward he just left days ago he chose to leave unopened.

'One more shot. Just one more shot *me lads* before my time is up!' That's what Ian Mc Larty, the tough Scottish gaffer promised himself. Then he'll show them!

As for Max' civil wedding? *Nix . Nada* . Nothing of the kind. Vivian knocked that on the head. She insisted on a proper wedding. They had promise of ample funds comming in to pay for it, and who could blame her.

A formidable matriarch was about to rise.

* * *

CHAPTER NINE

THE WEDDING

A compact crowd of revelers gathered at the stairway to the St Joseph's Cathedral. Amongst the late comers was Raymond de Villiers, Vivian's grandfather and the closest male relative remaining. He was given the task of giving the bride away to a new life. What with advanced age and frail constitution, he found the tropical heat exhausting. Even the sea breeze arriving towards late evening wasn't enough to restore his strength. He needed physical support to climb the stairway.

Right on time the organ struck notes from Mendelsson's Wedding March and the bride, all in white traditional splendour took the slow walk towards the altar. Two bride maids in tow. One of them was Maxine, the blue eyed one, doing quickstep, trying not to fall too far behind Loland on the other side.

Father Benetti, a very busy cleric, who'd only met this couple two days ago was favourably impressed. In his brief sermon, and that had a lot to do with Raymond's health condition, he commented:

"I can read it in their eyes. Love or hate. And in the eyes of this couple I read enough love to last a life time."

Vivian and Max exchanged the vows, embraced and sealed the union with a long kiss, watched by the enthusiastic crowd. Vivian became Mrs Horvat-de Villiers.

Celebrations continued at New Africa's Reception Hall well into the night.

Boss was the first to rise a toast.

"To our newly weds, our friends and associates, to their happy and lasting marriage!"

Others joined in. The bride tangoed with the Boss, and Max invited Aisha to the dancing floor. Aisha as bubly as ever spoke to Max:

"We want you here, you and Vivian. Welcome to our place any time, and promise you'll come!"

They changed dancing partners before Loland crossed the sights with Boss. She was on her feet before him. They made for an interesting couple. She was born inquisitive and he not easily beaten for an answer.

"Boss." She asked." What do you have in store for Max?"

Sisters would have been a lot happier with the wedding closer to home. Why did Boss insist on one here?

Whilst he carried a lot of sway as employer and senior statesman, he also owed an explanation and knew it.

"Well, it's like this **kiddo**. No use **fartarsingarund** Life as I see it, is a fight to the finish. A fight for every breath of air and every slice of bread we put on the table. Nothing comes free. And Max has one more mission to perform for our cause. I cannot do without him. More than this I should not be telling you. Not now. You'll hear it soon enough."

Loland far from satisfied with the cryptic answer felt the occasion didn't lend itself to further questioning. Instead she switched the conversation. Boss had been widowed for years.

"Didn't he think, ...well, all alone...at his age?

"I can see where you are headed Loland. At my age, the answer is no. I've still got the picture of my Agnes with me."

"You don't look a day over fifty, and one cannot live with a picture."

"Oh, yes, one can Loland. For as long as you carry the picture in your heart the love is not dead."

"You are a true romantic. For a man of your steely reputation that is some surprise, I must say."

"Be that as you say. So what is wrong with being a romantic? Just look at your brother in-law. He is a hard man. Up to his eye balls in love, at the age of fortyeight! And Vivian, a different person. A different woman altogether. And very, very pretty may I add."

"You are not the first to notice it."

"Well, there you go. Only love can do this to you."

He excused himself. He had to see Max and catch a flight back just before midnight.

"Oh, before I go Loland. Pass this on to Vivian. It is my wedding present."

It was a ring with a set of keys to a new Toyota Yaris. He left Loland open mouthed. first time in years, before she had a chance to utter another word.

Dinner was served and not long after third course, Jean spotted grandfather Raymond slumping in his chair. Sisters raced to take him upstairs to his hotel room. He'd forgotten about heart pills. Marc got an urgent call, and expertly revived the old man. They continued looking for the heart pills and searched the room upside down without finding them. It got left again to Marc to organize a replacement and save another sole.

At the same time on the far side of the hall away from the crowd, Boss and Max had a long conversation. Max was given detailed instruction on his new mission.

In a nut shell, he had to drop into Kishangani as inconspicuously as possible for a white man. Stay away from both Adam and du Plessis brothers. Undetected, yet close enough to render help if needed. With help of an agent assumed to be still loyal to Boss jump a four men team from BS and make them see 'reason'. Not fire a bullet unless in self defence. Avoid casualties and somehow short of miracle return home in one piece.

Of course, if at first all this sounded like a fairy tale Max knew better than to short sell Boss and his insights. There was a lot more to all this. He needed to know details. Boss watched him intently. He'd given this plan a lot of thought. That much soon became clear.

Nonetheless Max stood his ground.

"Are you sure that's all Boss? And another thing. There is no way I'm going in illegally."

"Look Max, if I thought this was mission impossible, what do you think. Would I give it a second thought?"

"Of course not, but I need a lot more to go on by. A lot more."

"You mean details. OK. Let's start with your departure. It's all *leg*. You are one of a party on a guided tour of DRC's National Parks. There have been efforts to revive tourisam of late. Visa will be issued at the Consulate any time, and your return ticket and reservations all inclusive are here in my briefcase. You fly from Nyerer's Airport to Kinshasa at 08.45 hours on Thursday. Use your new Australian Passport. That makes it in four days.

"Then what? Go around the jungle looking for Mr Tarzan, or the stone age man?"

"A healthy dose of scepticisam is good for you. No harm done. Listen! As you exit from the Kinshasa Airport an African dressed in a long sleeved green jacket identical to the one I got here in the brief case will approach you and ask for your name:*Che nome?* You'll answer Jean-Luke. He will swap places with you. Stay put and don't move. His blue Morris 1100 about 1950 vintage with Reg no K171 will pull up driven by his wife , to take you to an address on the periphery. Our man will contact you there with instructions. Stay away from night clubs, hotels and posh eateries. Cover your white face and do your best to look look grimy and unfriendly.Remember to swear in **patois.** Green berets are common.

"And there is one in the brief case I guess?" Boss nodded in acknowledgment."

"Starting to get a little clearer, I admit, but I still cannot see why du Plessis brothers need me. I mean, what they can not do I most certainly can not."

"Wrong. You are wrong and selling yourself short. To do what you did at Vukovar calls for a man with nerves and courage. I know. I followed the war. Those bastards in the White Hall had you Croats crucified. And that for the second time in 50 years. We the Scotts to this day and after centuries of bloodletting havn't forgiven them. I fear it will take just as long for you people."

"Hang on Boss. I was only pitching in to defend my country. Anyone else would have done the same."

"Oh, yes? Sheep don't fight. Even under attack. I fought in WW2. Don't tell me about every-man. A handful of braves saved UK in 1941. Even Churchill owned up. Remember his so few owed so much by so many? Croatia was the same in 1991. It is always the same. The brave get slain. The weak inherit the earth."

"You still havn't told me why?"

"Look here Max. Du Plessis stick out like a sore thumb here. Worse overthere. They make excellent bait though. What we need is surprise. We have to catch these teflon characters literally with their pants down. What helps our cause is the fact they are so cock-a-hoop after dealing with Palestinians. They really believe nothing can touch them."

"OK. So we catch them by surprise. Then what? Start a shooting war?

"No. You certainly don't start a shooting war, and fire only when fired upon. By the way use the silencers at all time. No. Ideally, try to corner and threaten them with delivery to Entebbe. There they would still recognize some culprits. I think, put under pressure these super heroes don't take long to crack. What we want is a written statement from the BA making certain they abrogate any rights to the one and only gold claim in the Itari provice. Claim no IT28/1989. That isn't so outrageous after all. If it wasn't for us they, the BS wouldn't have a clue. It is our work, and our money, and our technology that has found the gold. They haven't spent anything, other than bribe monies. Disarm them and see them off on the next plane of their own choosing. Take their fingerprints and guns. That should be enough. Well short of skullduggery common in the prospecting game without starting serious unpleasantries."

"Phew! And what makes you think they would take all this lying down?"

"You win some, you loose some. Nobody wins them all. If you don't fight you most certainly stand to loose the lot. I think they have other irons in the fire. This Itari region is bad medicine. If Adam had his way, he'd pull out tomorrow. Me? I say, give it one more shot lads, and the best of luck. And something else I have to tell you Max. You are damn lucky. That girl of yours, man."

"I know." Max freely admitted." At my age, for sure."

"At any age. You don't know it yet, but trust me. A woman can make or unmake a man like nothing on Earth."

"Oh I know, of this. I have had my share of torment."

They shook hands and Max wished him a good flight home. It was genuine and Boss exhausted just managed to wave back. The next moment he was gone and Max just stood there for a while gathering his thoughts. Vivian spotted him and came over to investigate the reason for his appearent discomfort.

"I don't know how to tell you this Viv. We have a three day honeymoon.'

"No news to me Max. Loland let on earlier on there was something of that kind going on."

"Just keep it quiet."

They continued partying as if nothing happened, until the last bottle of Granpa's 1982 vintage Frontignac was consumed. It came from Ray's Stellenbosh vinyard archived for the marriage of his favourite grand-doughter Vivian.

The morning after, Max overslept breakfast. He had a splitting headache. Not so much from Frontignac as worrying himself sick about the task ahead. Sure he menaged to get through Serbian positions in one piece, but he was only too aware of his shortcomings. He was no 007. For start, the little school French he spoke didn't go very far. He was heartily sick of war and violence. The whole shebang and theatrics. If he had a desire for anything, it sure wasn't for some fabulous riches, or chest full of medals. He refused to take medals in Bosnia when the Army took it as a sleight. But no matter how he looked at it, refusing to go now would ruin everything. He had to go, and to make the best of it. Vivian reluctantly accepted it. Had he decided to follow her initial wish to stay out of it, she would have thought less of him as a man.

'A man has got to do what a man has got to do.' Axiom as true now as ever.

So he did as instructed. Got the DRC visa stamped into his new Aussie Passport. He practiced French with Vivian. That installed some degree of confidence to his meager vocabulary. She also pointed out the African French major differences. They got Kinshasa's Le Monde latest addition. Vivian red it to him, article by article. It was a crash course as these go. He next thoroughly studied Kinshasa's city map. It was out of date by years. Not that anything of significance had been buildt in the meantime. Enough for Max to get his bearings without being hopelessly lost. He stopped shaving and having regular showers.

Another day passed by in preparations. Next something happened that turned this whole exercise on the head. The ball started rolling in Kinshasa. If anything, du Plessis brothers were a far more formidable combination than Boss gave them credit for. And it wasn't just the heavy weight judo black belt. Their brief was to keep an eye on Adam from a distance and ensure his safety. Instead, they went on the offensive. Du Plessis as they told what happened later on, got a valuable piece of information from a street vendor. For a price of course. They tracked the four men BS team, all full time Policemen as it turned out to a night club 'Petite Cherrie' on Kisangani Rd. A saucy strip show and Papa Wende the living legend performing. The place was choker block full. Standing room only. By the time du Plessis squizzed through, there was even less room to move in the dagga smoke filled hall.

The four were seated in a far corner and soon spotted the tall du Plessis approaching towards them. Their leader, a realy ugly looking brute went for his revolver. Connie, the older of the brothers got to him and yelled at top of the voice over the loud band music.

"Domkop! You pig head! What makes you think you can start shooting in here. Blacks will flay you alive. You f…..ng, stupid pig head."

"How did you know I was a policeman?"

"We know all about you bastards. Now put all your guns on the table. One by one. Nice and slow. The first SOB who tries anything stupid will end up a paraplegic, I promise you."

The element of surprise was complete. Physicaly, those four were easy meat for du Plessis and they knew it. Equally, to start a fireing exchange in a hall full of people, was a murder and suicide.

Stephen, the younger du Plessis frisked them out. One by one and came up with more of very interesting hardware, as he put it. Connie emptied all magazines, and returned the empty guns to the group.

"We don't want your guns. We don't want any bloody-thing from you. All we do want is to see your backsides on the next plane out of here, and take your pick where you want to go...By then the element of surprise had worne off. The ugly one suggested to calm things down, as the surrounding Africans became agitated. Suddenly, all of them whites, seemed threatened in peril facing the Negro mob. The ugly one went for the wallet.

"Let's pay and clear by Moses out of here before there is real trouble, and you two guys, or is there more? Congratulations. Now, can we talk to your leader and get some sense into this. What we have in mind is an offer your company will find hard to refuse. Here is the plan. No guns, no bloody drama, no Wild West. Let us talk business. Here is my card. Anywhere, anytime, bring in all the artillery you want. OK?"

They made off hastily just in time to escape the ugly mob, and drove off at speed in separate direction.

This encounter put a different complex on the matter. For start, Adam had to be contacted. Then of course the Boss. If du Plessis expected a dressing down from Adam for over-stepping the brief, they were in for a pleasant surprise. Adam commended them for taking initative.

"You got the better of those cops. It wasn't just the suprise."

"Now what?" Connie wanted to know.

"Since you insist, now we negotiate. You two demonstrated how to defend one's home turf. Now we play high finance stakes. These people have huge resources. It wouldn't hurt at all to have them on our side."

"You don't mean that Adam? Stephen protested." We nearly came to a shooting match only an hour ago."

"So what?" Adam was unimpressed." Look I've seen judo matches. That is as brutal a confrontation as you can wish for. You'd know all about that. What do you do once the bout is over? Half a cripple you still shake hands. What is so different here?"

"You are talking sport Adam. Rules apply in sport." Steven wouldn't concede.

"Rules apply in business as well. Some people call them The Rafferty Rules. It goes like this. Heads I win, tails you loose."

Exhausted from talking, the brothers suggested a drink. It had been a good session all around. Adam and the Boss can talk all the business they like, du Plessis have softened the opposition and everybody in the rough and tumble of mining game knew now you had to treat Shellberight Mines Ltd with a dose of respect reserved for more formidable outfits. Their next assignment was secure in coming after this mighty effort.

The one problem Adam faced now was to contact Boss on a secure line somehow. He thought of this and that, and no matter what, there was a certainty he could not have a communication with the Boss that was not compromised. So much for the vaunted technology. He had to fly himself to Jo'burg, speak to Boss, then return with new set of instruction. Or better still let Boss negotiate directly over his head with the BS CEO. He had no idea, in two days time Max was scheduled to land here. So much for the need to know regime. Thus he took a direct SAA flight to Jo'burg.

Boss met him on the OT Airport, and first decision he made was to contact Max supposedly still in Dar to stay put. Problem was Max and Vivian took a day tour of Zanzibar without leaving instructions at the hotel. This made Boss uneasy, feeling guilty. He tried and tried again. It was only late in the evening he received a return call from Max apologizing for the slip.

"Apology accepted Max, I want you to stay put. Your mission is off. As soon as there is more, you'll be notified. And keep your mobile on at all times. Oh.., something else just got to me. You sold off those bonus shares?"

"I needed the money then.

"Now after the yacht sale you can afford to buy them back. It may be a very wise move. I cannot tell you any more. Do you want me to buy them back?"

"I see what you a driving at. Buy them back and that many again. Wait I'll give you my bank details."

"No!No you don't. Not over the phone. I'll get those shares for you. Pay me back later."

"Thanks Boss, and what do I tell Vivian?"

"Ask Vivian if *oupa* Ray has any more of that Frontignac. The best *wee* drop I drank for years. And he can name the price. And…of course, give the sweet thing a hug from me."

Messages went backwards and forwards. BS was demanding their claim rights back and the mine field removed. By now Boss was cognisant of the ploy. They were agreeable to a farm in, with Shellberight Mines Ltd as operator on a 50/50 basis. To Boss that told BS would be happy to settle for lot less. One of the reasons was the dismissive report of their scouts in Kinshasa. They bribed so many it was embarrassing, only to concede it was money wasted. Security according to their report was not realistically achievable without an army. The opposition according to them also held most of the bargaining points. Actualy, all but one. The size. Compared to BS the Jo'burg explorers were a minnow. If it was attractive enough, BS would swallow this company in a takeover, friendly or hostile, no trouble at all, or so it was mistakenly thought at the time. To this effect their brokers in Jo'burg were busy looking into the shareholder spread. What they found soon started a buzz. Boss held about 28% of the stock. Friendly associates perhaps another 14%. That made a takeover a very interesting proposition. Within hours, and long before any announcement was made, there was a run on the shares at JSX.

Boss got wind of this soon enough. A cunning fox that he was, he asked for a temporary trading suspension. Due to an important announcement pending. All within days and rules. JSX had no reason to refuse. Max bought in just on time. Boss made sure of it. Twarted in their endevours once more, the CEO of the BS lost his temper.

"Never have I been so comprehensively shafted and copped so much crap from a bunch of no-bodies. We spend more on a monthly staff bonus and advertising than their market capitalization. How can that be right?"

He sent a telex to Boss offering 130% up on the closing price already at record highs. Boss politely refused. Then even more diplomaticaly, exolIted the prowess of BS and their profitability, only to offer a joint venture proposition on his terms. He had done the due dilligence, as the events unfolding soon proved.

First, the new lease to be jointly owned , with all future profits to be split 50/50. Second, work to be carried out by Shellberight Mines Ltd, and the capex in development to be met by BS, whose presence on the field would be esured at all times. Boss concluded: 'In view of your powerful financial position and banking connections we are of the opinion this fair proposal would deliver immense benefit to both companies.'

As for a hostile takeover possibility, BS would Boss was certain find more in the way of resistance…..Signed, Yours sincerily, Ian McLarty, CEO, Shellberight Mines Ltd.

This cought the BS by surprise. All the more so since the take-over target share options spent the last year under water without a single buyer for months on end..

"The old fox is playing hard to get." BS's CEO commented.

"Maybe not." His mining engineer was inclined to accept the offer.

"We have to be realistic. I think BS is doing well out of this. We haven't spent any time nor money on this. They have. For their size lots of it. I say we accept the offer. Before anyone else gets in on the scent.and we end up with nothing"

Mining engineer's advice on the past couldn't be faulted. The acceptance fax hit Boss's IN try in the night. It was all done at lightning speed , allowing no third party as much as a sniff.

At last Boss did have something to report. Substantial gold discovery, combined with joint venture with likes of BS. A jackpot! What more can one ask for, please tell me!

Final outcome ment Boss was winning. He could not necessarily retire, but set his mind on other things closer to his heart. Vivian and Max were to be offered positions others would grub with both hands. Let them have the honeymoon undisturbed first. His scheme could wait their return. Boss, finaly accepted, it was also most probable Adam was right, and that gold prospect will remain too dangerous for anyone to fully explore, much less profitably mine in his life time. All that was for his future successor to worry about. His time was nearly over.

As for Max, the shares he bought and hadn't payed for yet , looked as if all he had to do was sell back one eighth of what he bought. The rest was for free. And then a bundle of options he was strugling to find a buyer for before the announcement.

Now as to reveal the true bastardry of our human nature, Max wished he hadn't sold Kai Vai to the Elliots. He took on his own a taxi to the Sailing Club looking for the surgeon couple. Only Buzza was still there busy antifouling, yet again. Sue was on a sick list, starting to run a fiever. Buzza was hoping it was nothing worse than an attack by a *gastro*, but he wasn't at all sure. Wait for a day before we jump to conclusion.

That took the wind out of Max' sails for a while before he recovered.

"Would they reverse the contract?"

"Why?" He told them.

"No, no.." The answer bounced back. He was a *bonzer bloke*, but no. *Ta*.

"Thanks for the offer…Oh, wait, he and Viv were more than welcome to join on a leg or two sailing to Aussie. With the Captain off colour even more so."

That adage put things in perspective. Max was mildly surprised that during the pre-sale survey she was the one asking all the smart questions. He answered non committed.

"Mate! I'll have to have a *chin wag* with *me missus* first. Now I'd better go and see her." They were launching late in the afternoon.

"Max, please, let us know before, so I can organize *tucker* supply. That, or meet us in Zanzibar in a couple of days. See *yu*!"

Max wasn't so sure about the Kai Vai when he returned to the hotel to find Vivian on the phone. Soon he got so unsettled he wasn't sure about much else.

"Where have you been?!"

The Monsoon Drifter

She fired at him the eternal question men have been asked since the beginning of time.

"This phone drives me insane."

"What do you expect? No wedding congratulations?"

"That and heaps more. Look, just for start. Your mobile Nokkia is off again."

"No, it was on." He insisted, only to find the battery was flat.

"Boss will strangle you. As for Adam, I'd better keep quiet. He stays behind to run the company, while we are having a ball. Then that surgeon couple. He rang up just before you came in. Wants to talk to you. By the way, where have you been, I had no idea you left in the first place? Max, tell me what is going on?"

"All right, perhaps I should have told you this. Promise you'll keep it to yourself?"

"Goes without saying, Max."

"We in the circle have no secrets. Isn't that your own words, Vivian?"

"Max, circle is different. No comparison, though it is true we confine in each other."

"And you are dead certain that's where it all stays. None has got a loose lip?"

"I don't see what you a driving at. I can see we are having our first marital quarrel. On the second day of the marriage. Isn't the bliss supposed to last a little longer? Tell me, you have been married before."

That last remark did most damage. It was time to hit back, Max decided.

"I will tell you something else, more important instead. No, I havn't been out with a wench, nor to a gambling den, nor to get a fix. And I didn't tell you before I left, because I didn't want to wake you up. As for the rest. It was all going to be explained in good time without your hussles."

His tone became decidedly less friendly. For a good measure he added.

"Married I may well be, but remember Vivian for the good of both of us, don't drive me where I don't want to go. I promise to respect your freedom. In return you'll have to get used to me having a room to move."

She realized once more the old truth. It was easier to say it than to have it unsaid. Still spoiling for a fight, she put the foot in once more.

"It is all your fault anyway."

"And just how did you arrive at this conclusion?"

"You knew before you married me I had a big mouth. It didn't stop you then, now you deserve to suffer." There was a mischievous tone to this that didn't escape Max.

"Are you serious? So we're still on the war path.?"

"No of course not. I surrender unconditionally. My big warrier hero husband."

"All right." He tried again, "I don't know what the game is and less the rules. Let us talk some sense for a change, OK?"

"Go ahead, I realy would like to know."

"I will have to urgently contact Boss and Adam. It is almost certain, there is no need for me to barge into the Congo and upset the natives. Then, my dear wife, we have struck the jackpot. What from the yacht sales and double that from share sales profit. Your flat mortgage is in dire peril. To top it all, we may be lucky third time around, but this will have to wait."

"And all this was happening while I was asleep? Followed by another salvo."

"Noughty girl, I have the hide to make you a scene. There ought to be a fitting punishment for this."

"If so, you are hence on first offenders list and six month parole. Now enough nonsense for one day. Let me explain." When he took a breather, she refused to believe it was possible to make so much money in such a short time.

"It happens all the time. The stock market is the biggest gambling casino of them all. Win a millions on a punt, and more in one day, and loose it just as fast if not faster."

"So what are you saying Max?"

"Don't worry, I know I am simply a mug. I got lucky thanks to Boss. If I kept on speculating I am certain to get skinned. No my girl, we quit while ahead, and pay off your mortgage."

"There is only six months installments left on it to pay Max."

"You didn't tell me that."

"Well, I didn't want you to marry me for my riches. My handsome knight."

"I give up. You are too fast for me." Max finaly admitted defeat. " You win."

"No my dear husband. We both win this time. It calls for a celebration."

Then the phone rang again. Boss was on the line.

"I am trying not to sound angry Viv, I must have tried a dozen times to reach him."

"Wait , here Boss is the culprit himself."

"Blasted battery ran empty on me Boss. I am angry with myself you have no idea."

That was enough of **mia culpa** penance for Boss, so he got onto what he knew best.

"I can tell you Max those options of yours are worth a lot of money. If it was me, I'd sell them. We are trading again at JSX. At the moment it is all bubling along nicely. Tomorrow may be a different story. It often is. So what do you say?"

"Boss, I am just smart enough to know how hopeless I realy am when it comes to finance. Maths and high finance are different worlds. I can handle the first. As for the latter, if it wasn't for you I'd be a pauper. I owe you a big one Boss. One day I wish to be in position to do something for you for a change."

"Well". Boss chucked at the remark." One never can tell. Maybe the day will come." It was a hint if there ever was one, but hint of what? Max had no idea just then. Boss wished them a happy honeymoon and hung up.

"The next call, waiting on the line for some time came from Adam.

"Max, it is good to hear your voice again. Man, am I relieved to be out of that dump. You have no idea. Consider yourself very lucky you didn't have to go. I have so much to tell you. Those du Plessis brothers! Man, they cleaned up big time. As for me? Yeah man, Boss is retireing. I supose you know by now."

"Know! I just spoke to him minutes ago. Not a word of it."

"Don't forget he is past eighty, getting on and I fear for his health."

"Still as sharp as a blade. I wonder what he was like in his younger years."

"If you stay around these parts, people will tell you stories about Ian McLarty. Now, here is the latest piece of news. Boss has offered me to take over from him. One mining engineer stepping into the boots of another. Of course the Board has to approve."

"A mere formality."

"Not always, but then again I get on with most of them. What helps my cause is the fact one cannot get a mining engineer here for the love of money."

"What about the Africans. The BEE? graduates?"

"I have yet to meet an African mining engineer outside of Kitwe in Zambia. No man, they go for finance and military academy. Ask a bright African kid what he'd like to be, then see what answers you get. They all strive to become generals. Or if it has to be a finance guru. I have yet to see one who'd settle to be a shipwright or a plumber.

The sad results of this fallacy you can best see in the Congo or the wretched Zimbabwe. Anyway, enough politics. I hate it. How are you two getting on? With Vivian one has to slug it out at times. Otherwise she'd roll you like a Mac semi."

"You speak as if you knew and had skin missing."

"Look Max. It is like a boxing match. You cop a few, shake it off and then start another round. Same with Vivian. She wins one argument, fine, you make sure to win the next one."

"I can follow your tactics. It makes for an interesting duel."

"Now you're talking. Never a dull minute….So much for now. Greetings to Vivian. Wish you both a happy honeymoon. Forget the hussles man…Bye!"

Next call waiting on the line came from Frans. The warmest of greetings from him. He mentioned in passing there was some news, but it could wait. He didn't sound all too cheery, and Vivian asked him if he could handle the teaching lode she left him for a few more days. He wished them a happy and long married life, and then hung up. To Vivian it didn't sound right. She'd known Frans for over a decade, since she first joined the staff. Now she started a guessing game. What could it be? Going back over some bits of conversation that didn't appear important at the time.

There was this particular Teachers Union meeting when a fresh BEE Zulu graduate got up and gave an anti-whites tirade, spoken in *tsiZulu.*

Vivian got most of it, her nanny came from *kwaZulu*, and thought her the fundamentals. What he was driving at more or less was for a complete replacement of the whites in public institution. There were some dissenting voices, but the overall sentiment was for a change. It hit her now, and hard. She enjoyed the teaching and put all of her energies into it. Was her job on the line? She asked Max what he thought.

"Why? Of course. The pendulum has swung the other way. Just the way things are. Just the way we humans are. He remembered parts of a poem, he could now recite, with likely errors. It was a work of a certain Hopmann or Hoffman, he was guessing, it was so long ago, but the verse he could still remember went something like this

> for all the toil there be
> it cannot erase the primal fault
> for it rains and still the sea is salt.

We are a selfish breed. Everything on and about us is designed for our comfort and pleasure. All we seem to want is more, more, more. More of everything. The rich don't give a hang about starving children.

I remember one lunch I was having at an Italian resort at a place called Bentota in Sri Lanka. There was a barbed wire fence all around the resort, and armed guards patrols. As I ate my lunch I saw this girl about six years of age watching intently and saliving with every bite of food I ate. Every now and then the guard would chase her away. Finaly, I couldn't take it any longer. I took my plate with half a loaf of bread and passed it through the fence the best I could. What I saw next I'll never forget. A group of boys, about the same age emerged from nowhere and threw themselves at the girl and the food. Next the manager walked up to me and warned me not to do it again. I took off the next day, but it is not that Sri Lanka is any worse than most of Africa or India, or Bangla Desh. It is in the beast. No amount of preaching or moralizing will change that. Sure, there are some people willing to go hungry so others have a meal. There are exceptions, but taken as a breed, we are just no damn good. Of course you can object to those wretchedly poor breeding like rabbits.

"Thanks for lifting my spirits Max. Just what I needed."

"So let us think ahead. Things are in a flux, as I see it. You may loose your job, and me, I don't know if I still have one. But are we destitute or hungry, or threatened with violence. No no and no. So why despair and go into a depression. Cheer up girl, and give me a hug. Now, that's more like it, squizze harder..harder..!"

A few more calls later and ***oupa*** Ray was on the line. He'd found the heart pills. Oh yes. They were in the side of his hat all along. Enough for twice a daily dose. He just fargot. As having any more of that Frontignac in the celler? For a very special person like Boss only and free. And a big kiss on the lips to my darling .

Just when things got quieter towards dinner time another call, this time from Bazza. Sue was diagnosed with malaria. Their yacht adventure was off and full significance of this was to become clear soon.

The next morning, Marc, Jean and Loland ready to check out, dropped in to see the newly wed. Weren't they going to join? No need to call for two taxies.

Max was of the opinion, he and Viv would stay for another day or two, now Vivian's teaching position was lost, it didn't matter. And they would like a bit more time around Zanzibar. Bothas and Loland called in a taxi for the Airport. Now Vivian got agitated.

"What was that about some unfinished business you mentioned?"

"Let me come to the point. Bazza told me only an hour ago. Sue was confirmed down with with malaria. How that came to be he couldn't explain. They took Chloquine two weeks before. Never missed a dose and still. With Sue down, it was just as likely he was the next victim. That killed off all of their plans. You see."

"What about the yacht and the voyage to Australia?"

"I was coming to this. Sue is booked first class on the next plane to Sydney and Townsville. They have the best Tropical Deseases Clinique in Australia."

"What about Bazza? Isn't he flying with her?"

"Yes of course. That leaves yacht Kai Vai still on the hard stand. They decided wisely not to launch and we have unfinished business to deal with. We have to make a decision. The offer is to have Kai Vai delivered to the WA Perth or Carnarvon where their parents live. We can take our time and all expenses paid. I can name my price for delivery. These are wealthy people. So what do you say Vivian? Here is your chance to learn sailing and mine to rid myself of the nightmares."

"Now I see what you have been up to. Still, I suppose, we're financially no worse off and a free vacation on a beautiful yacht with a resourceful handsome husband. I'd be a hopeless fool to refuse. None is so stupid. No, you don't have to twist my arm, the answer is go for it."

"So I can tell Buzza you agree?"

"Sure, just one more thing. I have to get back to Jo'burg to pick up my car, pay bills and see Frans. You can stay here, I'll see you back within days, OK. Do you trust me to let me out of sight?"

"Shouldn't I? You are a tease Viv, did you know?"

Vivian hurriedly contacted Marc and asked him to hold the taxi. She was to join on the flight. For once the plane was only half full. No problem with late booking. This left Max alone for the first time in days.

* * *

Vivian returned to her flat from the airport to see a pile of bills and dust that somehow got in through the closed aircon duct. She called a taxi and took delivery of the Toyota Yaris automatic. A lovely city car and easy to park. It remained to decide what to do with the old Ford Fiesta cluttering parking space. She tought of giving it away, but could not think off hand of a person to give it to. It occured to her, poor Mawindy may do with it. Frans knew his mobile phone number, so she went ahead and asked Mawindy to drop in for dinner. She had a surprise for him.

He arrived punctualy. Just on seven o'clock, with a bunch of gardenias.

"Mawindy!" She exclaimed. This was a different creature altogether. He'd filled in. Wore clothes and shoes, only the best of the latest and as he approached closer, she took in a deep breath of that scent that made her nostrils flair up. It wasn't just the gardenia blossoms. There was all that musky scent of androsterone Mawindy seemed to exude. It was sending her dizzy.

She offered him a seat at the dinner table. He noticed right away it was dished out for two, so he thanked her, and lied, he'd eaten before he came in. No need to stay around and the **Baas** Max might not like it. She understood.

"No, you got it all wrong. **Baas** Max was still in Dar es Salaam."

The next moment she bit herself on the tongue, but it was too late. She poured him a Lion Lager and they silenty ate through the dinner. She offered him her Ford Fiesta. Unaware he just bought a new BMW coupe. He thanked her politely, and offered to paint her portrait for free.

Mawindy was big time almost overnight. Highly in demand. A toast of the town. His attelier a beehive of activity. She accepted, yes, if it was going to be a portrait. It sounded harmless enough.

He got down to work. Charcoal on matte cardboard. Suddenly he paused. If she could take off that turtle neck pullover hiding her neck lines. No harm done, she did as asked and turned the air conditioner up higher. Autumn evenings around Jo'burg can be quite cold. As she was wrestling with the tight pullover fit, her blouse top buttons got undone. As always she wore no brassiere. Mawindy's eyes went into a telephoto focus. Her natural pheramons not subdued by the birth control pill did the rest.

Scratch a fit African and he'll admit to phantisies about having it off with a white woman. Of course it works to some extent the other way as well.

In the multivariable calculus of life, what with older woman younger man;black on white;taste of forbidden fruit;that overpowering androsterone aphrodisiac; one or the other, or all of it together, we'll never know. Vivian felt aroused now comfortably resting reclined in a deep leather resting chair.

It didn't go unnoticed. Mawindy put his work pad on the table and approached Vivian side on. Next his left hand went for her breast cleavage. To Africans not the most erogenous zone. The whitness of that skin and the natural perfumes did it for the young **umZulu** stud. She was getting goose pimples. His other hand went exploring. She was past the need for forplay. He took her hard, still fully dressed. Later they withrew into the bed. It was a raw and powerful demonstration of what damage an eighteen year old can inflict.

The next morning with him departing quietly while she was asleep , Vivian could still feel where he'd been, and he'd been to places none had been before. She felt all mushed up, in a state of mental convulsion and turmoil.

The Ford Fiesta was still parked out on in the courtyard. By now poor Mawindy drove aboard his *Beemer* coupe with a payed driving lesson instructor. Her portrait Mawindy must have completed in the night. It was her, and all her down to depths of the soul. A masterpiece.

He signed it **Sala Kale**, farewell , Mawindy Lungule Nzuke. On a small sheet of paper he wrote **ukubonga**, thank you for all you two have done for me. I hope one day I can return some of your goodness. Words of gratitude and friendliness. That much Vivian knew from her childhood days nannie.

Now she was close to suicidal. She knew life with Max could never be the same again. She'd betrayed his trust and there was no way back. To make it worse, she just could not bring herself to confine in the sisterhood. One slip and you are out. Didn't Loland mention that. In desperation she left for the shopping centre hoping in vain to find some solace amongst the crowd.

* * *

Max met Bazza to organize the yacht delivery contract, and have it legally binding. That took longer than expected, allowing no time for a yacht trial. What put Bazza's mind at rest was the

Yacht Masters Off Shore Certificate Max had to his name. That had to be good you don't get much better.

On the financial side, Bazza agreed to pay a half in advance. The rest upon delivery. All verifiable expenses to be refunded in A$. The authority to navigate the yacht was signed and stamped by the Law firm. Max took possession of the keys, the yacht documents, and that was it.

Provisions, fuel and water had to wait until Vivian returned.

Another day went by, Max was by now the only one of the crowd still in Dar, and still no news from Vivian. He made sure the mobile was on at all times and fully charged. So that wasn't it. He rang up once every few hours and still no contact. He attributed this to her getting around on business. So many chores to do. It was no different for him. He was spending the best part of the day on Kai Vai. An ocean going skipper has to know every fitting of the boat and be able to find it blind folded. Another day passed, and still no news from Vivian. By now Max thought this odd, so he got in touch with Loland. She also expressed surprise. No, Viv hadn't been around, but she promised to investigate. Finaly watching the evening news the phone rang. It was Vivian.

"I apologise Max, I haven't been well."

"You are worrying yourself over that job again. Blow it. It is their loss more than yours. So anything else to report."

"Oh yes, that little Toyota. A real treat to drive. Automatic as well."

"I am happy for you. Myself, I like a bit more grunt in my wagon. So when do you think you'll be back. I've been here now for too long. And I miss you."

"Same here Max, I booked with SAA for late Tuesday night. Pick me up Wednesday morning and we can sail away. That is in two days time."

"You mean to say, without having a rest first?"

"If that is what you want."

"I thought you didn't feel too well. Now we are into endurance test."

"I leave it up to you to decide. I am feeling off. If you don't mind…"

"OK dear, have a good night. I love you!"

Once she hung up Max immediately felt uneasy. Something somewhere was amiss, but he couldn't put the finger on it.

Next morning he checked out. Antifouled once more fresh and launched the yacht in the afternoon. He planned to comprehensively test all systems before departure.

Sails, engine, nav lights, spreader and cabin lights and the search beam. The anchor chain power winch, the Flemming self steerer, radios, battery voltage, radar, air and fuel filters, propeller shaft gland lubrication adjustment, the bildge pumps and the life raft. It was all there and functional. The check list was fully ticked off, except for the crew.

Wednesday morning he filled with water, diesoline, and ordered supplies from a Port merchant to be delivered chop chop, hence picked the crew from the airport. She looked pale and Max was regretting the fact he'd checked out of the hotel. He suggested they go back, but she insisted to stay on board. It was hot and humid and water temperature at 29 degrees C was no help. There was of course no air conditioner on the yacht. That 12V fan was the only relief. Max knew how tough it was on a mooring so he hoisted the P pennant and put a request over the VHF Port channel for a clearance. He got to know the Port Captain personally. Within half an hour Kai Vai was cleared to depart.

They motored out into the the Zanzibar Channel and soon picked up the SE on shore breeze. Max set the sails up and rigged the Flemming self stirrer once out of the ferry traffic lanes. With this completed, he had free hands.

"The world is our oyster." He spoke to Vivian seated on the weather side of the cabin top.

"Just watch out for the boom." He warned her.

"So where are we headed for?" She asked.

"There are two ways open to us. One is we take a rough passage down the Mozambique Channel. Down the Agulhas Current and into the Roaring Forties. There in splendid isolation, with exception of a single speck of rock and no other land for the breath of the Indian Ocean, you freeze for most of the way and get thrown about night and day non stop. Mind you it is quick. Six weeks on the average ought to do it.

"Quick at six weeks? I don't think I like No 1. What is No2?"

"All together different dear. A lot of motoring to do. Some flukey wind shifts and doldrums . A lot slower, but much more to see and a lot more fun. It could mind you, take six long months, or even longer. Most of No2 takes place in the Equatorial tropics. Seychelles, Maldives maybe, Sri Lanka, a probability."

"I'm all for No2." She said." But you are the Captain. You decide."

"I tell you what. Here is our course. We give Zanzibar a day stay. Continue up northwards. Clear the Zanzibar Channel and set course for the Amirante Group in the Seychelles. That's where Sounion got sunk. What do you say Vivian? Oh yes, we pay a visit to that Belgian panick merchant Rene. I bet he'll flip out."

Slowly, Vivian began to regain the self confidence she'd lost there with Mawindy. The enthusiasam Max was showing was beginning to rub off on her. She decided to try her hardest to be of use, and not remain a self-pitying heap of misery. Fresh SE breeze was helping the mood. Kai Vai charging ahead at hull speed with a double bow wave left in the wake did the rest to cheer up our crew. That was cruising delights for you.

It took Vivian a little while to adjust to the regular movement of the yacht, but she soon gained the sea legs. Half way across the channel she retired into the cabin and stretched out leasurely on the starboard bunk. There she spotted Captain's Log within reach. She opened the Log. A brand new one, entering all the pertinent details about the yacht Kai Vai. Exact times and dates, next port of call and lastly, under crew heading her full name and in brackets'under probation'.

"I beg your pardon Captain, what was this under probation bit?" She called out loudly. Max in the cockpit could hear it clearly.

"Probation is dead right Vivian. We are all under probation. At one time or another. I had no idea, how you'd take it with no previous experience."

"So what would you have done assuming I made a hopeless crew? Toss me into the water? Feed me to the sharks, or sell me into slavery?"

"I'm not sure you'd fetch a top price. Arabs I met told me they like their women more rounded off."

"Some comfort you are. No I am serious, tell me." She insisted.

"OK. Two can play a game. Let's assume you are one of the majority who either get sea sick and cannot hack it. I would have kept in touch and met you in Mahe' or Reunion, or wherever. After all, it takes hours to fly what takes me weeks to sail over. So what's the problem?"

"You'd sail this yacht all by yourself?"

"I've done it before. It is very stressful, I'll admit, but if I could not do it I would never set out."

"So you don't need me."

"What's got to you? So belligerent since you've come back?"

Max was by now in two minds. To just ignore her sudden burst of foul mood or to try and get to the bottom of it. Anything for peace. He chose the former.

"All right crew, how about a hot drink, or something to eat. Come, I'll show you how to start that kerosene oven. Pump up a couple of times, then a spoon full of metho to prime, light a match and away you go." She did as instructed before starting another row.

"This thing stinks Captain."

"It does indeed, until it heats up. Now watch the gymbal, and never more than half fill anything."

"Yes, Captain."

"Good I'm pleased you've got that one right. Did you know by Maritime Law, your life is in my hands?"

"That means I have to be a good girl."

"Less argumentative, more prepared to share duties and take orders. At least while we are at sea. Yes, absolutely. Our lives may be at risk if we do not function as a unit. Most tragedies at sea happen because some smart arse didn't agree with the Captain. The sea is unforgiving. It always finds the weakest link. Anyway, how is that coffee coming along?" "Just about there Skip. Sugars, milk?"

"Neither, just not too strong. When you are through, just turn the kero off."

Mid-afternoon saw them dropping anchor off the old city and fair distance away from the dhows harbour.

" I know we don't have to call for Customs. Zanzibar is a part of the Tanzanian Federation. Although I have heard of yachsmen being hussled. More to do with pocketing bakshish, I think."

"Next order Captain?"

"Come on deck and watch how to stow the mainsail, then cook us a nice meal. Provisions are all marked. We'll have a rest later. I'll show you where the Sounion and Aisha's kidnapping drama began. I think, we are anchored almost on the same spot.

"I suppose it brings those memories back?" She tested Max.

"Not yet. The same place but different everything else. It was after dark in the wet season, a rain squoll, an Arab woman climbing on board uninvited. Look , the sun is blinding still. It is dry season and I have my good wife on board. Wait until it gets dark here, and it does it one, two tree, daylight gone."

"Tell me what made you leave. First SA, then, your own homeland for the second time, then Australia? You are a bit of a Gipsy, aren't you?"

"You have a point. There are those who stay on like immovable statues. No matter what. True to the bitter end. I'd put those whites still in Zimbabwe into that group. Is that good or bad, smart or foolish? I don't want to be anyone's judge. Even if appointed to do it, I'd refuse. We humans are all flowed characters. That is our weakness and our strength. Me? I follow the part where I hope I can do most good. Move out of harm's way to stay alive and fight a better fight, and fight to win, because that is really all that matters. Hystory pages have been written by the victors. The ones who lost fought dirty and caused the wars. Bloody history books. It is a con."

Then she fired back.

"Talking of con. Correct me if I am wrong. So you joined the Croatian war effort before ending up in Bosnia. Sick to the gills of war, you looked for a peaceful oasis and found Australia on the map?

Is that it?

You saved up and bought a tired old yacht to go around the world hoping to regain your sanity. Tested to the breaking point after the horrors of never-ending Balkan butchery.

Is that it?

Along the way you courageously saved an Arab libertine from here own folly. And now we're here aboard another yacht heading, guess where? In reverse direction. Back to Australia.

And I am here because I married the war hero who refused to be decorated, got locked up instead and saved by a miracle. Tell me, does that make me a hero or a fool?" Here was the Vivian of old devastating in a frontal attack. Max took it all on the chin

"Just as well you finished. I noticed ever since you have been back you'd changed. Man, I have never slaped a woman in my life. You'd be the first. Just please, cut it out."

He looked at her close up and noticed her unsteadily holding a half empty bottle of chardonney. She was drunk.

He finished the meal himself and let her be. She dozed off on the starboard bunk and fell asleep within minutes. Now Max knew he was in no-man's land. The woman he put so much trust into was getting drunk in order to get over something unpleasant. Him? What and who else? He decided to wait and thresh it out with her. He still loved Vivian and to lose her would have been a cruel blow. But he would not stand in the way if she decided to go. Loss of the job would have been a blow, but other people lost jobs before and didn't fall to pieces. Finaly, why was the only bitterness there aimed at him. Why? What did he have with loss of her teaching post? All this had to wait. He finished the meal alone, took his binoculars and climbed into the cockpit after hearing voices. Just in time to see two Arabs almost ready to climb aboard.

"Imshie!", he shouted at them, then grabbed hold of a gun from the cockpit locker. They got the message and departed in haste. That was just a forewarning, he feared. Max winched up the anchor, and left the anchorage for the channel, heading true North. Soon he had all the sail up and before dark got close to round off the Zanzibar Channel. He set a course NE for the Amirantes Group. She woke up in the middle of the night, asking for a cup of coffee and a headache pill.

"Did I muck things up?" She tried." And where are we, wait…this thing is moving, I can here it."

"All right dear", he tried gently, "tell me what is bugging you. Maybe we can try to do something about it. Be honest and let me know. Whatever has been bugging you I need to know. Whatever it is tell me please."

Now she got angry as a hornet, and went once more on the offensive. This time cold sober.

"You of all people should be saying this. How many times have I asked you to tell me about your problems. And the answers I get. Anything except the truth. I have to re-construct it from bits and pieces. Like a mosaic. You should be talking!"

That realy hit home, hurt and put him on the defensive..

"Look, I can see your point."

He tried reconciliation, sweet reason. Anything for peace.

"Let's patch up. Have a coffee with me. Give me your story and a hug. I love you Vivian. You ought to know all I want is to protect you."

That last sentence hit her like a body blow below the belt. She loved him just as much but there was no way she was going to confess to adultory. There are things and secrets one carries to the grave. Or so she thought…So she wisely decided to get on with the drinks.

Arising from the emotionaly charged confrontation, both of them, and for the first time felt a self-defence driven call to examine the state of the relationship. A stress test if you like.

She was hurt with his unwillingness to devulge much of his past.

For Christ's sake, what was it he was determined to hyde from her? Another wife hidden somewhere? Well..., who knows men? He wouldn't be the first by a long shot. A serious desease, genetic defect, vagrancy charges? War crimes? Who knows?

She did play up and put up a tantrum. That much is a fact, but did it come from nowhere?

In future, she decided to use her brains. More tact and less force. One way or another though, she'd get to the bottom of it.

As for Max. Late into the night he was still into the soul searching looking for answers. For him the speed of this relationship was threatening to overwhelm. It felt like being placed from an emotional ice bath stright into a steam cooker. And he was failing to cope. Pre-occupied so much he cought himself missing out on regular watch duties. This was bordering on negligence and could not be allowed to continue.

The next radar scan was due. Out in the open ocean with no land for hundreds of miles one could still not afford to relax. Even so, at their speed anything afloat would be picked up in a periodical radar scan soon enough. So he decided to turn the 12 miles Furuno on once every quarter hour. After a few scans with nothing to show have it turned off to save power. Not that he was short of it. Two 60 W solar power cells mounted on the stern post and connected to twin 120 Amp hours marine cycle batteries gave enough to run the lights, radar and an Engel 40 L fridge. A veritable luxury when compared to the previous yacht. Now a cold beer became a routine. And so it was with the rest of the gear. The Flemming self stirrer and the arrangement where all sheets and halyards led to cockpit ment a little child could run this yact. Far cry from the Sounion. Max, the sailor, felt spoiled, and felt a high that comes sailing at hull speed for hours.

The latest scan showed nothing, so he turned the Furuno radar off and returned to face his immediate problem. Back to emotional torture. He was beginning to realise, they couldn't go on fighting. He had to relent. There was no choice.

"All right." He conceded." Here is my story. We'll wind the clock back to May 1998.

She was ready to start taking dictation on the Dictaphone. Later in the night she'd edit, correct poor spelling of foreign names and words and transform the subject to a third pronoun as the shrink suggested. It took two more days and nights on and off before the Sounion's Log Book could be re-lived.

Life would never be the same again for either of them.

* * *

CHAPTER TEN

THE MONSOON DRIFTER

Yacht Sounion, 23.May, 1998. Zanzibar Harbour.
Since departure ex Chagos Archipelago, I noticed 2HP Mercury outboard missing.
Suspect: those kids milling around waving good by knicked it before departure.
Wind:NW to W 5 Kn max. Piss weak. Air pressure 1002 and falling. Low cumulus clouds promising another drenching. Dropped pick here @14.35 hrs. No sign of Customs. Mental state:RS. Physical state:*clapped out*. Starving and dying for a *tinnie*.

Vendors came along. Tanked 200 L diesolene and filled up with smelly water. Added 2 chlorine pills for a good measure. Groceries very expensive, bargain all you like. Some foreigners who refuse to bargain are too easy going. Those blasted cruise ships spoil it for us yachties'…

Vivian had the short hand slang expertly translated into Oxford English and the pronouns transformed.

Over its rich history Zanzibar has been in the thick of it. Just name it. Fought over by colonial powers;used by Arab traders for a slave market; scene of a savage anti-Arab rebellion; shaky union with Tanzania, and a peaceful period at last followed by a tourist invasion. The island is also famous for its spices. One can pick the scent of drying clove and vanilla pods wafting on the trade winds from miles away. Not to mention crafty silversmiths of the past and their fine filigranee. Of late, since the political turmoil settled down, growing hordes of Western tourist have been richly rewarded by its tropical splendour and the exotic setting. The island is blessed with miles of tranquil coral beaches and fringing coral reefs with a magnicicent green canopy of swaying palm trees in the background. Its people are a unique interracial breed.

But it wasn't any of the exotic attributes that drew Max Horvat a lone yachtsman to its shores. Not on this occasion anyway. A friendly piece of *terra firma* anywhere else would have been greated just as warmly. For him it was a sequence of things that went wrong. One blow followed by another. And little did he know it was only the beginning. It was mid-May by now, and he'd missed the reliable southeast trade winds. What wind there was, came unpredictable and accompanied by rain squalls. The only good that came his way were the hawkers. They supplied fresh food and diesoline. All at hefty premium. Until the next downpour saw them off looking for cover.

Max came to accept the theory of averages. If there is such a thing as a quota of good fortune deposited on the account of your average mortal up there with some mystique arbiter in command of decisions, as many do believe, upon who is to live and who to die, where, when and how, Max' account would have been overdrawn.

None can be forever lucky. Equaly, not forever bad luck. Things had to even out somewhere. If factual, having survived a typhoon, for him the pay back time had arived. For a start he found a vigilant watch was mandatory at all times. All the more so, after he noticed some commotion at the dhow harbour, which made it sensible to anchor further off shore.

The old faithful, 25 pounder CQR anchor dug into sandy bottom and Max felt releaved. Finaly, one could unwind, relax, then get a meal going.

It wasn't to be. He no sooner began to unwind and enjoy the long overdue rest when it all started to unravel. And fast, as the darkness fell.

Another rain squall moved in. Before long the noise of the wind whisling in the rigging, soon to be joined by loud polter of the tropical rain downpour destroyed all sense of tranquility.

And that wasn't all. In amongst that audio overload there was also a distinct sound of intermittent and loud tapping. No, this wasn't just a piece of driftwood banging on. And it was coming from the lee side. A few taps at a time. Then again. He traced it to the aft section.

All this spelled trouble. There was someone out there, uninvited and definitely unwanted. His senses went to red alert. Uninvited guests around these parts spelled big trouble these days. Still naked he raced through the cabin to reach the cockpit with a machette firmly in his right hand.

It was considerably colder on deck. Streams of rain lashing his body further increased the keen sense of a warrior ready to face the intruder. Two light beams from spreader lights threw about more moving shadows than useful light. He frantically began the search. How many were there he had to know first. He could see nobody on the deck and he'd just, passed through the cockpit. This placed the intruder on the outside. Then the sound of tapping came on again and with more urgency.

Sure enough, there was a body struggling in the chopped up water. Where and how it got here he had no idea. His yacht Sounion was anchored in four fathoms of water, half a mile away from the shore with a Q flag hoisted calling for port clearance. No other craft could be seen in the vicinity.

On the Equator the night darkness descends quickly, and the day light faded out fast. All that was before the rain. Now Customs would not come till next mornig.

He'd repeatedly tried on VHF port channel first then Channel 16 to alert the Customs about his arrival, until a voice rudely snapped at him, telling him to get off the air.

Following the direction of the tapping, then leaning over the lifelines, he sighted a head bobbing up in the chop, and a fist knocking on the hull. The head turned facing Max. At first he wasn't sure. As he called out and the head moved in closer, he recognized the female features.

"Are you alone?" That above all else was what needed to be ascertained.

"Yes, help me please!"

She called out, with all the voice power she could muster.

A quick search of the boat confirmed she was alone. That led to a hasty replacement of the machette with a boarding ladder stowed in the cockpit locker, and positioning of the boarding ladder abeam. Leaning over the gunwales he reached out in the direction of the woman. An iron grip reached for his hand. Their eyes met for the first time. Conveyed in the first contact was a sense of urgency mixed with fear. It was written in those eyes. Fear for once life and limb. Fear of a terrified victim hanging onto the last glimmer of hope. Fear of defenceless innocent victim about to face the torture master, and yet with a naïve hope against all odds right to the end. He'd seen it all before in Bosnia' war. She was on the run, no price for guessing that, but on the run from whom or what?

The fact that now inside the cabin and out of pouring rain he was still naked seemed so trivial it took some time before he became aware of it.

* * *

From the departure ex Sydney nine months ago on route to his birthplace island of Mljet in far away Croatia's Adriatic, this single-handed voyage was spooked with gear breakdowns, and foul weather leading to costly repairs, delays and unwanted detours.

A brand new auto pilot broke down when most badly needed, during a blinding downpour. Then the electrics started packing it in. What could break down broke down. The solar power cell leaked water through the inadequate seal, before the alternator bearing decided to pack it in. With limited power the radios had to be sparingly used. Not to mention the lights. Pulling into ports and waiting for spare parts cost him dearly in time lost. The best of the sailing season in the Indian Ocean was well and trully over. To make it worse, two exceptionaly early typhoons off Sri Lanka forced him to abandon the planned Red Sea route and head southwest running for his dear life before raging storm. Heading for safety of the Equatorial waters off African continent instead.

As it was he barely made it riding the wild waters. He coped a knockdown and the cockpit filled in more than once. It was high time to recoup. To dry out, and recover from exhaustion. A number of possible destination looked feasible. The closest one was the Chagos Islands. Choice helped by hear-say of the sailing fraternity. Easy going locals and no red tape. At first it turned to be true. No formalities to speak of indeed. No forms to fill.

'Just pick up your garbage!' The signs said.

Even getting to Chagos took a lot longer than planned. Frequent wind shifts, followed next by no wind of any kind all. He came to appreciate the despair of Vasco de Gama, Magellan and others facing the same trying conditions of the ocean belt better known as the Doldrums. Opressive humidity and lack of progress began to tell. He'd lost a lot of weight and became quite irritable. The beard he grew began to itch like crazy. He was getting more dispirited and lying on one side for too long would cause him discomfort in the rib carriage. He craved for some company. Still what he needed most was time and place to recover.

Man alone always gets beat. Why? By a hostile mob. Or the rough weather. Or by the system. In the end what does it matter? Who cares?

Nor was the tired, thirty year old fiberglass sloop Sounion in a better shape. A list of repairs to be carried out was growing by the day. Not to mention an aged and suspect rig that was to spell disaster.

He stayed on Chagos only long enough to careen the yacht twice to antifoul, and found the locals weren't all that friendly. Mega size cruise ships spoiled previous hospitality and reduced it to opportunistic trade. Read free market. Four dollars for a coconut. Not to mention the outboard theft. Physical fatigue induced new headaches. Back in a shipping lane in becalmed sea he'd start working on himself.

"You old fool, how did you end up here?" Solitude with nothing to do is deadly.

Torturous self-interogation went on and on! Sure, he could have headed for South Yemen port of Aden, but that had over the years accounted for more and more sailors lost never to be heard of again. Single-handed voyagers since give a wide bearth to ports along the East Coast of Africa, down to latitudes of Mombasa. Zanzibar looked like a safe proposition. A bit of R&R perhaps, and then on towards the Cape of Good Hope, and into welcoming South Atlantic. That was the idea. Facing the situation, the only one sensible.

Well, that was the ambitious plan before that woman showed up. This uninvited woman. His night time visitor who just climbed aboard.

And then, some woman. Late twenties? The moment she entered his world she spelled trouble. No wonder his senses were on red alert. But then he noticed she was shaking from exposure. Max opened a locker holding clothing. First wrapped a towel around his naked body and passed her another beach towel. He watched as her drenched cotton dress fell on the cabin floor and exposed a goose pimpled body of a well buildt and powerful woman in her prime. She seemed to be relaxed about his presence until he moved in closer to inspect what appeared as an open wound on the left shoulder blade. She pulled back in pain as he touched the surrounding muscle.

"Cigaretts. Mustafa's cigarettes." She spoke.

A number of burn marks extended to form what looked like a letter sigma in Greek. She had been branded. She spoke charged with emotion in somewhat halting English, yet gramaticaly correct and sufficiently fluid to make herself understood. There was also a hint of some speech impediment. She would tend to over-emphasize the second syllable and almost having a Sweedish accent by default in the process.

"Aisha". She introduced herself in a firm assertative tone and he took her outstretched hand becoming instantly aware of strong vibrations radiating from his visitor.

Over the centuries, Arabs, Shiraz, Negroes and colonial whites of many breeds have left their genes here in the offspring of a handsome race. The beauty and self assured bearing of their women folk was no secret. Tall and upright liberated ladies of Zanzibar mixed and did business with the best of men and knew how to dress in colour. They got liberated in 1964 uprising which after a blood bath put an end to Arab domination. That's what he found in the previous visits as a free lance reporter..

Now this woman! For the first time in months he was to share the cabin with another human being. He rightly felt her presence could only spell trouble. At first he was inclined to disbelieve her story. He insisted she repeat it all over again, looking for inconsistencies. There was none. In the end he had the gist of it.

He went through the lockers looking for something more suitable for her to put on. Along the way he got the kerosene stove going ready for a cup of coffee. She settled down onto the port side bunk with a hot cup of coffee on the midship table. The posture she took he found interesting. Back of the head resting on crossed hands behind it.

Aisha's story had more than a ring of terror. It was an inditement of man's cruelty and depravity.Yet none of this was his business. It was not at all reasonable to ask him, a total stranger to take sides. If these strange people practice their middle-age barbaric customs, who was he to interfere? It was preposterous to ask him, or beg him to take sides. And she did neither. She neither pleaded nor begged. She kept her dignity intact under most difficult circumstances imaginable. That made it far more difficult to dismiss. Max was convinced she spoke the truth. The amount of detail for start. Her voice had been close to braking point and still that aura of dignity didn't desert her. Nor a tear to be seen.

He'd been through to hell and back again himself and knew all about pain. Most people, young ones in particular nowdays had a low pain threshold. So what gave her the strength he was wondering. Others in her place would have been in tears by now. She had what the Polynesians call a big ***manna*** for a ***vahine.***

Her story started with Puccies, an Italian couple who used to run for many years The Park View Hotel. Five minutes walk from the Dar es Salaam's Oyster Beach. The beer garden used to draw them in after dark. All sorts. UN Fisheries inspectors, World Bank analysts, stray tourists, well off locals, pimps and good time girls. The leafy and flagrant beer garden had a lot going for it. Aisha would occassionaly hit a few bars on the old out of tune piano. On Sunday she'd play the organ at St Joseph's for Father Benetti's mass.

From an early age men were always drawn to Aisha. White men in particular. They came, lovers and sinners, one and all, then parted back to their home countries, until Enricco came along.

Much against her will theirs was a childless marriage. It was never the right time for Ricco. For him the overgrown child life was all play time. Until one early morning, six years into the marriage, the news came he'd been found in pieces on the road to Arisha. A fully grown kudu bull came out of nowhere. At 120 ***klips*** that bull was the last thing Ricco saw in this life. Wrackage of Ricco's Citroen was scattered over the lenghth of a football field.

Widowed, with virtually nothing, and too old for this part of the world to re-marry a local, she settled in with Puccies. Doing odd jobs, cleaning and serving drinks in the beer garden. Not a bad life altogether, considering the omnipresent poverty in these parts. She had a full board free. Money and tips on the side for the first time in her life.

Perhaps this would have gone on for how long none can tell, except a period of irreversible change was to put a stop to this type of existence. As everywhere else in Africa, once prosperous time for small, mainly white and Indian entepreuners was well and truly drawing to a close. In place of Puccies, Nashes of Malawi, or Jamesons of Zimbabwe, the big league was taking over. The Novotels, Sheratons, Hiltons etc were muscling in. The small privateers were easy targets. Mere denial to a Licence renewal was a death blow. Along the way a few blacks became rich overnight. Here Puccies saw this coming and looked after Aisha the best they could. They departed to Verona and the land they left in the childhood.

Aisha stayed behind and would have likely followed. She had a right to Italian citisenship, but for that faithful evening when a Somali seafarer she'd never seen before showed up.

Hamoud was a true free trader. You told Hamoud what is it you wanted and he made sure you got it. He could fix things. Escape from prison or silencing the witnesses. Arms smuggling in particular.

Hamoud had at one time or another done the lot. Under a number of aliases the Interpol had difficulty keeping a track of. All over twenty years. A record in this line of economic endevour. He'd seen many of African henchmen come and go. Only to see new ones emerge from what seemed to be an inexhaustible supply.

He was the master owner of the powerful luxury motor yacht Morning Glory with a crew of three.

Secret to one's longevity in his opinion was not so much in abundance of what passes for friends, but in fewness of those ***hombres*** keen to see you roasted on spit alive.

Otherwise he was a model for anyone starting up in this line. Painstaikingly methodical, and cat like in all he did. Those intensely burning black eyes exuding from handsome, typical Somali fearures told one facing him of inner strength and passion, as well as the menacing cobra like readiness to strike.

To augment his fighting qualities Hamoud was also cautious. He'd do his homework. Then do it again. Smiles to all at most times. It was all daggers behind it. He was of slight buildt, and cared for his appearance with a dose of vanity. He'd spend hours grooming. That pencil thin moustache a la' Errol Flynn in particular.

Purported to have been in the secret service of various intelligence agencies, a born freelancer, Hamoud was too smart to sell his skin for other's benefit.

According to his philosophy wars were all started by greedy elite and fought out by the moronic and misled masses.

He possessed no military training. Yet knew all there was to know about weaponry. When he struck it was with all the power he could gather and with military precision. As for personal courage and nerves? Text book stuff. Few have seen him loose self control and lived to tell the tale. His skills with knives were legendary. Oddly enough, he'd rarely resort to abusive language, wether this tertiary education or not had to do with it was a conjecture.

To top it all, one would never hear him boasting and he had for a bandit quite a few scruples. Except when it came to money. There Hamoud was not that much different from a typical multi-national CEO these days. As long as the bottom line was in the blue, how it got there was for most parts academic.

There was potential for makings of a capable executive except for his deeply ingrained distaste of those who shuffel paper work around, namely the lawyers. The dislike of the legal profession went deeper than the need to remain incognito. He'd never signed a contract. His word was good, and he did the business the Chinese way. On a word of trust. Any court evidence against him could have been no better than hear say of the anecdotal sort Western courts don't rate highly.

It equally didn't pay to do a dirty on him. Hamoud was respected for long memory and multi-lingual skills with fluency in a number of African languages as well as good working knowledge of German, Spanish and English. As a medical student trainee cadet, a part of the EEC's Foreign Aid deal, he had a short spell at Venusberg Clinic in Bonn, West Germany.

Until the German secret service got wind of secret arms deliveries destined for General Aidid's mob at Mogadishu in Somalia. Tracks led back to Hamoud who was expelled quietly. Within months he was back in East Germany. This time buying stolen Russian weaponry on the black market and sending shipments to Gen.Aidid's mortal enemy Gen.Ali Mahdi. There was no stopping the Somali. War and Hamoud seemed to go hand in hand. There were others of course. Nothing makes a buck faster than war, but they all worked as agent for powerful interest groups. Hamoud worked for Hamoud.

He was the only son of a rich land estate owner aristocrat. Guided by his father, he studied Medicine at Addis Ababba University in neibhouring state of Ethiopia. Before he was to qualify, the civil disorder and decay finaly cought up with Ethiopia. He left Addis Ababba in panic. Just in time to escape Russian trained state secret service killers by jumping through a closed second floor window. Since then the Pretty Flower, as the name of the city now translates had deteriorated into a slum. He was one semester short of qualifying when Col.Mengitsu took over.

By now, years later, all of East African coast, from Cape Town to Alexandria was for Hamoud an open book. With the exception of French controlled Djibouti. The Foreign Legion had a bounty on his head.

Hamoud's crew consisted of Mustafa, general deck hand cum cook, and two Bangla Deshi ex merchant navy officers.

Hamoud's relationship with Mustafa or Moos as Hamoud called him was bizarre. The two men couldn't have been designed more different.

Moos was the antithesis. A huge and ugly brute. With a walking gait and intelligence not much above that of a chimp. If there was a redeeming quality to him it was his absolute loyalty to Hamoud. There was no task too revolting, none too hard or exhausting Moos wouldn't unquestionably carry out on Hamoud's orders. His cooking was fit for pigs. His company equally trying. To watch him sweat profusely over a cooking stove was enough to turn one off food.

How Hamoud got onto Moos was an interesting side story. The story told of Hamoud a complete stranger at the time rescuing Moos from a Malindi stoning mob on a rape and pederasty charge. To pacify the enraged mob would not have come easy, nor cheap, but what price now for absolute loyalty from a virtual slave?

Despite all of his shortcomings it never occurred to Hamoud to replace Moos. The other two crew were payed on time and knew well to keep quiet.

The night Aisha was highjacked, it was on a Friday, and the beer garden started to fill in after dark. Hamoud walked in just shy of 9 o'clock. Well dressed, neatly trimmed hair style and that pencil moustache cought Aisha's attention.

She was of course unaware Hamoud had done his home work and knew Pucciees were in Italy and Aisha was practically alone. The photos of Aisha he sent to Sheik Ibn el Soud met with approval. The price was firm. One had to haggle if only for for the appearance sake. But most of all, he owed Sheik Ibn a big one. But for Ibn's intervention he was practically done for in the Saudia jail. Dumped and forgotten with other international misfits on charges ranging from spying following the Kuwait invasion paranoia , to liquour offenses.

Ibn was a much feared and high ranking official in Saudi Security Service. Hamoud did his level best to talk Ibn out of the proposed deal and suggested Ibn gets himself a Philipina instead. He was down to three wives. Ibn maintained Phillipinas were too fragile and had too many relatives. Hamoud knew, no matter how sick he felt about it, he had to accept the contract if he wanted his freedom back.

Now when it came to carry out the kidnapping it was all very straight forward. They tangoed on the packed dance floor full of bodies. Hamoud navigated through the tight gaps so light footed, he could have been walking over a mine field without setting it off. When Hamoud suggested they depart Aisha to tell the truth was only too willing.

She remembered boarding the motor yacht and the trans channel passage to Zanzibar, the champaigne they drank, and that was where the memory cut out.

When she woke up next afternoon it was with a sense of horror.

Facing her a foot away was the moon faced Moos grinning away, calling loud obscenities in Arabic and promising to have her sodomised.

"Where is Hamoud?" She wanted to know.

"Gone to Stone City to do the shopping with Rajid and Said." He replied.

"Won't be back till tomorrow morning. Just you and me, ha..ha.., Just you and me, sweet halva... you and me."

As she made efforts to rise up from the chair the force of the ropes pushed her back. She had been trussed to a floor bolted chair like a piglet. A splitting headache suggested knock out sedation dose was wearing off and a burning pain on the back of the left sholder suggested other dirty deeds had been inflicted upon her.

She looked at her wrist watch. It was late afternoon. Where the rest of the day went she couldn't account for.

A sense of panic combined with pain and revulsion made her try to free herself again, only to have the ropes bite back more cruelly into the flesh.

Moos was in fits. He'd never seen anything so funny. Hamoud told him before he left not to touch her, sure, but a bit of a tease that couldn't hurt.

Meanwhile fearing for the worst and coming to realise the predicament she was in, Aisha began to work on Moos. She saw that as the only chance.

"You, the strong one." She addressed him in a calm voice, realizing what a half wit he was.

"What is your name?" He got cought flatfooted. Nobody had ever spoken to him like this. And this just as he was ready to roll off another barrage of spicy insults. No, he thought to himself. This cannot be. She is only playing me for a fool. But Aisha picked the hesitation.

"Well common now, ain't you gonna tell me. I could be nice to you. I could be very very nice to you. If you'd only help.

"Noooo." He was firm. "I know where you are going. Sheik Ibn said for none of us to have it with you. Hamoud would kill me."

So that was the faith in store for her. Slave wife to some old pervert. No! No! And No! They thought in the West the slavery was a thing of the past. Ha! Litlle do they know.

"Now strong one, if I don't tell Hamoud and you don't tell Hamoud, how is Hamoud going to find out? *Ayh*! Think about it the strong one, and I let you do all those things to me."

She tried her best under the circumstances to appear seductive.

"*Ayh,* when did you last have it off with a woman?"

She was driving Moos where she wanted him. Moos was beginning to sweat profusely. The sweet talk was beginning to work.

"I like you." He said."

"I like your tail a lot. You have the sweetest tail I'd ever seen. Not like that old matrasse of mine back in Malindi." His breathing was becoming audibly heavier.

"Fat lot of good this will do you. All this empty talk. What are you? A man or a boy? Now come a little closer the strong one. Put your hand here." And she was motioning the head in the direction of the right thigh. All this was the final straw.

"Mustafa, the name is Mustafa. Hamoud calls me Moos." The tone was decidedly friendlier and Aisha felt she was winning at last.

"Mustafa!" She addressed him by his proper name.

"I'd love you to do all those things to me and promise not to tell Hamoud, if only you'd untie me first."

"And promise by Allah The Merciful?"

"Yes Mustafa, and promise as you wish."

Moos was a powerful man. The thought of her posing some physical threat to him never occurred to Moos. And she didn't have the slightest idea as to what she was going to try next. Anything beats being trussed like a piglet. She was also unaware that Hamoud, as careful as ever refused to tie up at the warf, but anchored a half mile at least away in the bay.

Moos got behind her and started undoing the 10 mm braided rope knots, watching here intensly and smirking away. His hands moved all over her buttocks, and he was getting a hard on. He began to undress her, wildly tearing at her blouse. Next instant with last knot released she rose. Unsteadily at first. The drug buzz was still evident until it gave way to white anger and revulsion. She rose up to full height then spun around to face Moos.

An eye to eye silent confrontation followed. As Moos red the wild look in her eyes he slowly began to realize he'd been cheated. Overcome with anger he became more abusive and finaly lost his self-control altogether.

"Yyyoooouuu, ..yyouu ffilthy, infidel, lying whore!" He screamed at her. When over-excited Moos would lapse into statter.

"And you stupid, ugly, filthy, imbecile cretin!" She fired back. "That's what you are, I'd rather die then let you near me."

Sadistic nature of Moos took over. Without being in control of himself he grabbed a heavy kitchen cutlass and led by an inarticulate shriek head bent charged at Aisha. She was in mortal danger. Jammed between the stove on one side and cabin stowage cabinet wall on the other, and nowhere to dodge the coming blow, she picked a heavy cast iron cooking pot half full with hot mutton stock.

"Dddye you will! He sreamed. She screamed back at him.

"*Imshie!*" Go away. All to no avail. Only a step away she cought Moos and tipped the hot mutton stock into his face. Blinded and screaming in pain Moos continued inertia driven in the same direction. The cutlass was just about to descend when she forcefully struck a sideways blow with all the strength she possessed.

The iron pot edge cought Moos on the temple. He lost the foothold on by now greasy and slippery vinyl galley tiles, then collapsed in a heap. He uttered a few incomprehensible grunts before his body went limb. She tried to step over him, only to loose foothold and stamble heavily on top of Moos. With horror she was petrified to move on at first. She looked at Moose again from close up. His eyes were still open focused on infinity. Moos was dead.

Wether he died from a massive heart attack or from the blow to the head she had no way of knowing, and no one was ever to find out with certainty. The deadly cutlass lay next to Moos in a pool of greasy mutton stock next to a sheep head.

It all happened so fast she was unsure it was for real at first and wished it wasn't. Yet the pain in the left sholder was real enough to remind her. So was the smell of burning human flesh with stench of tobacco smoke and that awful mutton head staring at her. She slumped into the same chair held captive before and began to sob. First tears of pain and sorrow then silent tears of loneliness and desperation.

At first she had no idea what to do next. The day light began to fade and there was a dark cloud over-head. As it began to rain she walked out onto the foredeck hidden from the shore view. Hard rain and wind outside gradually restored her senses. She raced through the bridge lockers and found her purse and a set of false ID papers, a Saudi Passport with her picture on it in another name. Nothing was locked, Hamoud trusted his crew. There were bundles of notes in American currency. She left the money untouched.

What to do now? She was panick stricken again. For an instant she thought of calling for help over the UHF radio. The call sign was there, but she didn't know how to operate it. Just as well. It wouldn't have done her any good. It would have given off her position and condition long before any help was likely to arrive. She thought of rowing ashore, only to find the dinghy was there already She could swim to shore and ask help from the Police. The same Police who killed her parents when she was a baby. And even if she could beat the incoming tide and wind and reach the shore, Hamoud was sure to get to her or buy his way out.

And then the Law. She just killed a man. In self defence for sure, but when did a woman ever manage to get a fair trial.? Least of all could she stay on board. Then she spotted outlines of a yacht some distance away with mast head light on. About the same distance away as the shore, but down wind. She made up her mind. Wind and incoming tide would help her swim the distances. There was no choice. It was desperation time. She slid from the stern into the dark waters of the bay clutching on a small parcel in one hand .

Not once did Max interrupt her. Then it was his turn to get angry. Why in the name of Almighty did this have to happen to him? Why of all the yachts in the Indian Ocean did she manage to seek refuge on his? Hasn't he been punished enough? No! He was resolute. It wasn't on. A man was dead. That was the last straw. And it was preposterous to challenge Hamoud in his backyard. She had to go. She had to go! He told her as much. Then he got onto the VHF calling the Port authorities. He tried Port chanells , chanell 16 as well with no one answering the call. At last the same angry voice butted in:"Didn't he know the time?" They worked office hours only if at all.

It didn't deter Max. She still had to go. He pumped up his Metzeler Aztec rubber dinghy and told her to get in. Without the missing outboard, fighting the current and wind Max soon found the inflatable was never going to make it through the chop with two of them on board. Even rowing with all the power he could muster he was making no headadway at all. If anything they were in danger of being swept away. Exhausted and defeated they turned back and slumped onto the cockpit seats. Too fatigued to worry about wet clothes.

She remained seated in the cockpit in the blinding rain. The faint glimmer of hope she had was all gone... She will have to own up to Hamoud. She did not mean to kill Moos. Her fate was in Lord's hands. The Christian fate she adopted from Puccies was the last bastion of hopes. She began to pray

"***Santa Maria ajuta me!***" She prayed in Italian. Loud enough for Max to hear it. Max got up then asked her to repeat it.

"Where did you learn all this?" He wanted to know." About the Holy Mary? He was convinced she was a Moslem. She explained. There was a long pause with sounds of rain poltering on the cabin roof and wind whisling in the rigging. He thought long and hard. What was he to do? Chicken out or…? When he spoke again it was in a low tone.

"Come inside and dry yourself up." I know I'll live to regret this. It is against my better judgement sense, but do come inside. Tell me this Hamoud character, a Somaly you say. Does he have a left hand small finger missing?"

"Yes. I noticed that on the dance floor."

"Be damned! Damned to eternity. This cannot be. He described Hamoud as he'd remembered the man from the Bosnian war five years ago. He lost the finger fending off two Afgani jihadists. Max' commander, the late Gen.Blaz Kraljevic was full of prize for the man. The Somali managed to deliver crates of Russian ***molotki*** anti tank grenades through an arms blokade. Only Hamoud called himself Arif in Bosnia.

How Hamoud managed to smuggle Iranian funded, Soviet arms abandoned by the routed Iraqi armies, collected over Kuwait battle fields, and then pass through the NATO blockade in the Adriatic into Croatia then Bosnia was a master piece. The man was a cool customer and a legend. Later on in the war the blockade was a sham. The US delivered shiploads of tanks and artillery to the Bosnian Moslems towards the end of the war, from late 1994 on.

But just then in the spring of 1993 when the Serbian onslaught found little if any reistance, Hamoud's arms delivery were God sent. The price reflected the value placed upon those weapons when it really mattered. One AK-47 was selling for a thausend $US. For this money one can buy a crate full in Africa. A light machine gun five long ones. Stories doing the rounds about the Somali were largely based on facts. Those two Afganies who cost Hamoud his left small finger were both found with their throats slit, and they were as fearless in close combat as they come. Max had never met him, but held the healthiest of respects for the Somali whatever his name was. It was only common sense and self preservation instincts that told him to hand her over…Until the foolish pride over a damsel in distress that gets most good men into trouble reared its head.

Damn the bastard, Max decided. Think, even if I hand her back, I am a witness to a kidnapping. He wouldn't want me around anyway…And, I'd feel like a creep for the rest of my days even if left in peace. All this moralizing was destructive self-searching. It had to stop!…Just try it! Easier said than done.

Anyone who thought making a tough decision was easy never had to make one. Then he turned to her with a wishful line.

"If only you could sail." More as a lament than a question. The last reserves of his energy were spent on that futile rowing attempt to reach the shore. He was in no way fit to handle this alone any longer. Nothing but wishful thinking, a drowning man clutching at straws, pure phantasy. He felt like a military commander who had just witnessed hist last reserves wiped out in battle. All the same, he decided it was worth another try.

"Can you sail Aisha?"

"Smaller boats, yes." She was quick to reply. Puccies were keen water rats and she'd spend weekends with them on the water. She also had a good knowledge of the coast line.

That did it! If you can sail a dinghy, you can sail! To hell with common sense, Max made up his mind.

He was going to take his chances and run for it. He just had to think through the tactics. It had to be good. For start direct run for Dar was out. It was the most obvious escape route and Hamoud doing close to 40 Kn would have him before he got there. Hamoud had a fast powerful vessel, he was certain to be well armed, and he could do without charts in these waters. If ever there was a mismatch this was it.

The second possibility open was to run with the wind and current heading South.

Equally open to likely capture. It soon became obvious Max had to embark on a course deemed if not foolish, then dismissed as most unlikely. That ment motoring due North into a squally front and so at least gain some precious time. Idealy Max was banking on the weather easing up, and with an early start be in the position to round off Zanzibar northern tip then head back into the vastness of Indian Ocean and work something out from there.

That ment there was no time to loose. That ment he had to run with all lights off and to stay clear from ferry lanes. He started the diesel engine, winched in the anchor and on low throttle quietly motored into the open waters. It was still raining but within an hour the sky cleared and the wind dropped. With half moon clear he had enough light to see ahead and engaged full throttle. That picked some speed but he was still doing 6 Kn only. She was on the bow watching out for traffic while he went down below to organize something to eat and drink.

He gave her the training suit he carried for colder weather. Now she volunteered to stay on the tiller and have him take a rest. He refused. Not before we leave this island behind us would he relax. Then we'll decide on roster routine.

Any bit of breeze that came to his assistance, Max would have the sails up in a jiffy and still the engine on full throttle. This helped cover the distance and they cleared the northern approach light to Zanzibar waters at Ras Nungwe at 4 am, with two hours to go before daylight. By then they were out on a close reach using the last of the off shore breeze and changing course to NE.

With sunrise soon it became dead calm, and he noticed the diesel starting to over heat. There seemed to be a blockage in the salt water cooling intake. Probably another plastic bag. That was the cause for majority of blockages.

This and a feeling of absolute exhaustion prompted Max to study the charts and investigate the possibility of finding a suitable hideout. The motor needed to be looked at and the two of them desperately needed a few days to recover.

The chart didn't have much detail covering the waters that were of interest, but there was enough on it to suggest a small lagoon surrounded by two uninhabited inlets and a narrow passage through the coral reef. With no depths given, it was a risky proposition, but they had little choice.

Max instructed her winched up in bossun's chair to the level of bottom spreaders what to look for. She was to indicate the current flow direction and the best course ahead. Meanwhile Max managed to remove the blockage and they were on the way. It was a hair-rising entry. All the more so because of the water clarity. A bottom could be seen clearly and menacing in ten meters of water.

They made it in a tidal surge and entered the lagoon. On both sides there were mature cockonut trees offering a protection from view. Max droped the anchor without delay and thanked the Lord for the lucky escape so far. Here holed up they could rest and unwind. There was no sign of habitation around them, nor any sign of litter. That ment of course no source of water, but they could with careful consumption last for weeks. His bilge water tanks were full with 500 liters of treated rain water.

The best was they were now out of circulation. Let them waste their fuel. Short of aerial reconnaissance and unforeseen intruders they were safe here.

* * *

CHAPTER ELEVEN

HUNTER TURNING GAME

The Sultan suite at Beytel Chai hotel overlooking the bay was made ready for Hamoud. His two Bangla Deshi crew were busy sampling sins of the flesh amongst the pale skinned backpackers escaping European cold and thirsty for thrills.

They were to meet in the market place out to purchase supplies of what Hamoud called the green stuff. He retired to bed early expecting company. First one then the other female companion joined in. Both local girls. To Hamoud the skin colour was irrevalent. And yet, despite all the wants and desires satisfied he was in deep thought.

It was all converging and starting to worry Hamoud. For the first time in years he was giving some thought to having a settled life. Wife, kids and family, all fruits of retired life. Life of ordinary people if that was still possible. Monies he invested shrewdly into rising UK stock market and cash deposited into Austrian banks ment there was sufficient funds to settle in a country of choice. He began to imagine living in Bavaria of all places. The Alpine scenery and Teutonic efficiency he admired so much. Trouble was, he had a criminal record there. Or Sweden perhaps? He liked the long leged sporty nymphs from the North. They knew all about love making there was to know and without hang ups.

The rain began easing off. Still in the early hours before dawn, and an uneasy premonition made him walk up to the balcony overlooking the harbour. As the sky cleared, he could spot the Morning Glory on anchor. Instantly he felt there was something amiss. Neither was there any sign of that yacht anchored in the bay.

At first he couldn't place the problem. Then it got to him. The riding white light was off.

It never happened before for Moose to disobey orders. For one it encouraged uninvited visitors to climb aboard. Moos was in fact instructed to keep the vessel well lit. Now Hamoud could not spot any lights at all. He returned to bed and decided to give Moos a good dressing down at first chance.

Next time he woke up both women were gone. The traffic and crowd noise from the Independence Rd was getting louder. He met the two Bangla Deshi and loaded the market produce with haste into the alloy dinghy, then started the 40 HP Honda outboard, and raced at speed to dock with Morning Glory.

It didn't take Hamoud long to piece it all together.

"What a bloody sucker!" He swore at the top of the voice, then kicked the cutlass out of the way. The Bangla Deshi stood by speechless. Hamoud turned to face them.

"Here! What a comprehensive bloody mess! A woman, an infidel Arab bitch did this. She killed Moos. But how did she do it, I don't get it."

She was to pay for this. Saudi sharia law can deal with her any time Sheik Ibn gets tired of her. One didn't live to draw pension in an Arab prison. Next he walked to where Moos' body lay and looked at his smashed wrist watch. Time piece stopped at twenty to eight. The body was cold that had to have been almost twelve hours ago, last night. For the last time Hamoud looked at the body of his long serving faitful servant.

"Kfaheri fundu." Farewell my friend. He mumbled the words more to himself. It occurred to Hamoud Moos was very useful, but that was as far as the sentiments went. He was to miss the willing slave worker more than he ever thought possible and before long.

Moos' widow was another worry. She had to be taken care of, lest she felt delt short out of her breadwinner's demise and had a revenge on her mind. This was going to cost more money. There was no social welfare here. Altogether, a most unprofitable morning session.

Hamoud felt a need to release the pent up frustration. He rolled himself a khat reefer. After a few puffs, the ephedrine stimulant began to settle him into his usual frame of mind.

As for Aisha, Hamoud was at first of the opinion she swam on shore and was hiding some place in the medieval Stone City. He left the crew on board and motored back to shore, then beached the dinghy as close he could get it to the Bab el Mandeb tea house frequented by dhow crews and harbour employees.

He put a thosand shilling bounty on Aisha, with bonus for fast delivery, then returned to Morning Glory once more. There was no time to loose. They had to dispose of the body and incriminating evidence.

Before departure the crewmen had to sign 'Missing at Sea Report' backdated four days. Hamoud passed two hundred dollar bills in smaller denominations to each to seal the silence. He equally backdated Captain's Log. Under the heading 'Disappearence at Sea', he wrote:

'Cause(s) unknown. Presumed fallen overboard during the stormy passage. A heart failure leading to it very likely in view of chronical heart problems.'

The galley was scrubbed clean. Hours later one could still smell that chlorine in the air. Hence there was no time to loose. Without further delay Hamoud walked to the bridge and started up the Daytona Merlin 450 HP twins. Having reached the open channel waters he gunned down the powerful engines and was soon skitting at 32 Kn heading for Dar es Salaam. The outside possibility of the departed yacht having had something to do with Moos' death also had to be investigated, Hamoud decided.

If that yacht was heading for Dar by his calculation it had to come into view within the next two hours. Both crewmen were on lookout. Scanning the horizon from the bridge, visually as well as using the 16 miles range Seacraft radar. Fibreglass yachts make for poor radar targets and can be easily missed. Along the way they overtook an American ketch a two master, another motor yacht and two Russian rust bucket fishing trawlers. And that was all.

Still steaming in the channel, Moos' body wrapped around with 50 meters of heavy spare anchor chain got tossed overboard. Without slowing down they continued on the same course. It was not possible for that yacht to be ahead of them and still Hamoud systematically checked the traffic, followed by phone calls to Seamen's Mission and Yacht Club. Barman on duty the red fez Hassan could not offer any useful information.

Failure on both fronts to find any sign of Aisha finaly forced Hamoud to admit his initial mistake. He began to suspect that yacht and not Aisha was instrumental in Moos' death. Information reaching him from the Stone City fuel vendor told of a single sailor aboard the yacht. If that was indeed so,

Hamoud began to realise he was up against a worthy opponent. Even more unsettling was the fact he could not get any of the coastal ports to provide information about a yacht fitting the description. And he tried them all.

So the single handed sailor killed Moos and hijacked Aisha, or what? One way or the other it took a man to do it. Moos was no pushover. He had to give it to his adversary. Whoever this man was, he had less respect for the red type than your average whitey *wozungu*. But what was to be done next? To help his cause he consulted the crew. Rashid was the first to offer suggestion. To his way of thinking the sailor had good sense to stay out of harm's way until things calm down, playing hide and seek. Hamoud agreed.

"Suppose you are right Rashid. Where do you think we should be searching next?"

"Oh, be fair Skip, I am not a magician. Hundreds of places to hide."

"Not for long. I've got my spies everywhere. From here to Pemba and a thousand shillinghi on her."

Even so, Rashid was correct. There were literally hundreds of suitable anchorages all along the Zanzibar west coast. Particulary around the maize of waterways next to Pangume.

Then Said picked a short message on a radio channel used by the Water Police. That was a timely warning to Hamoud. In order to pre-empt a nasty surprise he brought Morning Glory to a gradual stop then ordered all unlicensed guns already mothballed and hermetically sealed to be dropped overboard on a submarine marker. Just in time, or so he thought.

His sence of impending surprise was well justified, as out of nowhere a Police fast launch crossed their bow and ordered them to remain stationary, ready for boarding. Inspector Ngezi wanted to see the Captain's Log. He put on his reading glases and read the entries. To an untrained eye, not much of value. To Ngezi it was enough to find a number of inconsistencies that soon had Hamoud under crossfire.

"So you have a lost crew member?"

"Yes."

"Why did it take four days to report that? Why no call for help? Why no radio communication to the Police? Storm? What storm? Heart condition? Where was the medical evidence for this? Or was he Dr Hamoud passing free diagnosis?"

That last bit realy shook Hamoud. How much did Inspector Ngezi realy know about him? He hasn't been called a doctor for years. Grilling of the crew continued equally unmercifully.

"What were they doing in a blow? Everybody was on alert and knew it was bearing down. And carrying cargo? What cargo? Where is the cargo manifest?"

On and on it went for nearly two hours. Meanwhile they searched the vessel thoroughly for illegal merchandise. Not that Hamoud entered a single word of protest. On parting Ins.Ngezi called him to the side to have a quiet word. He passed a hint as to how costly this could be. For start, dumping those weapons overboard didn't go unnoticed. Now others, some a lot higher up would have to be made to look the other way. Some were a lot higher.

Checking through his returned passport forgery he found a Barklys' account in Nairoby and a figure of $5K beside it. That was just for starters. There were more hungry mouths to feed. Next the Police was back on their fast launch heading for Dar.

"The thieving jackals!" Hamoud loudly complained to Rashid.

"So much for the so called New Force as the media spin would have us belive it."

For a genius in planning and a man of legendary patience that Hamoud was reknown for, this was two big mistakes in one day. A lesson for undecided would be retirees. People do get retired generally for a good reason. Hamoud's mistakes were born by haste. He was being rattled by Ngezi. No question about it. His mistaken perception of corrupt Ngezi was to prove costly.

If there was a man in these parts next to incorruptible it was Ngezi. Those bribe monies were a ploy and trap to incriminate and compromise Hamoud. Monies eventually deposited Ngezi duty bound declared to Treassury and used to fund expenses in ongoing gathering of evidence against Hamoud. Bulk of it was soon used up for a leased light aircraft.

Hamoud didn't know it just then, but before long he was to regret not having taken the opportunity offered to him by fate to retire. And the esteem for Ins. Ngezi was soon to take a quantum leap. As the Morning Glory's crew was distracted by interrogation, two capable electronics experts placed listening bugs and miniature sound recorders into a number of hidden places.

One of them under the bridge cabin floor was to remain undiscovered. It was to provide valuable evidence so far lacking. In addition, a long range reacon in HF range was cleverly hooked up to vessels batteries and its HF antenna. It was to emit Morse MG code at 15 minute intervals, four calls in a group. This it was hoped would with aid of another RF finder fix Morning Glory's position in future.

* * *

For Max and Aisha the initial euphoria of having made the escape good wore off once the fresh supplies of food got exhausted. The vegetables and fruit purchased from the hawkers also had to be consumed first. There was no refrigeration on board.

Catching fish from the lagoon was no problem. Finding something green to supplement the sea food was more of a challenge. Here Aisha's local knowledge came to rescue. She was expert at catching crabs and turtle or tern eggs and knew which sea grases were eadible. They ate well, and Max found his physical condition improving rapidly. If they had a problem it was with sunburn of exposed flesh and sand flies in wind still corners. Mixing zinc oxide-castor oil burns paste from the first aid kit with olive oil and coconut milk when liberaly applied to feet and face gave protection from the sun burn. Certain areas were best avoided to escape the sand flies. Otherwise they wore long pants and long sleeved shirts most times.

A week went by then the weather conditions changed. From the variable winds of the transition period to a steady east monsoon **kavkazi.**

The wet season was on and with it increased humidity. The question arose once more, how much longer to stay here before making the break for the Seychelles. Returning to Dar es Salaam was still too risky and on limited budget knocking about expensive tourist resorts along the East Coast also not considered prudent.

The outer Amirante Group of islands was far enough from Hamud and also considered, wrongly as it proved to be less expensive. In order to make sure the trail got cold they decided to stay on for one more week. Without any more pressing repair and maintanance chores to perform they spent hours swimming and diving naked in the lagoon. Before long Max was forced to make another observation. He cought himself more and more watching his travelling companion. She was starting to do things to him he had almost forgotten about. It didn't escape her attention and she made the first advance. His one defence was the age difference excuse.

"Look, I could be your father." He protested."You do need someone younger, more of your age. This would be just my taking advantage of the situation."

She could not follow the logic of his. So she'd try another tack.

"Do you prefer boys? Or would you just play sport?" He would try and lough it all off as a joke, but soon found out there was nowhere to hide. One early morning while heading for the **mokutu** , plaited sun shelter she buildt close to the channel entrance and exposed to sea breezes, the most pleasant part of the isle, she ran him up from behind, took a rugby style tackle hold of him, and brought him down landing on the soft sand.

"Captain, I'm your crazy woman. More crazy today. I feel it is my time."

In the end he just let it be. He let himself indulge on the wings of the pagan surge. More than once he'd bury his face in her thick black hair and the long gone memories of his marriage and the brunette he loved so dearly would come flooding back to haunt him. So vivid and paiful as if all that happened yesterday. But why? Where was the rational explanation for this? The woman he loved deserted him when he needed her most. Gradualy the complex let go of him.

That last week they spent most of it in each others arms. Time ceased to matter. It was as if he was making up for his lost youth. Decades of emotional emptiness spent in fighting stupid wars or just fighting to survive. And each time it was back to zero hour. They were now as close to each other as our human capacity to love and share would permit. She made a comment:

"Look, I am airborn on a flying carpet and with a wish for Aladin. Guess what I'd like from you?" Boy or a girl? He stayed quiet.

Bringing babies to this world is one thing. Bringing them up in a good home is another. A home he didn't have to offer. On another occasion, she asked if he could hear the angels singing Mozart's Requiem. She could hear the Arcangel Gabriel playing the oboe.

"Crazy woman! In order to hear this you must be an angel yourself!"

"Me angel? Never. I am your crazy woman. More crazy today."

Then she'd go exploring through odds and ends boxes, and often come up with items he'd been missing for months.

On another occasion she turned up triumphantly holding up a CD with JS Bach's cantata ***Ich habe genug***. Play it for me , please Max." Thanks to her previous efforts in soldering, mulfunctioning solar power cell was back in operation. They had enough 12 Volt battery power to play her CD. Max had to translate the JSB's German to his disbelieving listener. How could anyone, no matter how pious be wanting to depart the land of the living before their time? She asked deeply disturbed. He had no answer.

When it came to discuss the Catholic Church, she was a fierce defender. Equal in fervour to any of the twelve apostols. Here she found Max with a different point of view.

"Why do you question the Christian faith?" She'd ask."You do believe in the Almighty I know for fact. So why question the belief?" He had to explain himself.

"Question I do, yes. The dogma and written scriptures. Up to a point. Never the faith. One cannot question faith. One has either got faith or remains atheist. I am absolutely unworthy to question anyone's faith and have no such intensions. In fact I am envious of those possesing faith. Blind faith, yes, because that is the only faith. Catholic faith that teaches us God made man in the image of himself. A merciful and omnipresent God. How then, can we account for attrocities and slaughter of innocents. I have seen enough with my own eyes. Men carved up in sadistic orgy of evil only Lucifer himself could be up to it. A child of six crucified. So take your pick. Is our Lord merciful and omnipresent, inferior designer, or have we as I suspect cooked most of this up. I fear we do not have the faintest idea how the Master of the Universe operates. Nor are we ment to have. As far as the church is concerned all this is heretical blasphemy.

Be it as it may, I do not seek to influence anyone. All I want is to be true to myself. I believe in God. Always have. Only a simpleton can mantain the complexity and beaty of the universe happened at random. Nothing of any importance ever happened at random that I can recall, or others can point out. I am not realy agnostic. Some of the top notch scientist could be also best described as such.

It does not make it easier to take a stand when science itself has a problem. How does one reconcile Darwinian Theory of Evolution that tells us of ever more complexity against the Third Law of Thermodynamics on entropy, that leads in the opposite direction? There are other powerful dilemas to which we have no answer. Why is the universe flaying apart ever faster, for one. The Big Bang Theory postulates the opposite. We are just ***ignoramus***. In the dark and pretending to know."

Exhausted by the revelation of his views on religion Max fell silent and withrew into his inner shelf. A chamber of horrors re-living the images of Vukovar, the Croatian Stalingrad and hell scenes from Bosnia that had him marked for life.

Hell worse than Dante's inferno. And yes, it was the Serbs in the main doing the dirty work. But there have been and will be others every bit as evil. It is in the heart of Man. The beast is both, selfish and evil, and this at every level. Starting from our genes up. Selfish at cell, gene, individual, family, tribe and so on. And this will never change.

At such times Aisha would back off. Not because her fighting spirit was lacking, but because she had too much respect for the man and could not watch him suffer.

* * *

There was a long pause before Max could collect his rational thoughts again. This Dictaphone exercise and facing Vivian who was stripping the pages from his past was sapping his emotional balance by now. To her it was a revelation and a complete suprise.
"I think I can begin to appreciate your predicament." She offered consolance.
"This is only the easy part Viv. Wait. You haven't heard anything about the war yet."
"Nor about how you got involved with Ngezi." She added.

* * *

Inspector Ngezi was back on the job after a six monthly training course in EEC countries. A part of EEC's Aid to Africa. This helped his already sound work ethics. He was a devout RC and a regular church goer.

Sisters of Mercy gave young John the first taste of Christian doctrine to guide him in his adult life. Into mid forties he remained single and lived in with his widowed mother. If he had a weakness it was for sweets and mum's dumplings.

Affairs with women never went further than an invitation to a ball, or one night stand at worst, to be mentioned to Father Benetti in the next confessional.

His job was to Ngezi more of a mission. Not that he was power obsessed. He preferred civilian clothes to a uniform and chose to remain out of limelight and media. There was no record of him taking advatage of the office. In the morning he'd coax the ancient Renault 4 back to life and drive himself to work over 1100 million or so potholes to turn up at the office before anyone else.

Stickler for details he detested sloppy work. One by one over time managed to suround himself with compotent assistants and dilligent staff. His favourite was John Thomba, a dual PhD graduate in Arabic studies and communications, at the age of 23. Good at delegating, his juniors would pay Ngezi back with results.

When it came to ensnaring the crims, Ngezi was systematic. He would take them behind bars when there was enough evidence to defeat even the most inventive of defence councils. Leading to it he would deliberately let them know they were in his gun sights, thus nervous and jittery, watch them make stupid mistakes. Like a python throwing a coil after coil over its victim. This earned him the nick name. ***Donga***.

A number of investigations were drawing to a close when a directive from the Head came to drop everything and clean up the coastal tourist resorts. The obnoxious ***papaasi*** beach boy gangs graduated in places to hard criminals. Tourist numbers were down. With it the major source of revenue. Hamoud's activities would have to be a part of that assignment.

Thus unbeknown to Hamoud, he was also under observation, and that was before Aisha's kidnapping. Her disappearance only put higher priority on it. When Aisha failed to turn up for Sunday mass, Father Benetti found himself without the organ player and had a word with Ngezi attending the mass. Witnesses had seen Aisha leave Parkview beer garden with a man fitting Hamoud's description. Ngezi failed to see the connection. Except for the fact Hamoud seemed to be implicated in both cases. He was also convinced Hamoud's alibi didn't stack up, but first he had to find holes in it. For now he had no choice but to let Hamoud go.

Back aboard the Police patrol boat after the thorough search of Morning Glory, Ngezi had more material to attach in Hamoud's file. Fresh finger prints and voice recordings were to join numerous photographs supplied by Interpol of Hamoud under a dozen or so aliases. Dressed in anything from a nomadic Arab robe to a Western busnissman stripe suite. Before a nose job and after. With and without a wig. At least two variations of moustache and none at all. Not forgeting the document forgeries. The very best money could buy. Worst of all there was no money trail.

To nail Hamoud, one tough customer, Ngezi knew he'd have to be at his inventive best. Fresh ideas were welcome.

* * *

Out of the Police clutches and two precious hours later, Hamoud returned to the position of the submarine marker and recovered the hidden weapons. They arrived at Pangume Island maze just before dark. Too late to start serious search using the cruiser. There were numerous mud banks and shallows. For most part unmarked.

Rajid suggested they proceed using the alloy dinghy, to which Hamoud immediately agreed. Said was left on board armed. Rajid took the outboard controls whilst Hamoud used a heavy hand held search light in one and a loaded semi-automatic in the other hand. They searched till 2 am and apart from running into a bull shark and a ray found no contact to report.

That was after combing mangrove channels, cays, estuaries and tidal creeks. Hamoud's temper thereafter reached a new low. He took a sharp pencil and drew on the detailed chart where they'd been. There was no way a yacht could be there left undiscovered.

"Damn it!" He cursed. Said just glanced at Rashid. They'd never before seen Hamoud loose his cool. In a way this was a warning to the pair to start preparing themselves. Just in case. There were possible kidnapping, murder, and money laundering charges. In all likehood add arms smuggling .

"They couldn't have just vanished, those two." Said tried to sound helpful.

"I say, we ought to hire a small plane. Pick them up from the air."

"And you think I haven't thought of that?" Hamoud was visibly angry." Just how long you reckon before *Donga* would be onto us. But you are right. Where else could they be?"

"I would try Mafia Island." Said suggested." It is a popular tourist and divers den."

"Any good anchorages there?" Hamoud was showing interest.

"Not in a serious blow. Otherwise no problem."

That clinched it for Hamoud.

"Get her going!" He snapped.

"At this hour Captain?" Rashid had other ideas.

"You heard me. Stay on the bridge and point the search lights ahead in a 60 deg sweep scan."

Dhows carried no navigation lights. Nor did they give off much noise as most Westerners do. One had to be vigilant. At times a dhow would cross one's bow arriving out of nowhere like a ghoust on a flying carpet. Add to this the illegal trawlers working the local fisheries after their own back home had been vacuum cleaned of all life. It was for legitimate safety considerations Rajid questioned the skipper.

After hours of motoring glued to the search light beams , they first reached then circumnavigated Mafia Island. And still there was no sign of the yacht. By now only one thing mattered to Hamoud. This chase was costing him plenty in burned fuel alone. Neither did it do much for his reputation. He'd noticed Bangla Deshi crew aside quietly.

conversing. Once more it was not in English. Most of all he came to miss Moos. Since his passing nothing was the same again. The SOB who killed him, he'll get that murderer and avenge Moos. No matter how long it took. All he could think of right now was revenge.

He contacted spies on Zanzibar and Dar and none had anything to report. That induced a state of depression. New to him, but not suprising. Being tired, deprived of sleep, angry and frustrated, all at the same time was a formula par exelance for inducing depression. Add to this the Police investigation. Sure he could pay them off once. And sure as peppers they'd come back asking for more. Bloody vultures!

The doubts he was beginning to find in his own judgement was like having worms eating your interstines. He was not accustomed to failure. Was he getting too old for this game? How much did Ngezi really know? 'Doctor Hamoud' remark for one. He hasn't been called that since University days. Should he retire after all? He'd made more than enough to live in comfort for the rest of his life. All that was sweet reason until it came to that blasted ***Wozungu***.

The crafty foreigner for whom he was by now developing a healthy dose of respect. Cheek of that infidel alone to challenge him on his own turf demanded grudging admiration. He could in fact have done with a man of such calibar. If only...Slowly Hamoud snapped out of self- searching mode, and decided once for all, retireing was fine. Once this business was out of way and not before. Unfinished business took precedence.

Trouble was , the weather facsimile showed a 982 mBar depression heading their way. He'd have to delay further search and ride out the foul weather first. There was time enough to refuel before storm. A slow process with frothy diesoline blowing back bubbles. They refuelled Morning Glory then looked for safe anchorage offering good holding. Hamoud left the crew on board and decided to call in at Spice Inn to pick one of those Nordic beauties. It was too damn useless to harp on one's failures. Life was too short for that.

* * *

Safe inside his lagoone hideout, Max wasted no time in going over and fixing up problems. Where spares were unavailable he had to improvise. Faulty solar power cell was a case in point. A poor soldering connection shorted one third of cell's voltage. He got to work and instructed Aisha in soldering techique. She was soon an expert at it. Now they had enough power to keep battery in top charge. And so on it continued. Her needle work on patching up worn out and chafed mainsail was alone worth a free passage.

With fresh food supplies bought from vendors in the harbour eaten within days, Max decided to bring down a few green coconuts. He repeatedly attempted to climb the tall stems only to finish up bruised. He couldn't do it. She had a go at it with equal defeat. So the diet remained restricted to fish, turtle eggs and eadible sea grases..

Next task on the list was to remove the radar reflector from the mast. This made the yacht a very poor radar target to all but most experienced operator. They discussed what action to take more than once.

Of the two distinct possibilities, the first one was to head for Dar es Salaam and contact the Police with all the risks that was sure to hold. Max didn't like the idea. Hamoud could flatly deny any of that kidnapping ever took place. She had no material evidence to prove otherwise. No witnesses she was aware of, and no photographs. Just hear say and Hamoud still free and around. How could she sleep at night? Getting her back to Dar was no big deal. Then what? It occured to her she was foolish in not taking that Saudi Passport with her.

Instead she had a suggestion out of the blue. He was her saviour. Could do with her as he pleased. She'd make him the best wife in the world. A promise. Could they go to Australia?

Now he had a real headache. Staying with diesel engine maintenance, setting valves, changing oil and the rest was child's play in comparison. Not that her suggestion was without merit. Back in Australia there was every chance of finding gainful employement.

Trouble was, Australia was far off and hard to reach from Zanzibar directly by a sailing boat. Against that, once through the Immigration controls, one was free to roam. Not only that. One could land in a yacht undeclared just about anywhere and an Aussie registred yacht would likely remain unobserved.

If he was to aim for that, Sri Lanka had to be reached first. Even there one only needed a reliable agent. So which course of action to take? Aisha was determined it had to be Australia.

With Puccies departed and Hamoud after her, how could he disagree? As for himself, he was also involved by now. Up to his neck into it. Playing by the rule book made no longer sense. They decided to sit out the incomming storm, take a chance on their luck trying to squeeze through the narrow coral reef opening, and head out for the open ocean waters. Almost ready, when Max decided to pick off some green coconuts. The lazy way. He fired the old Lee-Einfield .303 and harvested a few nuts. He'd done it before in other places. Only on this occasion he failed to muffle the gun shot. Wrapped wet towels are good for that. It wasn't a smart thing to do. Rifle shots were heard on the main island and the inhabitants didn't like it. Within an hour angry villagers surounded the pair. This looked nasty. A boat load of natives. Anger written in their faces and ***pungas***, sharpened machettes at hand.

"Who gave them the permission to harvest here?" The headman wanted to know.

"We saw none to ask." Max tried, then Aisha intercepted. This was no good.

She negotiated in ***kiSvahili*** the compensation. There was no choice.

"Ishirini dollari?"She suggested twenty dollars a head. A stiff price, a tonne of copra was worth that. This settled the crowd and they looked towards Max who returned from the cabin with the cash. The villagers departed jubilant to their long boat.

"Now what?" Max was uneasy.

"Oh, they're happy for now. In the night sure to be back for more." Aisha feared. There was no choice but to run for it. Their secret hideout was secret no longer and Max saw enough of those shiny machettes. Just before sunset, the high tide turned. They lifted the anchor deeply dug into coral sand, then raced out throught the foamy opening so narrow Max was certain some of his antifouling paint had been scraped off.

Once back in open waters Max thanked Lord for the help and set course 42 degrees True set for Seychelles backwaters.

Lagoon left behind them had no sign of their presence apart from a ***makuti***, a plaited sun shelter. One of Aisha's handycrafts.

* * *

Here Max decided he needed a drink before continuing on. No problem, Vivian had one on the way in no time at all. Coconut milk blended with Irish whyskey from the raid on the medical kit, with a tea spoonful of sugar made a good coctail. Max thought they'd done enough for one session, but no. She a hard taskmaster kept asking more questions.

"Was Hamoud still in persuit after two weeks?

* * *

Said Mukhta was older of the Bangla Deshi crew. Both experienced merchant marine officers. Certified and capable. Rajid in electronics and Said a marine diesel doctor as he liked others to see him, listening to each cylinder fireing with a scleroscope.

Hamoud rightly suspected Ngezi of planting bugs aboard the vessel and when inspection found reportedly none, Rajid was less than convinced.

For starters there was a drain on the batteries at idle and no appliances turned on of any power significance. Rajid kept the concern to himself and continued to look into the power drain testing circuitry. It wasn't until puzzled he tried the radio direction finder(RDF) on deck picking up a powerful HF signal that he could not line a direction on. No matter which way he turned the antenae signal strength remained the same. That ment Morning Glory was the source. Next he picked the Morse pattern MGMGMGMG. That led him to the expertly concealed emitter. Rajid continued searching and discovered all but one hidden listening bug. They had micro cassettes attached. Thus it wasn't only their position but their conversation as well being compromised.

Alarmed he decided to contact Said first. Skipper had to wait. In sotto voce he explained to Said what he'd found. Sending on HF using their own power and antenae. Brilliant piece of work. He was impressed. In his opinion there was only one thing for them to do. Keep tight lipped and go AWOL in the first port of call, then try back for UK and look for more traditional work. This whole thing was getting too deep for them, and was about to blow up. They were realy innocent by-standers. In the murder case not even that.

Said took it all in but disagreed. First of all, the more traditional work payed poorly. Indian and Philipino crews signed on for peanuts. Then Hamoud payed not only well but on time. He had been good to them, and diserved more loyalty. And lastly, didn't Hamoud manage to extracate them out of hot spots before? That should have settled it. Rajid in the past always looked up to Said. This was about to change.

Hamoud was catching up on lost sleep while the cousins continued discussion before splitting up without reaching an agreement, and both deeply in after-thought. For them this was a worrying development.

* * *

By now Vivian was totaly engrossed in the plot and pleaded with Max to continue. As it was, Max got the rest of the story from talking to Ngezi in a Dar es Salaam Blue Mango hotel years later.

* * *

Ngezi at his desk was given the telex transmission plot of the Morning Glory's position over the last 24 hours. He could follow the logic of Hamoud searching whatever it was he was looking for around Pangume. Prevailing wind and current would take anything floatsam down that way. But search north of Pangume on present plot made no sense. Conversely, what Hamoud was looking for wasn't Moos' body or other piece of floatsam, but something else. Possibly a missing organ player Aisha?

Reports of Hamoud look-alike leaving Parkview Hotel beer garden with Aisha Ngezi took with some reserve. Not impossible to be discounted out of hand. Equaly not plausible. Hamoud was a lady killer of first order. No need for him to go to such lengths in order to get his bunk full. No. There were too many other villains out there capable of rape and much worse.

Then just before morning tea break, a fresh report came in of a fisherman's net catch that changed Ngezi's thinking. Remains of a heavy male body wrapped in anchor chain came to surface. John Thomba went to investigate. He was reporting back to Ngezi. Barely enough flash was left on the skeleton for forensics. Estimated date of death five days, plus or minus two. No sign of broken bones nor bullets. No mention of jewelry either. A broken wrist watch stopped at twenty to eight. Without a date it wasn't of much help. Ngezi was disappointed. He needed much more information. That is when he called for help. Abdul Hasami, his school friend now senior detective in Stone City Zanzibar had to know more. This was happening in his backyard.

Over the channel by fast ferry Ngezi met Hasami for lunch. He came to the point. There was a woman missing and a dead body.

Hasami had his informers and heard of Hamoud's bounty on a woman. She disappeared. Just like that **Papabawa** perverted ghost. Without a trace. This gave Ngezi a lead. As reluctant as he was at first to associate Aisha's disappearence with Hamoud he was forced to accept the possibility after Hasami's input.

There was little known about Hamoud that could be classified as reliable information. His Interpol file mentioned a short spell in Saudi prison. This prompted Ngezi to call in Thomba who had good connections in Riad's royal circles and spoke perfectly Arabic.

"Go and find out what you can. Contact your informers. We need a breakthrough. Take your time. All costs are covered."

Thomba within days found out about Hamoud's shady past and his arm dealings in Kuwait that nearly cost him his life. After the Kuwait war there was paranoia in Saudi.

Every foreigner was deemed a spy. One saw spies everywhere and foreigners got themselves in trouble. Often beaten and locked up on most preposterous charges. A bottle of booze was enough. Not so Hamoud cought with a truck load of arms. So how did he get off? Little bakshish here and a little there, Thomba pieced it together. Hamoud owed his life to none other than Sheik Ibn-el-Soud. So what did the feared security boss want in return?

When told of all this on the open line, Ngezi smiled for the first time in days.

"Tell me Thomba, how many wives has Ibn got now?"

"My payed informer tells me he lost the youngest one a year ago. Down to three I suppose. Why?"

"I'll tell you when you get back. Your mission is over...Good flight John, you have done very well." Ngezi was satisfied he finaly had the motives for Aisha's kidnapping. Hamoud did not want her for himself. He got tangled up with Ibn and was desperate to find her before Ibn let his butchers loose on him. Perhaps Moos' death was connected with this somehow. In any case Aisha's freedom and possibly life was in danger. He got Thomba back on line and ordered him to hire a light plane with long distance fuel tanks.

"Try Nairobi. Without delay, chop, chop my boy!"

Within hours Thomba reported back. He could get over the Internet, lease of a tween engine Beechcraft four seater equiped with extra long distance fuel tanks for a week from Nairobi. All under four grand. Cheap? Would that do?

"You know about airworthiness. No need for me to remind you. Once you get that plane fueled up, ready to fly, contact me back in Dar. ASAP. Inspector Hasami had been most helpful." We owe the man one.

And it had to be Thomba flying. He was the only licenced pilot under Ngezi's command.

* * *

Two weeks passed after Aisha's escape. With each passing day Hamoud was getting angrier. He'd exhausted all likely sites worth investigating. Of course that excluded no brainers such as heading North into the storm fronts or returning to Dar es Salaam.

At a loss as where to try next he decided to begin visiting small settlements on the way up North. If there was anything out of the ordinary these people would be the first to know. Upon reaching a fishing village of Zemba he decided to disembark in persuit of female company. The Bangla Deshi crew were to stay on board guarding the vessel. The area had a reputation for poverty and violent crimes. Fishing was dead and price of copra at record lows. A promised tourist hotel in the village had the project stall. And the villagers found it wasn't worth the while to plant crops with all the new pest outbreaks.

Developers and traders were creaming off. Too greedy, leaving nothing for them. That's what the fishing folks were telling him. Hamoud tired of all the complaints interrupted, and asked the men point blank if they had any unattached women. He'd make it up to them.

Cought by suprise at first until an elderly villager spoke. One of his younger wives may pass. He was willing to lend his youngest. And sure she would not object. She never had enough anyway. When settled on price, Hamoud was shown direction to an isolated hut. It was a disused storage shed for spare nets and boat gear. There were no windows , but once the eye sights adjusted to dim light he saw the woman waiting for him wearing a smile and not much else.

In the early morning Hamoud left the village drained of all energy. Exchanging greetings with the old man first, then trying to find his beached dinghy, two younger men crossed his path. Yes, they also had similar proposition. He payed well, and their wives were prettier. That told Hamoud how desperate the once reliable breadwinners had become.

He also knew better not to refuse outright. He had understanding for their life struggle. In his diplomatic best he told them, all politicians were the same. One could not belive any of them. But developers? They'll be back. Just trying to drive a hard bargain. Maybe the next year?...But hang on. What was it he just overheard?

"What? A payback by a **Wozungu** for illegal harvesting?" And what! They knew more!" Sure", it came back. And?

"Wait", information costs money. So they settled on price first. The fishermen told Hamoud about the first, then second visit to Sounion four nights ago, when to their angry suprise they found the lagoon empty. The yacht was out of sight by then.

Fireing questions at fishermen Hamoud for the first time knew for sure what he'd only suspected by now. His quarry had good four days start on him. Villagers were honest enough to admitt they had no idea which direction the yacht took. Then it was their turn to ask questions.

"Did he know the foreigner? Did he know the Zanzibari woman? She was scantily dressed. Almost naked. No **bui bui** for her. Not even a head scarf."

Back on board Morning Glory Hamoud was jubilant and his customary air of confidence was there for all to see. He told Said and Rashid what he'd managed to find out. That businessman like drive had returned. All that confidence with it. He was still the best. Just as good as ever. To hell with retirement. He was every bit as good as the day he pulled the stunt on NATO arms blockade in approaches to the Adriatic and enforcing the arms embargo on Croatia and Bosnia. That was a special.

The Bangla Deshi had heard the story before but decided to tune in attentatively all the same. It was good to see the Captain back to his normal self.

Back in early spring of 1993 and the best of Mediterranian weather Hamoud hired a fishing trawler from Palermo in Sicily. With a local crew and a catch of slimy mackarel they set a course past the destroyer Erwin Rommel before acknowledging a request to take a boarding party. Hamoud not only sold the fresh fish at exhorbitant price to German sailors, but managed to put on a clown act. Both, the sailors and Sicilians were rolling in

stiches. Falling about from loughter. What the UN didn't, or more likely as later emerged didn't want to know was, what lay under the tightly packed dry ice boxes. Those **molotki,** sholder fired anti-tank missiles were worth their weight in gold. Mind you, the loud comment by the tall bearded German Commodore was none too flattering.

"Laute Halsabschneider!". It translates to a bunch of cutthroats. Thank you.

Years later it made be known Uncle Sam didn't think much of French and British obsession with Serbian empire. Those Russian anti-tank weapons were crucial in putting a stop to the onslought of Serbian armour previously unchecked. The Americans would later on bring in shiploads of weapons. But just then in 1993, it took somone with balls to do the job. The Bangla Deshi knew the background and were suitably impressed. Said more so. He came close to volunteer for Bosnian war effort.

Hamoud's self confidence was back. He'll get that **Wozungu** and the infidel bitch.....So the foreigner thought he was realy smart. And that yacht. S o u n i o n.? From Sydney Australia. Sounds like some commie SOB as well. Had he done Greek mythology he should have known better. Sounion was the birth place of Poseidon, the Greek sea God. No matter. He was on top of things once more. He felt elated and dizzy as if he'd drank a bottle of wine. He was in fact drunk on his perception of success.

All this was to be rudely put in place by his crew. Said finaly mustered sufficient fortitude to inform Hamoud about the listening bugs and the HF reacon. It was as if a bomb had gone off. Nothing short of it would have cut the air as deadly. Hamoud was speechless for a good while all that cheer and good humour was visibly draining from his posture.

"Bloody hell!" He exploded." What bloody radio transmitter?" He wanted to see it himself. Rajid signalled to him to stay quiet. They moved to top deck out of the listening bugs reach until under open sky.

"Why wasn't I told about this before?"

"Well Skip, we didn't see eye to eye on this, to be honest." Said played it stright.   "As it was, we only found out yesterday. Now we are with you Skip. We're all in the same pickle, 'xcept we'd want to be consulted from now on."

Hamoud thought hard and while still raging appeared to regain composure. He spun around to face them close up.

"In the pickle together, I heard you say. I think I like that. But that Ngezi. I under-rated the **Donga**. Next he brought the crew up to speed on information gained at the last anchorage. Four days start was no problem, but which way was the yacht heading? Back to Dar? That sailor had done what was least expected once. Was he likely to do it again?"

"No, I don't think so." Said thought he had the answer.

"And why not?"

"He knew to expect persuit on the way to Dar from Zanzibar. Now he is close to reaching open Indian Ocean." Said continued on his theory." He could be anywhere. An ocean going yacht is just that. Even a cruising yacht compotently handled can go close to wind nowdays. He is bound to be full of confidence. No more hide and seek. I say he could be just about anywhere."

"I beg to disagree." Hamoud objected." For start this anywhere bit. There is no such a place. Navigation means setting a course. Power or sail. No difference. And if the course is set it has to lead to a place. And a place has to have a name. I am convinced he'll do it again. He will set out the course least expected and do what he shouldn't be doing. One crafty SOB."

"You mean head back for mainland and Dar? I agree with Said Captain." That was Rajid's contribution." He could be anywhere."

"Thanks for reminding me to contact Hassan at the Yacht Club. He'll be onto them like a flash." That did it for Hamoud. Next he got hold of his chart table contents. Weather maps , wind calendar distribution , and Indian Ocean charts. The men studied all this intently. Finaly Hamoud concluded.

"I am convinced **Wozungu** is heading back for Australia. A long haul and not simple, but that alone makes any sense for one in his position. He has no choice but to head back. He is heading back to Oz with his new paramour. And that unless I've got the charts all wrong has to be via Seychelles and likely Sri Lanka. And he'd have to re-suply somewhere in Seychelles. As it is there is one official entry only. Victoria on Mahe'. And that's where we boys are off to. We carry sufficient fuel to do it at most economic speed of 18 Kn."

"Wait Captain". Rajid protested. You are saying one point of entry for the whole archipelago? What you mean of course is one legal point of entry. In his place I wouldn't even consider it for that very reason. It is too obvious. A yacht can pull in virtualy anywhere. As long as it is discretely done. And the wind is not on the nose. I've done a bit of sailing myself. Racing of course. I agree with you. He has set sail for Oz, but I am more inclined to see him landing around Farquhar in the Amirantes Group. If at all. With enough on board he can even try non stop to Sri Lanka. Is she likely to slow him down? I don't know. And another thing Captain. What is to be done with Ngezi's implants?"

Said suggested they leave the emitter on the island with one of the batteries. Rajid told him it wouldn't work without a proper balasted antenae. In any case , HF sets power consumption would drain a battery in days. Hamoud decided to leave it alone. What was Ngezi going to do out of his territorial waters juristiction? And what was he to use to catch up with Morning Glory's 1200 miles range? A Navy destroyer? Forget it.

Decision made, Hamoud settled the craft at 18 Kn heading for Amirantes Group. He wound up the radar to maximum gain and ordered watches at four hourly turns. Then withdrew into his cabin not feeling well. Before dawn he managed to struggle up the bridge during Said's watch. What he saw didn't please him one bit. He was pointing to a pile of dirty dishes.

"This ship used to be spit and polish. Starting to look more like Culcutta slums now. Just look at the mess! Said, man, how long before somebody does the dishes.?"

"Listen Skip." Said tried in a defensive tone at first." Since Moos is gone, well, you know, this is woman's work. Not chores for an officer."

Hamoud could not belive what he was hearing. But times had changed. He needed these men more than ever before. And they knew it. As no response came Said decided he'd done enough damage and decided to smoothen out the rhetoric.

"Why don't you retire and catch some sleep Skip. You don't look too good. We'll sort this out by the time you return. Then we can hold some man to men talk. OK?"   Hamoud nodded in acknowledgment and returned to his cabin looking for sea sickness pills.

The cousins tossed a coin for the dubious priviledge of doing dishes. It ended with Rashid looking for the f....g detergent. It didn't end there. Hours later, with daylight to assist, dishes all done and admirality brass on high polish, Hamoud turned up. Once he saw what the boys had done he felt elated. They wouldn't let him down. He was now certain of it. Sadly, replacement for Moos was hard to find. Instead the world according to Hamoud was these days stacked with smart Alec imposters. Decorated with degrees and certificates and full of hot shit. They'd seen it all on the box, or read it in the paper. They knew everything. They just had to Google it first. In reality they knew little to be of use...Full of fair weather sailors who melted to butter at the first sign of smoke...Sure, the machines were getting better, but quality of your men had gone the opposite way...Even so, he still had two of the best. In the past he'd never been known to go overboard on praize, only to go one better now.

"Right men. Let me offer you a drink." Although both Moslem they'd been for too long contaminated with Western indulgence to refuse.

"A shot of Chivers with soda, that's fine Skip." Said raised the glass. Rajid was in two minds. What was the old fox up to? He was acting out of his character. Until now he kept aloof. A master figure. As to answer him Hamoud raised the toast.

"Cheers to you men." He promised from now on they'd be consulted in decision making." From now on we'll be opcrating as a team." As the akward silence fell, Said decided to have a say, only to find a dry throat. So he took another gulp of the drink.

"That's all very well said Skip. We are happy to hear you appreciate our work. Yeah, that was fine, but what was all that goose chase about?" The words hit Hamoud where it hurts. Never mind, he had a ready answer.

"I see your point Said. Can't you see we are in danger for as long as she is there to testify? She has to be silenced."

Rajid watched all this shaking head. This was too clever by half.

"Quit frankly Captain, wether she lives or not this to us doesn't seem to be important, much less a big deal. If she killed Moos as you first said, Police would be the last place she'd want to see. And if it came before court it is our word against hers. Three to one. Any advocate would deal with this...

By the way, I had some fun with those listening bugs and cassettes." Proud of his handiwork Rajid was facing Hamoud with confidence. And Hamoud was proud of his crew when he should have known better. His men were deserving to be told the truth. But this Hamoud could not do. He feared Sheik Ibn above all. He knew if he crossed Ibn or failed to deliver, Ibn would get him. Nowhere on God's Earth was he safe if he failed to deliver Aisha. Ngezi was very capable in his work as he was finding out, but no more than a nuisance in comparison with Ibn. There were reports of men begging to be put out of their misery and released from his torturous interogation. Expenses to men like Ibn are meaningless. They always get their victims in the end. Bribe Achangel Gabriel if all fails.

Trying for something more cheerfull Hamoud gave them a bonus and promised to pay for the R&R expenses in Seychelles. And what the Creole belles could do was known far and wide. It was the stuff of the old sea chanties and nothing had changed there.

It wasn't long before Hamoud started to feel quizzy. Scotch didn't help. For all of his years aboard the open ocean swell would test Hamoud. Now bouncing at 18 Kn into a meter swell made it worse. He left Rajid in charge of the bridge and retired. Before long Rajid got tired of radar noises picking sea birds set at max gain. So he turned it right down to min gain. A costly mistake. Soon the tropical night fell. They motored for another day and night and passed a number of freighters and fishing trawlers. All fat radar targets. No sign of the yacht. Not on that radar setting. Hamoud stayed sick in the cabin. On the third morning they motored into Farquhar Lagoon. Legal point of entry or not. All of them dog beat, and Hamoud very relaxed about bending the rules in any case.

* * *

Having taken all of this down Vivian decided to call it a day.They would continue tomorrow on what unraveled in the Seychelles.

* * *

Intercept of Hamoud's phone conversation with Hassan landed on Ngezi's desk. The net was closing in. Monies deposited on Nairoby Backleys' account were also traced to a large Austrian bank. Interpol had satellite observed position of Morning Glory at Farquhar Lagoon passed on to Ngezi. For Inspector Ngezi this was no longer an enigma. It was like a mozaic with last few marbles left to fit in. The fact Hamoud was after an Australian registred yacht Sounion was a major breakthrough.

How Moostafa perished and Aisha got away had still to be determined. Sounion's skipper was a person of interest. So Ngezi got going with the routine Police bread and butter stuff. A port after port along the African East coast had no record of the yacht. From as far as Djibouti to Mombasa, and smaller ports, the answer was the same. Somali waters were out of question. Shifta bandits ruled there. This created a new headache. Failure to declare and clear ports was a serious offense. Yacht ceasure and prison sentence almost the norm for those cought. It follows one would not risk it , unles carrying drugs or weapons. This made Ngezi dig deeper. He checked with Australian Federal Police HQ in Canberra. They let him wait on the line while cross checking their records. Report faxed to Ngezi read:

'Darwin Port Authority stamped departure of an Australian Reg.Ship Sounion on 02.03.1998 at 11.47 hrs. Skippered, it read, by one Maximillian Horvat. Naturalised Australian, aged 44. A scientist and a writer. No criminal record. Crew of one. Next declared port of call Galle, Sri Lanka.'

Justifiably with high hopes, Ngezi got in touch with Sri Lanka's Galle, then Colombo. Neither had any records of the yacht. Ngezi was now back to where he started. What to do next? He got up from the desk chair and walked up towards the window overlooking the Lutheran Church. Buildt by the Germans pre WW1 and across the wide street. Nobody until now ever lifted a finger to maintain the building since the Germans got expelled. Cracks of the ochre coloured plaster were growing ever larger. This was to change for the better and we have Ngezi to thank for it. These days the Lutheran Church is one of Dar's architectural attractions.

He was pensive for a while before a gang of idle African youth cought his disapproval. Dressed in dirty rags, they'd been squatting for hours pefectly relaxed and passing around a gundja reefer.

"How can Africa ever hope to prosper." Despodent Ngezi sighed to himself.

* * *

CHAPTER TWELVE

BACK ON COURSE

Bouncing about in a small craft over open ocean installs in one respect for the row power of elements. It teaches one humility and respect for other creatures. It also puts human inter-relationship into a more practical frame. On land where most of us feel safe and cacooned in modern existence it can take a life time to realy get to know a person.

Confined within a small yacht at sea, it happens much faster. For start, Spartan living quaters offer no place to hide. One's weaknesses soon show up. Routine sets in after a day or two, and watch times and meal duties while under canvas become established. One soon gets to anticipate the next meal. No matter how meager the ingredients. Then there are rewards one only finds on open ocean waters. Night watch under clear sky for one. Southern Hemisphere's brilliance, an experience denied to a city dweller. Star gazing is infectious. One gets to phantasise of other worlds, other intelligent life and the Maker. Order or chaos. Which was the Nature's way? Did the laws of thermodynamics hold throughout the Universe? Max would spend hours remeniscing in the open cockpit and feeling priviledged to view the spectacle.

He tried his best to arrange some degree of privacy for Aisha. She was given the forecastle, right next to a washing basin. He would spend most time on watch or asleep on the floor boards. For one, sound travels faster through water and yacht's hull acts as an amplifier. It dawned on Max just how painfully noisy our sea traffic must be to whales and dolphins.

Of course the pair were concious at all times they were on the run trying to outsmart the enemy. Every day from now on was a guessing game. What was the mangy mongrel up to next? Max would ask himself. Their one advantage above all was the range. With water tanks full and some food they could stay away from shore. Not so Morning Glory. She had to refuel. As Aisha turned into a most capable crew Max got bolder in plans and decided without telling her to head stright for Equator on a NE course. Sooner or later they were bound to run into doldrums, counter currents and the rest, but Hamoud would by then be left behind. A yacht can and some had done it sail around the world non stop. Of course those sailors were much better equiped. For him just reaching Sri Lanka from here would have been an achievement. It is not a recognised sea route and for good reasons.

Then a third night out, laying on floor boards Max picked a sound of engines. Soon Aisha could hear it. She fearfuly walked up to Max and shaking assisted him to rise up.

"Morning Glory!" She pronounced panick stricken.

"How could she be sure?"

"Those engines. How can I ever forget!" This got Max up into cockpit in a flash.

There he saw the cruiser's mast lights, still miles away and closing. On present course it was going to pass them pretty close and upwind. Max let the sails out on a run. The farther away from the cruiser's course the lesser the chance of being picked up by their radar. Even so the best he could do was not far enough. Max knew anyone alert on duty would have him. Sure the radar reflector removal helped his cause. Sailing without nav lights was also prudent, but luck was to save them in the end. Morning Glory's crew put an s in front, ie they screwed up. Rajid after a long watch was half asleep and had the radar gain turned right down. To their relief Morning Glory continued on the same course without a propeller revolution dropped. This told Max they remained unobserved for now.

"How about we turn back?" He suggested. It made sense now.

"No!...No, please Max." She would rather die. This left him no choice but to continue. They reversed to previous NE course, trimmed the sails and found the wind was getting more and more on the nose. Finaly towards morning Max had the yacht as close to wind as she would go, and a very uncomfortable heel to put up with. That rig was under tremendous load. They sailed on at hull speed punching into the swell. At dawn a chatter of sea gulls alerted Max to scan for land. Sure, at first just the green palm tree tops and more sea birds riding on the thermals gave the direction. Then the sound of the heavy surf pounding into the coral reef on the port beam, and a line of breakers confirmed it. That had to be the Farquhar in the Amirantes. Max was pleased with the progress they made until the disaster struck. The tragedy to change everythig struck without warning.

Middle shroud on the port side snapped under full load. It went off like a bullet and shook the boat into convulsions. But for Aisha's instant reaction mast would most probably come down. In the cockpit at the time, she instantly luffed. It allowed Max time to furl the genoa in and bring the mainsail down. On examination he found the weak spot. Chain plate Norse fitting holding a 19 strand cable showed only four still had metallic shine before failure. Anodic corrosion and fatigue had eaten through the rest. Stainless steel wonderful material that it is suffers from these shortcomings. This changed everything. Now there was no choice but to land on engine power and look for help inside the Farquhar Lagoon they spotted in the morning. Under full power the Nord Ile channel entrance markers were at last in view. Ideally he would have prefered a night time landing, but there was no choice. After hours of motoring they entered the lagoon. Rounding the deep water channel and passing the warf, Aisha froze once more as she saw Morning Glory tied up to the jetty. Max forced himself to appear unperturbed and kept on motoring under steady throtle. Quietly running BMW engine was a blessing He kept on motoring around the next channel dog leg that put them out of line of sight. He anchored finaly almost on top of the shallows. As far as a keel yacht could venture on low tide and still be safe.

Morning Glory's crew arrived in the night and were at the time in the marina's office negotiating the price for rights of passage with *Monsignor* Rene, manager of the defunct copra plantation and the Law on the island. They were fully absorbed in huggling. Hamoud negotiating as hard as he could. He was paying in dollars after all, and not rupees.

Riding on anchor in eleven feet of water Max was busy examining the damage. Not only was the repair at best a make do arrangement. All of the standing rig's fitness was under cloud. What was to snap next? Or was he too fussy. Most islanders indulge in seat of the pants sailing. Only we in the West look for perfection. But we are what we are.

Insurance companies now demand a stainless rig be replaced regulary every eight years. It costs bucket loads of money to mantain a so called maintance free vessel. Monies he could not afford. Sounions rig when failed had stood up for 29 years. The rig failure was deadly in that it caused them to enter into a pocket. They were in a trap. Having illegaly entered was the least of the worries. Max swore loud in Croatian. Something he had not done for years. This was the low point.

Hours later, his resolve to fight the fate and his enemy grew stronger. He'd been in tight spots before, and he wasn't beaten yet. Desperate times call for inventive solutions. That much he knew from his war time escapades. Here they were entitled to some hope of remaining undiscovered until something hopefuly turned up. Against that, sooner or later they were sure to be found. Besides, just hoping is no way to fight. Soberly assesed, he was no match for Hamoud. Outnumbered, outgunned and now outmanouvred as well. Sure, some of it was just plain bad luck. Perhaps he was due for some good luck. Or was that dose already given in slack radar operation? Max came to the conlusion he had to even out the odds. He had to make use of one trump he still possesed. Hamoud didn't know they were here, or else he would have been onto them already. Max new that the element of suprise was to be used if he stood any chance. He'd seen in Bosnia what damage a handful of under-resoursed well motivated and led men can inflict on a batallion of heavily armed soldiers with their pants down.

Paramount to his improving the odds was putting Morning Glory out of action. Sink, or at least disable the craft and he had a fighting chance. But how? He knew enough about modern explosives as well as make-do stuff. But there was neither Semtec nor ammonium nitrate here. Not to speak of fuses and capsules. That got him searching through odds and ends lockers and paint cabinets. Petrol would have been useful but there was no point in stocking petrol since the last outboard was stolen. Now he had none. All this was enough to stop most people. Not Max. When on the verge of giving up he stumbled on a 2 liter half full can of #3 Polyurethane paint thinners left overs from the last top deck spray job.

#3 does to PVC plastic what water does to sugar. He found out the hard way once. And it is highly flammable. Read highly explosive fumes mixed with air in all proportions.

Experiments with 19 mm dia PVC off cuts took less then 15 minutes for solvent to break out. There was the idea! Stopper a short length of 19 mmPVC tube, fill it with #3 and stopper it on the other end. Place the device into the exhaust pipe of Hamoud'd cruiser and plug the exhaust pipe. Then wait for the first spark of the starter motor to set it off.

If it all worked out he had sufficient time to withrow in safety before the fireworks. There was a distinct possibility this would not come off. For a number of reasons. But what choice did he have? To just sit back and pray? No way. He prepared all the gear he had and decided to wait for darkness. Until then they had to lay low.

With sunset fading fast Max launched the Metzeler Aztec rubber dinghy. One inflatable design that rowes well. He rounded the hide out point in rhythmic action and headed stright for the cruiser. Her position had changed, now on anchor in the deep water channel. In his favour a cloudy sky presented a cover of darkness. Rowing closer towards the cruiser he could hear voices aboard. It was a call for the dinner table. Max gave it a last look then closed in to do the job. All accomplished in a minute and he was ready for getaway, when only a short distance away still, he could hear an outboard motor.

It had to be Hamoud returning from a social call to Rene, where he also met the Botha couple. Dr Marcus got a hint of Hamoud's line of business and made it clear he disapproved in strongest terms.

The Bothas, Marc and Jean arrived a few days before in a Bertram 35 cruiser, hired from Mahe'. For Hamoud the only bright spot was Rene's house maid Sharon. A cheeky little devil. But that will have to wait.

Approaching the davits, Hamoud got a nose full of that fish curry. All those blasted people could cook seemed to be curries. For an instant he thought there was something else in the air, a sweetish scent, but then dismissed the speculation. It didn't matter. Then he spotted it. A piece of something white close by and slowly sinking. He called out for a boat hook. Rashid was first to the scene with a boat hook and recovered the object then handed it over to Hamoud.

'Lawrie's Marina, Maloolooba. Sunny Qeensland.' It read on the baseball cap. Hamoud was jubilant.

"They are here! Drop me back in . He was half way up being winched on the davits.

"Quiet, not a sound!" he commanded. Rashid obeyed. Even so they could not hear a sound, other than an owl overhead. They had no idea Max was on oars. Puzzled Hamoud started his outboard and began at speed to circle the area. Until low on fuel and torch battery close to empty. He was furious with frustration. Once more the **Wozungu** got away. Or did he? He cannot be too far away. How did we miss him in the first place? This time there'll be no fooling around. No half measures. We'll get the Morning Glory with her powerful search lights going. When found, shoot just under the water line. We'll fish her out of water. And as for him? He's broken that many laws I don't think there will be questions asked. Just do a clean job and leave the lagoon without delay. That Rene is not stupid enough to give us a chase.

For his part Max knew, having lost his cap overboard, the element of suprise was gone. Hamoud was onto him. In fact came close to run over him. Fortunately, Hamoud was searching on starboard side as all right handers tend to do. On every occassion Hamoud took a fast turn, Max would row like hell, try to remain to port . Then over the chop towards the centre of the circle and head for the shallows. It was like a cobra and a moongose dance. Darkness helped no doubt. As Hamoud gave up and returned to Morning Glory, Max once more got to row. Back to Sounion on the reverse compass bearing.

Hamoud was highly strung and ordered Said to get the cruiser under way. He was not going to see **Wozungu** escape in the night.

"Leave the dishes and the curry for now! What spice was that sweet smelling shit anyway?"

Said thought to snatch a packet of Marlbhoro from his cabin first , then continued on the way to the engine room. Even with the cigarette lit in his mouth he could pick that faint sweet smell of paint thinners. Not alltogether unpleasant, so he chose to ignore it.

He went to start the engines as ordered and it was the last thing Said remembered doing. The explosion ripped one diesel's exhaust apart and cracked the hull in places. Flying shrapnell cought Said and a flame burst burnt his eyebrows and some hair. The same force also ripped the davits clean from the stern . The allloy dinghy was back in the water again.

Rajid who was aft at the time of explosion taking care of his kidneys discharge and picked the fresh paint smell as well, trying to remember the last paint job, when the superstructure lifted clean and tossed him into the deep water below. A poor swimmer that he was, Rajid began wildly to thresh the surface desperate to reach the shore. Just as he felt the goal was reached and touched the ground, a juvenile tiger shark, every bit as aggressive as a fuly grown one locked his jaws on Rajid's calf muscle and tried to drag him back into the deep water. Rajid fought it screaming and with closed fists. It only let go when hit in one eye and nearly on dry land.

This left Hamoud on bridge at the time busy on power anchor winch. He stopped for a moment, then felt the blast and the explosion. He turned back only to sea his beloved Morning Glory on fire. Next one diesoline tank cought on. Not that fibreglass needed help in combustion. It was clear to Hamoud the automatic sprinkler system had comprehensively failed. These much hyped gadgets will drench your bread toaster and work well in orchestrated demonstrations. Not so good in emergencies.

Now a chocking black smoke threatened. One could survive this for minutes at the most. Hamoud summed it up, took a few deep breaths of air and raced into his cabin. Water was rushing in covering the floor boards. He raced to lockers holding valuables and guns and on the way out spotted Said laying on the floor motionless. Where others might have panicked and left everything running for dear life, Hamoud knew what to do. He draged Said to the deck, returned once more for the guns and pulled the inflation plug on four men Zodiac life raft. Said was slowly regaining his senses.The pair managed through acrid smoke to launch the life raft then dive into the water after it.

To his next suprise Hamoud found himself next to a freed alloy dinghy, the outboard still attached. Given the choice he boarded the dinghy. Reserves of petrol were enough to reach the shore with the life raft in tow.

The explosion and fire on board soon brought Rene and Bothas racing to the shore. There was nothing they could do. Marc went one further . He suggested when fooling around with guns and explosives, that's what you get. That of course did not deter him from expertly applying first aid and surgery...

It took another ten minutes at the most and the cruiser sank out of sight.

Now the odds of survival fighting against his enemy stacked up against Hamoud. It was one on one from here on. All the advantages once in his favour were gone. Hamoud knew that better than anyone. Oh, how he hated that **Wozungu***!* But wait! He wasn't finished yet. Armed with ample cash, Rene in his pocket, or so he thought, Hamoud was more than ever determined to go after the impertinent foreigner. This was to be a fight to the end. Until there was only one of them left standing.

All this had to wait for daylight.....

Back on Sounion Max climbded aboard fully spent. Aisha couldn't wait to hear what happened. She saw the sky light up and heard the explosion, but what was the final outcome? He was in no position to be certain but had good reason to belive Morning Glory was out of action. Damaged or sunk. It didn't matter. Anything else had to wait. And he was certain the Morning Glory crew would come looking for him. No matter. He was ready for them. He went down below and unpacked the mothballed old WWI Lee-Enfield rifle he bought cheeply from an Army disposal store. Single shot but deadly accurate at long range. He cleaned out the barrel and checked out the gun. It was in working order. He loaded the magazine and took off the safety, then left the gun ready to fire laying in the cockpit.

They took four-hourly watches all night and turned off all lights, alert to any suprise. None came in the night, but around first daylight Aisha woke him up. There was an outboard motor she could hear and it was getting closer. Before long the 4.5 meters alloy dinghy turned around the point heading for them. Through the binoculars Max saw the Somali for the first time in his life. Hamoud had what looked from the distance like an M16 placed on the bow before him. Now the war was on.

Hamoud spotted his adversary and based on experience judged he had little chance of a direct hit .Instead aimed for the yacht with a long burst. Bullets ripped into the Sounion's stern port side and he could hear metalic pinge of a bullet hitting the diesel engine somewhere.

Max aimed but overshot. He took more care aiming next time with the dinghy riding the swell, and aiming for the chest and not head as previously. The next bullet hit Hamoud in the chest and made him slump to port side. The M16 fell overboard and the unbalanced dinghy at first still on high speed did a few uncontroled clockwise turns approaching closer to the yacht at times and in fact drawing a torroid locus. There Hamoud's grip let go. Dinghy slowed to idling speed and appeared to be heading for shallows away from Sounion. To Max this signaled the danger was over. But he couldn't hang around. There was a burst fuel pump leaking precious diesolene into the bilge. He could smell it. To reach the fuel connection he had to crawl on his side then squizze in a tight area between the engine and the shattered fuel filter. It was so tight in there it took a long time before he could reach the connection and that was with left hand only. Bullets that ripped the fibreglas allowed some light in. Then the unexpected happened. A tragedy that none could foresee comming.

Hamoud in his last act of defiance raised his head to spot direction of Sounion. Then with a superhuman effort got hold of the throttle and gunned the outboard full speed heading Kamikaze style for Sounion's weakened side.

"See you in Hell ***Wozungu*!**"

He uttered to himself. Aisha was terified, too slow to react. By the time she called out to Max it was only seconds away to disaster. Max couldn't withrow out of the pocket in time. Dinghy's bow rammed into the Sounion's side with such a force shattered fibreglass shreds cought Max on the throat and sliced his neck artery. Aisha became hysterical. Not helped by the fact the jammed dinghy kept rotating Sounion about the anchor chain. This went on until the outboard ran out of fuel. Hamoud's motionelss body lay slumped over the controls.

Meanwhile others were on the way to the scene of carnage and closing in fast.

Rene's pilot boat with Ngezi and Thomba aboard was the first to arrive. By then the dinghy's outboard coughed a few times to signal it was out of petrol. This allowed for easy boarding. What they saw sent Rene to snap and loose control. Aisha was still screaming and Max was covered in blood fading out fast. Hamoud's lifeless body lay in the dinghy. Rene at this point just lost his marbles.

For months he'd been keeping vigil at his wife's bedside. Beatrice, a Flamish redhead could never adjust to the tropics. Rene adored his wife and suffered more than he'd ever admit. Beatrice was diagnosed late with melanoma. Too late for surgery. Now this...There comes a point where a breaking point is reached. Any man's. The myth about superheros in B grade movies is just that. It's only that different people have different thresholds of pain tolerance. Rene's had been reached. All of his life work was getting undone in front of his eyes. His once peaceful island had become a crime scene with mayhem all around. His wife suffered on morphium dose high enough to bring down a rhino. He just could not take any more of this.

"Shut up woman!" He turned to Aisha. ***"Mon Dieu!** And you two!*

"Who told you to carry guns on my island? I am the Law here. Pass me those pistols over here! "He demanded. And to underline seriousness of the intent, he took the safety off on his pistol and started brandishing the weapon wildly. From experiance Ngezi knew it was no good to argue and antagonise the man. It was pontless in any case. Hamoud was dead, Aisha free, and all he had to do now was to write a report with few fingerprints and photographs to prove it, then close the case. Thomba did all the camera work. As for Hamoud they could burry him here or feed him to the blue pointer undertakers. Ngezi just wanted this over. The mortaly injured sailor implicated in murder, and God knows what else was as good as dead. That also simplified a lot of paper work. As for Aisha, she could fly back with them. All of the cosy summation came soon undone for Ngezi.

Bent over bleeding Max Aisha was trying to stem the blood loss. She had blood on her hands and clothes. Max tried to make her reach for the fist aid kit. Finaly she understood. Clumsily she applied bandage. It did little if any good. Then she cried out.

"Don't just stand there you men!

"It was no use." Ngezi told her. He needed expert medical attention. She eventualy accepted that, then turned to Ngezi with a new demand.

"Com'on John. Marry us! I am expecting a child I am certain. I don't want it to be called a bastard."

Stunned as he was, Ngezi a JP thought that was the least he could do. And he had done this many times before. As a routine he used to carry cheap one size fits all gold plated rings with him. But this had to be brief. Rene was once more into French obscenities. And more unpredictable by the minute.

"All right. Let's do it." He went down on one knee and asked Aisha to do the same. He asked still concious Max first if he was willing to mary Aisha to receive back a nod. He asked Aisha if she accepted Max as a lawful wedded husband till death do us part. She loudly answered in affirmative. Ngezi joined their blood stained hands and proclaimed them man and wife. She broke down sobbing and bent over Max to kiss his blood smeared lips.

Rene could take no more. He pulled Aisha up by force and ordered them to clear the yacht. Once more Ngezi urged Thomba to remain calm. This was way out of their base. They moved back onto the pilot boat with aluminium dinghy in tow and heading back for the Plantation jetty.

As the second party left the yacht scene the third one wasn't far off.

* * *

Jean Botha aboard the Bertram 35 heard first the Beechcraft plane landing. Later shots being fired and following the Morning Glory sinking previous night decided they had enough. This was supposed to be a holiday. Not a war scene they came for. They came to relax not to fight. Only to observe Rene join with two strangers Ngezi and Thomba boarding the pilot boat tied up next to Bertram 35. The pilot boat hurriedly motored away on full throttle heading for the lagoone, and out of sight. Dr Marcus Botha looked at his wife pleading for understanding.

"No, Marc, no please. It is enough. You patched up those two last night. We are leaving." She insisted.

"I may be the only doctor for this Archipelago. How can I just pretend nobody needs me with shots being fired. There are bound to be casualties."

She looked at him.

"My big hero husband. How can I not agree." She mocked Marc. This was an ongoing battle and Jean never won yet. Now she was resigned to it. Jean deeply loved and appreciated her husband.

Marc checked out his emergency kit. It was in order. Thermostated at right temperature. Now they would join the battle field and see if help was really needed.

Marc instructed Jean to take the wheel and stay at five knots over a deep water channel. He took a game fishing rod and dropped a bare hook into the stream. They arrived close to the dog leg point to see pilot boat returning for the Plantation jetty.

"Let them go Jean until out of sight!" Jean cought on. Next on full throttle it took only minutes to reach by now slowly sinking Sounion. The withrown dinghy left a big gap in the cracked hull with waves splashing over it. The bilge was already overflowing when they tied up alongside. From here on it was all first aid action.

They carried unconcious Max onto the Bertram35 where Marc went to lightning speed work and Jean assisting. A couple of expertly placed staples and stiches stopped the blood loss. But by then Max had lost so much blood Marc could not detect his heart beat. This was critical. Marc gave him all the serum he had and still no good. Max urgently needed a blood transfusion. Not knowing his blood group it was not on....Until Jean stepped in.

"I'll give him mine. 'O', the universal donor that she was. Marc rigged the transfusion and took close to a litre of Jean's blood. At last Max's heart beat could be faintly felt. Marc placed him under a cryogenic blanket and oxygen mask, then looked up beaming with pride at his spouse.

"In all the years I've known you I have never loved you more."

"The same here." She returned the compliment." Now I supose I'll have to clean up the mess. I feel a bit weak. There was blood all over the place.

"Yes please, while it is still fresh, while I go over and see if anything of importance can be salvaged before she sinks." Inside Sounion's quarters he recovered a sextant, Stainer's binoculars, documents, money and a photo album. It was too late for much else. Water was now freely rushing in. Floor boards were afloat. Before long 5.5 tones of lead keel won over and and gently settled the yacht in mud under 20 feet of water. The mast from bottom spreaders up was the only sign of a once ocean going yacht.

They departed the scene, continued on reverse course and past the Plantation jetty. Marc still seated in game fishing chair trawling a bare hook at five knots.

Upon reaching open waters they set course for Praslin Island. The nearest supply point. Marc at first had not the faintest idea as to who the man was. Nor why he was left for dead. All this had to wait for Max' explanation.

Over the next five days Max continued a rapid recovery gaining on lost weight. He also ate like a starved lion. By then Bothas got to know the story. They had to return to Mahe' Victoria and fly back to Jo'burg. Their holydays were over. Marc returned to Max all he managed to salvage from sinking Sounion and repeatedly refused any monetary compensation.

"You two leave me speechless." Max was lost for words of gratitude." I owe you my life, nothing short of it. Maybe one day, I hope I'll be able to do something for you in return."

He did just that only days later, as they parted company at Victoria's Airport. Max bought a one way ticket on Air Seychelles to Jo'burg. A ticket he was never to make use of but land in jail instead....

* * *

Here Vivian for once begged him to stop. She was simply overcome with emotion.

"My God, all this in one life time!"

"You havn't heard half of it yet. Should I go on.?"

"Do so please. Get it out of your system. Remember the shrink? Once for all time! Tell me what do you think starts a war."

"Oh, you're not asking a lot. But it is OK. I'll try my best and hope it does as you promised and rids me of my nightmares. We go to war next. Real war."

* * *

CHAPTER THIRTEEN

ABOUT WARS AND SAVAGES

Anno Domini MMII. Towards the end of the year the war drums were getting louder again as was the misinformation from the spin doctors. Price of gold and crude oil was on the rise, and Genneral Sharon forecast there'd be oil at $5 a barell. First of course one had to bring democratic sense to the Arabs and make them see the oil was no good. Only making them a target.

As it is, we don't seem to be able to function without a war somewhere on the planet. It seems war and not peace has become the natural state. Peace is what happens by default in between wars. Here the zealots and fundamentalists of all creeds find themselves in agreement. So what is war?

'War is continuation of diplomacy by other means.' According to Karl von Clausewitz. A Prussian noble and master tactitian.

'War is an unfortunate fact.' The comment came from Lt.General Peter Cosgrove, saviour of East Timor. A soldiers' soldier.

"**War is hell.**' That is how General William Tekhumse Sherman saw it first hand in the blood bath of 1862 at Shylo. A victor in tears.

Those who fought and suffered, those who became widows and orphans, it seems   they don't get asked. Even so, General Sherman was closest to the mark. **War IS hell.** Against that there are others exolting war.

'*War brings in men the best and the worst.*' As if there could be some noble quality in what is nothing but licence to kill and destroy. Soldiers of all armies are drilled in cold blood the science of killing. And if doomed to perish themselves to take as many enemy with them as possible.

On a higher level, it is for the victors to take posession.Write one sided history bestsellers and to multiply. The best the vanquished can hope for is mercy. It is Darwinian in a nut shell. Survival of the fittest. Wars serve as a crucible where those decaying and weak societies not serious about defence eventually go under and end up as scrap iron in casting of new order.

And when the returned soldiers come home as damaged goods, broken in spirit from foreign wars trying in vain to get on with their civilian lives, one can only shudder to think how much worse off are civilian casualties. Those left in the wake of carpet bombings, the napalm, phosphorous, cluster bombs and the rest.

And herein is the true nature of war. It is all about destruction, individual suffering on a scale beyond comprehension, and about cold blooded licenced murder.

Stuff all to do with democratic principles and the like. And the religions don't help. Take the commandement:'*THOU SHALT NOT KILL!*'

Who has't heard of it? It is present in all religions. Clearly, there are no exceptions. The commandement is clear. There can be no qualifiers like 'For God and King', or 'Gott mit uns', just to mention a few. In spite of this two millenia of Christendom have been written in blood. As often as not the sword and the cross have marshaled the forces together in wars of succession and conquest that have no end. And if once exuses of illiteracy and ignorance masked the guilt, has our information explosion improved the moral fibre? Not on the evidence available.

Once or so in a generation a collective outcry against the bloody business of war comes to surface, only to wither away under the pressures of modern living. Vietnam war was a case in point. Thousands went AWOL. Others rebelled, finaly those in power got the message and pulled out the troops. But not before millions were killed, maimed or countries destroyed, and for what?

So the war making machine could get new weapons and guns, more deadly than ever. And so the weapons suppliers and greedy war profiteers can make more money. Meanwhile we the public are deceived. An intrepid reporter in Vietnam came across a scene:

> On the banks of Perfumed river
> Lay charred remains of
> Eight buffalos
> Two pregnant women and
> Lorry packed with school children.
> All murdered in the napalm inferno this morning.

Describing the same scene General Westmoreland's communiqué read,
'Hue, South Vietnam, 53 Viet Kong killed in action this morning.' And there was no mention of the collateral damage.

The same spin if not worse continues to pollute the media to this day.

Homo modernicus, of the Silicon valley is in the ascendancy. Might is right.

Others are taking note. Not of what our propaganda in the West peddles ad noseum, but taking note of what we do. Muslim fundamentalists obsessed with thirst for revenge have taken it up another notch or more in mindless brutality. And there is no end in sight.

The seeds of the cursed wars and brutality are lost somewhere in the distant past. But one has to ask. Would it have made a difference if we and our forefathers had been less prepared to accept calls in the past to kill our fellow men for no good reason. Would it have made a difference if we'd taken our religion more to the heart?

Take the war cry to the Christian soldiers. Christian? Yes. Soldier? Yes.But soldiers are trained to kill. The commandements are clear. Christian soldier is a concientious objector. Christian soldiers? Seriously? Try again.

We Cristians invented this one. Now zealots and fundamentalists of other creeds come up with their versions of bigotry. As if to pay us back with vengeance and thirst for more innocent blood. The human kind has lost the plot. If anyone is hopeful in the next major conflict the loosing side will meekly surrender and not unlish a nuclear holocaust, they have failed to learn from history.

And left for last my Lord, why is our power to hate and destroy out of all proportions to our limited capacity to share and love one another. How can we obey Thy commandements when the dark forces rule our daly lives. The lost children of Thy creation of all creeds are desperately searching for an answer. All we seem to be assured of is there is going to be more wars. A war to end all wars. WW2, then wars of desintegration in Yugoslavia, Africa, Asia... Always one more war... If you are listening somewhere in the n-th dimension, we beg you Lord. Have mercy and go back to the drawing board. Re-design the beast, please!

* * *

CHAPTER FOURTEEN

THE GREAT SERBIAN REICH

For the third time in fifty years, USA under Clinton administration on this occasion exposed the narrow nationalism of the once great European powers for what it was. The nationalist propaganda sold to the masses in Serbia under Milosevic should not have had any support from the likes of France and Brittain. Two countries which fought the WW2 against the Nazies. As the history records prove, they not only remained on the sideline in the disintegration of Yugoslavia, but actively supported the Serbian aggression.

"Serbia is where Serbs live." So spoke *Slobo* Milosevic. Sounds familiar?

It was left to the Orthodox priest the **popa** to sprinkle some Serbian holy water over the estates owned by conquered non Serbs and the previous land records became null and void. Serbs and the Jews were the Lord's chosen people. They could take what they wanted. It was made official. Great dream of the Serb nationalists from generations back was to come true. All of this was no secret to the power brokers in London and Paris, who not only raised no objections, but in fact lent a helping hand. They managed on top of else to impose arms embargo on Croats desperately fighting off the invading panzers with hunting rifles.

It took the USA for the third time in one's life time to save the Europeans from their own folly and duplicity. The Americans got actively involved in the wars of the Yugoslav succession. Almost a repeat of the Suez Canal debacle. In 1956.

It was Richard Holbrook who negotiated some kind of peace and ultimate partition of Bosnia. It was the retired US Marines General Johnson (*I am Johnson*)who installed into Croatian military hastily cobbled together some sense of purpose and resolve.

And it was Mark Stinson a traumatology Professor from California who through the 'Contra Costa County' offered Max a hope of normal life once more, free of his Vukovar nightmares. Prof. Stinson was an expert. For a while the treatment seemed to work.

Now the nightmares were returning.

Post mortem discussions on the fall of the two Yugoslavias, the pre WW2 Kingdom and post WW2 communist regime, could fill many volumes and still end up in a raging argument. Turbolent times in Europe were reflected in Balkan upheavals better than anywhere else on the continent. Here the great powers saw the solution in imposing Serbian hemogeny on smaller South Slavs minorities. Not having learned the lesson after WW1 debacle, they repeated the same mistakes twice more. None emerges out of this war with any credit whatsover. Least of all the callous manipulators in the Foreign Office.

On personal level, the stakes were defined. His family background ensured Max could never have fair chance in Yugoslavia. For start, Grandfathers on both sides perished after WW2 ended. Rubbed out by Serbian ultranationalists. Mass graves hiding their remains are still unknown to their surviving kin.

His father, a small time shipping agent and devoted family man kept a low profile. This did not deter the Serbs to sentence him on trumped up charges. His home and business confiscated and himself behind bars as a political prisoner, Max was facing a grim future.

Relesed from jail a decade later, health ruined, his father passed away with Max and his brother Kresho still teenagers. After confrontation with Soviet Union, gradualy political situation settled somewhat. Horvats returned to their rainsacked, old, island home. His mother valiantly bore the burden and worked day and night to see the sons through the education system.

Max was a brilliant and inquisitive student. He graduated in Science and later on took up jurnoulisam spending years freelancing around the new emerging Africa. That explained his passion for the continent.

Then in the spring of 1971 when the revival of Croat's millennia long battle for independence threatened the Serbo Communist regime, the District Court of Pula had him sentenced to twelve years for a factual article on Serbian hegemony. He got practically a life sentence to be served on Goli Otok, an island penetentiary notorious for torture and deaths of many political prisoners.

His younger half brother Kresho was also on wanted list and thanks to his Serbian girl friend got tipped off on time to go underground. He also got news of Max' pending transfer to the island , and found out Max was in transit held in a poorly guarded holding prison.

Kresho, an electrician by trade was a born prankster. Forever in trouble with the school masters, unlike his brother also more down to earth and a sportsman of note. He reached the finals in middle-weight boxing division in the Balkans Games.

Now as luck would have it, the re-wired electrical and sound system for the holding prison were up- dated by a friend of his, another Croat on the run. He explained to Kresho the exact layout of the security system.

Just after midnight, as the streets went quiet Kresho approached the holding prison from the back street garden. He had with him a collapsible aluminium ladder used to reach the thick three meter tall wall lined up with imbedded pieces of broken glass. He was ready for this and wore heavy steel tipped industrial boots. Next he repositioned the ladder and slid to the ground unheard and unobserved. He quietly cut through two rows of barbed wire and advanced towards the prison dimly lit.

The night shift guard was by himself. Drunk and sound asleep Seated at the table, head resting on the folded up hands. In the heat of the summer night stripped down to short sleeved shirt. His uniform jacket was placed over the chair backrest. The rear window was wide open to allow fresh sea breeze in. Kresho was satisfied the fly screen could be removed without waking up the guard.

A short work with a sharp pen knife and the wide window was open. Kresho slid over the ledge and entered the room. The first thing he did was to look for guard's cell keys. They were in the jacket outside pocket. So was the service revolver.

Max emptied the magazine then placed it back.

Suddenly the guard began to stir, still full of moonshine *slivovica*.

Kresho grabed hold of the chair and spilled the guard on the floor.

This guard was a large man, with the neck of a bull, and before he hit the floor through the drunken haze mistook Kresho for his supervisor. He'd been on probation before for drinking and "other misdemoniours." This guard was none other than Stevo Hrndjak, a notorious torture master, who'd killed hundreds.

Kresho knew enough about the beast. Now the guard was apologetically talking his way out of the trouble.

"I got so tired beating this Croat my arms were falling off. Sorry I fell asleep. You promised he'd be all mine after trial, remember!"

"Sorry for nothing, you ugly swine. You are so good at beating men with their arms tied behind their back. Let's see how good you really are!"

The guard sobered up in an instant. Now he knew who his visitor was and a cruel snigger crossed his ugly unshaven head. He reached for the pistol and pulled the trigger, only to find the magazine empty. No matter.

"No, don't worry I could have shot you that's too good for you." Said Kresho then raised the voice and approached the guard still sprawled on the concrete floor.

"Get up!" Kresho screamed at the guard, who couldn't believe his luck. This upstart he thought to himself. I could toss him with one hand. But what Kresho lacked in size he made up in speed. The guard repeatedly insulted made a move for his knife.

"You hopeless fool. How did you get in here. I'll slit your throat with the blunt side. Just like the rest of your kind."

As the guard tried to rise from the floor his huge weight still resting on one knee Kresho moved in from the opposite side. He didn't move for the hand holding the knife but for the chin instead. Heavy steel tipped boot smashed guard's jaw in. The pain was excrutiating and the guard let go of the blade. Kresho kicked it out of the way and wearily sized up the guard who made a lunge for him. This opened guard's rib carriage to another blow.

"Get up you *chetnik* butcher! Get up and fight. You're not so shit hot." Max felt like killing the beast on the spot.

Instead he placed another blow. By now the guard had peed himself. He was begging for his life, just like so many of his victims did. Then his eyes went wide in terror. He saw Kresho moving in with a length of heavy gauge chain. The guard knew what that chain could do. It was his invention and a claim to fame. It was reserved for recalcitrant prisoners. Those refusing to comitt bestialities upon their fellow prisoners. First step in a systematic way of destroying self-esteem. That chain also made short work and hours of tireing beating reduced to fun.

On this occasion the guard found himself on the receiving end and he didn't have arms tied up, until later. Kresho continued , for how long he couldn't tell, that is until he couldn't lift that chain any longer. He opened the First Aid cabinet and used cotton wool to stuff up guards mouth then plastered the mouth with heavy gauge sticking tape.

He found Max beaten unconscious laying in the cell, arms still tied up with steel wire behind the back, a classical Serb method of treating prisoners.

Kresho looked at his wrist watch and found it was time to move on. He locked the guard up in the cell and left for the courtyard parked Fiat motorvan keys in hand, then quickly returned to fetch Max and dragged as much as carried his brother's injured body into the van.

With the motor running he opened the gates then drove out and headed for the Italian border. About two hours drive away. This was a run for freedom. He wasn't going to stop no matter what. Guard's pistol was loaded again and the safety off.

On the Yugoslav frontier post they readily recognized the Police van. The same vehicle was regulary used to bring back those refugees Italians didn't accept. Only the timing was out and the Albanian conscript guarding the post as much as queried the early crossing only to have Kresho sporting prison guard's Police head gear brutally abuse him. The Albanian conscript on back foot and half asleep wasn't up to it and did hastily as ordered to raise the boom gates .

Kresho waisted no time. He opened the throttle full up and had to jam the brakes in order to stop in time on the Italian side of the boarder.

It didn't take long for the Italian investigators to accept the bona fidi of the brothers seeking the political asylum. In fact, special care was taken of the pair to prevent Yugoslav secret cervices UDBA and KOS infiltrating and harming their targets...

Italy of course was only a jumping board to Australia, Canada or South Africa.

Within a year the Horvat brothers found themselves in SA goldmines making good money and starting a new life. This continued until Summer of 1991 when Yugoslav Federation began to follow the disintegration path of the USSSR. The only difference was Russians were prepared to accept smaller nationalities to gain their freedom.

Not so the Serbs. That's how the wars start. And Horvat brothers were soon in the thick of close combat. The worst of it was battle for the strategic key city of Vukovar. On the boarder with Serbia and banks of Danube it was in the way to any further invasion of now indenpendant Croatia. Serbs attacked with heavy artilery, armoured divisions on one side and river naval forces in a pincer movement, combined with aerial bombardement. It was going to take days at the most. World's military attaches gave Croats a week to comprehensive defeat. Then in order to ensure the desired outcome imposed arms blockade on Croatia. The attacking force was far superiour in numbers not to speak of weaponry. Arms blockade worked for Serbs as it was openly admitted by power brokers in London and Paris.

"We'll let the Serbs win." A quote from Lord Carrington once NATO Chief Commander. Mitteraund of France was even more blunt when asked. 'Give the Serbs what they want.' Three months later on the seage was still on. Until the defenders ran out of ammunition. Vukovar fell but Croats gained precious time to organize defence from virtually nothing. Those heroes who saved Croatia will live on in country's history. Their fighting spirit shown at Vukovar where barely a thousand poorly equipped men held the cream of Serbia's army, The First Guards Corps and inflicted massive casualty on the attacking force gained Croatia respect abroad in its fight for independence.

Not since Spartan King Leonidas. Not since the darkest days of Stalingrad and General Chuikov's defenders has anyone put a defensive fight against a far superiour force with such devastating effect.

By the time the Serbian armour poured into the city there was not a single building left intact. Cream of Serbian youth died at Vukovar. The once enthusiastic response for volunteers from here on died with it. Those jubilant Belgrade crowds showering the soldiers with garlands were a memory. Good many returning in tin coffins. Thousands of young Serb draftees absconded to Greece and Hungary to avoid the war. It remained to the fascist **Chetniks** paramilitary to continue their dirty work. Horrible attrocities were comitted on the civilian population and wounded prisoners alike. A mere handful of defenders managed to fight their way and reach freedom. Max was one of them...

* * *

Max didn't want to talk about it. Perhaps one day. He was still suffering Vukovar nightmares. Damn the bloody war! He was trying hard to get it out of his system and regain sanity before it completely corroded the belief he once held in the goodness of Man. Vivian decided not to interupt.

"Damn the nationalisam! Damn all the-isams!" He would rage." All they ever did was enslave the free and lead to more bloody wars.

"Thou Shallt Not Kill!" It says it loud and clear. All of the world's main religions are supposedly against war, and what do we do?"

"What happened to your doughter?" Vivian wanted to know.

"Serbs took her to Omarska, a notorious death camp outside of Prijedor township. There he lost track. Not until two years later in Bosnia's war would he discover the terrible truth.

"Was she still alive?"

"No. She took her own life." Hence he fell into brooding silence and clammed up. She could read the anger and pain in his face before he spoke again.

"Now please." He tried." Please, I beg you, let us talk about something else."

Viv withrew chastised into the cabin and opened Sounion's Log book while Max was in the cockpit on watch. There she found a poem he'd written. She read it and felt guilty at first of intruding into man's privacy, but then became overcome with a complex set of emotions.

"So my sailor, you are not much better off than I am." She commented to herself silently. "I am an orphan same as you. All we've got is each other and you don't know it." Then she began to read Sounion's Log book. Without asking for permission she opened up about the middle and found a poem he'd written.

Under the cabin reading lamp she read the poem again.

Darwin, 23.5.1996. To my ex wife.

THE VOICE

Your voice is still there with me
It eccoes from the cabin walls
It pleads with me surging with the
Gale and rides the wild wave crests
Leading me the Monsoon Drifter
God only knows where.

The voice wakes me up at night
Telling me your hand is still there,
In mine, in our web of emotions
That knew no Earthly boarders
When you was I and I was you
And neither knew what that ment.

And though you are world away
Your voice has been the guiding
Light helping me find a way
Through the labyrinth of my
Pain in the darkest of night.

For once Vivian fellt as an intruder completely ashamed of herself. That a man can feel for a wife who divorced him when he needed her most and still show deepest affections after more than twenty years was a revelation to her of absurd human complexity.

* * *

Sensation of a perfectly balanced Kai Vai clocking mile after ocean mile leaving behind a double bow wave and stern up like a Spanish dancer's skirt takes some explaining to a landlubber. Not to mention that gurgling sound that is pure music to a sailor. Reaching with sails full on the monsoon was what naval architect Boden had in mind. Averaging close to two hundred nautical miles a day was excellent progress. They were approachinge southern boundary of the Amirantes Archipelago strewn with coral reefs. Caution was needed. This ment visual observation at all times.

Soon Max picked presence of vegetable matter floating on the current. A flock of birds gliding on the thermals just on the horizon and confusing swell patterns, all indicators of a land mass not too far away. Timing was of the essence. One had to avoid sailing this close to coral reefs at night. A land fall had to be made during daylight hours. As the sun was about to set Max went hove to, intending to go closer to land early in the morning.

They'd been sailing together for close to a week and in the process getting used more and more to each other's idiosyncracies. Living in a city was no comparison.

As for Vivian, from being withrown, troubled by her indiscretion and unsure of her future, she was returning to that vibrant personality of old. Playful and capricious at times. More and more she would tease Max, who at first fell victim to her gamesmanship. Until he got to read that facial expression that spelled pure mischief and sudden changes of mood. They played games with each other and sang together. His course bass with her clear soprano. They sang hymns from early childhood. For most of those Vivian would teach him the lyrics in English. Her favourite was the hymn to Christian Soldiers. Max refrained from passing his opinion on the subject of Crusaders, the Inquisition and Christian Soldiers.

Gloria electis in Deu!

Her remorse was over finaly, completely healed. And she was in return nursing his war scarred psyche with all of her guile and charms. By now they knew each others body intimately. The all consuming raw magnetisam drew them ever closer together. No matter what the task was, they would end in each other's arms before long. As if to make up for lost youth. As if to make up for future uncertainty. It was the way a honeymoon is supposed to be. Time just flew.

That was, until the forth night out when in midst of another Vukovar nightmare he began to scream words in a foreign language she could not understand. She raced from the cockpit watch into the cabin and shook him up.

"Max, Max!Please wake up. I am here. Wake up!"

He had broken out shivering in cold sweat. The voice was thrembling as if suffering from malaria and he found himself using her long hair to bury his face in.

"My God Vivian…What?…Have I been talking in Croatian?"

"Relax now. Try and relax Max. I am here. The war is over. Finished. Fine. Finito.

"Do you hear me?"

She wisely decided to let that incident drop from their conversation. Any light on the matter would have to come from him alone. Max oblidged.

"Did you hear me say anything, any word you could repeat?"

"Yes". She replied."A few times I heard you cry out K r e s h o. I don't have any idea who or what that means." That was enough.

"Kresho, my younger brother, that was the last time I saw him, and what the Chetnik savages did to him. Kresho is no longer with us.

Bit by bit he told her the terrible saga of his escape from the war hell of Vukovar.

* * *

CHAPTER FIFETEEN

THE HORROR AND VALOUR OF VUKOVAR

A day before the ammunition ran out and the defence collapsed Max got admitted to the the bombed out remains of a makeshift hospital. Bleeding badly he came under the care of Dr Vesna Bosanac.

Small in statue, very average in looks she would have escaped attention in any crowd..Yet what this lady achieved in three months of the seage under continuous bombardement with rationed and almost no medication left towards the end, would go down in history of warfare medicine as an achievement in battle surgery without parallel.

Serbian gunners didn't spare the Red Cross sign. In fact it was the exact opposite. Catholic church spires and Croatian hospitals were prime artillery targets.

As for Vesna. She could operate for a day and night in a strech. What kept her going was a mistery. Some people suggested she ran on nicotine. The op room for one was always in blue cloud of cigarette smoke. Some unkindly suggested it was the nicotine as much as onset of freezing late autumn weather that prevented outbreak of gangrene amongst hundreds of wounded despite a lack of antibiotics.

Then the bad news finaly hit. One didn't need a messenger to know. T84 tank grenades were exploding all around them. Max decided he wasn't going to wait for the Serbs to take him alive. He had seen first hand of what they were capable of. Quietly he sliped through what used to be the entrance , reduced to a pile of ruins and rearranged with each new explosion. Spent insenduary bombs were still smoldering. With two companions the wounded defenders under heavy fire struck a course towards Mitnica, the last defender's post to fall.

The air was heavy barely breathable saturated with explosives fume, fine dust that wasn't given a chance to settle down and the acrid scent of tear gas still lingering in the surrounds. Autumn fog from the river Danub did the rest, cutting the visibility in places to no more than spitting distance. Street markers were destroyed long ago. As were whole city blocks. Just a pile of ruins remained from a once charming Austro-Hungarian buildt city.

And if they could barely see ahead in the direction they were heading, the bone chilling terrifying screams served to lead them in the direction to Mitnica.

Mostly crawling on all fours dragging the bad leg behind and trying everything to avoid the marauding T84 tanks towards the mid morning they arrived at the scene. A scene of Hell, worse than anything Dante could imagine opened up.

In a clearing was a surreal figure of what was only hours ago a fine male specimen with both eyes gauged out, broken bones hanging loosely from the torn jacket sleeves placed on the knees and a *Chetnik* officer slightly behind pulling on the hair of the victim. The second torturer was in the process of literally rubbing the salt into the wounds and flayed skin.

Terrifying screems continued. On the edge of the clearing were piled up bodies of other victims, now unrecogniseable, some still showing signs of ebbing life. All had the ears cut off, fetching DM50 on the Serb souvanier market. The men were captured this morning after Serbs dropped tear and nerve gas bombs on the last pockets of Croatian resistance.

What exactly happened and who charged first Max couldn't tell after the event.

Maddened by rage the escapees had the torturers knifed. The first one to fall was the **Vojvoda** a top ranking officer. Under his tunic Max found the white collar of the Orthodox order and a gold braided breast piece. Look of that hatred filled bearded face Max saw only briefly before he finished the beast would haunt him for years.

The other one Max thought was a Gypsy. Next Max turned his attention towards the victim. He recognized his brother Kresho. They fought alongside each other only days before.

"Kill me Max", he begged. "Kill me I cannot stand any more." He pleaded." Please, finish me off, and try to save yourself. There is no hope left for me."

Max couldn't take any more torment. He was beginning to crack up. He disarmed **popa**, the priest and loaded the pistol and fired with eyes closed..

"God, please give me the strength to end the suffering of the victims." Having done it he drew a pistol to his own head. When he pulled the trigger there was no more bullets left in the magazine. He was going to blow his own brains out only to have the fate deny him the opportunity.

"Farewell my brother. *Zbogom Brate!*" Eyes filled with tears he was as transfixed until there was noise of approaching traffic warning them it was high time to clear out. Max took prist's head gear a black fur **shubara** with skull and cross bones insignia and the semi automatic. They took temporary cover behid what use to be city's theatre and watched the passing columns of Serbian civilians enter the city in search of plunder and slaves. It was free for all pandemonium. Soldiers joined in.

One carried away what one could cary. All semblance of organized discipline had broken down. Furniture, machinery, cars, clothes, works of art, agricultural implements and boats, all were destined for Serbia. Then Max had an idea. They were never going to make it out on foot. His stiches were coming undone and blood was showing through the bandages. The other two were if anything in more trouble. There was only one way out. Seeing the table top truck towing a power boat on trailer gave Max hope. The way out of the city was limited by military traffic and throughfares partially or completely blocked. Max knew the same table top truck would have to wind around the old theater and exit on the other side. In crawling traffic they would have ample time to intercept the truck. Carrying the Serbian head gear nobody questioned his move when he ordered the driver to pull up. Very few words were spoken at first. Driver said he was heading for Belgrade. Max just nodded in agreement. Then a few more kilometers further past the Danube bridge now in Serbia and out on the open road, the driver became unaesy before downright suspicious.

It was the foot gear. Anyone of high rank wore leather boots not Chinese tennis shoes. Max watched him closely, and as the driver slowly reached for his pistol packed in the holster Max let him have it. Now they were free. He took the steering wheel and struck onto a northerly route, back to the river Danube.

Max was hoping to be able and launch the power boat then run for the Hungarian border some 16 kilometers upstream. On this occasion the thick fog worked for the escapees. The river was high after autumn rains and all they had to do in order to clear the sagging chain closing the river traffic was to head mid stream. Fortunately there was enough fuel to see them past the Hungarian boarder sign. That sign ***Magyororsag*** might as well have read heavens.

On the Hungarian side military took great care in their account of the battle.

Thousands of Hungarians had lived in Vukovar over the centuries. Loss of the city to the Serbs was in Hungary received as a shock.

The wounded were soon given best medical care, but the media was kept out of all this. One has to remember in Novembar 1991 the Serbs were on their high and military peak. Croats were starting from nothing. Add to this real angst of the Russian bear, Serbia's ally. Memories of Russian invasion in 1956 were still fresh in Hungarian psyche. All this dictated Hungary would stay on the side lines during the conflict. Notwithstanding strong army reinforcements on the southern boarders of Serbia and Croatia. If anything it was to send a signal to Serbs not to conveniently invade Hungary and storm into Croatia from the undefended north as openly suggested by some in Belgrade military.

News of what Serbs did to the Vukovar hospital patients and staff reached Max in Hungary. Serbs with French Red Cross officials closely behind charged into the underground wards and fell upon the sick and injured. In their hour of glory the French 'tactically'withrew issuing mildest of protests. Patients got thrown out through closed windows onto concrete floors. Over the next day and night they were continuously beaten and tortured. Over three hundred were buried into one mass grave alone at a place called Ovcara.

As for Dr Vesna Bosanac, only physical barrier erected around her by conscript Serb prisoners patients to whom she also offered all there was to offer saved her from a similar fate. She survived the Serbian concentration camp.

Max fully recovered and in spring of 1992 found his way back to Croatia. In Zagreb HQ he was listed as MIA with thousands of others. Now top brass wanted him back in action. He was one of the few officers with extensive battle field experience.

HQ wanted above all for him to join HVO units in Bosnia where Croats were in diabolical trouble.

Max was sick of war. Sick of butchery and killing. He wanted no part of it and was prepared to stand his ground until he heard his doughter was taken by the Bosnian Serbs and transported to Omarska, a concentration death camp.

* * *

CHAPTER SIXTEEN

BOSNIAN MADNESS #ONE

Max together with a few ex Foreign Legion experienced officers got dispatched to fight for the city of Mostar in Bosnia Herzegovina. It was a three way contest, a varitable free for all. Serbs, Croats and Bosnian Moslems all at each other's throat.

Presence of experienced commanders on Croat side saved the Bosnian Croat HVO outfit in the nick of time. They smuggled in some top quality hardware as well, and went on the offensive scoring some decisive victories against the Serbs.

Max' contribution was leading a night time crossing of the swift flowing river Neretva with field artillery making it across and only four men drowned, all four non swimmers. Element of surprise and accuracy of the German made howitzers cleared out the Serbs from the commanding heights overlooking the city. It was a well earned victory and Max Horvat got promoted to the rank of *bojnik*, on par with the rank of a Captain, received mention in the dispatches and to him far more desired ten days leave.

There was only one item on his list since joining in the Bosnian war. Max was desperate to find out what happened to his one and only child Daria. Going on hear-say the search led him to Livno. Once a Turkish stronghold and a strategic crossroad. It had commanding heights offering control of the fertile valley below it.

Max dressed in civics drove friend's old Fiat and parked it facing the High School taken over by the HVO military. Centry on duty had him frisked for weapons then given instructions allowed to proceed. Max walked the length of the dimly lit corridor and knocked twice at last door on his left.

There was no sign on the door and he patiently waited for an answer which came in a deep male voice asking him by his name to enter. He entered into semi darkness filled with tobacco smoke. It took Max a while to adjust his sights. What little light came arrived through a small square window facing the street. A tall, heavy boned figure of Magistrate Jozo Jurich rose to greet him with a customary handshake. A powerful man with iron hand grip and commanding presence. That is how Max summed up the host. Also the leader of the Special Forces commando unit that once liberated township of Kupress with nineteen good men.

"I have been expecting you *Bojnik* Horvat. Max was junior in rank and Jurich conveniently never mentioned the rank again, playing a host instead.

"Take a seat, be my guest."

"I don't think we have met before." Jurich continued." But I did my final year at Banja Luka's

Teachers College with your doughter Daria as you probably know by now. I went on to do the Law and she took a teaching position. As it was at school we had innocent fun and games and she was our class Princess."

Now all of Northern Bosnia, Banja Luka in particular was in Serbian hands.

"Yes, I recall Daria having mentioned your name." Max was deliberately avoiding to place a stronger emphasis on what at the time was known to him as a promising romance between the young couple. Instead he came straight to the point.

"You'd know why I am here."Jurich a hard man that he was and battle hardened never left his eyes off Max. This war made hard men cry. And he was struggling for words. What seemed a minute at least pased by in complete silence. A kind of silence one finds in an unattended church. Finaly Jurich struck a measured sentence that he'd rehersed within himself.

"All I can offer you Max is a hear-say rumours. Not much apart from this."

He opened a desk drawer and pulled out a typed witness statement from an Omarska death camp surviver exchanged for a Serb. Max approached closer to the desk and took the document. Some way down the front page was a brief mention of **Chetniks** raid on the High School and imprisonment of all non Serb staff. Men and women would be separated fist thing. What happened to those women the witness could only assume.

He didn't realy know. And neither did Jurich until later the same morning.

Still brooding and undecided as to what to try next, Max' attention got diverted by a wailing recital originating from the street outside. He moved closer to the window to find out the source. There on the other side of the narrow cobble stone street facing him sat a moustached man in traditional attire. He sat on the stone walked on by Turk and Christian over the centuries and worn smooth. The bard was dressed in black white and red.

Black bagy pantaloons, white loose shirt and red head gear. A flat top cap with red and white checkers and pony tail clipped to sholder height. Rich golden embroidery was a sign of distinction. Resting in man's midriff was an ancient single string instrument **Gusle** held by his left hand whilst the right hand was engaged moving the bow.

Bard was reciting in that monotonous five note all flat scale that finds Westerners brought up on their octaves shaking head. Max hasn't heard this for years and it wasn't the sound but the lyrics that made him uneasy. Words Kupres and trechery kept cropping up and the mournful notes spoke of Croat again killing Croat.

Max looked at Jurich in askance. Expecting some reaction no doubt. Jurich quickly cought onto that.

"No, no, no!" He insisted. I didn't invite the old man here. And certainly will not order him away. By the way, he lost two sons in Kupres disaster. Who can go and tell him to shut up?" Enough said, Max thought. On the other side of the smoke filled room and away from the only window occupying what used to be Headmasters desk sat a uniformed ham operator, busy scanning Serbian air communications on a civilian YAESU HF set. There was a lot of chatter.

Generally speaking the Serbs were sloppy, too casual to adhere to mandatory coding, and when using older sets could easily be listened into. A lot of useful information could be with due care obtained this way. HVO HQ was desperate to find out what the Serbs were up to. There have been a lot of troop movements and armour re-deployment reported by the front line scouts. As it turned out dirty politics was instrumental in dealings to carve up Bosnia. Milosevic was busy making deals with Tudjman to carve Bosnian Moslems and that with consent of the great powers. Nobody in the West at the time was prepared to contemplate a Moslem state in Europe. And none would later on to this day own up to their guilt, shame and supine complicity. And none at all gets any marks for this debacle.

Combatants had to deal with war profiteers at all levels. Serbs would hire Croats tanks and receive where land locked fuel supplies in return. All in cash Deutch Mark of course. Here they all played dirty and DM ruled the day.

Years later NATO got involved issuing idle threats time and time again. Contemptuous Serbs had French spies inside NATO delivering timely warnings. When NATO finaly struck with aerial bombardement of Serbia it was primarily to restore its tarnished credibility and a disgraceful capitulation of its Dutch contingent at Srebrenica.

Finaly, the whole disaster came to a conclusion at Dayton when the Serbs for all the war crimes and genocide got rewarded with half of ethnically cleansed Bosnia.

Emotionaly drained, the bard rose up and lit his **chibouk** clay pipe. He placed his instrument under arm pit and walked up the steep slope in that unhurried rhythmic gate of one who had been walking mountains from early childhood. A swarm of noisy children surrounded him until he disappeared out of bright sun light and sight.

Jurich was still busy in the filing cabinet searching for a particular document he was hopeful may provide more information for Max. Annoyed at not being able to find it he slammed the open drawer and called for his second in command, a fearless young man. Ante Raguz Jurich's deputy whos 80 year old grand mother had been butchered by **Chetniks** made it a personal score to settle. He had the prisoner they kidnapped from Serbian stronghold at Nevesinje in a night time raid brought in.

Hands tied up behind the back the prisoner looked a mess. He'd been more than roughened up. And still there was that unmistakable sign of arrogance, defiance and hatred written in his haggard face. Max could read the man and feel anger building up inside of him. An aura of menace radiating from the prisoner only made it worse. Deep farrows extending into the cheecks, the hollow eye sockets and scull and cross bone tattoo only increased the sense of revulsion Max felt.

"**Vojvoda** Grujich, Raguz announced. A big animal. A realy fat swine." At first he wouldn't talk, now we cannot stop him singing. And look what we found on the beast." Raguz went for his pocket and brought up a leather satchel. He emptied the loose contents on Jurich's desk. Amongs glittering gold, precious stones, wedding rings and pearl necklaces it was the satchel itself that attracted Max' attention.

He had a good close look at it and didn't need anyone's help to tell him what part of male human anatomy the skin came from.

Next Jurich turned to Raguz asking about the documents the commandos brought with the prisoner. Max was on his toes in no time. He wanted to be the first to look at those. The Cyrilic writing was no problem to Max, he had to learn it at school. It was compulsory. There were numerous files that demanded hours of thorough reading in order to gain the full benefit from them. To Max only one thing mattered. He wanted to know what happened to his doughter. Having scaned most of the files he was almost satisfied there was nothing more from his point of view to be gained in spending more time on this. There were two documents left only. And there at last, was the break he was desparate for. Both documents carried the signature of Omarska death camp Commander and signed Grujich Milovan.

After this Grujich could not deny anything. Max was into Grujich's face screaming at him.

"You animal! What happened to Daria Horvat?"

Grujich hesitated and did the best he could to avoid eye to eye contact. He was still denying any knowledge.

"*Ne znam*." He answered calmly, once more denying any knowledge.

Max knew he was lying, he had a proof and to this end produced the two documents implicating Grujich.

"Then what's this!"

"Don't know, eh, how convenient, then what is this?" Pointing to his signatures.

At this stage Max lost his cool altogether. Jurich just as angry decided to stay out of of the melee for a moment.

"Where is she?" Max screamed at Grujich again." Is she still alive?"

Grujich knew the game was up.

"*Gde, gde*, where, where…" He was defiantly mocking Max.

"What does it matter where. Now let me be." He loudly insisted." You can swap me for a dozen of your bastards held in our prison. The way you have been getting rolled by the Turks lately, you will need us to save your skins."

The term Turks was a derogative description for Bosnian Moslems. In a way Grujich wasn't far off the prophetic mark. Only weeks later a battalion of Croats surrounded by Moslems escaped the seage by crossing into Serbian held lines. All for a price of course. DM 150 a head. At this stage Jurich joined in.

"Prisoner exchange is not on. Why.? You have a few of my men that is a fact. It is also true that of those previously returnig from your exchange, not one is medically fit to do a day's work, much less fight. Systematic beating over the lower back practically ruining the kidneys was the standard forewell for those exchanged."

Jurich kept focus on Grujich studying his reaction, while Max could barely control himself from exploding. As for Grujich, refusal for exchange he knew was tantamount to a death sentence. His time was running out. But within himself he was relaxed about it. He'd been killing non Serb vermin since 1939. Now the cunning butcher wanted a quick end. He knew all he had to do was provoke Max.

"Ay you!" He turned towards Max, with defiance written all over him.

"You realy want to know what we did to your doughter and others like her? I'll tell you what. We had a lot of fun. A lot of good fun, four and five at a time, to make certain they fell pregnant and bring good Serb boys to this world. And did they complain. Of course not. Those pregnant with boys we let go…..And your doughter? Well…., she had a problem with our methods, even a severe beating couldn't rectify. We found here one morning. The silly bitch bled to death having somehow managed to bite through her wrists."

The words had the desired effect. Max was onto Grujich in a split second and grabbed him from behind by the long untidy hair.

"You criminal revolting butcher!" Max was struggling to put into words what he felt. Grujich limited in what he could do attempted a backward kick. Max knew it was coming. He cought the foot on the rise and gave it a vicious upward tug that caused Grujich to stumble awkwardly forwards, loose balance and crash headlong into the Headmaster's heavy oak desk. Sound of a smashed nose cathrilidge could be heard combined with groans and cursing on all sides. Grujich managed to stand up, as defiant as ever.

"We'll' slaughter the lot of you." That was his departing message to his enemies and repeat of the one his boss Karadzich declared to Bosnian non Serbs in 1992. Max could take no more. A karate chop smashed Grujich's Adam's apple in and sent him back on the ground. Grujich was rolling about all over the timber floor. At this point Jurich shot up from his chair.

"Damn it, damn it and damn it! Are we no better than them? We have to be. If for no other reason than to remain sane."

He pulled Zastava 9 mm pistol out of his holster and shot at the figure still rolling uncontrollably all over the floor. The first two shots missed sending splintered oak timbers into the air. The next one cought Grujich between the eyes. Finaly there was no more noise.

"Clean up this mess!" Jurich commanded." And get this filthy stinking carcase out of here. We'll swap him allright, dead or alive. Get sparky to contact his HQ at Nevesinje on HF. All this in a single breath, before just as resolutely he departed towards the toilet facility in time to throw up. Sometime later he returned and apologized to Max.

"Crazy people, we're all nuts. All of Bosnia has gone insane. This is a Bezerkistan. And the rest of the world not far behind."

* * *

Vivian asked him to explain a few points. War terminology was new to her. Then she made a contemptuous comment that got Max worked up

"So that is the civilised Europe for you!"

"And you realy think Africans have more compassion? Like hell."

"OK .How do you see Africans then?"

CHAPTER SEVENTEEN

ODE TO THE DARK CONTINENT

Place two individuals of the same gender into a confined space and before long one is certain to emerge in a dominant role. Similar outcome takes much longer to emerge with a mixed couple. For start, men and women live practically in different worlds. A mixed couple in love with each other, and one may never reach the point where the dominance is obvious. Vivian and Max where at that point.

She, somewhat unusual of all but some modern women had lively interests in the world outside. Polititics, economy, just day to day affairs, you name it. She was cognizant of what made the world go around and was keen to find out more. In Max she found a natural companion, and a worthy adversary when it came to argue the point. As for his nightmares, now she knew. It was enough to send anyone around the bend.

Finding a cure for it was another matter. Baring his sole to the world was supposed to remedy the syndrome. It remained to acertain if the pshyciatrist was correct. Time was going to tell.

There was another problem. Vivian found constant movement of the yacht forced her to withrow to the bunk holding the laptop firm before she could begin to edit the Dictaphone files. And once there she had to find a way around the Croatian alphabet. Converting the 32 characters alphabet into English was a headache. One had to compromise. Max offered the easiest escape route. Why, just bung c and h together and you've got phonetically at least close to the Croatian ch soft and ch hard pronunciation.

"Who cares anyway! Soft or hard. Better still, leave out the 'h' alltogether.

Once into foreign languages Vivian let him know she used to be reasonably fluent in Italian.

"I didn't know you were into linguistics." Mark was surprised.

"No, nothing of the kind. It was Gino. Her previous boyfriend Gian-Carlo as most Italian males insisted on her learning some Italian in return for all the embarrassment and patent inadequacies in English. Not to mention Africaans or God forbid any of the African languages. She admitted it was a torrid affair. Almost two years ego, before she found him too demanding.

"Oh, talk about dear Gino! *Come un mitrallista, Ra..ta..ta*."

Her lapse into Italian was only the latest surprise to Max. He was also fluent in street level Italian as were most of East Mediterranian people. Legacy of Italian colonial era more than anything. From personal experience Max knew more elderly people were still able to converse in Italian than English anywhere between Slovenia and island of Corfu in the Greek Ionian Sea.

And so the days just flew. How could one ever get bored was the question.

Not to be diverted by all the noise Vivian remained true to her cause. What she wanted to hear from Max was simple. Did he have any ideas why there was so much poverty in Africa. Now more than ever. If so, what was the cause in his opionion and most importantly, what was if anything to be done to overcome the crisis. Could one still help millions of destitute Africans or had it all gone too far and out of reach? What was wrong with Africa?

Max at first just looked at her speechless.

"Why do you expect me to provide answers when those payed fat salaries to do just that cannot."

"Precisely. Parrots on payroll are oblidged to tell the boss what he or she wants to hear. You are not. And you have traveled around the world more than anyone else I know. You are also I believe a fair and non biased person. Also well qualified to pass a judgement on what is fair an proper. And you know Africa. Not just the game parks."

"Check mate! You can realy put a fellow on the spot. Allright, I may have a few unpalatable words to say, but you asked for it. Remember that before you complain."

"Why are there so many poor? As you say, more than ever. I think this is the prime concern before one can look at anything else. The answer is easy is in the question itself...so many. No birth control.

The African for all of his natural resillience and resistance to most tropical deseases brings more children into this world than he can ever hope to support. And it is no different when it comes to number of cattle he can boast about. If the denuded pastures cannot support what he's got now, your African is just as likely as not to try and graze a bigger herd. If only he can afford to buy one. No bloody idea. Manure for brains, call it what you like. I have seen it all. One can still drive through the country side and be able to tell who owns the land just by looking at it. Most of the rest is minor, almost irrevalent. Try and tell them that, and you get told cattle means everything. Then what about the money. And if those famished beasts walk past you bones rattling, never you mind. It is the number that counts. And remember four cows buys a new wife." Fat or famished, it is all semantics to a Negro.

"My God!" Vivian was aghast. You sure can go ballistic!

"You asked for it. Did you not?"

"Not very subtle though."

"Make up your mind girl. You want to hear it the way it is or the way you'd like it to be."

"I am perturbed I must say. That is not what we given in the curriculum to pass on to the children."

"Do I look surprised? Would I expect it to be different? No. Truth can be very hard to digest. Almost unpalatable. But if one wants solutions, true nature of a problem remains to be quantified before anything. Idle talk is for the politicians. Bloody Mugabe promised every African a Mercides Benz, University education and a land holding. Now they have cholera, hippo piss to drink and nothing to eat."

"Boy, oh boy, just as well there is nobody else listening in."

"I should hope so. Enough of this futile nonsense."

"Wait man! Don't just chicken out on me. What about whites. Aren't they to blame? She was tenacious like a bull terrier and wouldn't let go.

"Whites, you mean the power brokers or working people, foot soldiers like myself?"

"Well, she wasn't so sure. I mean whites generally. Under apartheid you were priviledged, were you not? It is all the same. Is it not." That got him realy angry.

"ANC bulldust! *Domkop!* What else? I still had to work my back side off down in the guts of the Reef with men getting killed and maimed around me. What are you talking about? Every Rand I earned came by the sweat of my brow. Explotation! What rot….Oh, sure the whites were not without blame. For start, too much animosity between the races followed forceful confiscation of land.

Asked to choose between long term racial harmony or a short term gain from a land grub, well, you know the rest. And those dames from the working poor of UK arriving here to play high society. Maids and garden boys, almost aristocratic all over night. Many just got carried away. How many disgusting scene of racial intolerance I have seen by that lot alone would be enough to start a Mau Mau. Not to mention sundowners and those exclusive clubs. If only the whites had taken up studying African languages.

Those born here can do it. New arrivals including myself didn't think it necessary.

I picked up some Zulu out of just wanting to know. Even the click sounds with some effort. It can be done.

And the Aparthaid itself. It wasn't done so much on grounds of racial purity. South Africans mixed freely with other races for centuries before Aparthaid. Some were darker than Southern European new arrivals. It was an arbitrary decision. Portuguese did something similar. As long as a Mozambique or Angola African was fluent in Portuguese, that was enough to qualify for Portuguese citizenship. When they lost the drive to defend what they had, the blacks kicked them out just the same, and raped and killed bus loads of their girls, just the same in spite of all **assimilados in Clube Ferrovia at Lorenco Marques**.

"News to me a lot of this, I must confess. But what about explotation?"

"What explotation? Everybody exploits everybody ready to be exploited. Whites exploited whites, still do. Kids used to toil in coal mines and cotton mills of England and Belgium, just to name a few for 16 hours a day, payed pittance. Their lungs used to give up to silicosis about the same time as the onset of puberty. Of course of no further use to the factory owners. Blacks exploit blacks, or don't you ever hear of house maids abused by the nuevaux rich BEE boys."

A common sin is to portray the old colonial administration as wasteful, non-caring and oblivious to the problems of the less well off. Judged on what anyone can see, most of these accusations can be leveled at present administration and with more justification."

"Where is this getting us?" She objected.

"Sorry my fair maid, I thought all you wanted here was to find out how I saw it."
"Yes, but, where do you see a solution. Or isn't there any in sight?"

"It is like medicine. Of no use and no help until the desease is diagnosed. Pharmacy is stocked with drugs. Which one to take? You are right in one aspect of the tragedy. It relates to those in power. Those in ivory towers who draw straight lines in sharp pencil across the Africa and Asia separating tribes and call them next international border...They gave in to demands for independence way before the natives were ready for it. Why? I don't know. Political correctness? Or to apeace the electorate? Or because they genuinely believed the African was ready for **Uhuru** and democracy? I don't know. As the history proves it was a mistake. Maybe it is easy to be smart after the event. Not that Ian Smith didn't tell them so."

"Did you ever meet the man?"

"No. Once I met his widowed mother though , without being aware who she was.

At Selukwe, a small chromite mine township. My driver sprung a surprise on me. She was in the front yard by herself busy in the rose garden. No sign of any military nor Police about. I refused to believe it until later I read an article on growing roses. I recognised her features in the published photograph..."

"People were here supportive of him till de Clerk took over."

"I know. It had to happen. Thanks to all the bleeding hearts. Your Council of Churches mob in particular. Now Mugabe can do no wrong. WCC is yet to utter a complaint addressed to Mubabe's

Zimbabwe. What humbug! It makes one sick. Ian Smith was a statesman. Mugabe is a power hungry butcher, and as for who says that, talk to the Ndebeles around Matabeleland. And another thing, before I get carried away and be accused of pontificating. Rhodesia was a thriving economy. Work for everyone. We all know of today's Zimbabwe. But that ought to do for wasting precious time on politics. We are powerless to change things. Do your personal very best for your fellow men and that's about it…Now crew, my throat is dry .Any chance of a cup of coffee?"

Vivian took all this to mean she'd lost the argument and been rightfully put into her place. She was not a good looser and would fight on to win. Not on this occasion.

"Yes Captain! How many sugars?" Not until the next day would she pluck enough courage to ask him about the missing gaps. From Bosnia to Australia. Why not back to SA instead? He promised to tell her the end of Bosnian drama next and then about his stay in Australia. Now Max wanted a fix on the chart.

* * *

CHAPTER EIGHTEEN

BEZERKISTAN BOSNIA #2

Close to sixteen hundred meters above sea level and just below the Demirovac Mountain peak the early April chill in the air still came with a bite. Sprawled on the bare and icy cold granite outcrop JNA(read Serb)army Captain Manojlo Radich could observe through a pair of 7x50 Zenith Russian made binoculars movements of Croatian and Moslems jointly in a HOS unit dug in the routine trenches defence parimetar along the valley. That was the last time the two groups fought jointly and together against the Serbs and before their politycal masters stuffed up..

Hours of observation let the cold spread through to his joints and the binoculars began to feel heavy. He would have dearly loved to have a break and a drop of plum brandy, but under strict orders decided to remain in position uncomfortable as it was.

Not unusual for early spring occasional passing cloud formation would fog out his line of sight, otherwise he had almost a bird's view of enemies' positions. Even more useful, from his lookout he had a clear view of the vital Gate of Kupres, the only road acces cut through a mountain pass and leading to the township. Any troop reinforcement or supplies had to arrive this way. As for the other escape route to the west, that was also covered. Heavy artillery guns were in position ready to open fire. Trap was about to be sprung, and still he could not observe any hint on the other side of making some sort of organised defence preparation, nor any sign of concern of scouts, patrols, much less any re-inforcement.

There was something odd he thought. Perhaps another ruse. A decoy? Otherwise it didn't make sense. Captain Manojlo decided to contact temporary HQ at Vodica, some thirty kilometers away.

His superiour on the other side of the field phone was Colonel Vuk Martich, a Monte Negrian who was most appreciative of Captain's attention to duty. There was far too much slack elsewhere for his tolerance. All this despite a splitting headache from a last night's drinking binge hangover. If only I can get a clear head he thought. Then he cut the conversation short showing a dosis of skepsis that astounded Rajich.

"This mob of HOS *Ustashe* under Gen.Blaz Kraljevich was a bag of tricks."

Truth was, Blaz left a thriving business in Canberra to join the Croat ranks in the hour of need. His fighting methods were unortodox to say the least. Toyota 4x4 pick ups would emerge in foulest of weather and darkest of nights from nowhere and then disappear without trace leaving mayhem behind.

Just about ready to hang up, Radich bravely tried once more.

"How can you be sure it was another ruse Colonel?"

"If Blaz is leading the bastards, that's enough for me."

"But Blaz is dead. Killed by his own." Radich thought his superiour knew. Martich initially felt angry at being the last to know, and rolled off **kurvin sine** a number of saucy profanities questioning Captains pedigree.

"Why wasn't I informed?" He insisted." News travels fast, how come I haven't been told?"

"With respect Colonel, you have been informed. Just now. I only got the radio intercept this hour. We deciphred Tudjman's order to get Blaz out of way, as he put it. His killer commando of ex hard core criminals did us the favour. Croats are splitting all ties with the Moslems and busy killing their own."

As if by miracle Colonel's headache was no more. This was a gift from heavens. At a crucial time in war when Serbs were beginning to loose initiative, terrain and battles.

Moral was falling and glorious victories assigned to the memory. Easy plunder and slave females no more to be found. Now Serbs were actually being shot at with real guns and bullets were flying ever thicker.

Worst they had to fear in the past was bird shot. Molotov cocktails and even sholder fired anti-tank missiles had been reported lately. What next! Front lines had been overstretched and would have ceased to be defenseable but for mine fields. Day and night Serbs had been busy laying mine fields. Slopy work as usual left insufficient recorded details of these for future clean up, rendering large parcels of future productive agricultural land unuseable.

Now, as if by God's hand here was help from a most unexpected quarter. In his quest for absolute power over Croatia, Tudjman a self centred dictator that he became operated in the only way he knew how. He was after all, a communist and had Croat blood on his hands from WW2. Eliminate all of potential opposition. Croatia didn't need heros he pronounced. It was done under any and flimsiest of pretexes. And there was never a shortage of scum to do the dirty work. Yes, Croat was killing Croat. Yet again. Then he went one step further in his delusions and opened second front. This time against the Moslems. For the fist time in history those two ethnic groups were at war. Needles to say it was a military disaster. And a diplomatic setback of first magnitute. From a victim Croatia was by her age old nemesis in the West with some justification presented as co-agressor never to be forgiven. All this humbug and pretence by none other than the same political power brokers in London and Paris busy bending backwards to help the Serb conquest. By some magic they became concerned about the fate of the Bosnian Moslems…Or was it the tooth fary at work?

Suddenly Colonel Martich snapped out of his thought process. He was a professional soldier, not like some of the riff ruff around. As a professional soldier he recognized the opportunity when presenting itself. He began barking out orders.

"Stay on your post **bre** Manojlo! And wait for orders.Don't leave the observation post. If you stuff up, I'll hang you by the balls myself!"

He ment every word of it. Small in statue he had long memory and a fiery temper. That more than made up, and he was feared by junior ranks. Now he hung up and went into action. He was a soldier, a real soldier, who were those Croat peasants think they were fooling.

Soon he'll fill the valley with their corpses. He'll lead the attack himself. There were old scores to settle. If he gets this one right, General Mladich will have to take him back to HQ staff. He mounted a Jawa 350 cc motorbike and took a fire trail to reach the camoufladged tank unit hidden in the forest and positioned directly below Captan Radich's observation post. The scene for carnage was set.

The faithful day Kupres fell was none other than 10.April 1993, anniversary of the Independence

Day first proclaimed in 1941 and celebrated to this day by hard core Croat nationalists. As it was, only recently were the Serbs expelled from Kupres by 19 of Jurich's Special Forces men. They put a Serbian armoured unit battalion to flight. Most of the capable T-72 tanks managed to escape and were now positioned to extract revenge. Crews of those tanks were itching for it. They covered the engines with everything they could lay the hands on. Matrasses, carpets and blankets in order to muffle the noise. Then the move was on in bottom revs, engines practicaly on idling speed. One could barely hear the tanks gently clanking away only meters away..

Captain Manojlo faithfully carried out his orders and remained on the observation post. A call from the leading panzer with Colonel's voice wanted to know if there was anything to report.

"Yes, Comrade Colonel. I cannot see a single howitzer nor anti tank gun recoiles other than a few 80mm mortars in place. How bloody foolish. Sending men in with bare bums. I haven't seen them lay any mines either."

"Foolish maybe. Ever heard of trechery? Now get the artillery to line up 100 meter ahead of us. Fire only if ordered...

"Is that clear Comrade Captain?"

Within the last of the forest cover Colonel ordered tanks to stop, then sent scouts ahead. They were still unobserved. From the valley there was a delicious smell of roast lamb teasing his nostrils. Soon the Colonel was going to gate crash their party. Scouts reported back. First row of trenches was left unoccupied, deserted in fact. And the trenches were too shallow to stop T-72s advance. More sloppy work to be punished.

Only when the column of T72s fanned out at full speed, did the second line of defence spot the danger. By then from distance inside of 300 meters and rapidly closing, heavy machine gun fire at will, it was all over red rover. The lucky ones got killed on the spot. Others trumpled on or taken prisioner. Not one lived to see the sun rise again. And you won't find any of this in Croatian print.

It took 19 brave men to take Kupres and 500 ill equipped betrayed and poorly disciplined ones to loose it. But numbers are just that. They don't tell of treachery, of incompetence and bravery.

Forget the statistics!

* * *

"No more war for me." Vivian let off a painful cry." Like you, I am sick of it!"

* * *

CHAPTER NINETEEN

RETURN TO FARQUHAR

The Elliots couple couldn't have left Kai Vai in more caring hands. To Max this was a big improvement on Sounion in every aspect. Once under way there was little for the watch to do, other than keep an eye on the traffic. Used to have hands full on Sounion at most times, Max found time to work with Vivian on edition of Dictophone text. She'd interject at times not certain how to spell some of the foreign words and names. She was also trying to join some loose ends in the plot as well as to point out some things which at first looked insignificant.

When they departed from Dar es Salaam without telling Ngezi, Vivian thought it was better this way. Before darkness, they rounded off northern point of Zanzibar without anything to report. Similary, the three days sail for Victoria on Mahe' Island also went smoothly. There was though one fishing story that told Max more about Vivian than the fish.

Trawling for fish dinner he hooked a beautiful specimen of Dorado. They also make for top table fish. When Max went for the knife to promptly dispatch the fish, Vivian begged him to let the creature go. He paused telling her if so there is beans for dinner, and no fish. Then he felt her hands over his.

"Look at those eyes." She was pointing at the fish. They were following his every move. As if that wasn't enough there were grunting sounds coming from the fish. That fish fought hard for its life and knew it had help.

"How can you kill it? It is a God's creature. Same as you and me and diserves to live." He looked at her with a smile.

"I see, you are all for the fish. Then go on and tell the fish not to be fooled again by a piece of shiny metal. He carefully released the fish, allowed it to gain a breather half submerged then let it go. The discussion continued.

"Anyway, I don't mind beans, had them as child once a day, a staple diet.

"I would have hated you if you'd killed it, you know?"

"That's good to know. This way we all win."

They cleared all the paper work at Mahe'. No trouble at all. Garson's word was good. What did surprise, was the sudden and large increase in sea and air traffic. Seychelles had been well and truly discovered by the tourist industry. Those Shorts 360s turboprops went for scrap. Replaced by Boeing 737 jets. But the prices had gone up accordingly.

They sampled the local sea food delicacies. Some very spicy dishes among them. Tasted the local beer and joined the noisy crowd dancing and frolicking till late into the night. Two nights of this in succession put Max flat on his back with a hangover. He suggested to Vivian they set the sail for Farquhar.

"I am dying to see the look on the face of that character Rene." Said Vivian.

They left Mahe' at first daylight. Late in the afternoon the Farquhar Lagoon entry markers came into view. Motoring into the setting sun one had to be extra careful. Once more without problems. Max recognized the jetty, partially vacant at the time and decided to tie up alongside. Soon an agitated male wharf attendant showed up. They were not supposed to tie up here. It was reserved for fishing charter boats. Due back any time.

Max just ignored the man. Instead he told him to get Rene down here. The attendant had a good look at Max, shook his head, but went for the walkie talkie anyway. Rene got the call then asked the attendant in French, who was it wanting to see him.

"Tell Mr Rene, Mrs de Villiers wants to see him." Max tried.

Rene could not place anyone by that name, but *tres bien* he was comming down to the warf shortly to investigate. Within minutes Rene mounted on a bycicle arrived. Dressed in a Hawaiian shirt, white shorts and yachtsman's footware he cut a stylish figure, if somewhat overweight. Vivian a French speaker decided to converse in English. She wanted Rene on hot coals a little longer.

Max had a pair of dark sunglasses and a baseball cap on at the time. He took off first the sunglasses then the cap, and spoke in a calm voice.

"I believe Mr Rene we have met before. I am Max Horvat de Villiers."

Rene quizzingly looked at Max for a while. Over the last few years the coconut plantation wasn't making money, but the tourisam had taken off. Hundreds of visitors had been and gone. Who could remember them all? Try as hard as he may, Rene couldn't place the foreigner. Finaly he spoke.

"I don't think so Mr..de Villiers." He'd missed the first bit. His spoken English sounded much smoother. And he radiated self confidence. Max thought how best to bring it to him. "Do you remember a yacht by the name Sounion?" Max studied the man intently. Rene's bushy eyebrows first wrinkled up before joining together. It got worse when he recognized Max' scar on the left cheek. A narrow escape from a Serbian bayonet that nearly cost Max his life. Now Rene froze. The hear-say on Max' disappearence had to do with blue pointer sharks scavenging.

"*Mon Dieu! C'est impossible!* You are supposed to be dead.

"*Je non compre.*" Rene saw this as an act of God. Almost a miracle. A God fearing man he was. There had to be an omen to this. Max had it explained to Rene how he cheated death. Rene was still seeing a ghost. Just to convince himself this wasn't so he offered to shake hands. That settled him down somewhat. At last Rene was beginning to function again as a host.

He left the bycicle at the wharf. Instructed the attendant to look after the Kai Vai, and walked with guests the short distance to the house. Sarah, the house maid with three little ones milling around her met the visitors and introduced herself.

Oh, yes. The children were hers. All three from different fathers. She proudly owned up to that. Men liked Sarah and Sarah relished preying on men. Rene felt obligded to sound out the warning. He was one of the few Sarah failed to score. Rene did not approve of her behaviour. Equally he couldn't fault her work. And she was a good cheer in the house. Almost infectious. He was particulary thankful to Sarah for the help and understanding she showed when Beatrice was suffering towards the end. Now Beatrice's room left undisturbed since her parting was offered to Max and Vivian to move in. Once the couple understood, they politely declined and mentioned they'd be quite happy to sleep aboard the yacht.

Rene warned them about noisy neibhours and came up with a better idea. He'd rearrange the living room and have the satee converted to a comfourtable double bed. Vivian thought that was worth a try. To her it became obvious Rene had a guilty feeling deservedly so or not. Max wanted to know what became of Hamoud's body and what of his crew. But this had to wait for a more opportune time. As it was, he and Vivian were on a honeymoon. Things were looking up. They were on a high.

Boss refused to take his resignation, and asked Max to take his time making big decision. He felt for once, all the pressure was off his sholders. Pressure to make a living, pressure from obeying orders. He was free at last. That's how the rich must feel, he suggested.

Eventually, they would postpone the departure from Farquhar from four to seven days. Then a month and again for another month. In all that time Rene refused to take any monies. Max wasn't satisfied it was all due to feeling guilty nor hospitality. He was to find out before departure there was more to it. But just on arrival and their first month the couple enjoyed themselves in pristine surroundings. Swimming, diving, and surveying the rich marine life. This corner of the Indian Ocean was one of the last remaining natural environments that hasn't been thrashed. Not yet. Give it a chance.

In the evenings around the table Vivian would fiercely debate Rene on political matters. In French. At other times they'd go and play bocce. Rene was a passionate bocce player, and a bad looser. He wanted to know where Max learned the game, only to be told Croatia was the world champion in bocce for the year. Not that it ment much in world terms. Nobody outside Mediterran played bocce. But it settled Rene's anger in persistently loosing.

Away from his duties, Rene found the couple good company. He'd had a fill of the rich tourists expanding on and on about their ways of making more and more money. With his new guests Rene was engaging in topics of his choice and to his surprise found Vivian in particular more than capable to throw some new light on almost any topic. After week one they progressed further and Rene demanded to be called by his first name. Jean-Luke. Or just Luke would do. Sarah overhearing all this was dumbstruck. Rene was a stickler for formalities.

Next Sunday after the mass in Creole French held under canvas, Rene invited them to come along in his pilot boat to the other side of the lagoon. ***Ile du Sud*** and a three smaller inlets along the way. He had to time it on a high tide. They gathered at the jetty and Max noticed a ***boquett*** of tropical flowers in one hand and some ornamented candles in the other.

Vivian and Max looked at each other. They were off to a cemetery, this much was clear. There were no signs of permanent habitation outside of ***Ile du Nord***. They came across a party of fly fishermen from Nebraska and a local fisherman returning for his crab pots.

There was something odd about that barge though. It cought Max' eye, only to have his attention wilfuly diverted by Rene to the other bank. There was a white heron patiently waiting for a suicidal fish to carelessly approach. Nothing unusual to warrant extra attention. Still never mind, Max thought puzzled. One for the memory bank.

They disembarked in a narrow deep water channel leading to a jetty. A short walk led to a small cemetery. Rene led the way. Beatrice's resting place was out of character with the rest. Almost a small musoleum in marble, Beatrice's name engraved in gold leaf lettering. Rene lit the candles and prayed. He took death of his partner in life harder than most. Max and Vivian stood silently by. Then Rene apologized to his guests, he was aware English didn't openly display emotions. He just couldn't help it.

Max reminded him neither of them was English. It was no more than a language of convenience as French had once been, *a lingua franca*.

Somewhat relieved, Rene told them he had a surprise for Max. Max guessed it before Rene managed to jump a suprise.

"Hamoud's grave? Was that the surprise?"

"No more of a surprise." Countered Rene." And no more Hamoud."

So he led them to the far side, outside of the cultivated zone. There in a plot overgrown by weeds knee high was another tomb stone. Not in the sign of cross but half moon. The name painted in fading black paint could still be read: **ISMAIL HASSAN AIDID**. That was Hamoud's real name excluding two more middle names Interpol left out.

Max had a strange sensation, almost a sense of reverence for the man. After all, he was the one to deliver those priceless anti-tank grenades that stopped the Serbian armour. No more no less. In a way the man deserved better. He chased away a tern nesting on the tombstone and pulled out the weeds. Rene embarrassed silently watched him and promised he'd look after the grave in the future. They returned in time to beat the ebbing tide.

As customary, Sunday afternoon was a get together for the small island community. Spent in having a leasurly game of bocce and a social drink or two. Natives drank the palm vine Max was warned to stay away from. Fired by the drink and the occasion Africans would after dark lapse into the tribal dances origin of which had been lost in time. On about midnight the crowd fell silent and quietly dispersed.

Monday morning Max decided to make preparations for departure. Supplies ordered from Mahe' were due on the island supply boat in the afternoon. He needed 400 L of extra diesoline. Certain in the knowledge of encountering doldrums approaching the Equatorial waters.

Once more he went through the shopping check list and then headed towards the warf. There he saw it. The same barge that attracted his attention a day before. It was loaded with empty lobster pots and tanking fuel. Max approached the lobster man. Then had another look at the bow stainless steel anchor shield plate. This and the hard wood coamings rang bells.

Max enquired, only to have the fisherman explain mostly in sign language that the barge was recovered from the bottom of the lagoon. This added, up as Max looking for any signs of the wreckage of Sounion failed to see any, and he was certain of the position.

"That's really interesting." His comment to Vivian.

"Wait." She said." I think I know how Rene works. Leave it to me."

"All right with me." Max nodded in agreement. Obviously Rene intended for the matter of Sounion salvage to remain secret. Now he had to come clean. Not that he had anything to fear. By International Law of Salvage Rene was perfectly entitled to recover the wrackage and to put to good use what there was. All the more so, since no insurance claims applied. Max had Sounion uninsured. He couldn't afford the stiff premiums. What bothered Rene more was the emotional baggage. He felt a good deal of guilt regarding leaving Max mortally injured behind. Now this.

It was no secret any longer. Sounion was salvaged and the five-and-a-half tonne keel sold for lead scrap. Then the yacht cabin opened up and a conversion to a fishing barge completed.

"What a bloody disgrace! No yacht was supposed to end up this way!"

Max was disgusted. Now they understood why Rene was reluctant to take their money.

When it all came out, Rene explained he didn't want to touch upon old painful memories. Max reasoning over it came to accept it. There had to be some truth in that. Finaly they parted, and on best of terms with Rene and Farquhar. Rene had the permission to issue them with the Immigration clearance.

Next morning Kai Vai picked up the NW monsoon on the port beam and lifted the skirt doing hull speed. It was a sense of great joy to be back under sail. What happened to Hamoud's crew Said and Rajid, Max could not find out, apart from the pair acting as witnesses during his trial at Victoria's Court of Justice. It was all held in camera. Not a word leeked out to the media. Seychellois knew better than to publicise murder and crime. It all happened somewhere else. Like the neibhouring Comores Archipelago, avoided by the foreign investors like a leper colony. Max heard later both Rajid and Said recovered from injuries and got off with heavy fines. There the trail went cold.

It was high time to cover some milage. Returning to Australia's West Coast from Amirantes could not be done using conventional sailing routes. Only a lengthy study of Ocean Currents offered some hope. The Equatorial Current in the Southern hemisphere runs westward. To make it more difficult, NW monsoons were soon to peter out. Approaching Equator one runs into cursed doldrums. Just read the logs of Vasco de Gama and Magellan. It drove them suicidal.

On the surface enough to make one head south to the roaring Forties and the old clipper route. But wait! Vivian rejected this once before.

Max discussed the tactics before departure with Rene, who told him of information passed on by long line Korean fishermen. There was a powerful counter current at 5 knots at least, running easterwards. Somewhere about latitude 10 deg.South.

That's all it was. Max thought it was worth investigating. If not, he was prepared to motor two thousand miles if need be across the Equator heading for Galle in Sri Lanka.

He had enough diesolene and an engine just run in. And something much more precious the oldtimers didn't have. The hand held GPS units are now so accurate navigation skills of old are a dying art. To put it in proper contex with degree of accuracy to within a few meters, a plot can be derived within hourly intervals to clearly indicate the direction of the current. The old timers had none of these luxuries. In doldrums to test the theory one just had to stop motoring. For a strong current such as the Equatorial there had to be at least eddies or counter currents somewhere long before the Roaring Forties.

It was a matter of finding it. Sure there was an element of risk trying out a new route. It was also worth a try and a challenge.

Max decided to sail on NE reach for as long as his luck held out, and beat into ENE, until reaching latitudes about 10 deg.South, then test the counter current theory. He told Vivian none of his worries. Instead trained her on use of the radios and a man overboard routine. By now she could trim sails, adjust Flemming wind vane self stirrer and competently hold course without it. Running of diesel and safety equipment was next on the list.

She was a willing student up to a point. Then she'd get him wound up again. Before long she had an all over sun tan, and it never took long for male response to her open invitation. If anything since falling pregnant she was more demanding.

Still at sea, one has to keep a guard up. Running into submerged lost sea containers or sleeping whales amongst other things have wrecked good many sailing boats failing to keep a watch. There are other hazards.

Running into a two tones of solid sun fish is one of them and it was a close thing. Vivian saw it while on watch. It looked like more of that blasted plastic garbage on the surface, except she wasn't sure. She called for Max having a rest. As they got closer it became clearer Kai Vai was to run into a vast school of Velella Velella, a type of blue bottle. In the midst of it right on their course was a large sun fish busy feeding.

Then the man made hazzards. One night with dead silence all around Vivian on watch again noticed vibrations on the suspended tea cups. And it was getting louder. She raced to the bow and looked around the horizon. It was a clear night and there was nothing in sight. Soon Max heard it.

"Bloody submarine!" He cursed, then turned on the CD player on high.

"Just to let them know, we're here. The cowboys. Oh, big mucho men. They have sunk boats and fishing trawlers. Some couldn't care less. Every year list of missing boats at sea keeps on getting longer."

"Subs communicate on extra low frequencies. Either that or their propeller on extra low revs?" Soon it all became quiet again.

Kai Vai left Mahe' on the port beam and continued for another day and night. By then the monsoon was getting progressively weaker. They were still short of 10 deg.S. Max engaged the motor on half throttle to maintain the speed.

Two more days and the hand held GPS told Max 10 Deg 12 minutes S.

He noted the exact time and turned the engine off. The longitude 96.65E.This reading was most important if not crucial.Was the counter-current there or not?

There wasn't a breath of wind. Just humid heat. Vivian was profusely swetting. After half an hour had passed, Max couldn't wait to get the next reading. Meanwhile Vivian wanted to know what was the matter with the engine.

The next reading gave 10.12 Deg.S and 96.70E!

Max took a quick mental calculation and excited decided to repeat the experiment.

He got 10.15S and 96.76E!Bingo! Now to gain an extra pair of legs Max turned on the motor at three quarter throttle. In his calculation they were heading eastwards at at least 8 knots over ground. Not bad for a cruising boat of this size and windstill conditions. Not that counter current was continuous. More than once Max was disappointed with the eastward progress, fearing the counter current had run its course, only to continue on the same course of 90 Deg.T determined to find the stream re-emerging. Water temperatures and tides may well had something to do with it, the ebb and tide movement competing, but this was one for the Oceanographers. All Max could claim was the fact they recorded water temperatures up to 30 Deg. Higher than the accepted records.

Eleven days later, the diesel only got turned off to check the oil and top up fuel tank. By now most of the 20L portable fuel cans had been emptied. They had covered over 20 degrees of longitude, at close to the Equator that is almost 1200 nautical miles. The latest GPS plot put them just south of the Cocos Keeling. Max put it to his darling wife if she was too exhausted to continue. There was an airstrip and a twice a week connection to Perth. She just ignored the question and rolled him into submission once more.

Max had to decide weather to continue, low on diesoline and facing SE trades on the nose, or wait for the trades transition and the cyclone season that comes with it, hoping the NW trades would carry them closer to Western Australia. One way or the other, there was no free ride, and beating into a punishing trade wind for days on end was for the racing fanatics. Certainly not one for the easy going cruising crew of two. One of them expecting a child.

Yachts sail around the world westwards. The opposite course was for the brave individuals ready to absorb the punishment of the elements. Max decided to continue on the same course and contacted the Christmass Island Authorities on HF 2182 Hz chanell. He was given a clear home comming greeting. Case of another Aussie yacht returning home. He failed to mention the last port of call was in Africa. The weather forecast was mixed, there was a low approaching from the north, and some turbulence with it. Transition period had began.

Max reefed the main in anticipation and furled in the 140% genoa in. In its place was hoisted the heavy rust stained inner staysail. Sure enough within hours Max could see the front heading towards them. To make sure he put another reef into the mainsail. Not before time. It came down in buckets, and in your eye.

The first real rain they'd had in weeks. Vivian could not resist it. She walked into the cockpit stark naked enjoying the cool rain shower.

"For the first time I don't feel like a salted herring." She was elated. Until now water conservation allowed no more than two liters per adult per a day. One used a sponge soaked in fresh water to wash off the salt. Then it hit them. A sixty knot NW squall almost threatened to lift the yacht. Max let it fly. He estimated the yacht was powering ahead at about 10 knots surfing down some of the piled up wave crests. Before the storm completely abated Max found Chrismass Island just to the port side. One can be lucky and snatch a free ride. On the average the good and the bad had to somehow cancel each other. In line with Max' pet Theory of the Averages. They motored into the Cristmass Island Quarantine Station next morning. It was dead calm by then, the fuel tank was closing on the big E. And that's where their luck changed again. From bad to good to bad again.

Stringent quarantine regulations got imposed on them out of Africa. One took no chances. The yacht could be stuck here for weeks. Max used the opportunity and contacted Elliots in Perth. They were being held up at Christmass Island. Vivian spent a monthly allowance on phone calls. She wouldn't have reverse charges. Bazza Elliot had bad news from his wife. She was still in critical condition down with p.falciparum malaria. The deadly kind. How he got away with it, Bazza couldn't understand. The pair shared all there was. But he was keen to meet Max on Christmas Island and hopefully get some valuable sailing blue water experience completing the delivery along the way.

At about the same time Vivian was beginning to indicate she was in the need of expert gynecological care. Max jumped on that. He was glad the Dictaphone business was completed and felt relieved following her departure from the airport on a flight to Perth.

The last leg to Australia's shores was bound to be rough. Max wanted Vivian safe at home, so Bazza arranged a return ticket to Christmass Island with Vivian to use the return leg to Perth, then on to SA. The men received quarantine clearance on Christmass eve. How appropriate. At first, the twenty knots SE trade hit them on the nose. Nothing to do but tack and hope for the best. Soon anything not nailed down was on the cabin floor. Some baptizing for Bazza.

This continued for a fortnight. Beating into SE or tacking and motoring into the wind, until they reached the influence of the Australian festland and the wind direction changed to variable. In two more days they reached Carnarvon fully spent, with long beards and comprehensively starved out. Bazza's parents were at the Bowling Club to celebrate. Sue couldn't make it. She was still in Townsville on the critical list. The sailors cleaned up the club's menu.

Bazza sticking to the contract payed the remaining delivery fee in cash.

Before departure, Max popped a question. If the yacht was for sale in future, would he be the first to know? Bazza promised he would. To Max Kai Vai was a dream yacht. The punishment they took during the last leg of the delivery made him only more more appreciative of the fine quality.

They partied till closing time, to go their separate ways. The two sailors shook hands and parted in mutual belief they'd most probably never run into each other again. It happens every day. So many introductions and so few friends.

Now it was Max' turn to make it back to Jo'burg, his new home and new wife. A SAA Boeing 747 took off from Perth and for Vivian the next day.

Over the moon with joy, and flush with funds, plans for the future were open before him. Max was confident he'd finaly reached a point of finding some solid family prospects he'd been denied and badly missed ever since departure from his homeland when he was still a young man. He was tired of being a Monsoon Drifter. He wanted a family once more and a place to call home.

Little did he know about the turbulence ahead, and it was not of the atmospheric kind.

* * *

CHAPTER TWENTY

SMALL IS BEAUTIFUL

The inaugural meeting was organized impromptu. There was no written agenda either, and those present had no idea what to expect, gathered on Boss' private retreat. An accreage property at Schoemansville that could pass for botanical gardens. Overlooking the Hartbeespoort Dam on the south and Cheetah Reserve on the North side.

Guests were asked by Boss's secretary to make themselves comfortable inside a long conference room and to feel at ease. Boss himself was on the way, cought up in the traffic. He arrived within minutes and greeted them warmly as was his trade mark. He did have a way with people, and could tell one into the face things that were most unflattering, without provoking a thirst for revenge.

Visibly fatigued and fightning for second breath, he asked the audience to have patience. He was getting on and slowed *dun a wee bit*. Without taking his own seat, he turned towards Vivian seated half way down a long conference table.

"It has come to my attention you'd lost the teaching post, right *lassie.*?"

"Not wrong Boss, it is a blow, no ifs and buts. How can I fight the system that is stacked?"

"And you old warrier?"

He was addressing Max, seated next to Vivian."

"Now that you have done Kai Vai delivery to Carnarvon what can the Rainbow Nation do *fer* you? I can offer you a Reginal Manager job if you have a mind of accepting one. Very good money, but I'd be less than honest if I failed to mention what comes with it. It has become real dicey out there, Adam can tell you stories. And it isn't getting prettier. Do give it a good thinking, but before you decide, it might pay you to hear what I have to say to you all."

He rested for a while, gathering thoughts. In the stoney silence the only thing one could here was the astmathic secretary struggling for breath. Then Boss continued.

"To some of you who don't know me well what I have to say will no doubt come as a surprise…. As one who has done well out of the system, how can I bring myself to pick bones with it. Well, it isn't easy, let me tell you, but as you get close to where we're all destined to go, you ask yourself a question that just will not go away. It goes like this. How can we, the immeasuarably better off sleep in contentment with millions of our fellow men out there in wretched poverty? All of their human dignity trampled on? Now, before you jump and brand me a pinko, wait until you hear the rest, then call me what you like. I do not have to worry about that kind of gossip any more. That is one priviledge money bestows upon you. To speak your mind, and call it the way it is.

First of all, the economic system under which we live is badly flawed, designed to benefit the rich and propagate myths of some level playing fields. Let me tell you that's twaddle. Bloody ***voodoo.***

There is no such a thing as level playing field. The system is designed for poor to remain poorer. Or the other bit of revolting spin. That one takes the cake. It proclaims boldly that greed is good. Good for whom? Take the obscenly astronomical salaries Western CEO's pay themselves. It is nothing short of theft. It is the money stolen from the shareholders. Money that would otherwise filter down to the poor, one way or another. We can blame it on the politicians of this colour or that colour, nothing essentially changes apart from a handful who manage to clean up.

Just look at this country. Is the average African better off than he used to be under white government? Don't take it from me, ask them, and they'll tell you nothing much has changed. There is still no food for the hungry. A handful of party hecks have muscled into PS, and that's about it. Why that is so, the arguments abound of all sorts. Offered solutions? None I am aware of."

He paused again, visibly fatigued, fighting for breath before continuing.

"And why, I hear you ask, and what if anything are we supposed to be doing about it? You all know about the one dialogue with the Lord, a mortal asking for wisdom not to foolishly challenge what he cannot change, then for strength so he be able to change what he can, and finaly for fortitude to distinguish the difference. There is some truth in that I suppose, the flow in the argument is , one will never find out what is what until one tries.

Let's look at the first one. And here I owe my insights to Vivian, who saw through this long before me. It is as she calls it an upside down world. The quasi-science of Western economics puts things back to front.

The big are guaranteed to get bigger and uglier still. Until there is but one ugly monster brute to control the so called free market, which is in fact so tightly controlled already, it hurts anyone outside trying to get in. Wrong? Like hell.

There are supposed to be anti-trust laws out there making the petrol companies want to compete. So how come, they charge the same price. And change and manipulate it at will. The Governament doesn't regulate. It wouldn't dare.….

The Western type economics thinking also cannot sustain itself without an ever increasing consumption. We all know this binge of ever more cannot go on. The permissive behaviour of the big end of the town only tells you how much it would hurt the economy to spend another cent on cleaners meager pay, or on another hospital or another school. It doesn't try to equate cost of NOT building it. In other words, as brutal as it may sound, to the Western economist, there are only costs on the balance sheet. But not the cost that realy hurt the poor.

Like what cost a deceased bread winner at the age of 35. What cost rampant Hep B, because there is no money for sanitation and hospitals. In their balance sheets, the cost of human life, suffering and pollution of water and air doesn't come in. So the cost of human life is zero. "He slowed right down and one could hear a single fly buzzing about. Then Boss raised his voice once more.

"Are you then surprised at the outcome? What else can one expect. It only amazes me that there isn't a backlash in the public already. It will come, that is unavoidable. For as long as we are seduced by cheap imports from India, China and public still has credit to buy them it will be delayed.

Then as the jobs dry out, and factories still remainig pack up and join the rest employing cheap child and slave labor, watch out West for the next Hitler!

Here in SA we should have done better. A golden opportunity was missed. Maybe it is not too late, but unless something is done soon, we'll go down the slippery slope of the savage Congo and wretched Zimbabwe…..

What I suggest is no more than a very modest example. A practical example to start on a completely different approach. Again I owe Vivian. She recommended to me works of a late German economist Willy Schumacher who as a WW2 invalid sat in the Bonn Bundestag and wrote a book under the title:*"Small is Beatiful"*.

It should be compulsory reading in this country. Sadly, nobody until now has heard of it. That will change I hope. So now that you may have an inkling of what I am on about, let me give you a few more facts.

Africa has been good to me. It is **rooinek's** turn to give something back to Africa in return. At the age of 82, I don't have long to go. Before that I want to leave something behind of which a man can be proud. Being a practical man, I stick to what I know best. That is to make things happen. I leave the theory to those better qualified…..

This week I spent putting a few figures down. It appears following the huge success up North, our company shares have taken off North. So much so, I for the first time in my life have enough to make a difference."

He paused struggling for words. All attention focused upon him.

"Schumacher explains it much better than I ever could. I can only draw on his theories and try to put it into practice.

For example. The the big business reluctancy to employ people, unless it is absolutely unavoidable. Sure, the profit margin stands to go up, at least in the short term. Now you have supermarket chains employing fewer and fewer, soon even the check out girls will be given the boot. So the sad story continues.

Having closed down and put out of business thousands of family and small shops, big boys are still not happy until in their version of Nirvana there is no labour force left on the payrol. And then what, you ask!? With massive unemployement, who is going to be left there purchasing their goods?

If you think someone in the echelons of the fat beaurocracy would get up and have a dissenting voice, you'd be grossly mistaken. We, the public have been trained in obedience, just like the Pavlov's canines. It is left to the Joe Blow the average citizen to protest. And what can he do? Precious little. And if you think the Western media would have a crack at this, well, how can they. The same clique owns the media…..

But we my friends here may have a chance to try something different on a small scale. And here is what I propose."

He took another long pause and poured himself a scotch and soda with some medication, offering drinks all around.

"Well, I hope you have got your safety belts on tight, we are ready for take off. Don't get me wrong. Not for a moment am I suggesting any of us can get into an African's head. But what we can do is manage the economy better than any of them. We have five hundred years start to begin with ."

What Boss was proposing was not his idea, nor did he ask credit for it. The novelty in the scheme was a successful capitalist taking risks for no material benefit and in the process using his own not OPM(other people's money).

"What I am proposing may not be economical wisdom but it is worth a try. After all, should we fail, isn't that what the system would expect us to do?"

Here was his plan in broad terms.

From his finances Boss was to start a multicultural foundation, employing doers. Full time engineers, teachers, tradesmen and medicos. Nurses and women with domestic skills. No room here for lawyers, economists or politicians of any kind. A strictly NGO they were nevertheless hoping to eventually get some encouragement from the people in power. Their task was to lift the status and self respect of the tribal woman and to attract the African male back to the land. Offer them incentive and encouragement to find new prosperity and self-employement. Others in the land were also beginning to see the need to pitch in. He was by no means all alone. He mentioned a few big company CEOs who had shown some interest. At least, expressed privatly. According to his line of thinking, key to success was getting people back to gainful employement. Not welfare.

"We need artisans, weavers, tinkers and cobblers of pre and early industrial revolution. Small scale economies would provide jobs the large cities can never do. Back with their wives and children the men would be more content and less crime and rape prone..We can make our own shoes, sandals and leather goods. Why do we have to import this from slave labour camps of Asia? We can make our own cooking pots and repair what needs to be repared. Our women can still stich clothes and weave buatiful garments. There is a lot of artistic talent in the African as well that needs no more than a nudge to explode into productive creativity. Once an individual regains his or her place in society and regains the pride, we've won…..All this against a no hope squalour in stinking, and polluted crime and drug ridden ghettos. It shouldn't even be a contest that it is….Oh, I know it is a head full. It took me a long time to get around it. But just for starters, give it a thought. We'll meet again when there is a call for it. Vivian will take over from me" He paused for breath and went on…

"Now my friends, join us in the backyard for a ***braafleis*** and a sundowner…I"ll be back shortly. Let me clean out the spiders first, and thank you for your attention."

It was a commanding performance that had the audience stunned.

Boss excused himself. When he arrived back it was in full Scotts Guards piper's kit. Medals for bravery and campaign ribbons. The lot. He struck on his bag pipes the traditional Mt Lomond tune familiar to all. Vivian led the song,

> You take the high road
> And I'll take the low road,
> And I'll be in Scotland before you,
> And me and my true love
> We'll never part again.

Others joined in in a harmonious effort for a group that never rehearsed. Max' deep bass voice in particular. Those present would never forget the occasion. All this about his military past only Vivian knew before. Boss had been one of Ferggie's pipers in the Italian-Austrian WW2 campain.(Gen.Ian Fergusson for the uninitiated).

As he grew older, Boss noticed the faded out memories of long ago and his native land, coming back to life one by one. He'd lost a lot of condition lately. Visibly tireing, and it had been a long day, he took a breather, swollowed some more medication and spoke just once more before seeing the visitors out. A thought flashed through his mind.

"I just wish my Agnes was here to see this."

Boss failed to let them know, he was loosing the battle with the bowel cancer. Before the year was out he was to join Agnes. In his will he left Vivian expecting a child within months in charge of the ***Sanibonani Foundation***. To him she was a doughter he never had. Never mind the contracts, never mind the Manifesto, never mind the usual trappings of our litigious society where most people knew all about their rights spelled backwards and precious little about obligations. If Vivian promised she'd do it, that was good enough for Ian McLarty.

And she promised to make sure the funds were to go where Boss intended them to go. To poor and starving in remote **kraals**. To deserted wives. Too remote for the modern world to hear their cries of anguish...

* * *

Max arrived in Jo'burg in time for New Year festivities. He found a note of joy and optimisam in the Sisterhood. A fresh wind was blowing. Preocupation of all was planning for the offspring, babies' toys and clothes.

Loland was the last to fall pregnant and off colour. None of them had previous experience. Vivian was to lead the way.

Ousis was by now big and a butt of jokes she didn't take kindly to.

"Wait you scheming lot!"

She'd reprimand the twins." Soon it will be your turn."

Since the offspring was all due in coming year, Marc suggested they call the year after the pagan godess of fertility **Eostre.** None said it but all anxiously awaited to see those babies. Whose genes won the day? Little did they know.

It didn't end there. Heavy rains broke the worst drought in living memory. Parts of Sahara were flooded. Again Marc couldn't help himself.

"Who of your lot prayed too much!"

If there was a dark cloud it was Boss' state of health. He couldn't make it to their meetings and Adam although still to be officially promoted to the CEO position effectively ran the company.

Vivian spent days at Boss' bed side vigil in a private Cancer Ward at Bloomfontein. Mc Larty brothers droped in at times to call on their uncle both suffering from incurable malaria. Modern medicine could transplant a pig's head but could not cure malaria. It was a decease of the poor. And poor didn't have the money to buy.

The last time Vivian spoke to Boss he was visibly struggling for every word. And those he spoke warned her to look after her man. Boss had a warm spot for Max and belived Vivian and Max belonged together no matter what. As if he knew. Those words of a dying man were to be put to a critical test in not too distant future.

With two days to go to the New Year he quietly passed away. It was the biggest funeral the Presbeterian Church at Parkill had ever seen. A pipers band played the Last Post to the fallen soldier. Funeral procession ran for a mile. In his life Boss made a lot of friends. And many African miners amongst them. He spent many days underground himself holding a jackhammer eating dust and knew the conditions the miners worked under.

Funeral, wedding and Sisterhood celebrations all out of the way, the normal cycle of life and business resumed. For all of his benovelence and good intentions Boss left few if any specific instructions as to how to go about implementing his legacy.

Not surprisingly, suggestions came from all quarters. Some suggested simply distributing the cash amongst the poor. Others wanted to donate machinery and trucks to the remote communities.

Problem was none of them had any experience to handle this. Not surprisingly heated discussions followed.

After passively listening to numerous proposals advocating a cash distribution Max got up to have a say.

"Grettings to all of you. Those who don't know me well enough, let me tell you as a child I went hungry to bed every night. That qualifies me to speak about poverty. If you ask what I suggest, I have only one answer. Jobs and gainful jobs. Even a lowly payed job is a steady income.

Giving cash away is like winning on lottery. Easy come easy go. A steady job income gives a house wife something to budget ahead and hold on to. Women performe miracles with pocket money. Men gamble with fortunes. Jobs and jobs I say."

He took a seat in silence. No dissenting voices emerged. Just silence. Vivian looked around and decided to give her contribution without standing up.

"Max has the first bit correct. To draw those urban Africans from slums back to **Mnyama Thabas**, The Black Mountain and rural settings of their forefathers won't be easy. Jobs are indespensible for sure. But where are those people going to live? Ten to a roundavel? What are they to use for fuel. Dried cow manure? What are they to use for light? A stinking lard candle? Where is the power to drive any machinery we bring in? From the family oxen? Where is the water to come from? The sewage disposal? And I can go on!"

"Brilliant, that was the prospectus in a nut shell. I add to this. Who is going to treat the sick and where?" Marc's words.

Obviously a litany of neglect by all governments past and present was to blame. None disputed the facts. How to remedy the past mistakes? That wasn't so easy. Proposals for job creations were the first step. Again Max took it upon himself to offer a suggestion.

"If we want to be effective, most of these problems have to be treated in conjunction. As a whole, not one at a time. We have neither the luxury of unlimited time nor funds to do it. What I suggest is a simple practical scheme. It has to do with foam concrete casting in situ. I've done some home work on this before arriving here. Briefly, it is a relatively new, but proven technology only slowly finding acceptance in this country. Italian and Scottish builders perform miracles in this field…

Mullock heaps all around Jo'burg are a major raw material. We have available at practically no cost access to that technology.

It is possible to erect a foam concrete roundavel in four days. Big enough for an average family of six for less than R25K. A durable, hygienic weather and white ant proof structure. We have all the raw materials cheaply accessible and all this employing semi skilled labour. Few registred patents stood in the way. One could also ask for technical assistance from Europe. I am certain of success.

As for solar power cells and solar water heaters we can discuss it later. Sewage disposal solutions as well. Modern technology has ready and affordable answer for all of this. All the more so at our competative wages level. Ther'd be work for all."

Vivian finaly cought on where he'd been spending hours at a time. In the public library. This was a pleasant surprise to her, and she was all for it. It remained to thresh out the details. To provide the design she was to employ an African architect. A fresh graduate with new ideas. Those building structures had to be attractive in design appealing to the Zulu, as well as ergonomic and structurally sound and affordable.

Max suggested Mawindi for design. Vivian conveniently ignored him.

"More suggestions, please. Bear in mind we don't want to compete with tourisam ventures already in place."

She looked around. Plenty of suggestions came. From growing hydroponics for local markets to opening playgrounds for city kids keen to mix it and play with young animals. Some dying to ride a pony. It went well into the night. Vivian took transcripts and Dictaphone minutes before she tired out. When suggested she ought to take it easy with the baby due any time soon she just brushed off the idea with a dismissive hand movement.

They agreed to meet at regular intervals and to sound out Zulu chiefs, the *izinDuna.*

* * *

CHAPTER TWENTYONE

BABY BORN

Max would have made a poor public servant. No green and white papers, nor conferences tied up to endless meetings and subject to approvals ad infinitum for him. For his the inaugural meeting of the *Sanibonani* Foundation was clear enough. Action was needed to make up for lost time.

One of Vivian's aims was to consult the *izinDuna*, the Zulu headmen. They were vital to any chance of success. Max decided to head into the heart of the *kwaZulu*, perhaps a little naivly. When he explained what it was all about, the Zulu told him he was the last of the missionaries and two centuries after Shaka too late. Max realized where he went wrong and changed the approach. There had to be something in this for everybody. Of his own initiative, he offered two payed directorships to the headmen and or men of their choice. Finaly there was acceptance. How he was to convince Vivian remained for later. Max fell in love with Durban, and would suggest to Vivian to move the HQ there. It was everything Jo'burg was not. Particulary for a sailor. Now he was catching a flight back.

Upon arrival, reluctant to make unnecessary fuss, he left it till landing. Then tried repeatedly on her fixed line phone number, without success. It took Vivian years to even qualify for a socialite. Her expenses account was multiples of the old salary and still she'd baulk at paying for high fashion European goods. If away from home she'd cost the guest houses and bargain with their tariffs. Old habits do dye hard. Similary she had to be convinced to the economics of it, before purchasing a mobile phone.

Now she was getting close. As big as she was, Loland bet *ousis* was pregnant with twins, and she intended to ask Max if Croats sire such big babies.

Vivian underwent all the preliminary tests in Netcare Garden City Hospital at Mayfair West. It was decided to keep her. She was getting close.

Max got in touch with Loland who insisted he stay put. Their gardener Mzuma was going to fetch him from OT Airport. Upon arrival Loland brought him up to date, and promised to ask him something personal when he returned from the parked car with luggage. Max was trying to guess what that could be. Loland not feeling at her best was still a bit of a mischief maker, but he couldn't guess what she was driving at.

All of this jovial atmosphere was to turn into tears before long.

Loland offered Max to stay with them. It was more practical to drive together and visit Vivian after delivery. That took two more days than expected. The gyneacologist in charge decided late against induction in favour of a Caesarean to play it safe. She was getting on for a first born. Then the bomb shell dropped.

Loland received a call from the maternity ward next day late in the afternoon. It was the doctor himself calling. He had some mixed news to report. Loland's heart sank.

"Was Vivian all right?" The doctor reported she was doing fine.

"The baby? Well, ...was it a healthy baby?"

"Yes, the boy weighed nine pound two and was fine. A big sucker."

Loland was just not daring to ask the next question. The good doctor was also struggling for words before letting them have it. There was no choice.

"You see, we have one problem. Your sister insists there had to have been a mix up with babies. We are certain this was not the case. You see, for start, there were no white babies delivered in the last two days. Not a single one. You see. We would appreciate you come and talk to us before the husband gets to know. Come and ask to see Dr Prakesh first."

There he hung up.

If a lightning had struck the place it couldn't have done more damage.

Loland looked around. There was at the time none within earshot. What was she to do? Vivian of all people had a black baby. She decided to confine in Jean just arriving. Perhaps she had an idea. She had not. Not in the slightest. They in turn phoned Marc who was equally shattered. It wasn't the fact the boy was an African. They would have welcomed the baby no matter what colour.

No, it was Max they all feared would snap. Something had to be done. They discussed this for hours. Finaly Max unannounced quietly entered the room.

Yes, he overheard enough if not all. And he couldn't explain it. She was old enough and mature. If she'd been raped, she wouldn't be the first one. Jo'burg was the world capital for rape. Why didn't she own up and tell him? That hurt. He had to talk to her. He'd only just returned from a flower shop.

Marc returned from the clinic sensing trouble. They decided to go all together. Safety in numbers routine and hear what Dr Prakesh had to say. He was polite to a fault. After a short wait he led them in to see the new born.

Max knew it. Just one look at the baby out of the crib did it. He instinctly knew it wasn't a rape. He felt like running into a wall of pain. As if he had been knived into the abdomen with force. Or like one who had just seen his home go up in flames.

He also knew things would never be the same again. Still for her sake and all the happines shared until now, he had to talk to her. Bothas and Loland could wait in the corridor. He akwardly held the flowers and returned to the sister on duty to leave them there. Once there he couldn't fail but notice the snigger catching on amongst staff.

One African aid buildt like a Sumo wrestler was as bold as to loudly proclaim it was a bit of a payback for pale skinned Xosa boys. Max was shattered.

He could raise little Mawindi. He could for the sake of old times. She did more for him than anyone else in years. What he could not face was the snigger and derision. Sooner or later he was certain, he'd blow his lid, and retaliate. Only to end up in jail again. Life was too precious to waste it in a prison cell.

It still had to be explained. He wanted to hear what Vivian had to say.

"No." She calmly answered." No rape. I just got so carried away I couldn't say no. I'd never do it again. But it is no good telling you this. I know how you must feel. And I don't know what to do. Whatever I say it will be misconscrued. It is no good me telling you I love you more than you'll ever know. You won't believe me anyway. But I do. Now please. Leave me, and let me cry alone!"

Again, he wasn't convinced she was telling the truth. They made love passionately dozens of times. How is a possible just one act of indiscretion can undo all that. If his sperm moved at five centimeters an hour, did it follow African sperm traveled at fifty? That was all nonsense. And he couldn't think of anything else to say. She was crying, face covered in her hands. Max approached her with a heavy heart. Face twisted in pain..

"Vivian, I don't know what to do. I don't want to do anything silly.

Let me take a break... Do the work on foam concrete technology in Padova and Dundee, South Pole or anywhere... We need a bit of distance between us for a while. You and me."

Impact of this, the latest blow upon his already suspect self-confidence and emotional balance was devastating. It left him exposed bare and valnurable. Towards the end, it disarmed his last defences. Just like a flood torrent sweeps dead wood out of sight.

He paused, feeling lost in space. Feeling wounded as if in battle, and trying to sound rational for his age. He felt the room beginning to turn and close in on him. Images and colours of those in front of him began assuming deviations from the normal.

He was right on the edge of sanity. In the dying moments of retaining self control he managed to utter one more verbal message barely audible and coherent.

She heard him say how he appreciated her being open. Not trying to avoid the blame. What followed was either in a foreign language or gibberish. She could not tell. Apart from a repeated call of 'black baby.'

With these words he parted. Head low and eyes fogged up. He staggered past Loland, Jean and Marc oblivious to their presence. Hence continued, as if on auto pilot towards the exit door.

Marc watched him exit. He got up from the waiting room bench. Only to have Jean pull him right back.

"Just where do you think you are going, my hero husband!"

"He is sick. I am worried he might do something to himself. We can't just sit here, my wife!"

"I am forced to agree." Jean rose up.

" OK. Let us talk to Viv first."

They walked into post-natal ward to find Vivian. Head buried in the bed pillow!

"Viv! Jean called out loud. "What did you do to Max? Now snap out of feeling sorry for yourself *ousis*. Marc thinks Max is dire strights. Common get up, we have to do something! "

Vivian slid out of bed. At this point Marc took charge. He brought up Vivian's clothes and hastily slipped her morning gown over the night dress. With her starting to do up hair, Marc found the hat and slammed it on back to front..

"Never mind the bloody hairdo. Let's not waste any time."

They walked back into the exit corridor hand in hand with the Matron in hot persuit, demanding the bill be settled first before release papers. She insisted they stay put seated in the corridor and wait for the release papers and bills...Half an hour gone and still nothing to show for, Marc decided he had enough of inaction. He was worried about Max. Where could he be? He used Viv's mobile and called up Max from the memory bank. The phone rang twice before cutting out.

"Yack!" Marc swore more to himself. "He hung up on me. That is even more of concern." He told the sisters to wait for him in the casualty entrance and raced ahead himself. Just in time to claim an ambulance delivering a road casualty. Within minutes Jean and Vivian arrived. Both winded from running. Loland stayed back to see the Matron. Marc commandeered the driver to head for the airport with the sirene blazing away. A check with the Telecom provider confirmed Max' mobile was somewhere in the OT Airport Departure complex soon within sight. They hastily alighted from the van and charged into the Departures hall. It couldn't but alarm the security personnel.

Max seated alone in the middle of a three seat bucket row found the darkest of his
inner self taking a strangelhold. Aloneness can be testing. When idle it is even more corrosive. He felt there was no point in going on. The black dog was onto him. What the hell. A million miles travelled. Fortunes spent. Wars fought. All in vain. He had nothing to show for all that. A life wasted. Fritted away. That's what. All hope was gone.

Once more he felt like the Monsoon Drifter of old, with nobody in this big world to cling onto. He took the revolver out of the carry bag and loaded the gun.

Marc was the first to spot him and rushed in. What he saw only confirmed his suspicions. In next to no time, he had Vivian out of breath by his side and both facing Max. Security guards and lagging Jane not far behind and rapidly closing in.

"Give me that thing Max, please!" Marc begged him. Max showing no emotions.

Next totally unexpected, Vivian stepped forward and opened up the night gown.
"Shoot me Max! Shoot here! It is my fault. Shoot me! You diserved better."

It was Jean's turn next. She'd cought up. Marc experienced in dealing with highly distressed individuals instantly recognised the sympthoms. Max' life was hanging by a very thin thread. He silently passed a hint to Jean. She red it, approached Max from behind and ruffled his hair by running her hands through it. Then kissed him with all the passion she felt and could master.

"Listen Max! Listen, please! Our dear friend! We cannot let you do it to yourself. You are one of us. One of the circle. You carry my blood in your veins. It doesn't matter what happens next. You belong here. We need you and the foundation needs you badly."

In a bold move she stepped forward around the bench seat. Next calmly took the gun out of his hand. As if she'd been doing it every day and it was the most natural thing to do.
"Marc just put you on the sick list for a month. And I am your nurse." She said. "Not Viv, doing time in purgatory. I am in charge! And we are heading for home. You hear me! Home, our dear friend. Our home."
The guard arriving first to the scene got there just in time to take possesion of the gun.
This concluded the airport act of the drama. But for the news hungry reporters charging in. Morning newspapers splashed across the front page featured our true hero Dr Marcus Botha back in action saving another life.

They took Max to Botha's place in an ambulance. There is a finite limit on capacity of a man to take punishment before cracking up. He'd had a ride to hell and back twice. Hence he was to stay under day and night observation and expert care for weeks. Before Marc with Jean's assistance would slowly wean him from benzodiazepine tranquilisers and continue long rehabilitation.
There was a glimmer of hope at last. He was in loving hands of the circle.

* * *